SINCE

Longarm fired back at the muzzle blast and adjusted his aim when a second ball of flame blossomed. At least two pellets ticked the brim of his Stetson, and then Arnold had fired his own two cents' worth, and they could all hear the separate thuds of meat and metal hitting the dirt in the inky shade.

Two rifles being more dangerous than one spent shotgun, Longarm got over to the ones by the wall first, got no response when he kicked each in the face, and moved across the stable yard behind the trained muzzle of his .44–40.

Longarm called out to Arnold and O'Hanlon, "I make it three down. Stay put whilst I make sure this one ain't playing possum."

Then he moved in, rolled the fallen ambusher over on his back, out in the moonlight, and hunkered down to feel for a pulse. "This one's sincerely down, too."

O'Hanlon hunkered down for a closer look. "This one was at the bar earlier. But, then we've just established the three of them was up to something sneaky!"

"Sure, but what?" asked Corporal Arnold.

Longarm had noticed that most old boys were better at checkers than chess. He wearily replied, "At the risk of sounding swell-headed, I was the likely target of this Anglo rider's dirty little game."

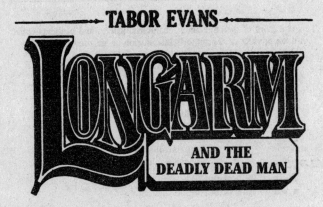

TABOR EVANS

LONGARM

AND THE
DEADLY DEAD MAN

JOVE BOOKS, NEW YORK

LONGARM AND THE DEADLY DEAD MAN

A Jove Book / published by arrangement with
the author

PRINTING HISTORY
Jove edition / June 2003

Copyright © 2003 by Penguin Group (USA) Inc.

ISBN: 0-515-13547-X

A JOVE BOOK®
Jove Books are published by The Berkley Publishing Group,
a division of Penguin Group (USA) Inc.,
375 Hudson Street, New York, New York 10014.
JOVE and the "J" design
are trademarks belonging to Penguin Group (USA) Inc.

PRINTED IN THE UNITED STATES OF AMERICA

10 9 8 7 6 5 4 3 2 1

Chapter 1

Reporter Crawford of the *Denver Post* had learned the hard way to double-check his sources. So he was walking weary as well as tall and wide when he parted the batwings of the Parthenon Saloon in a wilted checked suit, with his soggy derby in hand, one hot dry Wednesday noon in August.

To his relief, the leg-sore newspaperman spied a source indeed at the free lunch counter. Deputy U.S. Marshal Custis Long of the Denver District Court was even taller, but not as wide, as Reporter Crawford and didn't seem as hot and bothered in spite of the three-piece suit of tobacco brown tweed he wore under a coffee brown Stetson and over his stovepipe cavalry boots. His double-action .44–40 rode cross draw, with its tailored grips peeking out from under the frock coat.

As the reporter joined him to slap a ten-dollar gold piece down on the bar between them, Longarm, as he was better known west of say longitude 100 degrees, howdied the older man, then observed that the overworked redhead on the other side of the long bar might just hate making that much change for the needled beer you were required to order if you meant to dig in to the cold cuts, rat cheese, devilish eggs and such in such a fancy joint.

Crawford placed a more reasonable two bits in silver by the half eagle as he told Longarm, "Put your gold away before we confound the poor gal, then. It's your share of a bar bet I won off Whipple from the *Republican Tribune*."

The tall, tanned lawman made the welcome ten dollars vanish as the snows of yesteryear as he observed, "Lord knows such winnings do come in handy out here in the deserted wastes betwixt paydays. But what did we bet Reporter Whipple about, old pard?"

Crawford chortled, "The *Trib* ran yet another interview with that ever modest Calamity Jane Canary. When I demured at the Press Club about her notorious common-law relationship with the late Wild Bill Hickok, Whipple bet me an eagle there was no way to prove her sad story wasn't true."

Longarm washed down some cheese wrapped in sliced ham before he observed, "The good-natured but pathetical old bawd can't tell the truth when it's in her favor. Have you ever seen the circus posters featuring Miss Agnes Lake, the bareback rider James Butler Hickok had just married up with when he rode up to the new gold fields around Deadwood to see if they'd hire him on as town marshal?"

Crawford grinned dirty and replied, "I surely have, and she seems to be riding bare of ass as well as bareback."

Longarm shook his head to reply, "Pink tights. Miss Agnes ain't no soiled dove and old Jim had to marry up with her lawsome before he got to see anything she had under that bodacious riding habit, or so they say. I wasn't there. Neither was Calamity Jane."

Catching the barmaid's eye and pointing at Longarm's beer scuttle, Crawford replied, "The Widow Hickok, being a lady as you just suggested, has given few if any interviews since she journeyed west to have her man dug up, repacked and buried in a regular cemetery, after a church service Calamity Jane did not attend, according to the guest list. I found that wasn't enough to convince Calamity Jane's admirers on the *Trib*. But then I recalled what you'd said about federal court records and, recalling Cockeyed Jack McCall had been convicted in a federal court after beating the rap in local court and, worse yet, bragging about how slick he'd been within earshot of another federal deputy, I sent for the transcripts of both trials, which agreed the late James Butler Hickok had left his bride in Cincinnati to wend his way west ahead of her, with a view to sending for her as soon as he had a job. He arrived in Deadwood in late June to be shot in the back by Cockeyed Jack McCall in front of witnesses in the Number Ten Saloon on the second day of August. The name of Martha Jane Canary does not appear as a witness or courtroom spectator in either trial. There is not a shred of evidence she was anywhere near Deadwood at any time in the Year of Our Lord 1876, nor in '78 when Miss Agnes had him dug up and replanted with half the territory in attendance."

Longarm reached for a pickled pig's knuckle as he chuckled fondly, and recalled, "Miss Calamity once told another reporter she turned yours truly down when I tried to console her for the loss of the only man she'd ever loved. I told his paper I'd come after them personal if they didn't print a retraction. Talking to Miss Calamity, Lord love her, is a waste of time."

As the barmaid slid a beer his way, Crawford reached for the same, saying, "I've had less luck this morning with another legend in the making, Longarm. Didn't you tell me, some time back, we'd seen the last of the one and original Clay Allison of the Cimarron Country?"

Longarm nodded to reply, "I did. I had to. The homicidal son of a bitch busted his own neck falling off a wagon, crazy drunk, in the summer of '77."

Crawford said, "That's what I told my editor. He told me to check my sources because tales of Clay Allison keep coming along the news wire out of Texas."

The reporter inhaled some suds and added, "Following your advice to put more faith in official records than the uncertain memories of self-appointed historians, I've

3

wired high and I've wired low for the brass-tack details and, quoting this federal deputy I know, I'll be switched with snakes if I can find any evidence of Clay Allison dying of a broken neck or any other misfortune anywhere along the Cimarron. No state or local authorities the length of the Red River have any record of Allison's infamous gunfight with the late Chunk Colbert, and didn't you tell me Allison was about to be arrested for the killing of three soldiers blue when he saved the taxpayers the costs of a federal hanging by busting his own neck?"

When Longarm simply nodded, Crawford demanded, "Then how come they have no records to back your play anywhere in Texas?"

Longarm easily replied, "Texas would have no records of Allison's mad-dog doings of say '74 to '77 because they all took place down by the Colorado–New Mexico line. He gunned Chunk Colbert in Red River Station, *New Mexico,* near Santa Fe, not along the Red River of Texas. He shot Pancho Greigo in *the town* of Cimarron, New Mexico, nowheres near that Cimarron River running through the Texas panhandle. He shot those three troopers of the colored persuasion in the same hotel taproom he'd shot the Mexican. Saint James Hotel in Cimarron, Colfax County, New Mexico Territory, near a smaller Cimarron *wash* running into the headwaters of the Canadian. I sure wish you newspaper gents would get your western geography straight."

As he raised his improvised sandwich, he added, "Trying to fit news items from the Red River of the North to the Red River of the South, or mixing up the Virginia City of Nevada with the Virginia City of Montana can surely lead to unlikely yarns."

Crawford put his beer scuttle aside to break out his notepad as he grumbled, "Colfax County, New Mexico. What about those stories of Clay Allison being run out of Dodge by one of several lawmen, depending on whom you ask?"

Longarm had to swallow before he replied with a shrug, "I read the brag of Bat Masterson. Couldn't have hap-

4

pened in the summer of '77, as he brags, because Allison was holed up in New Mexico, not Kansas, with myself, amongst others, packing federal warrants on his surly hide. My boss, Marshal Billy Vail, wanted a word with him about the perjury before a federal district judge in Pueblo, Colorado, earlier in '77. When Judge Henry couldn't hang Clay or his brother, Jack, for the murder of a lawman named Faber in the Olympic Dance Hall at Las Animas, in Bent County, not goddamn it Las Animas County, Colorado, we broke out that older killing of them three troopers south of the state line. So Allison ran home to New Mexico, not Kansas or Texas, to die there in a sort of fitting way when you consider the results of a federal rope dance."

Proceeding to encase a devilish egg in a slice of ham, Longarm went on to assure the newspaperman, "It's all on record when you know where to look. The trouble with Ned Buntline and the rest of you Wild West recorders is that you'd rather shoehorn might-have-beens into a fuzzy grasp of recent history and considerable geography. I swear I could tell one of you newspaper dudes I'd just run Black Jack Slade out of Denver because he'd insulted my true love, Lola Montez the Spider Dancer, and the story would run with embellishings!"

Crawford smiled sheepishly and confessed, "I wish I *could* run with that ball, Longarm. But haven't Black Jack Slade and Lola Montez been dead for some time?"

Longarm shrugged and said, "You know that, and I know that, but I wasn't surprised to read about Clay Allison't adventures in Dodge as he lay dead and buried in Cimarron. I understand Joaquin Murieta has been stopping the Wells Fargo stages out to the Motherlode, riding with a mysterious road agent called Black Bart. But you have my word they played the dead march and laid the sod over Clay Allison in the summer of '77 and, like the Indian chief said, I have spoken!"

The newspaperman washed down some salami and sighed. "Since you have yet to lie to me, Longarm, I'm going back to the press room to assure my editor of the facts you just related. But that leaves us stuck with an otherwise fine lead about the notorious outlaw Clay Allison beating a Texas Ranger to the draw down in the Big Bend along the border."

Longarm shook his head knowingly to reply, "Clay Allison was never an outlaw, exactly. To give the devil his due he was an otherwise honest cowpuncher inclined to kill folk when he was drunk. Served with honor, albeit as a Confederate spy, during the War Betwixt the States. Captured and condemned by the Union. Shot one or two guards as he got away and drifted westward, restless as an unreconstucted reb with some other noisy habits, to hire on as a foreman just north of Cimarron. Had his own spread further south by the time he died in his late thirties."

Longarm sipped some suds and continued, "By this time he'd married up and settled some, so they say. Member of the Cattleman's Protective Association and active in civic improvements north and south of the nearby state line. Gave handsome to the construction of the Pueblo Opera House and his woman's chapter of the WCTU. Never stole a horse nor even a cow to human knowledge. Simply had this mean streak that came out when he'd been drinking, and he drank a lot."

Crawford asked, "How do you like the notion of that ranger down in the Big Bend losing to some *other* badman going by the name of Clay Allison?"

Longarm dryly replied, "I like it better than that Texas Ranger must have. A man who shoots rangers or anybody else under an assumed name sounds more possible than a mean drunk crawling out of his grave in New Mexico to show up along the Big Bend in high summer. There's at least two Billy the Kids to the southwest at the moment, if not three. Billy Bonney or McCarty down along the Pecos and a Billy the Kid Clairborne out around Tombstone."

He grimaced and added, "Tombstone sports its own Buckskin Frank Leslie, not to be confused with the gent who puts out Frank Leslie's *Illustrated Magazine* and of course we have three famous and original Deadwood Dicks—a colored cowhand, an English remittance man and a plain old American drunk. All claiming to be the one and original Deadwood Dick made up in London Town for an English Wild West penny dreadful."

Crawford sighed and confessed, "I bought a drink for the English one before the other patrons warned me he was full of it. Someday, when they try to sort this all out, writers are going to have a time with names, dates and places that don't add up."

Longarm smiled thinly and teased, "Why wait? You boys have been getting lots of things wrong with the smell of the gunsmoke still fresh and the witnesses still breathing."

So they finished their free lunch on a lighter note, shook and parted friendly, so's Longarm could get it on back to his office before Billy Vail sent somebody after him.

The courtroom duty Longarm had pulled that morning had ended short and sweet with the fair but firm Judge Dickerson informing the soon to be late accused, "And there you shall be hanged by the neck until you are dead and may God have mercy on your soul. Court's adjourned for the day because there's a sale at the Denver Dry Goods and I dare not let my wife and daughters go alone!"

Hoping against hope his boss might have escorted his own old woman through the same dangerous shoals, Longarm strode back to the federal building with that ten-dollar windfall and a fine box of candy for a new gal in town in mind. But when he entered the marshal's office on the second floor, young Henry, the squirt who played the typewriter out front, told him Marshal Vail wanted to see him. So he headed on back with a sigh, reaching for a three-for-a-nickel cheroot along the way and lighting up in self-defense before he entered the smoke-filled inner sanctum of the very smokey Marshal Billy Vail.

As he entered the oak-paneled private office, the somewhat older, somewhat shorter and way fatter Billy Vail looked up from behind his cluttered desk, through the fumes of his own stinky cigar, to declare, "Watch where

7

you flick them ashes and don't bother to sit down without my permit, Custis. Henry is typing up your travel orders and you just have time to get on home and gather your shit. You got a train bound for Raton and points south to catch this afternoon."

Longarm said, "I'd rather go to a temperance meeting than south of Raton in August. But ours not to reason why. So how come you're sending me where in such a considerable expanse, Boss?"

Vail replied, "Tanktown, Texas, in the Tiswin Basin of the Big Bend Country. An old Texas ranger pal asked for you by name, seeing you get along so well with border breeds, ain't been beat to the draw as yet, and still hold a warrant for the arrest of Claymore Allison of Cimarron and points south."

Longarm cocked a dubious brow to reply, "You, too, Brutus? I was just now telling Reporter Crawford the late Clay Allison sent his own fool self to Hell with a busted neck back in the summer of '77!"

Vail nodded soberly and replied, "We were wrong, which makes more sense than a mad-dog killer from Hell beating two Texas Rangers in a row to the draw! Until you bring him in or prove him dead for keeps, the case of These United States against the murderous Claymore Allison stands open as a whorehouse door on a Saturday night!"

Chapter 2

There was no sensible way to get to the Big Bend Country because few if any sensible folk wanted to get there. Sensible Indians and a whole lot of Spanish-speaking folk had found it easier to swing north or south of the confounded rock piles and white-water rapids inhabited by poison-mean Chiso-Apache and other thorny flora and fauna. The Big Bend had only been settled by some few nominal Christians, Anglo or Mex, since the Chiso-Apache had been cleared out a scant few summers back.

A geology-teaching gal Longarm had engaged in pillow converstaion about the impossible streambed of Colorado's Gunnison had explained to him, betwixt kisses, how a sluggish, meandering river could appear to have run up and over a mountain range to carve a canyon through the same. She'd explained how the Gunnison, Colorado and of course the Rio Grande had been there first, before the mountains had slowly risen a few inches a year like a slab tilting under a stationary saw.

It could thunderghast a mere mortal to consider the millions and millions of years it must have taken the bottom of some ancient, nameless ocean to buckle miles into the winds and rains of the western sky and end up as literally rocky mountains. But Longarm knew it must have happened because there the mountains rose, with meandering rivers as old or older cutting though them at unlikely angles.

So like the canyonlands of the Four Corners Country to the west, the Big Bend of the Rio Grande meandered, unlikely if not impossible, through a series of canyons neither properly mapped nor completely explored along some stretches. Uncertain thunder in the mountains to either side of the border could shoot flash floods as well as more boulders to churn the coffee-colored rapids that made the Big Bend improbable if not impossible to run. Some few brave souls, or awful liars, claimed from time to to time to have run the Grand Canyon, gone over Niagara Falls in a barrel or gone clean round the Big Bend on a raft.

Such troubles lay downstream from where Longarm's mail coach took him, up Bottleneck Canyon into the surprisingly green Tiswin Basin to the last stop at Tanktown, where Tiswin Creek had been dammed to form a pond, or tank in Texican terminology.

First things coming first, Longarm dropped off the open mail coach covered with mustard colored dust from head to toe, with his store-bought suit in a saddlebag and just his traveling denims to worry about. He hauled his heavily laden saddle rig to the grassy banks of the tank, paying no mind to the quartet of curious Mex kids trailing after him.

They doubtless knew their own creek was named after the home brew the Chiso-Apache had whipped up from its limestone waters and corn mash in their shining times. Nobody north or south of the border had worried about Chiso-Apache getting drunk as skunks on their home brew. The trouble with a Chiso-Apache full of home brew was that he just refused to stay *home*. But that was now ancient history.

So as Longarm spread his rig and saddlebags on the grass to shuck his hat and empty his pockets, he did so without such history on his mind. He took off his gunbelt and spread it on the grass beside the McClellan. The kids all laughed when he whipped himself some with his Stetson, stepped shin-deep into the tank to bend over and fill the crown with water, then poured it all over his dust-covered leather goods.

It took more than one hatful, and more kids had drifted over from the dusty 'dobe town to stare and giggle by the time he had everything spread on the grass gleaming wet but clean. Anybody could see the blazing Texas sun would dry everything in no time. So Longarm put the contents of his pockets, save for the double derringer he hung on to, in the crown of his now-clean Stetson. Then he belly flopped, dusty duds and all, in mountain runoff that felt cool and clean as that old swimming hole back in West-By-God-Virginia.

The kids weren't the only ones laughing as Longarm rose like Venus from the waves, soaked to the skin but free of trail dust at long last.

An Anglo gent as tall as Longarm was laughing boyish as any Mex kid, and Longarm was just as glad the stranger was wearing a ranger star when he regarded the .45-caliber Colt '73 worn sort of low and tied down. As Longarm bent to pick up and buckle his own sidearm back in place, the ranger dryly observed, "If you're that federal deputy we've been expecting, I'll be proud to carry you over to see Captain Kramer, now. If you're somebody else, I'll thank you to keep that .44–40 in its holster with your hands well clear of it whilst you introduce yourself. In either event I'd be Corporal Arnold. José Arnold. Before you ask, though, there ain't no greaser in me. My momma come west with a romantic nature and it got her all excited to have me in San Antone under a roof of Spanish tiles. She named my poor sister Juanita and used to sprinkle chili pepper on our flapjacks."

Longarm was fixing to pick up his saddle and possibles when one of the bigger Mex kids volunteered to tote them. So Longarm told him in Spanish he could tote everything but the Winchester saddle gun.

Corporal Arnold waited patiently till they got that

11

sorted out, but as he led the way over to his ranger station he asked Longarm where he'd learned to talk such pure greaser.

He thoughtfully added, "You ain't . . . of the Spanish persuasion, are you, Deputy Long?"

To which Longarm dryly replied, "I aint an Indian, neither. But I know enough Sign to explain my appearing of a sudden on a prairie rise, and I've likely saved some needless pain for all concerned."

"We heard tell you had a way with redskins and greasers," Corporal Arnold replied with the innocent arrogance of the ignorant, as yet another ranger appeared in the doorway of a 'dobe catty-corner on the far side of the dusty market street and the wide stretch of an even older Mexican wagon trace down to the Rio Grande. He added that the older gent ahead was Captain Kramer and asked, "How come you get on so well with redskins, greasers and even niggers, to hear tell?"

Longarm dryly muttered it seemed a natural gift. He knew it would be a waste of time to tell the tall Texan he seldom called Indian Mex or Colored Folk redskins, greasers and such. So he asked what Arnold could tell him about the two rangers dying at the hands of a man who'd been dead for some time.

Arnold said, "Those were the good old days. He got two more as you were on your way down from Colorado. I wasn't there. So our Captain Kramer, yonder, can say as much as any of us knows for certain."

This turned out true. Arnold shook in the doorway with the graying Captain Kramer, who asked how his old pal Billy Vail was before he ordered another ranger to take Longarm's load off that Mex kid.

When Longarm tried to tip the young Mex, the kid smiled shyly and said it had been an honor. So Longarm asked how he was called. When he tried to tell young Ricardo Chavez who *he* was, the kid said he'd already known that. So Longarm followed Captain Kramer and his shit inside.

Captain Kramer found a pint of tequila filed in a drawer

marked "T to Z" and poured drinks atop the desk in the center of the reception room, as he told Longarm, "I've lost four good men to the son of a bitch, so far, and the last two, Page and Summerhill, were not only good but teamed up two to one and had the drop on the spooky son of a bitch!"

As he handed Longarm one of the shot glasses, he added, "I know you federal lawmen say Clay Allison lies dead and buried many a mile from here. But I say if it looks like a duck, walks like a duck and quacks with a .45 Schofield . . ."

Longarm threw back his shot of tequila to be polite and managed not to let it show as he protested, "Slow down. You gents are too far out ahead of this child. I've had time to read all you wired Billy Vail as I was wending my weary way down from Denver for the better part of a week with nothing better to read. But before we worry about whether your current problems could be inspired by anyone at all resembling the late Clay Allison, let's drive home some brass tacks."

With the Winchester in his other hand he pointed at his saddlebags on the floor and added, "I got some photoprints of a known clear tintype of the cuss, enlarged to six by four, along with a list of his known kith and kin. None of whom hail from South Texas, by the way. Clay Allison was born and reared in Tennessee to serve as a scout for the Confederate Cav and busted out of a Union stockade to head west before the war was over. Wound up in New Mexico Territory by way of the Texican panhandle. Never kissed one gal nor fought one man south of your Canadian River, as far as anyone can say. So let's talk about how come you think he's down here on the border, doing what, from the beginning, with less speculation as to exact identities if it's all the same with you."

As Longarm placed the shot glass on a corner of the desk and bent to slide his Winchester back in its saddle boot, Captain Kramer refilled the glass, saying, "I follow your drift. Let's say some tall blond stranger walking with a limp and tied-down side-draw rode into view this spring with a quartet of greaser buckaroos and a dozen head of Spanish saddle mules along with their scrub ponies. He bought a round of drinks at the Toro Negro Saloon and declared he meant to carve his own Lazy A spread out of the high country to the east. When Pud Ryan off the Rocking X tried to tell him the high country over yonder wasn't fit for man nor beast the stranger materialized a Schofield .45 from thin air, shoved its muzzle in Pud's face and intimated it could take years off a man's life to call Clay Allison from Cimarron a liar."

"He offered that name and home address?" asked Longarm.

Kramer said, "He did. Polished off more bourbon than one mortal man would have thought possible. Laid three whores at Mama Felicidad's and vanished into the night with his stock and vaqueros."

Helping himself to another shot, Kramer continued, "That should have been the end of it. Such range as may be in this verdant but limited basin has all been claimed. The local stockmen raise just enough beef for the town, here, and breed riding stock and army mules for all the military posts along the border from say Castolon, upstream to Fort Bliss. So when he heard the Lazy A had sold some mules at Presidio, we figured the bragging Clay Allison had settled over to the west."

When Longarm made the mistake of downing his second tequila, the old ranger refilled it, saying, "Then we commenced to get complaints about missing mules and ponies, unbranded stock set aside for the personal or military market. From a trickle at first it commenced to tally a heap of missing stock, before a Caddo breed who hunts for bighorn along the ridges to the east came in to report a good-sized home spread and a handsome herd up a box canyon say a day's ride east by buzzard. So I sent my Lieutenant Weiner to interview Mr. Claymore Allison about his increase. But Weiner never came back."

Longarm turned his glass upside down with a politely firm comment about the day being so young. Kramer sighed and said, "You're right. Like I was saying, Weiner never came back. So I was fixing to send Henderson when word came in that the tall blond cuss called Allison was holding court at the Last Chance, four miles downstream. You'll have noticed Bottleneck Canyon. A jasper called O'Hanlon runs a water, grub and likker hole over yonder near the entrance."

Moving to put the tequila back in its file drawer, Captain Kramer continued, "Seeing he didn't have a whole day's ride ahead, Henderson rode over to the Last Chance to find Clay Allison, or this cuss who calls himself Clay Allison, lazing against the bar with the benign and sleepy smile of a dangerous drunk. Before you ask, Tim Henderson was an experienced ranger who read such warning signs and he could toss a tin can in the air and draw and fire, accurate, before it hit the dust."

"What happened to him at the Last Chance?" asked Longarm.

Kramer soberly replied, "He got swatted like a fly. Introduced himself to this real or imaginary Clay Allison and allowed they had to talk about a missing ranger and a whole lot of missing stock. So he was likely expecting some verbal answer. But the owner of the Lazy A drew quicker than spit on a hot stove, dropped poor Tim with one round in the center of his forehead, then helped himself to some free lunch after he'd reholstered his Schofield and purred he was at the service of any motherfucker there who wanted to ask dumb questions."

Longarm whistled softly and asked how the surviving rangers knew such details.

Corporal Arnold piped up. "I was the one who took down the statements of everybody who'd been there that afternoon. The Cap, there, sent me and Quirt Page out yonder as soon as O'Hanlon sent poor old Tim back to town in his buckboard."

Kramer sheepishly explained, "I know Texas Rangers seldom feel the call to work in pairs. Arnold and Page were red-faced about it at the time, but I insisted, seeing this mysterious Clay Allison or his spook had got the drop on two lone rangers in a row. I got the transcripts of the statements Arnold took, along with the more recent ones we got just yesterday, if you'd care to go over 'em."

Longarm said he would, later, adding, "I got to find me a place in your town to bed down and use as my own base of operations. Why don't you just tell me about the more recent killings?"

Kramer sighed and said, "Ain't that much to tell. We were fixing to mount an armed expedition into that tangle of canyonlands, knowing a forted-up desperado with a rifle could hold an army at bay amidst all them echoes. But then we got word the big blond bastard was drinking over to the Last Chance again. O'Hanlon sent a greaser kid to tell us he was there and making everybody nervous as hell because he wouldn't let anybody leave the party he was throwing."

Nodding at Corporal Arnold, Kramer said, "Jose, here, was serving a warrant over to the west. So I sent Quirt Price along with George Summerhill. They were both good men."

He paused and added, "They weren't good enough. They entered the Last Chance with their guns drawn and leveled, having heard they were up against a quick-draw artist. But, one damn way or another, what they'd taken for a human being lounging at the bar with his gun hand holding a tumbler of bourbon just let go the glass and somehow shot both rangers before the glass shattered on the floor."

Corporal Arnold volunteered, "We're missing something about that shoot-out. It ain't possible things went as a room full of witnesses claim. The murderous son of a bitch has some trick way of doing that. Nobody can draw and drill two rangers who already have the drop on him!"

To which Longarm could only reply, "When you're right you're right. They say that back when he was alive, Clay Allison was inclined to draw sneaky as well as sudden."

Chapter 3

The summer morning had been grinding to a halt when Longarm got off at Tanktown. So *La Siesta* had set in serious as he toted his heavily laden saddle along the deserted camino toward that Toro Negro Saloon Captain Kramer had suggested when he'd politely but firmly declined an invite to board with the *capitán* and his *mujer* during his stay in the basin.

As Longarm had explained to the older lawman, it wasn't as if he felt too proud to board with anybody. He just didn't want to be a bother, and the hours he was inclined to keep, on or off duty, had been known to bother many a lady of many a house considerable.

On the take-home pay of even a senior deputy marshal he had had no choice but to hire a furnished room up Denver way. But his Denver landlady had given up holding grub in her oven for such a night owl and never forgiven him for that time he'd busted her bedsprings with the help of another night owl he'd flown home with and snuck up the stairs in the dark.

A Mex cantina called Del Toro Negro would have already shut down for *La Siesta*. But despite the black bull painted over the entrance, the Toro Negro was a Tex-Mex saloon serving customers that didn't follow the customs of Old Mexico to the point of there being no place in town to get a damned drink before late afternoon. Things just slowed down, with a skeleton crew serving the quietly serious local drinkers and any new gents in town. Corporal Arnold had told Longarm as much before he'd trudged all that way under a blazing white sun in the center of a cloudless cobalt blue sky.

Owned and operated by an Anglo widow woman now, the tile-roofed adobe and sun-silvered timber complex had been an important if not too well charted trading post, built by the shady breed of Mexican trader recalled with distaste as "Comancheros," albeit they'd been as willing to trade firewater and firearms for stolen stock and other loot gathered by the raiders of any Indian nation north or south of the border.

The rest of the town had grown like the weeds of an untidy garden around the original water tank, corrals, trading post and such, with friendlier folk, Anglo and Mex, finding it as easy to build with free 'dobe and cottonwood for the cutting all along Tiswin Creek. Tanktown now served the far more peaceful basin as a market town, with its own post office, Western Union shed, ranger post and a few other saloons.

Longarm didn't ask about Mama Felicidad's when he went inside and draped his heavily laden McClellan across the limed oak bar of the Widow Whitehead, whose hair was really rusty red and worn in a bun.

She started out friendly as most fat women of a certain age and got even friendlier when Longarm showed her his badge and I.D. whilst he explained he was in town with the advice and consent of their own Texas Rangers. He explained he only needed a base to store things he wasn't using as he went in and out at the odd hours his job required.

The Widow Whitehead confided her man had been a lawman. A county brand inspector and an honest one, too, before some dirty drygulcher had murdered him in the badlands off to the east, summer before last.

18

They agreed on four bits a day with the linen changed once a week and him buying his own food and grub off her or anyone else as he went tumbleweeding in and out at all hours. She reached under the bar for a cowbell, and when she clanged it, a regular, dozing at a corner table, awoke with a start to call her a name no man had a right to call any woman.

She reached across to grab Longarm's sleeve as he started to turn, saying, "Let it go. He's so drunk he thinks he's home with his mother. But I thank you for the thought and hold on whilst I ring for that lazy Yzabel again!"

But before she could, the bead curtains down at the far end of the bar parted to admit a mousy little barefoot mestiza in a frilly Mex blouse and wraparound black skirt trimmed in red. She wore her hair parted and braided, Caddo style, and her high cheekbones and big sloe eyes betrayed more Indian blood than most border Mexicans were prone to own up to.

Longarm knew that was more a social than racial distinction down Mexico way of late. The Spanish Empire had nipped its own "Indian Problem" in the bud by declaring everybody who cared to exist a subject of His Most Catholic Majesty, expected to put on some duds, attend Mass regular and speak some damned Spanish. Indians who'd been stubborn had been run up into the rough parts the "Spanish," red or white, hadn't thought worth fighting for. Then the "Spanish" left had sorted out the best land and political plums along the lines of who could claim to be most *sangre azul* or blue of blood. Those blue veins didn't show worth mention under Indian hide or an honest suntan. So the current El Predidente Diaz of Mexico claimed to be *sangre azul* and wore face powder to prove it, even though he had as much Indian blood as a heap of the *péones mestizo* he was inclined to spank for their own good.

The widow handed Longarm a key and told Yzabel to bed him down in room 2-K at the far end if he aimed to traipse in and out at odd hours. The little mestiza reached for Longarm's load and fought him some for it as he insisted he'd rather carry it. When she asked if he implied she was too puny or too untrustworthy to handle his old McClellan and Winchester, he confessed he had a treasure in his saddlebags and she smiled radiantly.

Most border Mexicans cottoned more to being called a thief than a weakling or, worse yet, a coward. Many a Mex who'd just laugh if you called him a horse thief would cloud up and rain all over you if you implied he might be a sissy.

As Longarm was trailing Yzabel, the widow called out to ask if he'd be about at suppertime. He told her he had to ride out of town with a ranger pal as soon as things cooled off some. She told him in that case she'd figure on him eating with her and the help around six. She had no other guests upstairs, and it wouldn't be cool enough to ride before an hour after sundown, being it was high summer.

Yzabel led him back through an empty kitchen and up an outside flight of stairs overlooking the sunbaked stable yard. Longarm knew he was imagining bats and cobwebs all around as he followed Yzabel along the dark empty corridor of the second story, because the 'dobe walls and peeled sapling ceilingwork smelled old and dry and the Widow Whitehead had told him he'd be all alone up yonder.

The bitty mestiza gal must not have worried about him feeling so lonesome. Because she commenced to get undressed as Longarm draped his saddle over the foot of the bed in the small and dim-lit chamber she showed him to. Longarm waited till he'd removed the heavily laden saddlebags, leaving the Winchester in place for the evening ride to come, before he glanced meaningfully at the open hall door to calmly ask if they usually greeted guests so warmly at the Toro Negro.

Dropping her skirt and blouse on a handy chair as she turned buck naked to shut and bar the heavy oak door, the surprisingly friendly little thing said, "Is not every guest who rides for *La Causa, El Brazo Largo*! When

20

Ricardo Chavez first spread the word you were in town, I was how you say hoping against hope you would be staying here at the one *posada*!"

She moved over to the bed to throw her pretty little self down across the same, rolling on her back with her chunky little thighs spread in welcome as she hopefully added, "Is too much for to assume you were not expecting for to be met by some other *mujer* on this side of the border?"

Longarm silently hung his gunbelt and Stetson on a bedpost to give himself time to study his answer. Border folk didn't like to be called liars or, worse yet, fools. So playing dumb and asking who *El Brazo Largo* might be could be asking for more trouble with the locals than he'd get from more distant Mex *rurales* anxious to collect the price El Presidente had out on the head of a pestiferous Yanqui called "The Long Arm," or *El Brazo Largo* south of the border.

He assured the pretty little thing, who hardly seemed out to collect the bounty posted by a dictatorship most decent Mexicans had no use for, that he hadn't expected to meet any gals of her cause down this way. He sat down beside her to unbutton his shirt as he confided he was on a secret mission.

She closed her thighs to perk up and get to work on the buttons of his pants as she chortled, "That is what Ricardo thought! He has only told those of us who can be trusted for to resist that *chingado hijo de puta* who stole our *revolución* from the dead eyelids of our most beloved Benito Juarez! After *La Siesta* we can tell Ricardo how many riders you need, and *adonde* you wish for them to ride with you! *Pero* first we die together for a while, no?"

Longarm knew what she proposed would never meet with Billy Vail's approval, whilst Lemonade Lucy Hayes, the not-bad-looking but mighty prim First Lady who'd inspired the pesky current dress code for federal lawmen and refused to let them even drink to *her* with hard liquor, would doubtless throw a hissy pissy if she ever got word

21

of a deputy U.S. marshal enjoying carnal knowledge of a teenaged maiden with Indian blood that showed. But Miss Lemonade Lucy was a long way from Texas, and Yzabel was surely going to hiss and piss if he acted like a priss too proud to treat a mestiza as a natural woman.

So by the time the two of them had him naked as her, Longarm had a couple of fingers in her ring dang doo to wriggle in time with the tongue he had in her mouth, whilst she moaned and groaned and took the matter of his manhood in hand.

That felt swell, too, but as he cocked a leg over a once more wide-spread thigh, Yzabel gasped, with his tongue in her mouth "*¡Ay, Dios mio!* I was told me *El Brazo Largo* was *muy hombre, pero* this is so much more than I deserve! I am not certain I can . . . *No, espérte,* what do you think you are doing and, *Dios mio,* you are *doing* it, and if I die I die, *pero vida es breve. Vamanos pa'l carajo y joder toda la fregada siesta!*"

So they let themselves go to hell and fucked away the whole fucking siesta, or most of it, before they ran low on new positions and sweet things to say, inspiring the pretty little thing to ask more serious questions as they shared a smoke atop the rumpled sheets.

Longarm had been afraid she might. So, during a spell of dog style, he'd come up with a yarn meant to keep his local Mex admirers happy whilst mayhaps helping him some with his real mission.

He made her force it out of him, knowing women prided themselves on seeing through glib sweet talk. He knew what she was going to say when he confided he meant to jump the border alone to hook up with some rebels pals down Chihuahua way and bust some other rebels out of a *federale* prison camp.

Yzabel pouted. "*Que pesado.* I have given you my all at both ends and still you do not trust me! We both know neither *El Gato* nor *La Mariposa* are at war with *los federales* within a week's ride of *our* crossing! Not even *El Brazo Largo* would wish for to dare the most dry crags of the Sierra Burro without a guide. So you must wait

22

here for someone from *La Causa* to join you, no?"

He put the cheroot they were sharing betwixt her pouty lips as he sheepishly confessed, "Trying to slicker such a woman of the world seems beyond my limited talents. But if I tell you the truth, do I have your word you won't tell anybody? Not even your pals here in the basin?"

She asked how he could doubt a woman who loved him sincerely enough to swallow, and so, as she commenced to stroke him some more, Longarm spun her the line of bullshit he wanted her to cast far and wide for her own kind to hook on to.

He told her he was pretending to work with the rangers north of the border to lull any *federale* spies as to his true concerns as he went through the motions of hunting for a gringo killer who'd been dead a spell. She kept stroking as she said she'd heard the most terrible Clay Allison, who hated *La Raza* and shot *Negros pobrecitos* on sight, had killed four gringos recently. But that was all she was able to tell Longarm about the mystery. Nobody she knew all that well was missing any stock, because most of the folk she knew all that well kept goats, pigs and chickens.

Having drawn him back to attention with her languid hand job, she rose up to fork a tawny thigh across his hips and spit herself on the monster she'd created, sighing. "*Ay, que linda!* When do you intend for to jump the border, *querido mio*? I do not think I will be able for to get enough of this in less than a year!"

He wistfully allowed he doubted he'd be staying there a year, but when she pressed him for tighter figures, he said, "I've already told you more than I should have. I ain't officiously supposed to cross the border at all, see?"

And this was the simple truth when you studied on it, for Longarm had standing orders to stay the hell of out Old Mexico since the last time he'd caused an international incident down yonder. That was what they called it when you had to gun a *rurale* or Mexican Ranger, an international incident.

Longarm had never set out to tangle with El Presidente Díaz and the thugs he had riding herd over the republic he'd rustled from the less ruthless members of the Juárista party after old Benito had died, leaving them rudderless. But there was something about an Anglo lawman who wasn't inclined to lick their boots that brought out the blood lust in illiterate riders who'd been assured they were lords of all within rifle range. Longarm had tried to work with *Los Rurales* when trailing U.S. federal wants in their jurisdiction. He'd even managed to work with the few halfway decent Mex lawmen he'd met up with on rare occasions. But, being only human, he'd had to fight back more often and this had somehow led a heap of Mexicans in general and the several rebel factions in particular to dub him *El Brazo Largo* and claim him as a member of *La Causa* whether he wanted to be or not.

Longarm and the inquisitive Yzabel lost the thread of the conversation for an all-too-short, delicious spell. Then they both came again, and being a woman, she picked up where she'd left off about his secret mission south of the border.

But before he had to make up any whopper that might satisfy her and all her kith and kin, they heard the distant but insistent sound of that cowbell. So Yzabel rolled out of bed with catlike grace to dress with astounding speed as she muttered awful things about *chingado vacas* of the gringo persuasion.

As she slipped out, Longarm rose to bar the door after her, meaning to catch forty winks before that ride out to the Last Chance, seeing he'd been saved by the bell.

Chapter 4

Longarm caught more than forty winks by sundown and got up feeling fresh to eat supper downstairs in the kitchen with the fat Widow Whitehead and her stable boss at one table, served by Yzabel wearing a fresh blouse and the innocent expression of the proverbial cat who'd swallowed the canary and Lord only knew what else.

The red-haired Widow Whitehead commented on her *chica*'s Mona Lisa expression when Yzabel joined the other kitchen help to eat her own grub. She murmured to Longarm, "I suspect that girl has been sparking her own cousin, young Ricardo Chavez. They were buzzing out back like flies above a cooling pie on the sill, and this evening she sure looks pleased with herself."

Longarm prided himself on his poker face. But he didn't risk commenting on the implied incest, even when the widow smiled dirty and speculated on how the snippy little mestiza was going to put it to the padre at her Saturday confession session. He excused himself and his grin by allowing he had to get back to work for her and other taxpayers.

Nobody argued. So he went back up for his stripped-down saddle and Winchester, then took them through the dusk to the ranger post, to see they'd been expecting him and had a spanking paint pony waiting for him, bridled with a Spanish bit and saddled with a centerfire roper. So he draped his McClellan over a corral pole, switched his rifle boot and Winchester to the Texican rig and forked aboard to ride out to that Last Chance with Corporal Arnold.

With Arnold showing the way on a black-tailed buckskin barb, they rode down the wagon trace between ever narrowing bluffs to the south. The trail took them through glades and alamedas of black willow and cottonwood, or alamo as they called it, well watered on either side of that creek, with the slopes rising ever higher to their left.

Trotting some and walking some, it didn't take a full hour to rein in out front of the Last Chance in the moonlight. Longarm had to take it on faith that they were dismounting in the dooryard of an adobe-and-pole sprawl even bigger than the Toro Negro back in town. It was right tough to make out more than lamplight spilling out narrow windows and a wide front entrance as they tethered their mounts with others to a long hitching rail out front.

As they did so, Longarm noted that two of the other ponies wore bare-tree Mexican saddles with the broad flat dally horns and suicidally high cantles favored by the dyed-in-the-wool vaquero. So he was expecting to spy at least two traditional Mex sombreros amid the more natural hats bellied up to the bar or seated at card tables inside. But he didn't spy *one* as he trailed Corporal Arnold to one end of the bar to meet up with a big burly cuss with curly black hair, eyebrows as met in the middle, and features Irish as Paddy's pig.

Liam O'Hanlon shook with a grip that would have made a milkmaid wince and confided they hadn't been visited by Clay Allison or any of his Tex-Mex hands since the shooting of Price and Summerhill over by yonder doorway. He added, "There was two riders dressed Mex a few minutes ago. But I doubt they could be riding for the Lazy A, for nobody here had ever laid eyes on them

26

before and they was asking the way to Tanktown. So that's where they must have headed."

Corporal Arnold proved he knew his job when he replied, "They're still around here, somewheres, unless they decided to leave two Mex saddle broncs out front and *walk* four miles into town."

O'Hanlon grinned dirty and confided, "I might have known they'd heard about them white trash gals camped down by the creek in the sticker-brush. One of 'em looks pure Chihuahua. The other looks to have more white blood. Them two Mex riders, not the gals down by the creek. What sort of pizen can I serve you boyos? I don't serve the clap nor the blue balls. But you can have anything from bourbon to white lightning, on the house."

Longarm asked if they served Maryland rye. When O'Hanlon allowed they surely did, Longarm said he hadn't had the real thing in a coon's age and asked how many of the regulars in the crowd all around had witnessed the ranger's shoot-out with the quick-draw artist claiming to be Clay Allison.

As O'Hanlon moved down to fetch a fifth of Maryland rye from his back bar, he asked regulars he passed to join the lawmen toward the back. So by the time Longarm got his Maryland rye there were three other witnesses to back O'Hanlon as he declared they were missing a half dozen others who hadn't ridden in that evening as yet, if they meant to, on a workday night.

Longarm allowed that the words of the three fairly sober gents dressed for riding, along with a cold sober barkeep, would likely be enough to hang a man who didn't have a mighty fine excuse.

As the four of them repeated what they'd already told the rangers about a blur of motion in the tricky light of a late afternoon sun, blazing through that big front entrance to outline Page and Summerhill with their guns drawn for certain, Longarm downed his free shot of rye and broke out the blown-up photo prints of the poison-mean but sincerely dead Clay Allison.

As he handed them out and asked his witnesses to study

some before they made up their minds, he didn't stress the date of Clay Allison's death, lest he influence their replies. But he had to ask if they were sure when all but one declared the prints were fine likenesses.

The cowhand who wasn't dead certain said, "He aint wearing a hat in this picture. The stuck-on-hisself face looks familiar, but I'd be a whole lot surer if he was wearing his hat."

When Longarm asked what sort of hat the man they knew usually wore, they all agreed on a gray cavalry-style hat, fairly new and likely Stetson brand to go with his grade-A riding outfit and serious gun rig. There was some argument as to whether his spurs had been Mex or Cav. They all agreed on his .44 or .45 six-gun being a nickel-plate Schofield he could pluck from thin air like a stage magician.

Longarm put the pictures away as Corporal Arnold repeated, "If it looks like a duck and walks like a duck . . ."

O'Hanlon refilled their shot glasses as Longarm cocked a brow to decide in a dubious tone, "Let's stick with something as *looks* like a duck! The trouble with all these yarns about King Arthur, Barbarossa or Black Jack Slade still being alive somewheres is that they fail to account for what these famous dead who faked their deaths have been *up* to all this while!"

He downed his drink, told the generous O'Hanlon he'd had his limit whilst on duty and explained, "Clay Allison's dubious fame rests on the fact he killed men, lots of men, all along his trail from that Union prison camp to both sides of the New Mexico–Colorado line. In just the two years before his officious death in the summer of '77 Clay Allison gunned at least two Mexicans he accused of stealing stock, three colored troopers he accused of being uppity, a Colorado lawman, and two quick draw artists almost as famous as himself. He sat down to supper with the dangerous Chunk Colbert at the Clifton House in Red River Station and shot him for dessert for reasons as vary with the reporter. Some self-styled authorites put

Red River Station just north of Santa Fe in for Pete's sake Texas!"

"You mean that shoot-out *wasn't* in Texas, near Allison's ranch on the Washita?" asked Corporal Arnold.

Longarm smiled thinly and said, "I read that wild guess, too. But for the record the Washita River runs through neither Texas nor New Mexico. Clay Allison never had no ranch in the Indian Territory. But I digress. He shot it out with the dangerous Pancho Griego in the taproom of the Saint James Hotel in Cimarron on an autumn eve of '75. In the spring of '76 he was drinking at the same stand when the three unfortunate colored soldiers offended him by standing in the doorway. All three wound up dead on the walk outside, and did I leave out a young Texas cowboy named Bowman the sensitive Mr. Allison swatted like a fly at a dance? At any rate, near the end of '76 Clay Allison and his brother, John, shot it out with a Constable Faber in Las Animas, Colorado, and somehow, likely by crossing some palms with silver, persuaded the local grand jury to let them off on a plea of self-defense. Anyone could see a lawman trying to enforce a municipal ordinance against wearing guns to yet another dance was a homicidal maniac."

Longarm reached under his denim jacket for some cheroots as he told them, "Federal District Court in Pueblo didn't see things that way. As in that case of Cockeyed Jack McCall being arrested federal after he slickered a local court, federal charges were devised so as to end the tedious killings of Claymore Allison and . . . By the way, might your own Clay Allison haunting the badlands over to the east have a kid brother, wife or children with him at his mysterious Lazy A?"

Nobody there had heard tell of anybody other than four or five Mex vaqueros backing the play of their own Clay Allison.

Longarm said, "There you go, then. When I was sent to serve Allison with a federal warrant back in '77, his kith and kin had just buried him in New Mexican soil and, far as I know, they're still up yonder."

29

A skinny Mex kid joined O'Hanlon behind the bar to pluck at the big Irishman's sleeve as Longarm was pontificating, "What we got here is some *other* homicidal maniac who heard he looked like the late Clay Allison and took it as a compliment."

The cowhand who hadn't been sure about that missing cavalry hat opined, "If he's just a gent as *looks* like Clay Allison, how come he draws and *shoots* like Clay Allison?"

Longarm said he'd never seen Clay Allison draw and shoot in any of his incarnations, adding, "For all I know your local boy could be better or worse. Meanwhile he has the charges being filed against Clay Allison, not against whoever in thunder he really has to be!"

O'Hanlon leaned foreward to confide in a softer tone, "Hector, here, tells me I was wrong about them two Mex riders playing slap and tickle down by the river. He tells me they're out in our 'dobe-walled stable yard to the south. With their big hats on the ground and saddle guns in their hands, covering the way in here!"

"Or the way *out* of here, you mean!" Corporal Arnold scowled, adding, "Wasn't Dick Brewer and that Billy the Kid hunkered behind such a wall in line with a front street when they ambushed Sheriff Brady over to Lincoln County, New Mexico, a spell back?"

Longarm smiled thinly and replied, "These other gents could have read about that down Mexico way. We'd best ask 'em. Could you show us a sneaky back way out of here, Mr. O'Hanlon?"

The burly Irishman reached under his bar as he replied, "There is and I'll show it to you."

Then he yelled for someone called Pop as he produced a ten-gauge sawed-off Greener.

Pop turned out to be the grizzled old-timer who'd been waiting on the card tables. O'Hanlon directed him to take over the bar, and as they changed places the bigger and younger proprieter of the Last Chance told young Hector to stay with Pop as he led the way back along a dimly lit corridor to the shithouse yard, then sideways as he whispered, "Nobody who dosen't work here is supposed to know how to work this gate. Them Mex riders must have come over our stable yard wall from out front."

Longarm clutched O'Hanlon's sleeve, his own six-gun drawn, to say, "Open it and then stay back of me and Arnold, with that Greener aimed at the moon, old son!"

O'Hanlon worked the deliberately compex bolt of the narrow gate at the far corner of the main building and changed places with the two lawmen. Longarm stepped into the stable yard, hugging the wall. Corporal Arnold moved in after him, further out from the corner, as they both threw down on the two dimly visible forms hunkered behind the four-foot 'dobe wall to the west.

Longarm silently signaled the ranger to keep quiet and stay abreast as he moved closer, six-gun trained but aiming to get closer in such tricky light before he ordered the two sinister strangers to drop those saddle guns and grab for some stars. Corporal Arnold seemed to cotton to his notion, and the two of them closed half the distance side by side before O'Hanlon, from the corner gate, called out in a no-bullshit manner, "Behind you! Under the ramada!"

So Longarm fired on the two by the wall as he was crabbing to one side and dropping to spin on his knee, as another shotgun blazed in the black shadow of the brushwood ramada shading the front of yonder stable, to send a load of double-O buck through the space Longarm's back had so recently occupied.

Longarm fired back at the muzzle blast and adjusted his aim when a second ball of flame blossomed three yards along the ramada from the first. At least two pellets ticked the brim of Longarm's Stetson, and then Arnold had fired his own two cents' worth and they could all hear the seperate thuds of meat and metal hitting the dirt in the inky shade. So Arnold yelled, "Hot damn! We got him!" and Longarm warned, "Don't count your chickens before they're hatched and get over in the shade of the main building to cover me as I have a look-see at what we have wrought this evening!"

Two rifles being more dangerous than one spent shotgun, Longarm got over to the ones by the wall first, got no response when he kicked each in the face, and moved across the stable yard behind the trained muzzle of his .44–40 to duck under the ramada and hug the stable wall and find that, sure enough, he could see the dark sprawl up the way a heap better with the moonlight bouncing off the dust on the far side. Longarm called out to Arnold and O'Hanlon, "I make it three down. Stay put whilst I make sure this one ain't playing possum!"

Then he moved in, covering the figure sprawled face-down by another sawed-off shotgun and a Texas ten-gallon that had parted company with his curly head. He rolled the fallen ambusher over on his back, out in the moonlight, and hunkered down to feel for a pulse with his free hand before he called out, "This one's sincerely down, too. Come on over and see if either of you can say who in thunder he might have been!"

As Corporal Arnold and O'Hanlon joined him, Long-arm saw that others had started to spill out the back of the Last Chance. He roared, "Get the fuck back inside and stay there!"

Corporal Arnold added, "In the name of the law! We both mean that!"

O'Hanlon hunkered down for a closer look before he said, "This one was at the bar earlier. He didn't seem to be with them Mexicans. But then, we've just established the three of them was up to something sneaky!"

"Sure, but what?" asked Corporal Arnold, observing, "If the three of them were laying here for the two of us, wouldn't they have done better shooting us on sight, as we dismounted out front without a care in the world?"

Longarm wearily replied, "This Anglo gunslick was too slick to do us that way. Don't you see what the sneaky bastard had in mind?"

Chapter 5

Longarm had noticed most old boys were better at checkers than they were at chess. So as O'Hanlon ducked into his stable to fetch a lantern, Longarm explained to the ranger, "At the risk of sounding swell-headed, I was the likely target of this Anglo rider's dirty little game. I'll get to that notion once we have more light on the subject. I can't speak for yourself, but I told more than one in town we'd be riding out this way after dark. So they had plenty of time to get set up. But setting up an ambush is one thing and getting away clean is another. So this one with the ten-gallon hat and twelve-gauge Parker meant to sacrifice them two pawns over against yonder wall in order to crawfish back into the Anglo crowd assembled, as outraged about the cadavers of you, me and the two dirty greasers we took down with us."

As O'Hanlon came back out with the oil lantern already lit, Longarm added, "He figured that even if somebody in the crowd speculated on us tangling with more than two Mexicans, they'd be looking for some strange Mexican, not a wayfaring Texican stranger just passing through when the shooting started."

As O'Hanlon's lantern light spilled over the sharp features and sleepy smile of the dead man at their feet, Longarm nodded knowingly and said, "I was right. This would be the late Hardpan Harry Hoffmann, a notorious bounty hunter and gun for hire. He knew who I was, too. I reckon somebody in these parts shares your Captain Kramer's faith in my rep for solving puzzles. Hardpan Harry's going price for a killing was five hundred bucks, or a year's wages for a top hand. Lord knows what sort of a tale he sold his poor tools over by the wall. Getting them killed instead of having to share the payoff must had made him feel too slick to stand himself."

Corporal Arnold still didn't seem to get it. O'Hanlon was the one who said, "Jasus, Mary and Joseph and I see it all now! As you just said, had they fired on you boyos coming *in,* they'd be riding for their lives with a posse on their heels and a good description of at least two of them on the wire! But this professional knew a lawman like yourself would do just what you did when we found out, as he expected us to find out, two mysterious gazoons were in wait with saddle guns, covering the dooryard!"

Corporal Arnold blinked and marveled, "Well, sure he did! He knew we'd try to pussyfoot around behind them while he was covering the whole stable yard with that twelve-gauge and . . . How did you spot him in time, O'Hanlon?"

The man who owned and operated the whole layout said, "I only knew there was somebody moving in the shadows of my ramada. The shade ain't total as it looks. Slivers of moonlight slice down through those willow branches, but when something's moving through them the flicker gives away less form than motion. I'd have never spotted him if he'd been smart enough to stand still over here!"

Longarm meant it when he allowed he was just as glad O'Hanlon had.

He asked Corporal Arnold, "How do you cotton to the notion of the two of us riding for that Lazy A with the news before anybody else can carry it to our suddenly shy Clay Allison?"

The ranger said, "I've always sort of hankered to screw Miss Sarah Bernhardt and have her pay me a million dollars for the job, too. I just ain't sure how I'd go about that. Lieutenant Weiner wasn't able to fill in all the details, but it's my understanding he had Caddo Flynn, the breed as stumbled over the canyon spread, show him the way."

"Hasn't the same ridge runner told anybody else where the layout might be?" asked Longarm.

Arnold replied, "Well, sure, he's *told* most everybody who'll listen how he tracked a wounded bighorn up over a sandstone hogback to see a bitty Garden of Eden on the far side, watered by a summer stream and shaded by cottonwoods galore. Flynn claims he counted over two hundred head of contented stock grazing stirrup-high alfalfa and wild mustard, with a ranch house big enough to pass for an old Spanish mission and so on, till you try to pin him down to map coordinates. Old Caddo don't know how to read anything on paper. After that he aint clear as to how you'd reach the place from the river road before it peters out. He likely showed Weiner the way over hill and dale."

Longarm frowned and demanded, "What do you mean, *likely showed*? Didn't you gents take a statement when he came back without the lieutenant?"

Arnold answered defensively, "Caddo wasn't there to make one. Some say they seen him hither whilst others say they've seen him yonder since we lost track of Weiner over a week ago. Captain Kramer's put out the word we want to talk to the wandersome breed; Caddo likely aint heard, yet. He's a good old boy who's never been in trouble with the law, or had a permanent address he can be reached at. He'll likely come in any time now, and so . . ."

"So we can't hope to find that Lazy A spread in the dark, tonight." Longarm cut in, adding, "By the time we can ask Caddo Flynn to show us the way, if he shows up for morning roll call at your post, the mothers who sent *these* mothers after me will know what happened here, and I am not refering to anybody's Mother *Dear!*"

35

Liam O'Hanlon volunteered, "I've taken some interest in this hidden ranch in the canyonlands to my east, seeing the gazoon who's said to live there keeps killing people in my saloon. But none of the Anglo riders I serve know that rock pile more than a few twisted miles in, and even the Mexicans I've talked to make that sign of the cross and swear they're content to let a cow straying more than say a score of bends up any of them winding canyons have its fucking freedom if it's that *loco en la cabeza.*"

Arnold volunteered, "More than one greaser's told me everything say south of Emery Peak to the hairpin bend of the river is haunted as well as unexplored. I make that many a square mile, with the spooky Lazy A most anywheres amongst 'em!"

Longarm said, "Let's see about loading up these boys before they get too stiff to lay straight. Then we'd best run 'em into town before everybody there calls it a night, and see if anybody there can tell us who they used to be."

O'Hanlon called out to the crowd striving to stampede through that gate, and in no time at all they had the three cadavers laid out tidy in O'Hanlon's buckboard, with plenty of volunteers helping Longarm and Corporal Arnold into town with them. They made it well before ten, and seeing they had no opera house in Tanktown, the turnout for the show-and-tell was bodacious.

But despite the crowds milling by lamplight past the three strangers propped up on planks outside the ranger post, none of the three save for Hardpan Harry Hoffmann could be identified, and Longarm seemed to be the only one there who could identify him. So it was decided the trio whose ponies now stood tethered to the ranger's hitching rail had never crossed the nearest fairly safe ford of the Rio Grande in cloaks of invisibility. A local Mex with Chihuahua kin he visited a heap opined, and others there agreed, it was nigh fatal to ford the river farther downstream and not much safer higher up. It seemed the floodwaters of the rocky Bottleneck Canyon had formed the best ford for miles as it dumped sand and gravel into the main stream as fast or faster than the current could carry it on down through the hairpin slot to the southeast.

Corporal Arnold held, and Longarm had no serious objection, that a hired gun and two dumb greasers riding out of the hills to the east from that mysterious Lazy A made sense enough to him.

That raised the question as to who in that late-night Anglo-Mex crowd might know the way to the hidden ranch of the officiously late Clay Allison.

Nobody in town that night could offer an educated guess. As if Longarm, being a stranger in town, needed a local geography lesson, more than one townee and twice that many local stockmen repeated how the half dozen fair-sized outfits and mayhaps twice that many small holdings were strung like beads along the narrow river valley, on range too steep and rocky for any cash crop more tender than riding stock. Hither and yon an acre or ten of flat-bottomed basinland did provide a toehold for a homespread, a truck garden or even a small town like Tanktown. But the share of the rugged Big Bend Country one could inhabit at all depended on grazing ever steepening slopes within an easy ride of the creek-side trail along the narrow floodplain, and allowed no sensible livestock to stray much farther from the creek than the scent of water in the thin dry air.

More than one local gent seemed willing to posse up, anyhow. But Captain Kramer decided, and Longarm agreed, it made more sense to find that fool Caddo Flynn and ask him to show them the way.

So, Caddo Flynn being nowhere in town that evening, they called it a night by turning the three stiffening cadavers over to Doc Fletcher, who served as their coroner and undertaker when he wasn't pulling teeth, and agreed to talk about it some more in the morning, after they located Caddo Flynn.

Since Longarm had left his saddlebags at the Toro Negro, he left his McClellan and bridle in the ranger's tack room for the time being and headed on home with his Winchester, still wide awake but having nothing better than Yzabel to fool with after he stopped by the one-room

Western Union shed to wire a progress report back to Billy Vail at night letter rates. He knew his boss hated to waste a nickel a word unless the message was important, and all he had to report, for certain, was the shoot-out with three pissants at the Last Chance.

He hadn't been sent all this way to kill or capture Hard-pan Harry Hoffmann and some possible beginners. So he had to admit like a man that he still had no idea what was going on down this way.

Back at the Toro Negro word of his actions at the Last Chance had proceeded him. So the taproom was crowded, the Widow Whitehead was serving, and everybody wanted to buy him a drink.

He'd only downed a couple of beers before he'd determined half the faces in the crowd were gents he'd already talked to up to the ranger post, and that none of the ones he hadn't talked to yet knew any more about the uninhabited rock piles to the east-southeast. Experience had taught him how tough it was to excuse oneself from such drinking occasions. So he muttered something about putting his saddle gun away and just crawfished backward through that beaded curtain to find himself alone in the dark kitchen.

That had been his plan. Before anybody could miss him, Longarm made it out the back and up the stairs, felt his way along the deserted second-story corridor and dropped to one knee outside his hired door to feel the bottom hinge.

The match stem he'd wedged in place was still there. But he had a round in the chamber of his Winchester '73 when he unlocked the heavy oaken door and followed its muzzle inside.

When he kicked the door shut to plunge the room into total darkness and struck a match in an unexpected corner, Longarm saw he was alone up yonder after all. So he barred the door from inside, explaining to it, "I aint usually such an old maid, door. But I don't usually meet up with hired guns after supper, neither."

He leaned the saddle gun against the lamp table as he

lit the oil lamp atop the same. Then he hung his six-gun even handier on a bedpost and used the other three to hang the rest of his outfit tidier than usual, save for the boots on the floor, to kill time as he waited for Yzabel to join him.

He hadn't seen her down below, so that meant she was off duty, Lord love her sweet brown behind, and he knew she knew he was waiting for her up yonder, if she was anywhere in town. For the whole blamed town was still abuzz with his riding back from the Last Chance alive.

But as he lit a cheroot, seated on the edge of the bed in his birthday suit, all that seemed to be rising to the occasion was his fool organ grinder.

A man didn't have to invite his privates to throb like so after a close call. It seemed to be human, or male animal nature, to feel like shitting when something seemed out to kill him, and like fucking after he'd killed it instead. That Professor Darwin over in England had allowed that the winners got to fuck whilst the losers didn't, and that was why they called it Survival of the Fastest.

He told his throbbing erection to behave itself, lest they scare poor little Yzabel or give her delusions of grandeur when he opened the door to admit her.

But, naturally, talking sense to a stiff dick was as futile as talking sense to a woman who'd made up her mind. So Longarm rose to trim the lamp and smoke more modestly in the dark.

He'd smoked his cheroot down and, telling himself it was still too early to worry, commenced to light a second when he heard some timid tapping on the oaken door.

Rising to snub the smoke and draw his holstered six-gun, Longarm called out, "*¿Quien es?*" to be answered in whispered English, "It's me, silly! Open up and let me in before somebody sees me out here!"

So he did, lowering the six-gun to his side and reaching out with his free arm to haul the pretty little thing in for a French welcome.

The perfumed and silk-shimmied shemale kissed back

in kind, sucking on Longarm's tongue as she kicked the door shut behind her with a bare heel.

Longarm tossed his gun on the bed to bar the door, as any man in such a ridiculous situation would have wanted to, before anybody on earth caught him swapping spit, bare-ass, with the big fat Widow Whitehead, unless there was somebody else on the premises wearing her perfume and weighing over two hundred pounds!

The middle-aged redhead seemed to have some brawn under all that lard as well. For the next Longarm knew she'd literally swept him off his feet, or up on his toes at least, to waltz them both over to the bed and he was sure they were going through the bedsprings as they crashed down across it.

But the bedsprings held, as the lady who owned them had no doubt foreseen, and then Longarm lay pinned to the mattress with his six-gun digging into his bare ass and a whole lot of woman going up and down the maypole as she stripped her shimmy off over her unbound red hair, laughing like a mean little kid before she declared she'd known all along he'd been as anxious to screw as she'd been, since first the two of them had met downstairs.

Longarm was too polite to ask what might have given the fat old gal such an odd notion, and once a man studied some on how swell it felt in such an imaginative old gal, it seemed only common courtesy to roll her over on her big broad ass and treat her like a lady.

Chapter 6

If it was true all cats were gray in the dark, a halfway sober man could feel the differance betwixt a tiny tawny mestiza and a great big strapping redhead twice her age and experience. Experience could make up for a hundred pounds of excess tonnage when it opened wide, said, "Oh, yessss!" and clamped down to move like a schoolboy jacking off with a greased-up velvet glove.

She kissed so good it was hard to recall what she looked like with the lamps lit, and as she dug her nails into his back to hug him to her heroic naked breasts, it didn't seem to *matter* what she *looked* like.

So a good time was had by all until, having come with her, Longarm moved to holster his six-gun and light a smoke for them to share.

The widow begged him not to strike a match, confessing, "I don't know how I'll ever face you in the light again, after all those silly things I was begging you to do to me, before! I can imagine what you think of such a dirty old woman now, and I just don't know what came over me tonight!"

Longarm knew why she didn't want him to strike a light. He wasn't sure he wanted to break the spell, either.

41

So he turned to take her in his arms again and kiss her, tender, before he said soothingly, "Nothing came over you that didn't come over me earlier, ma'am. I was showing it hard when you came through the door and I reckon we were both sort of inspired by all the exitement. I remember lying in this billet the night after Shiloh when these farm gals out of nowhere . . . but that's another story and I'm sure glad you came."

She giggled and jiggled closer to toss across his gut a thigh big around as your average corral pole, and reply, "I came more than once and I'd almost forgotten how good the real thing felt! For how would it look if I gave in to every wayfaring stranger who tempted my . . . ah, womanly feelings?"

Having no certain answer, Longarm just nuzzled her neck.

She decided, "I expect it was all that talk of blood and slaughter in the bar downstairs, after hearing those Mexicans had tried to kill you over at Liam O'Hanlon's place. They thought it was Mexicans who drygulched my Danny, and it all flooded back on me how I'd refused my man the night before and sent him to his death the next morning with no satisfaction for either of us!"

Longarm was too polite to say he wished women wouldn't drag other men into bed with him. He'd yet to mention to a newfound friend he'd just come with the late Roping Sally or other gals he'd loved and lost, and how might this one like it if he told her he'd had little Yzabel less than twelve hours back on the very same sheets, or that Yzabel had needed a pillow under her own rollicking rump, which was more than present company could say? But recalling Yzabel in that same bed, and how the tawny little thing had said she was looking forward to some more in the same, inspired an uneasy feeling indeed as Longarm pictured the scene to follow should Yzabel come tapping on yon chamber door in the near future!

He didn't really give a shit, but he politely asked, "How come you held out on your man like so, ma'am?"

She sighed and said, "I guess it's all right, considering,

42

if you were to call me Flo, in private. I've often tried to recall what our spat the night before had been inspired by. My Danny and me usually got along, or at least made up by bedtime, or once we were in bed. He was a natural man and you may have noticed I have feelings. But spat we did, over one silly thing or another, and I never forgave myself when they brought him down from Emery Mountain after the buzzards had been at him. Other widows have told me they were left with the same empty aches about thoughtless words and unimportant arguments. So I fear all married couples bicker like so."

To which Longarm could only reply, "That's the simple truth. Reckon nobody can feel lovey-dovey twenty-four hours a day."

He felt no call to add that was another good reason for a man who packed a badge to pack one *alone*. For he'd learned the hard way that just as the sweetest little thing you ever saw couldn't shack up with you a full month without asking why you couldn't find a better job or at least not clean your gun on the kitchen table, she preferred to be told a lawman sparking her was more worried about leaving a young widow than getting it on down the road to see what might lie around a bend beyond. The nicest thing about widow women, aside from knowing more ways to pleasure a man, was the way they seemed less desperate to marry up with every man they fornicated with. He sensed old Flo, Lord love her, doubtless enjoyed being the sole proprietor of the Toro Negro, free to indulge any sudden temptations and not keen on marrying up with any gent who wasn't a way better catch than a lawman passing through. So mayhaps when and if Yzabel showed up, it might be possible to get old Flo to act like a sport about it and . . . Great balls of fire! Wouldn't *that* make for a night to remember?

"You're getting hard again." Flo giggled, thrusting her moist pubic thatch and gaping slit teasingly to kiss the trembling tip of his old organ grinder as he inspired it further by picturing big old Flo and tiny Yzabel in a mighty sassy position.

So, seeing he only had big old Flo to work with, and a gal with a behind like that needed no pillow under her ass, he rolled her on her back to remount her as she marveled, "This position again? So soon! My God, Deputy Long, when was the last time you had a woman?"

"Not since this afternoon," he truthfully replied, inspired as much by the brazen truth as she was by what she thought a silly brag, and his mighty mixed feelings about the possibility of a sudden shy tapping on the hall door had him at her hard and heavy as he strove to come whilst the coming was good. For if she recalled sending a man off to work with an unsatisfied hard-on, Longarm remembered how awful it felt to pull out of a gal and roll out of her window when a husband she'd never told him about came home early.

It was just as well old Flo was horny natured and hadn't been getting as much of late. For she found his enthusiasm flattering and came even faster, grateful as all get-out, to hear her tell.

But he took another uneasy breath when she confided, as they lay limp as two satisfied dishrags, that he'd more than lived up to her daydreams about such a notorious lady-killer.

Then it turned out she was talking about all the bullshit going around about the famous Longarm, not the *El Brazo Largo* her kitchen help might have been jawing about. He knew better than to ask her what, if anything, little Yzabel might have been saying downstairs about anybody or anything. He knew better than to mention Yzabel at all. For Flo was older than him, possibly smarter, and he knew from his own questioning of suspects how a cuss with something guilty to hide was inclined to ask innocent questions about the safe he'd raped or the maiden he'd cracked if nobody else brought them up.

So, seeing Flo was set against his striking a light, and being there was nothing you could do in bed with a woman but screw her or talk to her, Longarm worked the two of them into a more comfortable position for some pillow talk and resigned himself to hearing the story of her life, hoping she had some local gossip he could use for Billy Vail.

Flo Whitehead did. Even the sad story of her sending a man to his death with a hard-on added to the picture Longarm had been building of a West Texas settlement branching off the wilder downstream or upstream approaches to the Big Bend.

Flo said her Danny, after riding through the Battle of Glorieta Pass unscathed in Sibley's Texas Brigade, had bought the Toro Negro off the Mex family who hadn't been able to make it pay, with results one could see downstairs. Danny Whitehead had made a little extra on the side as a county brand inspector. It hadn't paid much because there hadn't been much to do until, two years earlier, there'd been a sudden spate of serious rustling in the modest local herds.

She said, "They told me, later, it read as if my Danny had cut sign where a dozen head or more had been run up a canyon everyone else had always considered dry and blind. The sheriff's deputies trailing my Danny when he hadn't come back for two days picked up on the cow and extra pony tracks as well. Danny had followed them through a narrow cleft in the side, not the end, of that supposedly blind canyon and trailed them on, and on some more, a dozen miles deeper into those uncharted crags, along a zigzag route the thieves had found, until, in a deep black canyon running down from the slopes of Emery Peak, they figured, they found what was left of my poor Danny. Shot in the back and half-eaten by buzzards!"

Longarm patted her plump shoulder soothingly and asked how come they had a name for any peaks in an uncharted wilderness.

She explained, "You can see Emery Peak from any rise in these parts. It looms head and shoulders above all the others between it and the river. Nigh a mile and a half above sea level, or so they say. They never said they found my Danny *on* that mountain. The cow thieves who murdered him must have been trailing the stolen stock *around* Emery Peak, see?"

He said he did and asked how come he hadn't met up with any county lawmen since he'd arrived, come to study on it.

She explained how after Danny Whitehead and a county deputy called Frenchy Cartier had been drygulched by that person or persons unknown, the newly reorganized Texas Rangers had set up that post under the Captain Kramer he knew, with results that hadn't surprised anybody familiar with the Texas Rangers.

Set up back in the twenties to cope with Indians and outlaws, the Texas Rangers had fought Mexico, twice, as irregular troops. Fighting the Union in the more recent War Betwixt the States had resulted in them being disbanded and replaced until recent by a far less popular state police force, until President Hayes, a decorated Union vet who could stand up to the radical wing of his party, had issued his generous blanket pardon to all Confederate vets and allowed the Texas Rangers to get back in the saddle, to the dismay of many an outlaw who'd been riding rings around the Texas State Police.

The old gal who lived there told Longarm things had been downright peaceful around Tanktown with the rangers scouting for strange riders with running irons. Or they had until that mysterious Clay Allison had ridden in to make his brag, claim that canyon farther in from the river and commence to shoot folk.

Snuggling her hugely naked flesh closer to his own, Flo confided, "It was when I heard his Mexicans had tried to kill you I decided I just had to have some of your sweet manhood in my lonely twat while you were still alive and manly. They told me Mexican outlaws killed my poor Danny, and as it all came back to me I suddenly felt so *hot*!"

Not yet feeling up to what she seemed to have in mind, Longarm asked how anybody could say her man had been murdered by Mexicans, adding, "Fair is fair and that mysterious Lazy A hadn't hired Mex riders yet."

She demured, "They'd come up from south of the border, silly!"

He demanded, "How come? To what end, if they were residents of Old Mexico? Don't get the notion I'm soft on border raiders. Lord knows we get our share of 'em. But wouldn't Mexicans riding up out of Chihuahua to steal cows drive them *back* across the river into Chihuahua instead of in the general direction of Chicago via Emery Peak?"

She started to object. He said, "I ain't finished. I was about to say Mexicans from south of the border would have no call to murder a Texican brand inspector. A cow thief could *brag* on the brands of a stolen herd in Old Mexico and be called a hero. What made them say your man had been done in by Mexicans to begin with?"

She said, "Sign. When they carried poor Danny out of the rock pile, they told the rest of us they'd read the sign as Mexican. They don't shoe their ponies the same, any more than they fancy the same saddles or sensible hats. They found some of those Mexican wax-stemmed matches and butts of those black cigarettes they smoke down Chihuahua way. Above all, who *else* would have been stealing stock from around here? All the Anglo cattlefolk know one another!"

He decided she couldn't be that much smarter than him, after all. He might have sounded as if he was bragging had he gone into all the times he'd caught best friends stealing everything from one another's wives to the fillings out of their teeth. For if any lawman could tell you three out of four burglaries were inside jobs, old Flo wasn't a lawman and he didn't feel comfortable talking about dead husbands in bed with lusty widows.

So they talked of other things as he drew a tighter map of the range up and down the river until he could tell by her breathing she was asleep, and wasn't it swell a gal with such lung capacity didn't snore!

He caught himself dozing off, worked his arm out from under her ample charms lest he awaken with gangrene, and rose to make certain the door was solidly barred before he slipped back in bed with her.

That woke her up, with a start, to gasp, "Good heavens! I can't go to sleep with guests! I'd best go back down to my own quarters unless you want to come in me some more."

He said he'd have no hard feelings if she spent the rest of the night in her own bed. So they kissed and parted friendly, with him wondering whether he could get it hard at all if Yzabel showed up as soon as the coast was clear. For it seemed likely the pretty little sneak had tiptoed to yon door by this hour, had she meant to come back at all, but hadn't cared to ask if the boss lady wanted to be a sport about playing three in a boat.

So Longarm wasn't looking forward to facing the two of them down in the kitchen come morning, and decided to just slip down the stairs and have breakfast somewheres else.

But Flo Whitehead caught up with him in her stable yard, wearing more perfume and looking younger and more relaxed in a fresh dress, with her rust red hair bound softer. She whispered, "Good morning, darling. Please don't tell anyone, but I fear half the Mexicans for miles around must have heard about us by this time!"

He asked what made her say that and wasn't as surprised as he let on when she said Yzabel had lit out sometime the night before, with no sign her own bed had been slept in.

Flo said, "I know the little snip's a churchgoing Papist but . . . honestly, what right does that give her to judge a Baptist widow who hasn't had any loving for ever so long?"

Longarm made sure they weren't in anyone else's line of sight before he kissed the fat redhead and said soothingly, "Some holier-than-thous can be like that. They just can't abide others having a good time. I suspect it makes them feel left out."

Chapter 7

Longarm soon discovered that, as he'd hoped, they served grub at the coach terminal, albeit in truth the coffee wasn't good as Flo's kitchen help made it and he suspected the chili con carne had been simmering on the back of the stove long and indefinite. Like Irish stew, chili con carne could be preserved by constant cooking instead of refrigeration, and to a point, both improved as the cook ladled well-cooked servings out and tossed in fresh ingredients. But in this case that point had been passed. So Longarm only had one order of chili con carne and topped it off with a generous slab of tuna pie with rat cheese, washed down with their acrid but strong black coffee. He acted as if he'd never heard it before when the cook at the stage terminal explained the tuna pie on their menu wasn't made with fish. For she wasn't a bad-looking señorita and it was easy to sound as if he gave a shit when she confided "tuna" was the crimson "pear" of the prickly pear cactus, infested with pesky black seeds but sweeter than any pear pulp, once you ran it through a strainer to bake in what a stranger could take for a cherry pie with a soapy aftertaste.

She allowed she was called Consuela and said she'd

49

heard about the gunfight at the Last Chance, looked those dead Mexicans over and had no idea who in tarnation they or the dead Anglo they'd been riding with might have been. She said most every stranger passing through ate there or at the Toro Negro across the way. She sounded as innocent when she allowed that a chum who worked at the Toro Negro had never laid eyes on the rascals, either. Longarm didn't ask how well Consuela might know Yzabel, or whether Ricardo Chavez had mentioned *El Brazo Largo* to her yet. For as in the case of poker, it was best to hold one's own cards close to the vest when playing "I wonder if you know that I wonder what you know about what I know."

After filling his gut and tipping a handsome dime, Longarm mosied over to the nearby Western Union shack to see if his home office had wired him care of the telegraph company.

They had. The skinny gray clerk handed Longarm a night letter sent by Henry, their prissy file clerk, instead of the boss incarnate.

The night letter explained how Billy Vail had sent Deputies Smiley and Dutch down to New Mexico Territory to interview the survivors of the late Clay Allison. Judge Dickerson of the Denver District Court had told Billy not to be silly when he'd requested an exhumation order. Smiley and Dutch had found Jack Allison calmed down and willing to jaw with them. They'd gone along with his request they leave the young Widow Allison and her kids alone. But they'd made certain they were way closer to Cimarron than the Big Bend, and they'd found others in town who'd been at Clay Allison's funeral, held with a closed casket because they hadn't been able to get the contrary cuss to straighten up and lie right after that wagon wheel had rolled over his neck like that. Smiley and Dutch had paid a call on the undertaker, with copies of that same photograph. The undertaker had seemed certain the corpse he'd done his level best to tidy up had been the same cuss, perhaps a tad older and gone more to seed *before* he'd been run over by a loaded wagon.

He'd offered Smiley and Dutch the professional opinion that an exhumation order might or might not settle the matter once and for all.

According to a gent who likely knew, there was just no saying what a body buried since '77 might look like now. When the Widow Hickok had had her man dug up, reboxed and replanted in '78, Wild Bill had been in the ground two years and looked fresh as if he'd been buried the day before, save for being pale as candle wax, with mold growing on his duds. Other bodies, on the other hand, would commence to go bad before you could bury them. Some king of England had disrupted his own funeral services by swelling up and exploding his fine casket to stink up the cathedral just awful. So the undertaker in Cimarrón had opined that the body in Clay Allison's grave could look fresh as a daisy or more like the bottom of a cesspool, with an average expectation of being hard to identify for certain on sight. Clay Allison had been given a decent Christian burial, and at high altitude in dry ground, a body embalmed worth mention tended to mummify rather than rot. But as the undertaker had pointed out and even Billy Vail in the end had agreed, comparing the face of a mummy with that face in an old photograph wouldn't add up to final proof. So it was *possible,* albeit unlikely, Clay Allison had faked his early death with the help of his kith and kin. So Longarm put the night letter away to show his ranger pals and trudged up to their post with his Winchester '73 attracting odd looks in passing as he cradled it polite, with no round in its chamber for Pete's sake. When a wide spot in the road had no opera house or roller skating rink to occupy idle minds, the least thing out of the ordinary seemed more interesting. But Tanktown was a for God's sake cow town by the border, not some prissy place like, say, Boston or even Austin.

At the ranger post Captain Kramer said Corporal Arnold had taken some of the boys to handle a complaint up Tiswin Creek a ways. Longarm showed the captain the night letter. Kramer agreed it would hardly make sense to stage your own death if you meant to show up somewheres else to brag you were still alive and ornery as ever.

Handing back the telegram, Kramer moved over to the file drawers as he opined, "But it's tough for a leopard to change its spots and there's no indication Clay Allison ever tried before his sudden death at the age of thirty-seven for Gawd's sake! I mean, if a mean drunk hasn't reformed by the time he's a thirty-seven-year-old man with a wife and kids at home and a cattle business to tend to, it's safe to assume he just isn't the reforming kind!"

"He may have meant to, more than once," Longarm pointed out to be objective. As Captain Kramer poured, Longarm added, "Playing devil's advocate, how do you like a well-to-do but nasty cuss with a federal warrant out on him staging his own death to queer the do and . . ."

"Who could anyone ask to take his place?" Kramer cut in, pouring himself another as he demured, "They had to have *somebody* up yonder in Cimarron to bury, didn't they?"

Longarm swallowed his own tequila bracer before he easily replied, "Dead bodies with broken necks ain't that hard to come by in cattle country, Captain. Grasping at straws, like a man wanted for killing three soldiers in cold blood might, what if some ranch hand with even a slight resemblance to his boss died accidental as well as convenient? They'd have had to bury the cuss in any event, and I for one never insisted on exhuming the remains when I showed up too late with my own warrant."

Captain Kramer started to pour himself a third shot, decided not to and put the bottle back in its file drawer as he shook his head stubbornly and insisted, "I don't know what you were taught about man hunting, old son. But I was taught to look for motive, means and the opportunity. A wanted man with a convenient corpse on his hands would have the means and opportunity to fake his own death. But it falls apart as soon as you study the *motive*. Say Clay Allison faked his own death. Say he deserted his family, abandoned his herd and got away clean. Then ask yourself why in tarnation he'd show up here in West Texas to declare himself alive and well and meaner than ever?"

Longarm replied, "I can whistle more than one chorus to that tune. Many a mean drunk has busted a gut to reform, reformed for quite a spell and then given in to the same old habits. In either incarnation our hard-drinking, quick-drawing, poison-mean and cold-blooded son of a bitch seemed or seems to glory in letting everybody know who he is as well as how awful he's behaving. The real Clay Allison liked to have it known he was the winner as the gunsmoke cleared. He bragged who he was to witnesses who hadn't known his name. Just the way the cuss who gunned your four rangers, more recent, bragged."

Kramer shrugged and asked, "What if some *other* surly son of a bitch is out to lay the blame on a dead man none of us can hang?"

Longarm said, "That's possible. If the cuss is putting on an act for some deliberate reason. But whoever he may be, he looks like the real Clay Allison and, more important, he's as *good* as the real Clay Allison, if not better. I don't recall the Clay Allison of legend going up against two Texas Rangers, or two serious gunfighters of any sort, to draw and blow them both away when everyone there agrees *they had the drop on him!*"

Kramer grudgingly conceded, "He would have had to be good, damned good, no matter what his real name was, wouldn't he?"

Longarm said, "He would indeed. So how come he ain't famous in his own right? I've searched high and I've searched low in my mental files on famous gunfighters, past and present, on both sides of the law, and I'll be switched with snakes if I can recall a tall blond handsome cuss who walks with a limp, drinks like a fish and performs magic tricks with a six-gun drunk or sober. Your turn."

The older lawman shook his head wistfully and replied, "I follow your drift. No matter who the big blond bastard might be, he's too ornery to be running loose without a leash and too good with a gun to be human. So now that

53

I study on it, any growing boy with such bad habits *ought* to want to claim the discredit. You don't see Billy the Kid claiming to be Jesse James or, worse yet, the long dead Wild Bill Hickok. A modest mad-dog killer is a contradiction in terms. Anybody with sense enough to pour piss out of his boots already *knows better* than to shoot it out with Texas Rangers and not even cross the handy river into Old Mexico. What was that about it all being some sort of an act?"

Longarm said, "Just covering all bases. Haven't thought up a motive as makes sense to me. It's *possible* to mayhaps use stage makeup and a damned good gunfighter to give the impression Clay Allison didn't die back in '77 after all. Anyone can limp if he puts his mind to it and I never shot myself in the foot the way they say Allison did that time. But to what end? Any fake name would work as well and doubtless seem more convincing if the owner of that mysterious Lazy A is out to hide his true identity. I can't make the piece fit any sensible pattern."

Captain Kramer allowed that made two of 'em. Then Corporal Arnold came in with the two rangers he'd ridden out and back with, trail dusted and chagrined, to report, "Ain't sure there was any crime at all. Dead sure that rounding up strays is no proper chore for the Texas Rangers!"

His boss told him to explain himself less witty. So Arnold tried. "We ride out to the Bradford place like you told us to. Rose Bradford said she's just wrangled a mule contract off the army over to Fort Stockton. Far side of the Glass Mountains."

"Damn it, Arnold, we know where Fort Stockton is!" snapped Captain Kramer, adding, "Would you like me to guess where Pecos County might be whilst I'm at it? The Flying B won a War Department mule contract. Then what?"

Arnold said, "She sent her hands out to round her herd up and cut some army mules out for the soldiers blue. That's when she noticed she didn't seem to be grazing half the stock she'd thought she had grazing the rocky slopes and canyons all around. She figures she's missing one hell of a remuda of mules. Seems to expect us rangers to do one damned thing about it. I told her we were officers of the law, not cowhands popping brush for strayed mules. When she insisted her stock had been stole, I told her we needed dates, times, places and an infernal corpus delicti before we'd posse up. I don't reckon Miss Rose followed my drift. She couldn't seem to grasp the difference betwixt lost, strayed or stolen. I tried in vain to show her there was just no saying whether a pony or mule was even missing, since last you tallied it without so much as a simple sample of your brand on its hide! I told her missing stock, in the absence of any evidence of a felony, was a matter for the county sheriff and the Cattleman's Protective Association up to Alpine. She wailed that the county seat was over a hundred bumpy miles to the north and intimated I was a piss poor excuse for a lawman."

Arnold chuckled fondly and added, "Miss Rose was too much of a lady to say piss. But she purely came close."

Captain Kramer brought Longarm up to speed, explaining, "Miss Rose Bradford runs the Flying B for her folk, being she's a woman growed, her ma don't know how to manage even a small cattle spread and her dad ain't been right since a mean bronc throwed him and stomped on his poor old head. Miss Rose is all right, but inclined to get testy when she can't have her own way, and Arnold here was right to tell her stray stock is not a chore for the Texas Rangers."

"What if her stock has been stolen?" Longarm asked.

"Then we'd go after the thieves and bring 'em in with the stolen stock," the older lawman answered easily, before he insisted, "That's not the matter before the house this afternoon. The matter before the house is four dead rangers, a killer who claims to be a dead man, and his unmapped home spread we can't find without the help of Caddo Flynn, and nobody can tell us where Caddo Flynn is, cuss his half-breed hide!"

Longarm picked up the Winchester he'd been resting

on the desk as he casually asked directions to that famous Flying B.

Kramer said, "Follow Tiswin Creek past the first three spreads until you come to a gate with a cow skull on the crossbar with the Flying B brand burnt into it. That's a B with bitty wings, as if it was fixing to fly up and away."

Longarm said he knew what a flying brand looked like. Kramer told him, "You'll find Miss Rose a looker, but they say she don't put out, and how in blue thunder do you expect to find unbranded stock that have wandered off into the unknown or drowned in the river weeks ago for all anyone up yonder can surely say?"

Longarm shrugged, hefted the saddle gun and headed for the door as he soberly replied, "Can't say before I ride up for a look-see. You're likely right. I may not cut sign that stale and uncertain. But on the other hand there's not much I can do around here before you gents can find me that guide to the Lazy A. So I may as well give this Flying B a try this morning."

Chapter 8

The rangers helped Longarm select and saddle a spanky Morgan mare from their handsome remuda out back. She matched the coffee color of Longarm's pancaked Stetson, save for her white blaze. Riding light, he followed the main drag to the edge of the settlement, where it turned into a two-rut wagon trace running more or less north on up the creek as the rugged hills rose to either side.

The long northwest to southeast spine the Rio Grande cut through to form the Big Bend had many names as well as complex geology, as it served to seperate the valleys of the Pecos and the Rio Grande. They called the craggy red ridges the Sangre de Cristos up where they'd officiously buried Clay Allison. Farther south, where they'd held that short but bitter Lincoln County War, the same high stretch was called the Sacramentos, Guadalupes and what all, before it ran down into West Texas to become the Davis, Chisos, Burros and so forth, all depending on which angle some distant surveyor had been looking when he mapped the jumbled ridges by guess and by God.

Whatever you called the rises to Longarm's right as he rode along, they fed draws and canyons, all dry in high summer, into the main streambed of Tiswin Creek, which was still running over rocks and sandbar stretches that late summer morning. Cows, mostly scrub, with some black Cherokee longhorn, grazed hither and yon on both sides of the creek, paying no mind to a dimly perceived form moving on four legs. It was a man afoot who had to watch out for half-wild longhorns.

He rode past a brushwood jacal with its five or fewer acres of truck snake-fenced with cottonwood poles, with standing timber and a way higher limestone bluff rising behind it, closer than usual to the creekbed. The limestone of the Big Bend Country eroded capricious as it's layer-cake strata tilted every which way in shades of vanilla, chocolate and more orange than strawberry.

He passed more cows grazing on open range, cows seldom straying far from cool clean water, with more pole fencing enclosing the way larger pastures you needed to hold horses or mules, both breeds being more adventurous, or stupider, than cows in semi-arid country. The wheat-stem, gramma and other short grasses on either side of said fencing grew swell, with their roots well watered in the "terra rosa" bottomland you got in limestone country. Stock grazing on such fodder grew strong bones. The higher limstone karst all around the basin was naturally useless as all get-out for anything but postcard scenery. The widely scattered summer rains that far west soaked into the rocky heights all around to reappear as bottomland springs, leaving the crags above bone dry betwixt gully washers.

But down here in the basin the grass still grew green at the roots, and things would have been swell, had their been a mite more of it.

Then Longarm came upon a gate with that sun-bleached cow skull. It had a flying B burnt into it. So he dismounted to open the gate, as a pack of wolves howled at him from the sprawl of 'dobe and cottonwood timbers with a salmon-pink bluff looming not too far behind it.

The yard dogs stopped baying, as if somebody who meant it had told them to. The distance being short, Longarm led his borrowed pony in after shutting the gate behind them. A tall, thin ash blond gal in a riding habit of tan whipcord came out on the veranda to howdy Longarm, as a barefoot Indian kid in white cotton tore out into the sunlight to take the reins of the Morgan away from him.

Longarm didn't argue and left the Winchester with the saddle to show he trusted the Flying B, as the gal who had to be Rose Bradford said that whoever he was, he was just in time for the coffee and cake they were about to have inside.

As Longarm doffed his Stetson to follow her in, he told her who he was and what he'd come for. She brightened and declared that in that case the two of them would be served in the parlor because her mom and dad in the kitchen tended to get upset when she had to report a theft.

Longarm was too polite to say he'd heard her ma was stupid whilst her dad was tetched. She sat him down on a sofa before a baronial cold fireplace of sandstone flags, and whilst they waited for refreshments Rose Bradford told a federal lawman what she thought of the Texas Rangers and, whilst she was at it, the Sheriff's Department in far-off Alpine, adding, "The stock thieves were never half so bold when we had our own undersheriff and a dozen or more part-time deputies who knew the country and all our neighborhood brands!"

Longarm said soothingly, "There's a heap of mighty rough range to patrol and, no offense, how can one be certain unbranded stock has recently been purloined?"

An Indian gal came in to set coffee and cake on the low oaken table betwixt the sofa and fireplace as the young lady of the house explained, "The army prefers its own brand on its horses and mules. They like to buy stock young and barely trail broken so's it can be trained their way."

Longarm said, "I spent some time with an army in my mispent youth, Miss Rose. So I know what they mean about there being three ways to do anything."

She dimpled and agreed—"The right way, the wrong way and the army way!"—as she cut and poured.

She added, "I know how many mules we've lost because I keep a stud book to show prospective buyers. As an old soldier you doubtless know the cold cash considerations that make it more profitable to peddle mules to the army rather than cows to Chicago, west of the Pecos?"

Longarm did indeed. Beef on the hoof worth say sixty dollars a head in New York City only sold for forty at a western railroad town and, being a cow could only be driven ten to fifteen miles a day, profits fell off alarmingly by the time you could get a West Texas steer anywhere worth mention. So unless you could wrangle a government beef contract to supply nearby army posts or Indian agencies, and that had been the one true motive for the infamous Lincoln County War, you had to breed and sell stock more profitsome than beef on the hoof.

As he washed down some raisin cake with mighty fine coffee, Longarm knew better than to lecture a mule-breeding gal on the economies of raising horses and mules for an Indian fighting army. He was sure she knew the army remount service bought Trakehner and other such taller and cooler saddle breeds rather than the smaller more spirited Spanish stock preferred by Anglo and Mex riders alike for working stock instead of charging Indians.

Longarm knew from weary experience that any army used up ten times as many mules as cavalry mounts, and paid nigh as much a head, preferring the Missouri mule sired by a jackass to, say, a Friesian dam, yet willing to spend some good money for a so-called Spanish saddle mule, bred to a Barb or Arab dam by a Mexican burro stud.

As if she'd been reading his mind, Rose Bradford proudly informed him her jackass studs were French. He resisted remarking on the charms of French lovers. He told her his friends called him Custis, whistled softly when they established she seemed to be missing over fifty head, and wondered aloud about a badman born and bred in Tennessee knowing so much about marketing mules down West Texas way.

60

She said she failed to see what such an observation might have to do with her missing stock.

Longarm insisted, "The Clay Allison from Tennessee already knew how to handle a gun when he dropped out of a war and headed west. They say he worked a spell as a ranch hand up Cimarron way until he learned enough about the western beef industry to start his own herd, on the east slopes of the Sangre de Cristos where, no offense, it's a whole lot easier to raise beef! So don't it strike you as sort of odd a Tennessee farm boy by way of northern New Mexico Territory seems to know more about raising stock in this Big Bend Country than you Texican and Mexican folk who got here first?"

She washed down the morsel of cake she'd been chewing before she told Longarm, "I've heard gossip about that strange bully boy having a hanging valley paved with alfalfa over in the Chisos. The Mexicans tell me those Seven Golden Cities that Coronado was hunting for are still out yonder, somewhere east of Eden and west of Nod. But it's not true yonder high-dry hills are completely unexplored. Our Anglo mapmakers and even the majority of our Mexican neighbors may have given up after finding their ways back to water after a scared spell up a canyon maze. But the Indians tell me it's possible to thread one's way through the Chisos if you take your time, don't panic, and live off the land their way until you wander out the other side."

Longarm asked if any of her Indian informants had mentioned a green oasis such as Caddo Flynn had reported.

Rose Bradford shook her blond head to insist, "That old breed has a vivid imagination as well as a drinking problem. He's not the only hunter who's ever wondered what lay over the next ridge and the next in the Chisos, Santiagos or whatever you want to call them from a distance. You have to understand how dedicated to survival our long established border folk—red, white and in between—can be. How long do you think secret mountain meadows such as Caddo Flynn describes would remain undiscovered within no more than twenty miles at the most from settled or at least well-mapped country?"

Longarm swallowed some of his own coffee and replied in a conversational tone, "Not forever, for certain, but if there's anything to Caddo Flynn's story, that hidden green valley *has* been discovered, and then taken over from whoever discovered it by somebody calling his fool self Clay Allison."

She started to object. He raised a hand to hush her as he went on, "I know that mysterious stranger just drifted in with a small herd a few short months ago. I know he couldn't have known this country as well as those of you he sort of horned in on. But they tell me he was riding with some Mexicans. So what if one of them Mexicans had told him of kith, kin or mayhaps enemies already set up in a secret ranch they paid no taxes on because they'd never seen fit to pester the U.S. Interior Department with their earlier discovery?"

She frowned uncertainly and decided, "That would explain the ranch house and other improvements this Clay Allison and his small crew had no time to set up, and I fear some of the older Mex clans tend to be secretive around the rest of us. So are you saying my missing stock has been driven off to Clay Allison's secret ranch in the sky?"

Longarm shook his head and replied, "Too early to call. Like you just said, Caddo Flynn might have been fibbing. But we do know there's a jasper calling himself Clay Allison somewhere in these parts, bossing at least four Mexican vaqueros and grazing at least the mules they showed up with, somewhere, on something. So I reckon I'll go have a look-see, Miss Rose. I'd take it kindly if one of your hands would ride over into them canyonlands with me and my borrowed pony, as far as ponies can make her. For once the going gets too tough for horseflesh, I mean to push on by shank's mare with just my rifle and, could you and yours spare 'em, a couple of water canteens and mayhaps some grub to wash down with the same."

She rose first from the sofa, saying, "Well, of course

we'll send you off with all the food and water you can carry, ah, Custis. But you were so right about a man not knowing this country having a tough time finding anything out yonder! What if you wind up lost and can't find your way out before your food and water run out?"

As he rose higher, Longarm replied with a modest shrug, "I'll wind up hungry and thirsty. But I don't lose easy, Miss Rose. Scouted in the Dakota Badlands for the army a spell back without getting myself totally lost, and I've yet to see country more confusing than them Dakota Badlands!"

Longarm followed the willowy Rose on to the kitchen, where an older couple sat at a pine table. The woman who had to be the blonde's mom was feeding soup to a white-haired and empty-eyed man who drooled at least half of it as he hung on to the table as if it was the railing of a hot air balloon and he was scared of heights.

Rose Bradford got to work at a counter as she told her mom who she was fixing a basket lunch for. The older woman asked if she could tag along and added she'd always enjoyed picnics under the cottonwoods along the creek. Longarm liked Rose Bradford better when he noticed how gently she told her dotty old mother they weren't going on any picnic but she'd ask the help to serve her supper out on the veranda so's she could watch the sun go down. It was no mystery to Longarm why she hadn't included her father in the invite.

He didn't ask about that, since the rangers had already told him about old Bradford's bad luck with a mean bronc. But as they went out to the stable to saddle up, with Longarm holding the food and water she'd fixed him up with, Rose Bradford said, "My dad's not stupid or crazy. He got hurt, riding harder and braver than most men half his age. I 'spect that in his day my dad could work twice as hard as you and lick you at checkers besides!"

That helpful young stable hand hadn't unsaddled the borrowed Morgan. So as he saddled a palomino gelding as matched the willowy blonde's hair, Longarm lashed the two canteens and straw pannier filled with sandwiches and canned grub to his McClellan.

So about the time *La Siesta* would be ending down Tanktown way the two of them were wending their way up the canyon Rose Bradford had advised for as deep a penetration of the Chisos as she knew of.

As the canyon walls rose ever steeper and higher to either side, Longarm saw that they were unlike the Dakota Badlands, where clay and marl in horizontal layers had been carved into an intricate maze by a lot of time and scattered rainstorms. The harder shale and limestone beds down this way, like the rest of the ranges breaking ever higher along the continental divide, had started out level enough on the bottom of some long vanished ocean, then they'd set harder than clay or marl, to be slowly but surely lifted into the sky at crazy angles, with the bedding planes complicating the drainage one way for thousands of years, only to tilt at a new angle and set the erosion patterns some other direction. So something awful had happened near the head of the box canyon they'd been riding up a spell. But Rose Bradford didn't seem at all surprised when she reined in, waved at the eight- or ten-story cliff ahead and told Longarm, "This is far as you go, aboard that pony. Do you really think you can work your way up to the rimrocks above with all that food and water?"

To which Longarm could only reply, "Not hardly. But I reckon I got to try."

Chapter 9

With the willowy blonde's help, Longarm commenced by getting the load he was stuck with distributed as evenly as possible. He crisscrossed the canteen straps to pack a half-gallon army canteen on each hip, for a total of eight pounds and change. They got the straw pannier holding two days' rations high on his back, held in place by its braided-straw pack straps. He slung his Winchester '73 from his right shoulder and naturally had his .44-40 side-arm on the opposite hip. Then there was nothing left to do but set his hat more firmly and start climbing. They didn't know one another well enough to kiss goodbye.

He didn't look down. He didn't dast look down as he felt with his bare hands and booted feet for holds to work his way up. The cliff didn't rise sheer, and in places there were friendly crevices a man could wriggle up without feeling way in the middle of the air. But he was grateful as hell and gasping for breath when he finally hauled himself over the gritty rim, where harder iron-rich rock had fought erosion better, resulting in such a sudden drop.

Rolling over on his butt, Longarm peered over the edge to feel his ass pucker as he took in how bitty Rose Bradford and the two ponies looked to him now. He waved his hat to the good sport down below as he softly declared, "I don't believe I climbed that far. It ain't possible."

Rose waved back, shouted encouraging words he couldn't make out and turned to ride home with his borrowed pony, leaving Longarm all alone atop the asspuckering cliff. So he turned around to get his bearings and that hardly helped worth shit.

As far as the eye could see, clear to the shimmering horizon, there was nothing but rock, a heap of rock, rising like the waves of a petrified sea frozen solid in the middle of a hurricane. There were big waves and bitty waves, with jagged crests of wind-carved shale or limestone, save for more distant swamping peaks surveyors had managed to name and map from some ways away. Off to the east rose the ominous groundswell of the Deadhorse Range, with the aptly named Grapevine Ridges looming on the northeast horizon. To the north loomed Emery Peak, sixty miles north of the Rio Grande and a mile and a half above sea level if those maps meant shit. A stranger could hazard more than one guess as to which white limestone crag out yonder might be the one and original Elephant's Tusk. For the topographers had charted at least two, whilst off the other way, on the far side of Tiswin Basin, rose a choice of Mule Ear Peaks. Other peaks, at least on the survey maps, indicated water-holes or tanks whether they rose high enough to spy from a distance or not. Longarm was about convinced the maps weren't worth all that much as he lined up on a distant crag to keep himself from wandering in a circle as he headed away from the basin.

The sun hung high to the west. But thanks to the altitude and dry, nearly constant breezes, his sweat dried fast as he could put it out and it only felt too hot by half as he worked his way east down a far more gentle incline.

As he did so, he saw that the cliff he'd just scaled was the steeper edge of what they called a hogback ridge up along the Front Range west of Denver. Something awsome had tilted a square mile of once-flat seabed up like a tabletop with two of its legs busted off. Farther down the sere naked rock gave way to a flat patch of high chaparral as seemed to be growing from a sandy flat. As he made his way through the stickerbrush to the far side, Longarm saw bare rock rising the other way and figured the scrub was growing in the sand-filled bottom of a sort of stony hammock. When he got up on the next rise, he could see by the distant Emery Peak he'd trended farther south than he'd thought. He went back down to bust off some branches of scrub oak, which was what chaparral meant when it wasn't short for mesquite, catsclaw and such.

Moving back up to the rock ridge, he wedged a spring of green where chaparral didn't grow and told it, "I'll thank you to stay put and show me the way back, stickerbrush. This is turning out worse than expected, but if I turn back no later than four, I ought to have the sunset at my back descending that fucking cliff and, oh my, won't *that* be fun!"

Gazing about for the most sensible route, Longarm followed the ridge northeast to where it hairpinned or ended against the edge of another limestone massif tilted another way. As he followed that one, he saw more chaparral and some expanses of dry mesquite grass in the depths to either side. It was easy to see why hunters such as Caddo Flynn followed the crests of this choppy sea of stone in preference to beelining, or trying to. It made Longarm's legs hurt just to think of sliding down and scrambling up such rocky slopes.

The next time the natural ridge route he was following zigged to due north, Longarm found a patch of sheep turds in the shade of a boulder perched uncertainly, like a cork float atop a breaking wave. He made a mental note of the handy landmark and declared to Caddo Flynn, wherever he might be, "You were telling it true about bighorn roaming about up here. I figured it had to be something like that overgrazing the ridges up here. The herd would be healthier with a few more hunters to cull it. Or at least a family of mountain lions. I doubt wolves could manage, in such poor country for running things down. That's likely why them bighorn stay up here on such piss poor range to begin with."

The missing ridge runner didn't answer. Longarm hadn't expected him to. He still said, "All right, Caddo, where's that green Valley of Eden you promised me? Up to now I ain't even seen a seep of wet rock up here!"

Knowing it was easier to follow cardinal directions, and having no better bearings as yet, Longarm kept working his way due north toward old Emery Peak, leaving a patch of greenery against the sky or making note of some easy landmark each time he dropped out of the far-off crag's line of sight. As he worked his way farther north, he saw he'd struck what looked to be a game trail running the ridges in a generally northbound series of zigzags. There was no way to ask the bighorns why, or whether they took bearings on the highest wave in their ocean of rocky swells. He'd long since known why game trails followed ridges. Critters didn't care to slide down and clamber up slopes any more than a man on foot might, and like the parts along a hairy critter's spine, such stickerbrush as grew in busted-up terrain tended to part as naturally where the stone rose close to the surface along such ridges. On top of all that, a critter worth eating felt safer on high ground, where it could gaze down all around and about for anything more dangerous than vegetation.

Longarm had food and water enough to roam the stormy sea of stone forty-eight hours or more. But he'd made up his mind to call it a day and turn back by four unless he spotted something more interesting than yet another breaking wave of jumbled rock.

So along about three-thirty he sat on a sandstone slab under a wind-tortured mesquite to wash a ham on rye sandwich down with canteen water and enjoy a smoke before turning back, having decided a stranger wandering about up yonder without a guide was a sad case of the blind leading the blind at midnight.

Then a shift of the breeze carried a whiff of perking coffee and rancid pipe smoke through Longarm's meager patch of shade. So Longarm muttered, "What the hell? I brung no coffee and I'd never smoke such trade tobacco outside an infernal tepee, as a *captive*. For I swear it smells worse than them shitty cigars old Billy Vail smokes back at the office!"

Wetting a finger to hold high and make certain which way the wind was blowing, Longarm slid the Winchester off his shoulder, levered a round in the chamber and slowly and silently rose to his full considerable height, nostrils flaring, to follow the scent downslope and around a steamboat-sized boulder. He could see as well as smell the smoke now, rising from a draw forty rods beyond the big, erratic lump of shit-colored mudstone.

Dropping to his gut with the Winchester cradled across his forearms, Longarm crawled through dry grass and rabbit bush until he could peer over the edge, where, sure enough, a coffeepot perked on the coals of a small camp fire, a bedroll hinted at where somebody had been sitting, and a burro munched on the pods of the mesquite it stood tethered to, on the far side of the draw.

As Longarm was taking the scene in, a voice from behind him calmly asked, "Might you care to drop that gun and tell me what the fuck you think you're doing out this way, Mister?"

Longarm managed not to gleep like an old maid with a mouse under her skirt, albeit that wasn't easy, as he let go the Winchester to roll clear, prop himself up on his left elbow and nod up at the scarecrow looming over him with a double-barreled twelve-gauge.

Longarm said, "I'm scouting for lost, strayed or stolen mules. I'd be U.S. Deputy Custis Long. Might you be Caddo Flynn, sir?"

The ragged-ass, bushy haired and gray-bearded man staring down from the shade of a tattered straw sombrero replied, "Never heard of him. I'm Pepper MacLeod, prospecting for gold, of course."

He motioned with the double muzzle, meaningfully, as he added, "I ain't one to call another white man a liar without just cause. But if you're the law, you ought to be

69

able to prove it with a badge and your warrant."

Longarm reached slowly for his wallet as he allowed that seemed a reasonable request. He waited until he'd flashed his badge and I.D. and seen the shotgun sagging like a satisfied dick, before he sat up straighter to ask, "Prospecting for gold in shale and limestone, Mr. MacLeod?"

The old-timer snorted. "That don't sound as foolish to me as you hunting for mules up here in the middle of the air. Didn't they first strike Colorado color in Cherry Creek, and don't Cherry Creek drain the red sandstone hogbacks of the Front Range, Mister Know-It-All?"

Longarm rose to one knee and, meeting no objection, picked up his Winchester, observing, "The way I hear it, the placer gold in Cherry Creek ran down into sandy seabottom off granite bedrocks further off to the west."

The grizzled prospector said, "There you go, then. Can't you see all this shale and limestone must have started out on the same swamping seabottom, ages and ages ago? If you'd care for some coffee, get up and circle down to meet Flora."

Longarm didn't ask who Flora might be. Lots of elderly loners were sensitive about discussing their feminine companionship. Another old-timer had once assured Longarm, "Show me a desert rat who's never fucked his burro and I'll show you a man who can't get it up!"

As he followed the older man south to a natural cut in the rim of the wash, Longarm asked if MacLeod had heard tell of an outfit called the Lazy A, somewheres up here amid the confusion of ridgelines and said to be spring watered and summer green.

As they moved north again to the thrifty fire, MacLeod called out to his burro, "This young feller is searching for ridge-running mules and the estate of that giant Jack found at the top of that beanstalk, Flora. You mind that Mexican sharpy who tried to sell us that map of a lost gold mine up this way?"

Flora didn't even bray. She just went on munching mesquite as the older man hunkered down by his fire to pour a tin can full of coffee for their unexpected guest.

Things got even more neighborly after Longarm shrugged off the pannier, hunkered down beside it and produced the last sandwiches Rose Bradford had made, along with the cans of beans, tomato and peach preserves.

Longarm said, "I was about to turn back in any case, so you may have more use for this grub than I'd have, climbing backwards down a cliff."

The old-timer allowed he'd save the sandwiches for later. Then he sniffed and marveled, "Jesus H. Christ! That's real rye bread and I aint et nothing but sourdough since Flora was a virgin!"

He bit in and moaned with sheer delight, "Store-bought mustard with sardines in this one, and I'll never forget this gift of the gods, Deputy Long! I only wish I had something better than camp coffee to offer in return!"

Longarm bit into a cheese on rye and sipped some coffee lest he offend the old cuss. The coffee was as bad as it smelled. But the pungent mustard and cheese helped. He asked old MacLeod how they were fixed for water. When the prospector said he'd found a seep the next draw over, Longarm allowed he'd hang on to Rose Bancroft's canteens and asked how come MacLeod hadn't made camp closer to that seep.

The old-timer snorted. "I can see you ain't prospected much in Indian country, old son. Your hair stays closer to your skull when you camp within earshot but clear of handy firewood and water. I mind one time in Mescalero Country when I awoke with a start to hear fool Apache chopping wood on the far side of of the hill and . . . never mind. Just don't never fall asleep next to a water hole the redskins know about."

Longarm vowed he wouldn't and asked how far to the south MacLeod had prospected. The old-timer said, "To the river and back, of course."

Longarm insisted, "All of it? Every hill and dale of all them hills and dales?"

MacLeod reluctantly conceded, "Course not. We're

71

talking many a square mile of unsurveyed mountain scenery. Take a man years to explore every nook and cranny. Doubt they'll *ever* get the Big Bend properly mapped without taking photographs from a mighty high observation balloon or that flying machine Mr. Jules Verne wrote about."

"So there *could* be a fair-sized stock spread somewhere up amidst all these crags and canyons?" Longarm asked in a weary tone, seeing he was in the same fix no matter how the older man replied.

But it didn't help a lick when old Pepper MacLeod replied in a far less worried tone, "Shit, for all anyone can prove without one of them observation balloons and plenty of clear ballooning weather, ain't no saying *what* in thunder a man could hide just behind many a ridge in these jagged-ass hills!"

Chapter 10

Thanks to his having seen how pointless it seemed to wander through such a rocky wilderness without a guide, Longarm was saved from a no-doubt pointless night atop some unmapped rock pile. Thanks to his own common-sense generosity, he was saved climbing backward down that ass-puckering cliff.

Pepper MacLeod left his Flora and newfound grub near his camp fire to lead Longarm the wrong way back to the Flying B, or so it seemed at first. Then the old-timer who'd spent more time up yonder pointed out a shallow draw running entirely the wrong way and confided, "If you follow this draw, it'll turn into a gully, and do you follow the gully, it'll turn into a canyon, and do you follow the canyon, it'll spill you out on the floodplain of Tiswin Creek six or eight miles north of where you left your horse and saddle, old son."

Longarm reslung his Winchester next to the empty pannier on his back and regarded the draw doubtfully, deciding, "Well, if you say so . . ."

Pepper MacLeod said, "I say so and have faith, my son. Before you get back down to the creekside wagon trace, you're gonna be certain I have given you a bum steer to perdition. But when all seems lost, I'll thank you to consider that did I want to make you vanish from this earth, I had the drop on you with two loads of number double-aught buck before you ever heard me say a word, true or false."

So they shook on it and parted friendly, with Longarm only starting to worry serious after he'd followed the wildly twisting draw all over Robin Hood's Barn, until the walls to either side were too steep for a Doubting Thomas to scale without considerable risk. He could see by the afternoon sky the route was meandering most every direction but down to the west he wanted to reach before sundown. He figured that wherever, whenever this water course had commenced to run after the scattered rains out this way, it had formed its wide, lazy loops on nigh flat mudflats, to just keep cutting its original channel ever deeper as the flatlands buckled into a jumble of hogback ridges, mesas, buttes and rock formations too grotesque for such easy handles.

He was glad he was zigging and zagging under a bright blue cloudless sky, for in places the dry streambed dropped over ledges that had to be waterfalls, or through boulder fields that had to be white-water rapids when it rained enough to matter. Getting caught between such steep walls by a summer thunderstorm would be no fun at all, and they got bodacious thunderstorms off the Gulf of Mexico, mostly in high summer after a hot spell out this way.

From time to time he'd consult the railroad watch clipped to the opposite end of the chain he held his derringer with. All his watch told him was that he'd been following the winding route like a turd through the famous sewers of Paris, France, for hours, with no end in sight.

He swigged canteen water, smoked cheroots and regretted having been so generous with those sandwiches by the time he found himself heading west more often than not along the cobblestone floor of the now substantial canyon. As he spied patches of sedge and scattered clumps of bunchgrass, the canyon widened and the walls to either side rose gentler as well as higher. Then, rounding a bend, Longarm found his way barred, official, by four strands of fairly fresh barbwire, strung on rot-resisting albeit twisty mesquite poles.

It didn't stop a man on two feet, anxious to stride free of the now darker shadows of the otherwise tedious canyon. He could see it was a drift fence, meant to discourage cows from grazing farther up said canyon. As he rolled through the taut strands, he followed the drift of the unknown stringer of the drift fence. Cows grazing farther up stood little chance of getting lost before they were stopped by that last dry waterfall he'd scrambled down. But they'd never make it out of the slot alive if the canyon flash flooded of a sudden.

Longarm swigged canteen water and strode on to spy first one and then half a dozen more longhorns ahead as the canyon widened out to a grass-covered alluvial fan sloping down into the floodplain of old Tiswin Creek, on the far side of all those damned cows.

Longarm stopped where he was and slowly but surely shrugged his Winchester off his shoulder and around to port-arms as he regarded the grazing cows, and vice versa, with considerable uncertainty.

The Texas longarm, like the wild Hispano-Moorish critter it came down from, had been hunted by two-legged critters who'd painted its picture on the walls of Spanish caves too long ago to fathom, and for reasons best known to that Professor Darwin, the final results fled a human on horseback and figured a human on foot was an object of derision and revenge. But, seeing they seemed unusually contented cows, for West Texas, only one chongo-horned calico lowered her head, raised her tail like a battle flag and charged up the slope at him, with the two behind her loping his way more like curious, frisky pups.

Longarm levered and fired three fast rounds into the dust betwixt them as he crabbed sideways to his left. The gunshots, geysers of dirt and one screaming ricochet, inspired the more serious longhorn in the lead to pause but stand its ground, pawing more dust, with its tail still raised in defiance.

Longarm kept crabbing, neither advancing nor retreating, since either could provoke a pissed off critter, to where he could see chimney smoke hanging above a willow grove farther down the valley. Then, sure enough, there came four riders, stirrup to stirrup, with their own guns drawn as they charged him, or at least his way. So Longarm lowered the muzzle of his Winchester with his right hand and waved his Stetson at them with his left.

They slowed and the beefy older rider to their right, and hence a tad upslope, holstered his hogleg as he rode forward, taking in the scene with a sardonic smile by the time he rode within easy earshot to shout, "What happened to your pony, Little Boy Blue? Have our mean old cows unsettled you?"

Longarm called back, "Only that chongo. Left my pony at the Flying B, downstream. Name's Custis Long. I'm the law. U.S. Deputy. I just came down yonder canyon after a look—see up above."

The older man reined in to ask, "Find anything? I'd be Hank Borden of the Rocking X and I had that canyon fenced off to keep cows and curious kids from getting lost up yonder. I've noticed how mean that chongo's been getting. 'Bout time we ground her up for chili con carne. She's too old and ornery to be served as beef. Start walking with us on my far side. She won't charge the five of us, if she knows what's good for her."

Longarm got Hank Borden's black barb between himself and the ornery range cow as the owner of all there was to survey in those parts said he was just in time for supper and allowed he'd heard a federal lawman who thought he was the bee's knees had come all the way down from Colorado to help the rangers catch Clay Allison.

As they moved toward the willows, Longarm said he doubted they could be talking about the real Clay Allison and asked if Borden or any of his hands had seen the mysterious cuss.

The local cattleman shook his head and said, "Never laid eyes on him, albeit we have missed some riding stock and our cash-crop saddle mules since word got around about that Lazy A somewheres off in the Chisos. If the cuss druv a small herd into these parts this spring, like some say, he never druv 'em north around the Chisos to the Pecos by way of Santiago Pass. Must have druv on up the Rio Grande out of the stretch the greasers call the Journey of Death. Ain't *possible* to git *down* the Rio Grande around the Big Bend."

Longarm asked how possible it might be to bring stock alive and well through the *Jornado del Muerto* north of say Mesilla, New Mexico Territory.

The stockman, who likely knew, said, "Aw, the stretch from El Paso north to say Socorro ain't nigh as tough today as it was when them old-timey greasers named it. Fair is fair and it's thanks to later greasers that the Journey of Death ain't as deadly no more."

Longarm didn't want to dwell on a distant stretch of cattle trail that might or might not have doodly shit to do with the coming and goings of the mysterious owner of the uncertainly located Lazy A. Longarm had been over the *Jornado del Muerto* more than once on earlier cases. He didn't need a lecture on how the early Spaniards had made the dry country of the American Southwest more like the dry hills of the Old Spain they'd first grazed stock upon.

But as if he was an infernal dude, Hank Borden gave a lecture on the Hispanic habit of sewing seed from the saddle or wagon seat as they rode from one water hole to another, whenever it looked like it was fixing to rain.

Longarm could see the 'dobe sprawl of the Rocking X home spread through the trees ahead now, as the three younger riders loped in faster, while their boss held his barb to an easy walking pace and droned, "It was lack of fodder, not water from the nearby Rio Grande, as made the stretch north from El Paso so rough on wagon teams going and coming from Santa Fe. To begin with there was nary a clump of anything but cactus east or west of the river because the river runs through a rain shadow betwixt the north-south mountains east or west. But it do rain, everywheres, now and again. So them old-timey greasers knew they just had to get more greenery going than the jackrabbits and other wild critters could nip in the sprout. It was pretty slick to start by sewing mustard greens. You can always tell where greasers were the first settlers because of the stirrup-high and canary-yaller mustard blooming in the spring. Cows and such *can* graze mustard if they're really *hungry*. But it's pungent enough to get a leg up on the wild grazers, along with the anise and other such peppersome shit as the greasers seed dry range."

To slow him down, Longarm wearily cut in. "I've seen wild mustard saddle-horn high out California way, where the Spanish had as good a head start on us, with better weather. They companion-crop esparto and then ever more tender grasses to where the rest of you stockmen could learn a lesson from 'em, no offense. Might you be any kin to them Texas Bordens who invented condensed milk?"

The old-timer snorted. "Do I look like a fucking dairy farmer? My daddy did once say Gale Borden had been a distant clansman, all us being Scotch as well as Cow. My daddy bragged more on Captain Ewen Cameron of the Texas Rangers, who commenced the Texas cattle industry during the Mexican War by coming back from Old Mexico with all them longhorns him and his boys had rounded up, once they had no greasers left to fight. Gale Borden was a more sissy Scotsman raising cows the old English way along the Brazos, you see. Fair is fair, and of course, being Scotch, he naturally wound up with more dairy cows, yielding more milk, than anyone in Texas was about to drink. So he invented that way to condense and can it, just in time for the war, with both sides pouring Borden's Condensed Milk in their coffee and ain't that a bitch?"

As they cut through the willow shade, a woman fatter than the Widow Whitehead but not as pretty was waving her apron at them from a back door. Old Borden dismounted to just let go his reins as a Mex kid ran over to take charge of his pony as well. The Mex kid led the black barb toward the same pole corral they kept the rest of their remuda, as Longarm and his host joined those other riders and the lady of the house in the kitchen, to be served at a long pine table by a brace of young Mex gals.

Despite the 'dobe decor and Hispanic help, the Bordens of West Texas ate steak and potatos, mashed and cratered like volcanos to hold the gravy thickened with white flour and black pepper. The coffee—to be drunk with the meal, Rural American style, and not served, damnit, with dessert and everybody thirsty as hell—was Arbuckle brand. So Longarm commented on that, knowing a guest was supposed to notice when they were served quality shit.

Mrs. Borden looked so pleased with the both of them Longarm was minded of a biddy hen fixing to lay a grade-A specimen. But she didn't seem much for talking. Longarm had noticed in his travels how either the lady of the house or the man of the house usually did most of the talking, and they'd already established that Hank Borden was a talker.

Nobody else at the table tried to put an oar in as the old-timer, who seemed to be daddy to one Rocking X rider, the uncle of another and the just plain boss of the third, elaborated on their recent lost, strayed or stolen stock. Borden confirmed Longarm's suspicions about that barbwire up that canyon being new, and added that it hadn't helped.

He said they'd had a slow, steady leak of their cash on the hoof, and decided, once Longarm asked, that the losses *had* been worse since somebody calling himself Clay Allison had been making others edgy farther down the creek.

Washing down a heroic chaw of steak with a great gulp of Arbuckle, the beefy stockman declared, "Can't say we've seen hide nor hair of that tall blond stranger with a Schofield and a pronounced limp. Ain't seen any strange greasers up this way, neither. Neither Rose Bradford to our south nor the Winslows to the north have spotted total strangers trespassing round their spreads, and anyone can see you'd have to drive stock from here north or south along the creek. The slopes to east or west being impractical."

Longarm demured, "Impractical, sure, but are you certain that ain't *possible,* Hank? Like I told you, I just came down off the ridges to the east. The going up yonder is mighty rough. But hither and yon you do see patches of fodder and seeps of water."

One of the younger hands gathered his courage to ask Longarm if he'd seen cattle sign up that canyon they'd fenced off. That was what you called cowshit at the supper table with three women in the room, cattle sign.

Longarm gravely replied, "Nope. The drift fence you all strung saw to that. But there must be dozens of other routes where a night rider could drive a head or more at a time, through canyons never properly surveyed by the land office, to that mountain meadow where, according to that bighorn-hunting Caddo Flynn, a small herd passing through just last spring has expanded considerable in the last three or four months."

Chapter 11

After Longarm apologized for having to eat and run, their hired hand, Chad, ran him over to the Flying B in their buckboard so's they'd neither force a guest to walk four miles nor wait too long for the return of a pony. So Chad had to set down for more coffee and at least one slice of cake whilst Longarm filled Rose Bradford in on his hike through the neither far nor well-known high country to the east.

She said she'd told him he wouldn't find much on foot up yonder without a guide, and he had to admit he hadn't learned a whole lot from old Pepper MacLeod.

Both Rose Bradford and the young hand off the Rocking X knew Pepper MacLeod, albeit only Chad seemed dead certain the old prospector was totally insane.

Somebody had told Chad you didn't prospect for color in limestone.

Rose said she'd heard you might find copper or even silver veins in lava rock. But Chad insisted there wasn't enough lava rock over yonder to matter. Longarm said he didn't rightly care about the rock formations of the Big Bend all that much, being they hadn't sent him there to file a mineral claim.

Chad said he had to get on back to the Rocking X. Rose seemed sort of put out when Longarm allowed he had to be on his way as well.

She followed him out to the corral, pouting they still had so much to talk about. As he saddled his borrowed Morgan, he assured her he'd have been proud to talk to her clean through to breakfast if only he hadn't been on duty at the moment.

By that hour the evening sun hung low and red above the hills across the creek to the west. So it was hard to say whether Rose was blushing or paling when she looked away, protesting, "I guess I never invited any man to spend the whole night with this child! Does it have to be all or nothing at all with you, Custis Long?"

He said soothingly, "Not hardly. I've been known to jaw past midnight on a porch swing with a lady I walked home from a church social, Miss Rose. But this evening I'm really busy."

As she helped him saddle and cinch, she asked what he expected to discover back in Tanktown, wistfully adding, "I've never found it all that exciting of a Saturday night in roundup time, if the truth be known."

Longarm chuckled and confessed, "I've been to bigger cities, albeit I suspect there's some action to be found in any town if you know the right inhabitants. I'll tell you what I'm going to do for you, seeing you've been so helpful, Miss Rose. I'm going on in to see if I can find out what in thunder's been going on, and then, if I live through it, I'll come back out here and tell you all about it."

She said they had a deal and stood on tiptoe to seal the bargain with a schoolgirl kiss sweet enough to make him wonder whether a lawman without the least notion of his best next move might not find his way to spare a lonesome little gal a few more minutes, or mayhaps a few hours. But he knew what Billy Vail and his own morning-after conscience was likely to say to that.

He had no call to ask what a gal past her teens with looks and brains was doing wasting so much of the little time there was on such a modest spread so far from the bright lights and music. He'd met her childish ma and helpless pa. But as if she'd read his mind the willowy blonde stared up at him through the wistful shades of sundown to tell him, "I guess I've seen the valley and I guess I've seen the hill and I guess I've even been to the ladies' seminary in San Antone. But then my dad got stove in and . . . things don't always turn out as we plan."

Longarm smiled down at her to say, "I'll be back, when we have more time to talk about . . . San Antone, Miss Rose. But now I got to get it on down the road."

He couldn't quite make out what she called after him after he'd shut that gate and rode south a furlong or more. The sunset had commenced to get serious. But the gloaming sky glowed lavender enough to read the store signs as he rode into Tanktown close to eight that evening.

He tethered the coffee Morgan at the hitchrail shared by Western Union and that chili parlor next to it. He went in to wire another progress report to his home office at night letter rates, knowing how Billy Vail felt about spending a nickel a word for straight telegrams declaring continued confusion. They had no wires from Denver for him. Old Billy wouldn't spring for a night letter unless he had orders or a seriously helpful suggestion to offer. They'd both known before he'd left Denver that Longarm could conduct routine procedure without his head being patted often as you'd pat a bird dog.

Coming out of the Western Union, he saw that Consuela, that Mex waitress from next door, had carried a bucket of water out to his borrowed mount. She was petting its withers and declaring it *muy bonita* as Longarm joined them in the gathering dusk. He thanked her but said, "You'd never know it from just looking at such a born actress, Miss Consuela, but she's been loafing about with plenty of fodder and water most of the afternoon."

Consuela, who seemed a tad older, a tad more filled out and likely half-again more *sangre azul* than little Yzabel over to the Toro Negro, shrugged the tawny bare shoulders as showed above her frilly Mexican blouse to opine, "My people have a saying about not getting a horse to drink unless it is thirsty, and I am not forcing this one's head into that . . . how you say *cubo en ingles*?"

He said bucket was the word she was groping for.

She said, "*¿Es verdad?* This sounds like something much more rude I have heard *vaqueros gringos* shout when something annoys them when they have been drinking. Would you like for to come inside and allow me for to serve you something for to drink as well?"

He told her he had to get it on up to the ranger post. She nodded knowingly and managed a gallant smile as she said, "Buck it, eh? I understand. Forgive my forgetting my place, señor. Is a most quiet week night and sometimes I feel . . . *solitario* when business gets so slow."

He asked how late they stayed open. He wasn't surprised when she said she worked there from four in the afternoon to midnight. Mex folk that close to the border were like that. He allowed he might be by later, after he tended some chores of his own. She sniffed and warned him she shut for the night on the stroke of twelve, and added, "I am not a woman to be despised."

He didn't ask what she meant by that, either, as he led the Morgan up the street on foot to wake his legs back up. Folk who didn't savvy the ways of the Southwest tended to think Mexicans lazy because they shut most everything down around noon and napped until three or four. But Longarm understood the logic behind *La Siesta,* taught to Spanish Christians in their old country by North African Moors, in spite of that Spanish Inquisition. Getting in out of the hot sun and trying not to move too much during the hottest hours of a sunny clime only cost precious business hours when you kept the same business hours they kept in London or New York, and having been there in high summer, Longarm wasn't sure New York wouldn't be better off following the hot weather hours of Old Mexico.

The Mexican business day started well before dawn. When they knocked off at noon, most Mex banks and such had been open way longer, and they made up for *La*

Siesta by staying open way later in the evening, when it was more sensible to move around outdoors. Albeit Consuela staying open to midnight was pushing it some, doubtless to catch Mex trade as it headed on home for the shorter nights it took when it slept more than once out of every twenty-four. Her intimating she took no shit from any man could be taken as many ways as her watering a man's pony without being asked.

It seemed a shame, Longarm thought, that he'd never know for certain. Old Consuela had a somewhat more cameo face than old Yzabel and a different figure entire. But the same romantic natures that made Mex gals such swell kissers made it prudent to kiss no more than one in the same town unless a man had no use at all for his hair or hide and, hell, she'd just *said* she'd get on home alone if he showed up a second past midnight.

Up to the ranger station, Longarm helped their wrangler unsaddle, water and rub down the Morgan before he left the McClellan in their tack room but held on to his Winchester and mosied around to jaw with their night desk.

Despite their military-sounding ranks and the way they organized as companies on paper, the Texas Rangers had always come in smaller lots than even platoons. They'd started out as nominal Mexican subjects, as a twenty-man force under a captain. So Longarm doubted Captain Kramer had that many, divided into night and day shifts. But he refrained from asking as he brought a Sergeant Farnsworth up to date on that run out to the Flying B and up that cliff.

The older, leaner and balder Farnsworth allowed that Captain Kramer had told him to watch out for their federal guest before heading home for his supper. Farnsworth added he knew Pepper MacLeod and considered him set in his ways, totally ignorant of geology, but harmless.

The older lawman explained, "He's never found a nickel's worth of color in them limestone hills, but he will keep prospecting 'em, and local merchants who ought to be ashamed of themselves will keep grubtaking the poor old loon for shares in that goldmine in the sky he means to find most any day now. I suspect they'd rather have him up in them hills, lecturing his burro on the subject, than holding forth on his odd notions in a barbershop or barroom."

Longarm asked if Sergeant Farnsworth knew that hunting breed Caddo Flynn that well.

The ranger made a wry face and declared, "*That* old loner is crazier than Pepper MacLeod. Nobody *wants* the rack of a bighorn as a trophy unless he shot it his fool self. The hide's worth no more than a goat hide you can buy off many a Mex farmer, cheap, and such meat as Caddo can pack in before it spoils is, let's face it, *mutton*!"

He rose to rummage in that same file drawer marked T to Z while he volunteered, "Not that old Caddo *finds* many bighorns over in them dry, uninhabited hills. He claims to be part Indian. Arnold swears he's a greaser. Either way, the real Indians in these parts don't consider that range a good hunting ground this far south. They say you do see deer and even elk or bear far south as the parts of the range you'd call the Guadalupes. But the way both Indians and Mexicans tell me, the deer-hunting Mescaleros, who straddle the range up Roswell way, hunted out most everything betwixt their mountain agency and the Big Bend long ago. I tried to tell him that the first time I met up with Caddo Flynn. Anyone can see how long it would take to restock hunted-out deer country with the Rio Grande to the west and south, the Pecos to the east and a whole tribe of deer-famished Apache to the north. But he wouldn't listen, even though he was pestering us to buy a side of mutton he'd been carrying around too long by far!"

As the older lawman poured, Longarm mused half to himself, "Since I have yet to have the honor, and nobody seems to know where I might find Caddo Flynn this evening, I wonder how long it would take the Bureau of Indian Affairs to locate and lend me a Mescallero who might be even more familiar with the high country down this way."

Sergeant Farnsworth allowed he'd drink to such a grand notion. So they clinked shot glasses and Farnsworth decided they'd best do that some more. But Longarm demured, saying he was still on duty and might want to get it up later that night.

The older lawman wisfully remarked he just hated to drink alone, but, seeing he'd started to pour . . .

Then another ranger Longarm hadn't met yet barged in, demanding, "Sergeant Farnsworth! You mind that federal lawman they sent down to help us identicate that ornery Clay Allison?"

Farnsworth laughed and pointed at Longarm to reply, "I did hear some mention of the ugly cuss and I was about to ask him what he thought he was doing down this way, seeing that's him, standing there with his bare face hanging out!"

"You'd be Deputy U.S. Marshal Long? The one they call Longarm?" the younger lawman stammered, holding out his hand to toss in, "I'd be Andy Steiger. It's an honor to meet up with a lawman so famous, and I'm ready to back your play at the Last Chance, Longarm!"

Longarm exchanged puzzled glances with Sergeant Farnsworth, who put the cork back in the tequila bottle as he asked, "Play? What in the blue blazes are you talking about, Steiger? Have you been bumming drinks off Liam O'Hanlon on duty?"

The ranger shook his head and protested, "Ain't had a beer since I came on duty this evening, Sarge. I patrolled down the creek like the captain ordered, turned back where the basin peters out beyond the Tumbling Sevens and naturally reined in at the Last Chance when they hailed me from their dooryard."

"Then what happened?" Longarm asked before Sergeant Farnsworth could beat around the mullberry bush some more.

The ranger said, "Then I went inside, of course. The place was night empty. O'Hanlon said it had emptied out earlier when old Clay Allison had shown up, alone, but drunk as a skunk and waving his six-gun crazy. O'Hanlon showed me the new holes Allison had shot in his ceiling tin. Then he said the crazy bastard had ordered a glass of that Maryland rye they said the great Longarm fancied."

"He mentioned me by name?" asked Longarm.

Steiger said, "He did. Then he opined any man who drank such sissy whiskey could hardly be man enough to fuck his own mother, likely sat down to piss and didn't dare to meet the one and original Clay Allison for a friendly drink before dying."

"Is he out yonder right now?" asked Longarm quietly.

The ranger replied, "I can't say. I never saw him there. O'Hanlon told me that after he'd made his brag Clay Allison declared his intent to lay four sisters camped down by the creek and that he'd be back in an hour or less to have that drink with Longarm, here, if anyone there was man enough to carry word to the . . . never mind what he called you, Longarm. I hope you understand I am only repeating his words."

Longarm turned to the sergeant to say, "I'd be obliged if you all would lend me another mount this evening."

Farnsworth said, "I can do better than that, Longarm! What say we send you to have that drink with Clay Allison along with all the night riders we can rustle up on such short notice?"

Longarm calmly replied, "What for? Didn't Steiger, here, just tell us Clay Allison had invited me to drink alone with him, *mano a mano*?"

Farnsworth nodded but cautioned, "What if he's not a man of his word and, even if he is, what makes you so certain you can beat him to the draw?"

Longarm motioned Steiger to the door with his Winchester as he told Sergeant Farnsworth, "The only thing any of us can be certain of is death and taxes. And sometimes I wonder about taxes."

Chapter 12

Riding down the creek with Steiger on a borrowed buck-skin, Longarm suggested they'd get there nigh as soon and a whole lot quieter afoot, leading their mounts the last half a mile in the moonlight.

Since a horse ran faster but walked slower than a man, Longarm had time to jaw with the local rider about what lay ahead. He'd had time to ponder Steiger's earlier words. So he asked, "How come you managed to ride *back* from that Tumbling Sevens spread if Liam O'Hanlon's Last Chance sets beside the exit of this basin, old son?"

Steiger explained, "On this side of the creek. The Tumbling Sevens grazes a fair-sized box canyon facing the Last Chance spread from the west side of the creek. Ain't no regular stream down that canyon, but the water table's high enough for plenty of wells and they get enough sky water for short grass on good bottomland."

"Enough bottomland to matter, up a side canyon?" asked Longarm.

Steiger laughed and replied in an easy tone, "I can see you haven't explored this Big Bend Country all that much. This basin is only part of the range around Tanktown, all told. It's true you don't get much bottomland in one slice up any canyon feeding into it. But they have a shithouse worth of canyons to both sides of the Tiswin floodplains. They call the Tumbling Sevens spread the Tumbling Sevens spread on account of its home canyon running back into the south cliffs in such a tumble. After they cleaned the Indians out of that maze, they found it offered seven branched box canyons, with flat loamy bottomlands dammed behind dry waterfalls in a series of drop-offs."

Longarm whistled and asked how much acreage they were talking about. The younger lawman shrugged and said, "Couple of sections at the very least. Mayhaps more. I ain't rid higher than the first dry falls behind their headquarters spread half a mile up. But before you ask, Captain Kramer's been over the survey maps and they were telling the truth about their Tumbling Sevens being a sort of pitchfork of box canyons. Ain't no way in Hell to drive stock any way but out the main entrance of that canyon, past the housing and corrals of their main spread. So that's likely why, so far, the Tumbling Sevens ain't lost any stock they know of."

Longarm said, "They'd doubtless notice if Clay Allison or any other haunts rode past on the way to the Last Chance."

Then he silently called a halt where the trail ran through a dark patch of cottonwood shade, saying, "This looks like a handly spot to leave these eight steel-shod hooves."

Steiger started to say something dumb. But then he nodded and said, "I follow your drift. A sneak staked out a ways to watch for us ought to be listening for hoofbeats, not pussy feet!"

They hugged the same shade as they led their mounts off the beaten path into thicker tanglewood closer to the creek. Then they tethered them out of sight from the trail to brouse cottonwood leaves high or gramma and sedge grass low.

Longarm took the lead with his saddle gun at port. Steiger tagged after with his own Winchester for only a few paces before he softly called out, "The trail's over *that* way, no offense."

Longarm said, "None taken. Didn't they say Rangers Page and Summerhill strode into the Last Chance by way of the front door, with their guns already drawn?"

Steiger decided, "Now that you mention it, entering from the shithouse side might be more prudent."

So the two lawmen worked all the way over to the bluffs rising from the narrowing floodplain of the creek and hugged the natural wall to approach the 'dobe complex around the Last Chance down an alleyway of cliffside shadows. They rolled over the 'dobe wall of that corral and worked the tricky gate leading to the shithouse yard Steiger had first suggested.

Longarm made certain there was nobody in the shithouse before he followed the muzzle of his cocked Winchester along that dark corridor toward the dimly lit barroom, where he could make out Liam O'Hanlon quietly polishing glasses behind the bar.

Since that was all he could make out from where he stood, Longarm stood there until the burly Irishman glanced his way, blinked like an owl caught taking a crap and waved them on in.

The place stood empty as a jug of rum on a Sunday morn. As the two lawmen joined O'Hanlon behind the bar, saddle guns trained on the open front door, O'Hanlon said, "You just missed him. Came in twenty minutes or more ago, asking for you by name, Longarm. Ordered drinks for everybody in the house but before I could pour there was nobody but him in the house. I'd have left myself but he might have taken it the wrong way. He said some awful things about sissies in general and you in particular before he stormed out again, and I don't mind telling you I was just as glad to find myself with no customers at all till you boyos showed up just now."

"Did he say where he was headed?" asked Longarm thoughtfully.

O'Hanlon nodded and replied, "Tanktown. Said something about some mountain not coming to its momma. He was drunk as a skunk and might not have known what he was saying."

Longarm said soberly, "I know what he was trying to say. He had a point. I'm more likely to find him in town than down this way now."

"Don't you boyos want any for the road?" the saloon keeper called after them as Longarm headed for the front door with young Steiger in tow.

Longarm addressed his words to the ranger as he cautioned, "Crab to your right as you step outside with the lamplight behind you. I will have already crabbed to my left. We'll discuss our next moves once we see how we made out getting that far!"

But once they'd both made it out front with their backs to solid 'dobe and their outlines lost from anybody farther out, Longarm had to sheepishly admit, "O'Hanlon *said* the asshole had headed into town. But let's pussyfoot some as we work our way back to our mounts."

They did so without incident. As they'd hoped, the mean drunk who claimed to be Clay Allison had apparently ridden past the ponies they'd tethered off the trail without noticing either.

So they mounted up and rode back to Tanktown, reining in before the Western Union a little after ten-thirty.

Longarm's notion to wire another progress report was foiled by a printed notice hanging in the unlit window of the one-room telegraph shed. It explained how in view of local telegraph demand, the company only kept one operator in Tanktown and he had to rest up now and then. The notice gave the street address of his boardinghouse but begged would-be customers not to pester him when he was off duty unless it was a matter of life or death.

Longarm decided a night letter informing his office he might or might not be fixing to meet up with Clay Allison at last wasn't worth that much bother, yet. So they left their mounts tethered out front to go into the chili parlor and have some black coffee whilst they decided what they ought to try next.

Consuela seemed proud to serve them, and as she bent

over her counter, Longarm noticed she'd slathered on more lavender water since last the two of them had been alone together there. When they asked, Consuela said she hadn't heard a thing out front that evening about Clay Allison or anybody else on the prod.

The ranger suggested, "You might want to reconsider sitting in here in lamplight with that homicidal lunatic most anywheres out in the dark with that Schofield, pard."

Longarm said, "I doubt he's prowling up and down the streets of Tanktown with a drawn gun. Somebody would have noticed and that ranger post you may have forgotten is in line of sight just up the way. If he's in town at all, and not just bragging, he's laying for me. Laying for me somewheres he's expecting me to go."

Steiger asked where that might be.

Longarm said, "I've been down this way long enough for some to gossip, and they say he has some Mex vaqueros riding for him."

He nodded at the waitress on the far side of the counter to assure her that hadn't been meant disrespectful of *La Raza*.

She dimpled back at him to say she'd heard he was *muy simpatico*. He didn't ask what else she might have heard about him. Mex folk he met along the border knew or didn't know about that bounty posted for *El Brazo Largo* by *Los Rurales*.

Longarm told Steiger, "Like I was saying, the rascal has likely heard I'm working with you rangers whilst staying at the Toro Negro. He could be laying in wait or planning to bust in on me at either of them locations. If he has a lick of sense he's planning to lay for me in the taproom of my posada or come calling after I'm upstairs in my hired room. If he stood willing to take on your whole ranger company, for all his bragging, he'd have done so by now and you would be drinking to his memory as I packed up to head on home."

Steiger suggested, "Why don't I scout the Toro Negro's taproom, then? I only know him by description. So he's never laid eyes on me and I don't look at all like you."

Longarm started to say he didn't let other men stick their necks out to save his own. But on reflection the ranger's suggestion made sense. So Longarm said, "Mind you don't lock eyes with any big blond rascals or study on their guns as you just ask the Widow Whitehead if somebody else, neither me nor anybody riding for the rangers, has been by tonight. When she naturally tells you she don't know such a gent, just leave, casual."

As Steiger rose from his stool, Longarm added as an afterthought, "If the widow ain't tending bar, you'll likely find Miss Yzabel of the Spanish persuasion behind the same. The plan is the same in either case and, just in case either should ask, you never heard of me."

Steiger asked why either old gal might ask about him.

Longarm replied in a desperately casual tone, "Because I've been boarding there and nobody there has seen me all day, of course."

So Steiger left a nickel, tip included, by his drained cup, to leave Longarm alone with Consuela in the otherwise empty chili parlor.

When the pretty but sort of hard-looking waitress commenced to trim the oil lamps above the mirrors on her side of the counter, he asked, "Didn't you say you stayed open till midnight, Miss Consuela?"

She calmly replied, "Most nights I do. This is not most nights. Do you take me for a deaf woman? Do you think I did not hear what that other *prole* just said about that *tiro malo* out there in the dark with you for his chosen *objetivo*?"

Longarm dryly replied, "I suspected you might be listening, Miss Consuela. Didn't you hear me tell him the surly cuss would likely be planning to finish me off at my *posada* in the wee small hours?"

She said, "*Sí*, that is for why I am not going to let you go back to the Toro Negro tonight. Since nobody could have told any *tiro malo* of our . . . *amistad,* he would never think for to look for you at *my* place, *comprende*?"

Longarm wasn't dead certain he did. *Amistad* translated as no more than friendship, platonical, albeit he hadn't thought they'd got *that* far along already. Taking the bull by the horns, he replied in a firm but not unkind tone, "I'd as soon face a gunfight in one bedroom as one of them fancy mannered stage plays deciding who gets to sleep on the sofa, no offense."

It was too dark by then to read her expression as she asked in a sort of throaty purr who'd said anything about anyone sleeping on any sofa.

So it was just as well Steiger gave Longarm time to study some before he came back to peer uncertainly inside, saying, "You in there, Longarm?"

When Longarm allowed they both were, the ranger reported, "Nobody answering to Clay Allison's description has been anywheres near your posada as far as the Widow Whitehead can tell. I never seen the Mex gal you mentioned, albeit I heard Spanish jabber coming through this beaded curtain. Jawed some with some old boys I know from right here in town. They said nobody strange has rid in since sundown, far as they know. But when I asked if they'd noticed *us* riding out and back, they confessed I had 'em stumped."

Joining them at the counter so he could make out what Consuela was up to when she poured more coffee, Steiger added, "I naturally asked at the livery stable and municipal corral. No rider sitting tall with blond hair and limping afoot left a pony either place. Our two mounts out front are the only ones tethered along the *camino* at this hour. Do you reckon it was just a drunken brag?"

Longarm found himself holding hands with Consuela when he reached for his own coffee. But all he said was, "Reads like a drunken brag until you consider he's gunned four rangers so far, here in the basin alone. Whether he's the real Clay Allison or some lunatic following in his footsteps, a lot of men died up Cimarron way after dismissing what they took for the drunken brags of a big blond cuss with a limp!"

Steiger asked what came next. Longarm said, "I'd be obliged if you led both ponies on back to your post and put my saddle with yours in the tack room. I'd best hang on to this Winchester."

The ranger said he could do better than that. He offered to turn out the whole outfit, day shift as well as night shift, to sweep the streets of Tanktown until they caught up with Clay Allison.

But Longarm said, "We don't know if he's Clay Allison or not, and I don't want to run him out of town. I want to *catch* him and find out who he might be and what makes him so mean. So why don't you see to our mounts, report to Sergeant Farnsworth and tell him I'd just as soon work alone tonight and let you all know in the morning whether I found out the price of beef in Chicago or tea in China."

Steiger finished his second cup and left. As he led the two ponies off in the darkness, Consuela laughed softly and murmured, "*Bueno*. Is better he does not know you wish for to be alone with me, eh?"

Longarm smiled wistfully and told her, "I know we're both likely to wind up hating me, come morning, Miss Consuela. But I got to find me a hunting blind to stake out the riverside trail out the south end of town. They say the mysterious owner of the Lazy A makes his way home from somewheres along the same, and when he don't find me at the Toro Negro, he'll surely head home before daybreak."

Consuela said, "*Bueno,* I have just such a place for you. Since first coming here from Chihuahua I have live alone by the creek, just outside of town, to the south. From my bedroom one can see the trail by moonlight, as long as we light no *lampara pendeja,* eh?"

Chapter 13

Since at Consuela's own suggestion they never lit no fucking lamps, they didn't take as long as usual to get down to brass tacks after she'd shown him how one bedroom window of her 'dobe on the outskirts of town overlooked an open moonlit stretch of the riverside trail.

Knowing they'd hear hoofbeats better than anyone outside might hear bedsprings, Longarm stood his Winchester on its buttplate with its muzzle against the sill before he took Consuela in his arms, kissed her some more and lowered her to the bed as she got to clutching at his buckles and buttons.

Not daring to break the spell, as he had more than once with an overly exited señorita, he hoisted her sateen fandango skirts out of their way and, with nothing else to bar further progress, entered her with his pants and gunbelt on, which she seemed to find an exciting novelty, judging by the way she was moving with her sandal heels dug into the edge of the mattress to either side of his denim-clad hips.

After he'd made her come that way—it was easy— Longarm stripped her to the buff as she lay purring in the afterglow, hung his six-gun on the bedpost closer to the open window, and shucked his boots and duds to treat her even friendlier.

Consuela responded in kind, and though she and little Yzabel were the same border breed, it was a thundering wonder how different two gals could get without either of them being ugly.

He never said so, of course, and for another wonder Consuela was one of those rare women who could screw just swell without telling every man they screwed about that cherry-popping brute who'd taught them to screw so swell. The only indication she gave that she'd ever had a past at all was when she mentioned hearing about *El Brazo Largo* knowing how to treat a *mujer* before she'd ever left Chihuahua.

He didn't bite. He just fumbled for his shirt on the floor for a cheroot and some waterproof Mex matches without letting on whether or not he'd heard tell of such a pal of *La Causa*, and as he'd already seen back at the chili parlor, Consuela was a quicker study than little Yzabel and knew better than to press a man when he failed to answer a veiled question.

As he made certain nobody was passing by out yonder and lit a smoke for them to share, Longarm decided he liked Consuela better, and that seemed a shame. For of course, when came the cold gray dawn, he was going to have to tell her Yzabel had seen him first.

When a man had to choose between two border Mex gals he was well advised to show preferential treatment to the dumber of the two. You might be able to explain how things had to be to a *smart* Mex gal and escape with no more than a tongue lashing. They all tended to be sort of touchy, and the dumber they were the more likely they were to cut a man where it hurt the most.

But the cold gray dawn lay in the future and Consuela was still warm in the magical here and now. So she had something bigger than a cheroot between her soft pretty lips when they both heard hoofbeats outside, moving sudden along that moonlit trail. So Longarm hissed at her to hold the thought as he rolled bare-ass off her bed to prop

98

the Winchester across the sill and cock it. He'd levered a round in its chamber earlier.

But the Mex on a Spanish saddle mule, dressed in white cotton under a big straw sombrero, with a high sugarloaf crown, was riding into town instead of for wherever in blue blazes the Lazy A might be. So Longarm let him live, put his Winchester down and rose to attention for good old Consuela again.

She seemed to like it dog style, missionary style and most any style but hostile, punctuated by scattered moments of anxiety as they had to break off for another rider passing by outside.

None of them looked anything like Clay Allison was described, and not a soul rode by after two whooping and laughing vaqueros appeared to have called it a night. Consuela said she recognized the dirty laugh of one, said he rode for the Spanish Hat and asked Longarm to come back to bed and let her get on top. So he did.

But the next time they got to sharing a smoke with the pillows under their heads for a change, Longarm questioned a gal who likely knew about that Mex spread with such a fancy Spanish-style brand.

She said she'd heard the Fernandez family were *sangre azul,* left in place by the generous terms of the peace treaty ending the Mexican war. She said they were considered quality by the local Anglos but didn't have much to do with anyone who wasn't what Texicans called kissing cousins. She sniffed and added they'd never invited a mere waitress to supper, even if her great great somebody or other *had* marched against Montezuma under Cortez, *sin duda!*"

Since she'd just said she'd never been invited to visit, Longarm had no call to ask her to describe the lay of the land that far down the creek. If the Spanish Hat raised enough stock to matter, they had to have access to yet another grassy canyon running back betwixt the high red cliffs down yonder.

As if her mind was dwelling on the high-toned Mex

family, Consuela suddenly blubbered, "*Yo no soy una mierda, por Dios!*"

Longarm cuddled her bare hide closer to his own as he assured her anyone could see that, even though he'd never even *hinted* she was just a piece of shit. Her remark about some Spanish don whupping her Indians ancestors under Cortez betrayed how mixed up she felt about her mixed heritage. A man who was pure white, or pure anything, had to be careful about the touchy pride of an uncertain border breed, and he wasn't looking foreward to telling her about Yzabel.

So he didn't, even though his common sense warned him it was better she hear it from him than from other Mex or, God forbid, Yzabel herself in such a small town.

Blowing thoughtful smoke rings in the dark, Longarm composed more than one respectful explanation with an earnest plea for understanding.

That part wasn't so tough. Fair was fair, and even a woman should be able to see that any slap and tickle a man might have been up to before they'd ever met hardly counted as deliberate spite, and after that, a heap of women sort of cottoned to the notion they'd taken a man away from most any other gal.

It was somewhere along in there that the confession trail commenced to get treacherous. Most gals would go along with that other gal not having as winning a disposition or as satisfying a ring dang doo. But after that they wanted to hear you cuss the day you ever gave in to such an ugly slut and swear to be true and never go near that other woman again.

Swearing to be true to Consuela, as long as he was in town, would not have been such a hard row to hoe. If Consuela wasn't built quite as tight, she was somewhat prettier than Yzabel and way tighter and compact than the Widow Whitehead. But were either Yzabel or the Widow Whitehead likely to approve his shacking up down to this end of town with another gal entire?

Weighing the odds as he finished his cheroot, whilst

Consuela moved skillfully on top to finish what *she* was enjoying, Longarm wondered how long he'd manage to play Yzabel and her redheaded boss against one another at the Toro Negro without a hissy fit and likely the loss of all three gals. So he snubbed the smoked-down cheroot and rolled the bird he had in hand on her back to fully enjoy what he had whilst he still had it.

Consuela took that as a compliment, but as she responded with some passion, she sobbed, "*¿Ay, que mas y que tanto, querido mio?* Forgive me for being such a *colegiala*, but I am not used to being treated as a how you say gang bang? How many times have we died together, tonight, so far? Don't tell me! Just die with me again and then *por Dios mio* let me put my legs together and close my eyes for just a little while!"

Longarm was willing. For in truth they'd both fornicated to that show-off stage new partners fornicated into, getting to know one another well enough to admit their true feelings. He kept at it to where she asked more than once if he was almost there. Then he faked it, same as she had, and rolled off to stare at the herringbone willow ceiling pattern he couldn't make out without more light, wondering how Yzabel might take it if he warned her the widow she worked for might fire her unless they sacrificed some passing passion in the interests of her steady job.

It seemed even darker now, outside as well as in. He glanced out the nearby window to see he couldn't make out the trail half as well. The moon was setting. Or it was clouding up.

Snuggling Consuela closer, he quietly asked how well she might know the Mex help over to the Toro Negro.

She answered with a purr betwixt a contented sigh and a gentle snore.

He didn't think this would be a good time to wake her up and ask the same question. He wasn't certain how he wanted her to answer it.

There came a deep rumble that fit as distant gunfire or thunder, closer. The darkness outside minded Longarm more of thunder. He sat up and swung his bare feet to the braided rug, softly humming that old trail song as went with

"Cloudy in the west,
Looks like rain,
And I left my slicker
In the wagon again!"

Consuela stirred in her sleep to purr, "¿*Que paso, querido?*" So he drew the counterpane up over her bare charms as outside, as he'd feared, it commenced to rain, scattered drops at first. Then there was a nearby thunderclap and it commenced to come down fire and salt as Consuela woke up to gasp, "Close the shutters! Is no glass and I do not wish for to have everything ruined!"

Longarm rose to draw the slatted jalousies in place, but as he did so he heard hooves, a heap of hooves, thudding and sloshing through the downpour as somebody encouraged the stampede with whip-crack pistol shots.

Longarm let go the shutters and picked up his Winchester to aim it out the window into the wind-whipped rain, as a literally thundering herd of around twenty mules sloshed by, tails up and long wet ears gleaming on and off and the sky above crackled from limelight to nigh total darkness. He could have dropped more than one rider whipping down with slickers buttoned up and hats pulled low, but he had no notion who they were, up to what, so he called out, "Slow down in the name of the law and tell us what's going on!"

Nobody answered till he called out, louder, "Make that federal law and explain or I'll shoot!"

Then somebody answered with a shot pegged close enough to splinter the window frame to his left and thud into the 'dobe behind him, so he ducked as Consuela screamed, "¡*Ay, mierda!* ¡*Nos vamos a morir todos!*"

Then she wanted to know what he thought he was doing as he fumbled to get dressed without raising his head above the level of that open window and the noise outside commenced to fade away.

He told her, "Got to get my pants on before the posse chasing them tricksters shows up! Then I got to run clean the hell up the other end of town and throw my saddle and self across a bronc to chase after 'em. The sons of bitches have slickered me! It was all what this stage magic gal I used to know called *misdirection*. Sucker the know-it-all peace officers into expecting a showdown with a mean drunk and . . . Never mind. What they done's been done and now I got to see if I can undo it!"

Strapping on his six-gun and setting his Stetson at a determined tilt, Longarm kissed the naked gal when she rose to the occasion. Then he chased his Winchester out into the rain at port-arms and, just as he'd feared, got soaked clean through his summerweight denims before he'd made it far enough uptown to matter.

He sloshed on, idly wondering how come a second bunch of riders had yet to slosh downstream after the first bunch. Up ahead, beyond the cluster of shops and such around the stage terminal, he saw lots of lantern or torch lights, moving or stationary, through the shimmers of the pouring rain. So he picked up the pace as he jogged on toward them, muttering, "That's one hell of a way to run a railroad or to posse up! Them stock thieves were driving that herd lickety-split in cold night air with one hell of a lead to begin with!"

As he joined the crowd gathered out front of the ranger post, the just as wet and even more confounded Captain Kramer caught up with him to demand, "What's going on, Longarm?"

Longarm knew better than to ask an older lawman who'd likely been fast asleep and who'd just now intimated he didn't know what in the hell they were gathering to celebrate.

Kramer having the local Indian Sign, Longarm let him bull their way through the crowd and tagged after him toward the open doorway.

There, once they got close enough to see, sprawled

103

Andy Steiger with his head in Sergeant Farnsworth's lap. The young ranger stared up blank, and despite the rain pouring down, or mayhaps because of the extra moisture, the whole front of him glistened red as a shot-up can of tomato preserves. Catching Captain Kramer's eye, the night desk said, "I didn't see it. Slim Putnam, here, says he did. I was inside at my desk, of course."

Corporal Arnold joined them as Kramer turned to a tall skinny kid in a ten-gallon hat and a yellow rain slicker.

Slim Putnam, as he was so aptly called, said, "I was sleeping one off in the livery hayloft when that thunder woke me up. I went over to the corral where I'd left my saddle over a pole and my roan free to wander. Time I had my slicker on and shook out a loop to rope my roan and move her over to the livery, I heard Andy there calling out for someone to step out of them shadows and explain his fool self to the Texas Rangers. So by now my poor roan is soaked to the bone and if she dies she dies."

Captain Kramer said, "Never mind your pony, damn it! What happened?"

Slim pointed down at the dead or dying man with his chin to reply, "You can plainly see what happened. This taller cuss stepped out into view from between yonder corner of your post and the shuttered shop beyond. Andy yelled, "Jesus H. Christ!" and went for his gun. The tall cuss beat him to the draw, easy, and dropped him in his tracks. Then the next thing I knew the winner was coming my way, limping some, and I didn't know whether to shit or go blind as he nodded at me, sort of friendly, to ask if I had any objections to his just heading on home for some peace and quiet."

Slim hesitated, then sheepishly confessed, "I never answered. I never said shit or moved a muscle as he limped on by me, allowing that was what he'd thought."

Somebody in the crowd whistled. Kramer asked, "Did you get a good look at him, Slim? Could you describe him if you saw him again?"

Slim Putnam replied without hesitation, "Nothing to describe. It was him, Clay Allison. Wasn't the first time I'd seen the moody cuss, albeit tonight was the first time he ever spoke to me, and I don't mind saying I'm just as glad I never answered!"

Chapter 14

Doc Fletcher, their deputy coroner, turned out to be a fussy old soul so worried about his suit and tie he depended on an umbrella as well as a black slicker to fend off the rain. After opining that Steiger needed neither a dentist nor a doctor, he asked why in tarnation they hadn't carried him in out of the rain. So they did.

By this time Longarm suspected, by way of the blank looks he kept getting in answer to his comments about mules, that nobody else had noticed that thundering herd. He was sure nobody had first when he asked Captain Kramer and then when they both asked Sergeant Farnsworth. Nobody else crowded around the body on the floor inside had noticed a herd of cows being driven through town just now, either.

Longarm said, "They must have driven them through the high chaparral along the bluffs behind all your shithouses, at a walk, at the time or shortly after all that gunplay out front drew the attention of everyone here in Tanktown."

Captain Kramer gasped, "Thunderation! Are you intimating this poor kid was murdered just to provide a distractication?"

Slim Putnam piped up, "It was a fair fight, Captain."

Kramer snapped, "Shut up, Slim. Let us be the judges of how fair it might be for an experienced man killer to slap leather on a green kid!"

Then he turned back to Longarm to decide, "It don't take outlines in chalk on a blackboard to see what they planned in advance. Figuring on heavy weather tonight, they let it be known Clay Allison might be in town, on the prod for another gunfight, so's all the law for miles around would be expecting trouble here in town and not out on the range in the dark."

Longarm suggested, "They likely had them expensive mules selected in advance or already rounded up and bunched somewheres. They waited out this storm with the gunplay misdirection set up to get the stock past this bottleneck and merrily down the stream."

Sergeant Farnsworth said, "Poor Steiger there told me about Clay Allison gunning for Longarm here. Since Clay Allison gunned Steiger instead, I can see he was just out to attract attention. But how could they have known in advance it was fixing to cloud over and rain so hard? The day was clear, as was the evening sky when the sun went down and the moon came up."

Longarm knew. But he let the Texas-bred Captain Kramer explain in a weary tone, "We've known all along about that mysterious Lazy A being on higher ground. You all should know by now that our notorious West Texas summer cloudbursts start as thunderheads over the Gulf of Mexico to come at us from the southeast by way of Chihuahua, forced ever higher and angrier by the rise of the land till they trip over serious ranges as rips their bellies open. By three or four of a dry West Texas afternoon, you can usually make out thunderheads heading your way from Old Mexico if you've eyes to see and high enough ground to stand on."

Kramer nodded thoughtfully at Longarm as he did the arithmetic in his head and decided, "They had the stock they meant to purloin ready to drive up to that Lazy A whilst they waited for the right time to do so. We'll worry about where they could have been holding them for a romp in the rain after all the outfits upstream have had time to tally their herds some more. It's safe to assume they couldn't have been stolen from anybody *down*stream. The bunch you saw just now were driving 'em for some pass through the Chisos and . . . By the way, where did you say you were when you spotted all them stolen cows, Longarm?"

The federal lawman replied, "My personal habits ain't the subject of this discussion and the rain outside is letting up. How do you feel about us gathering and deputizing a serious *posse comitatus,* Captain?"

Kramer pursed his lips thoughtfully before deciding, "All the rain we just had ain't fixing to leave a heap of sign to follow by broad-ass daylight and it's still dark outside."

Longarm insisted, "It'll be dawn by the time we round up at least two dozen riders and get 'em moving down the trail. How much sign do you need to trail that many head along the only route on an ever more narrow flood-plane? All we have to do is ask along the way about that modest but noisy trail drive until we run out of folk on the trail who heard the ruckus, see?"

Kramer grinned like a mean little kid and said, "I do indeed. It's as simple as ABC. The mules were druv past you or they weren't. If they never passed you, they turned off the trail somewheres betwixt you and the last folk upstream who heard 'em pass."

Slim Putnam horned in with, "You get ever fewer places to turn off as you move downstream, Captain. Time you get to our turnoff, the old creek laps so tight against the trail the boss is worried about there *being* no trail in twenty years or so."

Kramer muttered, "Slim rides for the Tumbling Sevens." Then he said, "Go get your pony and bring it back here with any other Tumbling Sevens hands you meet in town." He raised his voice to announce, "We're fixing to posse up. Don't want nobody who can't knock a can off a fence post with a pistol at twenty paces, hear?"

As the gathering around the dead man on the floor commenced to thin, Longarm ducked outside, saw the storm had blown over, and sloshed on back to the Toro Negro, the ground underfoot still soaked to the bone.

The Widow Whitehead caught up with him in his hired room as he was changing his wet socks and breaking out his own slicker and a box of fresh cartridges from the saddlebags he'd left in her care. The fat redhead wore a flimsy nightgown above floppy slippers as she shut the hall door firmly to demand, "Custis! Where have you been all night? I was worried sick about you *before* all that shooting up by the ranger post!"

He told her he'd been working on that case he'd told her about, and this was the simple truth when you studied on it, some.

She moved in to take him in her plump arms, gasp and declare, "Oh, my poor baby! You're all wet and icky! Why don't we get you out of those wet clothes and into something warm and cozy, namely me?"

Longarm chuckled fondly but tried to sound wistful as he told her his spirit was willing but his flesh had to posse up. She ground her ample charms against his wet denim, warming it some, as she begged him for just a quick one, and damned if he didn't feel tempted.

But he just kissed her French, fondled a big tit that felt nothing at all like Consuela's, and told her to hold the thought whilst he did his duty in the name of the law.

But it sure beat all how, by the time he was back at the ranger post, his old organ grinder was giving him hell with a hard-on that made it tough to mount up in tight wet jeans.

He had time to study on that, and laugh at himself, as the rest of the fourteeen-man *posse comitatus* mounted up and mustered in the middle of the plaza by the first light of dawn.

Captain Kramer called out, "Gather round and listen tight! The bunch we're after moved down an ever narrowing bottomland route with the obvious intent of turning up one side canyon or another. The Lord only knows how far up amongst the crags we may wind up. So let's all keep our wits about us and husband our horseflesh till it's called on for serious riding. Follow my lead, which won't be faster than a a slow trot until I figure out where we're headed. I mean to start by asking directions along the way. I'll want everybody but Longarm here to stay on the trail with Sergeant Farnsworth and cover us as we ride into each dooryard along the way. Somebody along said way may be a big fibber. That's all I have to say, for now. Let's ride."

They rode. By then most everybody else in town was up despite the hour. It was not the custom of riders on a serious mission to wave back at the gals in passing. So Longarm just nodded when they rode by the Toro Negro, and when they passed Consuela's more modest 'dobe, she wasn't waving from her doorway half as hard as the Widow Whitehead. But of course, Longarm reasoned, the shapely Mex gal hadn't had near as much recent rest as that fat old redhead.

That likely accounted for the perverse mental picture of a big pale rump a man might have dog styled with wet jeans on, damn it, flashing through his mind, unbidden.

"Don't you never think about anything better?" Longarm asked himself with scorn, only to answer, in all innocence, "What else *is* better?"

He knew his mind was a tad fuzzy from lack of sleep and the breakfast he'd been planning on having in bed. As it got light enough to see colors, he spied a patch of fresh cowshit pounded paper thin by rain on the rain-smoothed pony track ahead. So, riding abreast with Captain Kramer at the head of the column, and Sergeant Farnsworth bringing up the rear, Longarm commenced to search for sign.

You could read rain-pounded cowshit from horseshit by the color. You couldn't say which way way a shitty mule had been going, alone or in a bunch, and there were no hoofmarks to mention out ahead. But it hardly mattered, seeing that the bluffs across the creek and the closer, ever steepening slopes to their left were seldom

110

more than a furlong either way and the scattered cows chewing cuds and staring stupidly at them as they passed had obviously not been stolen. Slim Putnam and other stockmen in the posse checked the brand as they passed each and every one. They all belonged about where they were grazing that morning. It was Slim who suggested they must be near the sneaky turn-off to that Lazy A up in the hills, seeing the mysterious Clay Allison hadn't cared to excite near neighbors by running off *their* stock.

Longarm asked how many head the Tumbling Sevens, ahead, had lost since that tall blond mystery man had first appeared that spring.

Slim answered easily, "None and, now that you study on it, the mean cuss who gunned Andy Steiger did seem to recognize me in passing. You reckon that means anything?"

Longarm said he'd ask the killer when they caught him. When Slim asked whether Clay Allison couldn't claim self-defense, seeing poor Andy had called him and slapped leather, it was Captain Kramer who snorted in disbelief and demanded, "Have you been reading them Ned Buntline yarns about some Code of the West as requires us lawmen to challenge an outlaw to a formal duel and offer him an even break if he chooses to resist arrest?"

When Slim sheepishly admitted he'd heard some say the same, it came Longarm's turn to suggest, "Don't ever count on a plea of self-defense when you gun a lawman, fair or dirty. Cockeyed Jack McCall thought to get off that way for the murder of James Butler Hickok. John Wesley Hardin offered a more reasonable plea of self-defense when he stood trial for the gunning of Sheriff Charlie Webb in '74. It could at least be argued Webb was on his feet, going for his own gun, when he died. But Hardin was wanted for earlier killings, and as a lawman Sheriff Webb had the right if not the sacred duty to draw on him. So as we speak, John Wesley Hardin is doing hard time in Huntsville Prison for winning *that* fair or unfair fight."

Captain Kramer expanded some to add, "Texas Ranger

named Armstrong tracked Hardin all the way to Florida and took him alive in spite of his brag no lawman would ever do any such thing. And Armstrong was sick at the time. Poor cuss had caught the consumption, tracking down outlaws for Texas. Last I heard he'd resigned to go home and die with his boots off. Hope it ain't true. Let's ask at the Gomez farm over yonder about the outlaws *we* are after!"

As the others waited along the pony track, it only took Kramer and Longarm a few friendly minutes in the dooryard of the friendly Gomez clan to establish they had indeed heard and seen perhaps twenty mules moving downstream through the stormy darkness, punctuated by flashes of lightning. Old Arturo Gomez said he couldn't say what time it had been because he didn't own a clock. He said twenty head sounded about right for the herd, but he couldn't describe the riders herding it. He explained he only worried about his own goats and chickens to begin with and thought it imprudent to ask armed gringo riders what they might be up to on a public right-of-way.

They got much the same answers as they kept working southeast, with the creek creeping ever closer and the limestone slopes looming ever higher and steeper. The tree-lined creek banks were indented here and there with modest backwater coves. The eroded slopes or sheer cliffs formed larger pocket meadows or canyon mouths overlooking Tiswin Creek, but such possible escapes from the overgrown gully called the Big Bend were where the local folk had built their home spreads, and while they kept agreeing someone had driven hard past them in the stormy darkness, nobody recalled any mule thieves busting through their garden walls or drift fences. So the *posse comitatus* kept riding.

They rode through a narrower natural bottleneck where nobody had laid claim to such land as lay between the creek-side cottonwoods and the limestone cliffs they likely shaded some at sundown. Then they made it to the eight-or ten-acre amphitheater occupied by the Last Chance layout of Liam O'Hanlon.

As they all reined in out front, the burly owner of the former Mex establishment appeared in his doorway wearing his undershirt and a puzzled smile. As Kramer reined in, he raised a hand to call out, "We're taking ten here either way. Take your leaks, drop your loads and smoke if you got 'em but be advised you'll not be drinking on duty with the Texas Rangers!"

O'Hanlon joshed, "Aw, *you're* no fun!" as Kramer and Longarm were first to dismount near the saloon's ever-open front door. Then Liam O'Hanlon asked in a more serious tone what everyone was doing up and about so early.

Kramer asked, "Can't you guess? Didn't you wonder at all about a score of mules being rawhided along yonder pony trail in a thunderstorm last night?"

The somewhat younger and way bigger O'Hanlon frowned—not a pretty sight when a man's bushy eyebrows met in the middle like that—and told Captain Kramer, "I don't know what you're talking about. When was all this supposed to happen?"

Longarm said, "They passed me, closer to town, either side of four A.M. Figuring they were driven at the same pace, they'd have passed by here within an hour at the most. How do you like just before dawn?"

O'Hanlon sounded certain as he replied, "I'd like dawn better if my old leghorn rooster didn't make such a fuss about it every morning. I was awake well before dawn. That rain had let up and some birds along the creek had commenced to sing. But I'll be a protestant if one mule moved between here and the creek this morning!"

Chapter 15

Captain Kramer sent Slim Putnam and three others across the creek to canvas the Tumbling Sevens and the canyon claimed by the Spanish Hat, even closer to the only known exit from the basin. He ordered them to catch up as he led the rest of the posse back the weary way they'd just ridden.

They wound up having a welcome breakfast with Mom and Pop Cooper, raising pigs and chickens in a four-acre hollow. Captain Kramer said, and Longarm agreed, whilst the motherly Mom Cooper's back was turned, he purely doubted you could hide a score of mules or even goats under a henhouse or pigsty. Longarm pointed out, "If Pop Cooper was a mule thief, he'd expect us to ask up and down the line to check his story. So when he says they heard nothing at all passing by in the wee small hours, I vote the mules were never druv this far south and that means Liam O'Hanlon was telling us true as well."

They were polishing off Mom Cooper's fresh-baked sourdough biscuits slathered with goat butter and sage-brush honey when Slim Putnam and the others caught up to report nobody at the Tumbling Sevens or the Spanish Hat knew toad squat about any predawn trail drives. So

114

Slim and his bunch had to down their biscuits in the saddle without coffee as the *posse commitatus* retraced its route along the rain-pounded dirt road.

They investigated a bat cave a rider recalled some kids talking about. But there was nothing to be seen inside but bats and batshit deep enough to hold hoofprints, had any hooves entered for years.

So they rode on, and just before they got to that Mex spread where they *had* heard hoofbeats in the wee small hours, the beaten path to the east of the creek swung closer to the same because of a massive limestone buttress jutting out from the cliffs north or south. Limestone eroded like so, given enough time and sparse but patient summer rains. So they had to ride *off* the beaten path through the sage and sunflowers, closer to the cliffs, before they could see the narrow slot that made the buttress more like a natural arch when you looked tighter, and once you took that in, you noticed the slot ran back to the east as a mighty narrow canyon mouth nobody riding with Captain Kramer had ever noticed before.

The nigh hidden entrance was littered with scree and was treacherous under hoof. Longarm held off suggesting they dismount and lead afoot, because he doubted stock could be drove where a drover couldn't ride. Thieves driving stolen stock at full gallop through the night would likely aim to make some distance before the sun got high enough to matter. They had a hell of a lead as it was, afoot or mounted up. So this seemed no time for the posse to slow down.

As he rode behind Kramer, Longarm caught an occasional whiff of mule or horse shit. The two smells were too close to call. That was no big deal when you considered the jackass ancestors of a mule were closely related enough to fuck their horse relations and for all Longarm knew he was smelling Kramer's horseshit. The smell came with the times. A Victorian miss who'd blush beet red if a man admired her shoes never noticed the horse apples falling from under the tails of the carriage team taking them to or from a fancy dress ball. For there was

115

just no avoiding the sight and smells of steam and horseshit in a world that ran on steam and horsepower.

Cowshit smelled different. Not as strong, for one thing. But as in the case of every critter that lived on bulk vegetation, cows had to shit constant, and a hidden stock trail was a hidden stock trail.

When he called ahead for the ranger officer to watch for cowshit, Kramer called back, "I'm ahead of you, old son. But all that fucking rain has washed all these fucking rocks clean enough to eat off. Any cowshit, horseshit, chickenshit or strawberry jam has been washed too deep for us to detect. But I keeps seeing *flies,* and flies don't live on rocks alone."

Longarm agreed the increasingly unlikely route didn't seem hopeless yet. So they wound onward and upward to where the slot they'd been following up forked on them.

The two feeder canyons had carved a somewhat wider stretch below their doubtless swirly meeting place when the waters rose. But the fit was tight as Longarm moved up beside Kramer's roan on his borrowed paint to ask, "Do we choose one or split into two columns, Captain?"

It was a good question. That was why Longarm had asked it.

The experienced ranger leader asked how many riders Longarm had counted moving that modest herd under cover of stormy darkness.

Longarm shrugged and said, "Six or eight. I couldn't get 'em to hold still for me to tally. If you're worried about odds, we might as well quit whilst we're ahead."

Kramer warned him not to get sassy, twisted in his saddle, then called out, "I want the closest dozen men in line to follow me along this canyon to the left. Rest of you follow this wise-ass federal man up the right fork."

He turned back to Longarm to add, "Take Farnsworth with you. If you come to another fork, I want you to split your dozen with my sergeant. But that's it. I don't want fewer than half a dozen pushing on into country where one man with a rifle on the rimrock could hold off a troop of cavalry. Do these canyons offer more than two more shuffles, I want your word you won't risk thinning this posse out past common sense."

Longarm nodded soberly and said he'd order his bunch to reassemble at the first fork or, finding themselves alone there, ride on back to town and await further orders. They shook on it, and Longarm edged out of the way up the slot to the right as the head of the column followed Kramer up the other. Then he called back down to Sergeant Farnsworth, bringing up the rear, "Did you hear them orders, Sarge?"

The ranger called back, "Not hardly. I'm deaf. What are you waiting for, a kiss goodbye?"

Longarm chuckled, yelled, "¡Vamanos, muchachos!" and heeled his paint up the even narrower but not quite as deep left branch.

It wasn't easy. His borrowed mount got tougher to manage as the slope got steeper and the loose rocks under its hooves got looser. Reining in whilst the reining was good, Longarm called back, "We'd best dismount and lead afoot. This would be a hell of a place to have to shoot your pony and tote your saddle. Make sure you all hang on to your saddle guns as we figure out where the fuck all them mules *went*!"

Suiting his own actions to his words, Longarm forged onward and upward, with the reins in his left hand and his Winchester leading the way in his right. Albeit he wasn't sure what good it might do him if some son of a bitch up above braced another rifle over the rimrock to shoot fish in a barrel, or dismounted riders lined up in a narrow slot.

The range for such a rear-guard sniper closed as the canyon floor they were following rose ever higher. Then Longarm led the way around another bend to see they'd come to another fucking fork!

Seeing there was barely room for a man to squeeze by pony rumps and gritty red sandstone, Longarm told Slim Putnam to lead his paint and the next half dozen men in line up the left fork a ways and wait.

That allowed him to consult with Sergeant Farnsworth

at the fork. They didn't waste time on a long powwow. They'd both heard Captain Kramer's orders. So they shook on them and parted friendly.

It took Longarm way more time to wriggle his way on up to his own paint. When he saw that branch had narrowed more than he'd expected, he told Slim Putnam, just ahead, "I fucked up, Slim. It's easier for you to take the lead with me reading over your shoulder than it would be for me to haul this paint over you and that bay!"

Slim Putnam, who'd been wearing a dapper Mex charro jacket and two-gun rig under that yellow slicker, laughed and allowed he'd always hoped to lead his own *posse comitatus*. So he moved on, afoot, with the grade getting steeper as well as narrower by the furlong.

You don't have to yell too loud to make yourself heard with solid rock just inches to either side. So when Slim yelled back that he thought he smelled stock, Longarm called back, "Keep moving and hold it down to a roar. If they did drive the stock up this canyon, let's not tell 'em we're coming. Let 'em *guess*!"

As he passed over the cobbles Slim Putnam had been sniffing, Longarm paused, hunkered down and couldn't make up his mind whether he could smell mule shit or whether Slim had him imagining. When he rose to move on, he called out, "Hey, Slim? Are you a smoking man?"

The lean and hungry-looking cowhand called back, "Used to. Gave it up when the sawbones said I looked consumptive. Told the old goat it was only pneumonia, but by the time he agreed I might live I'd kicked the expensive habit. Why do you ask?"

Longarm replied, "I've quit the habit myself, over and over again. You just gave me another good reason. Your sense of smell ain't dulled by tobacco as mine. Let me know if you smell or see more shit. Otherwise, let's keep it down."

Slim protested, "Suffering snakes! *I* wasn't the one as broke the code of silence with remarks about sniffing shit or tobacco, was I?"

Longarm agreed and added, "I usually wake up by this

late in the day. Reckon I should have got more sleep last night, and some breakfast coffee might have helped."

As he trudged on after the swishing tail and occasional farts or worse of Slim's bay, Longarm was dying for a smoke as well as that black coffee he'd planned on sharing in bed with Consuela. But aside from not wanting to dull his own sense of smell, he knew how far the smell of tobacco could carry in canyon country, and how mean it would be to forbid all the others to light up if he gave in to temptation. Slim Putnam's boyish ambition to lead a *posse comitatus* or anything else came from never having been stuck with leadership.

Longarm had often found it hard enough to save his own ass in the line of duty. Having to worry about other asses, and the sick self-loathing that came over a leader when he failed to carry all the eggs safely back from the henhouse, made it way more comfortable to work alone.

So when Slim Putnam called back, "Another fork just ahead!" Longarm raised his Winchester high to halt the column and worked his way past the fat-ass bay to join the leaner rider to regard, with equal distaste, the two upslope routes to choose from.

He said, "Slim, you hail from these parts. Have you notion one as to where either of them glorified gutters might be coming down from?"

The Tumbling Sevens rider shook his head morosely and demurred, "I don't hail from around these parts. My outfit grazes stock on *grass*! This is the first time I've been up in *these* parts, and from what I have seen of 'em so far, they ain't good for nothing but getting from hither to yon. One branch or the other may lead to that Lazy A we've heard so much about, unless Sergeant Farnsworth or Captain Kramer is on the right track. Either way, it's a safe bet one way or the other we get to choose from leads nowheres anyone with a lick of sense would care to go, and the captain said not to split up into groups of less than half a dozen, remember?"

Longarm said, "I do, and I gave my word. So why don't you take this bunch back the way we just came, wait at

119

least an hour at that first fork down below and ride on back to town if nobody joins you? There ain't much point for half a dozen men to loiter in a hole in the ground all day. The others will rejoin you in town unless they took the right fork. They'll tell you later how it all turned out if they did."

Slim Putnam said, "I'll carry them back down to the riverside pony track. But I'll be fucked with a corncob before I'll ride back to Tanktown with my tail betwixt my legs. I ride for the Tumbling Sevens and I most often relax my nerves at the Last Chance. So that's where I reckon I'll be headed as this dull party breaks up."

Then Slim smiled uncertainly and asked, "How come we're having this conversation, Longarm? Captain Kramer put you in charge of us. So why did you just order *me* to take over?"

Longarm calmly replied, "Somebody has to. You heard me promise Captain Kramer I wouldn't split you boys into smaller bunches than the bunch we're hunting. So being a man of my word, I'm sending this half dozen back and going on by my lonesome."

Slim Putnam protested, "Longarm, that's just silly! Clay Allison on his own would be bad enough to meet up with in this maze of never-mapped side canyons, and didn't you just say you counted at least a half dozen night riders with him?"

Longarm shrugged and wearily replied, "Me and my big mouth. It ain't certain our quick-draw artist from Hell was riding with the bunch I spotted, even if he's really from Hell and not some sort of lunatic pretending to be a dead man."

Slim demanded, "What does it matter when you get right down to the brass tacks? I was there last night when whoever it was beat old Andy Steiger to the draw with time to spare! Before I seen it with my own eyes I'd have sworn no mortal man could draw that fast!"

Slim repressed a shudder and added in a worried whisper, "Maybe no *mortal* man can. I know they say there's no such things, but don't the Good Book make mention of hombres coming back from the dead now and again?"

Longarm grimaced and replied in a certain tone, "If there be one thing Clay Allison could never be mistaken for, dead or alive, it would have to be a saint out of the Good Book. But whilst we stand here arguing theology, the son of a bitch, whoever he may be, already has a hell of a lead on me. So *adios, amigos,* and I reckon since I can only choose one fork ahead, I may as well choose the one leading off to the southeast."

"You're fixing to get yourself killed!" Slim Putnam warned as the taller and more solidly built lawman led his borrowed paint up the sloping slot to his right.

Longarm didn't answer until Slim shouted after him, "You've fucked up my whole morning! I got to lead all these old boys back to Tanktown, now that you've put me in command, cuss your hide!"

Longarm called back, "We all have our crosses to bear, Slim. I'll buy you a drink in town, later on, if we both make it."

"What if you don't make it?" Slim almost wailed.

To which Longarm could only reply, "I just said that."

Chapter 16

The route he'd chosen wound around to the east-northeast before branching again, and then once more after Longarm had chosen at random the way to keep going. As he saw he was working his way topside to the frozen limestone waves he'd navigated before, Longarm saw that the walls to either side sloped ever more gently until in point of fact he was leading the paint through what seemed the troughs between the salmon waves of the limestone sea. In lower patches they crossed pockets of mineral-rich but dusty terra rosa soil, already dry despite the recent rain, with hither and yon a modest clump of tumbleweed or cheatgrass. The paint balked at being led up onto the bare stone crests to either side. Longarm decided it had a point once he'd scrambled on up afoot with his Winchester to gaze all around for miles and miles of miles and miles that looked about the same, save for where a bigger pile of rock peaked higher. He could tell by triangulating the two distant Elephant Tusks with the even farther-off Emery Peak that he was south-southeast of where he'd met up with old Pepper MacLeod atop all this karst geology. But otherwise it looked about the same, and if there was a secret Garden of Eden just over the next ridge, it was surely tough to tell. Old Pepper's suggestion about hot air balloons hadn't been dumb. It just hadn't been practical. Longarm wondered whether a man atop one of those taller peaks, say with a spyglass, might read the lay of this tortured land clearer. But of course the fly in that ointment would be making it halfways to any of those higher peaks all around. From where he stood at a way lower elevation he could see countless ridges to be crossed if one beelined. The Widow Whitehead had said her brand-inspecting husband had been drygulched closer to Emery Peak, in a canyon leading that way from the Tiswin Basin. That route had to have beelining beat.

He allowed as much to the paint when he rejoined it down below and decided, "This way, Paint, since it seems to lead more downwards than upwards and we know nobody's grazing stolen stock on bone-dry crags."

The paint didn't argue. It perked up when they rounded a bend to come upon a shallow pond of rainwater in a wind-carved basin of less porous shale strata. Longarm slaked his own thirst from a canteen. The rainwater looked clean enough, but there were buzzards circling high above and the notion of sipping buzzard shit . . .

"What are them ominous birds so interested in, up yonder?" Longarm asked the watering paint as he stared skyward. He didn't expect any answer. He just figured talking to a pony had an edge on talking to himself, and those two big birds skating across the cloudless cobalt sky in big figure eights seemed to be worth talking about.

The turkey vulture or buzzard of the western skies flew lazy for long distances as it searched the earth far below for sign. With an empty stomach and time as well as itself on the wing, a buzzard who hadn't spotted anything kept drifting along up yonder to keep *looking* for something interesting. When it found something interesting to gaze down upon, it circled back for another look, and mayhaps another, whilst it made up its mind whether to circle on down or not.

"Them birds have spotted something unusual, somewhere up here amidst the ridges, and somewhere *close*,"

Longarm decided as he watched one big-ass bird circle back directly over him and his borrowed paint.

Working up another draw toward whatever the other loop of that miles-high figure eight denoted, Longarm confided to the paint, "They're interested in you and me because you're a pony and they know you don't belong up here. They're hoping I'll bust one of your legs and have to shoot you. They're just as interested in something or somebody half a mile to our north. So let's mosey on over and take a look at it our ownselves!"

The draw opened out to a surprising patch of greenery that might have convinced a water witch to drill for water if he or she was not familiar with the prickly pear or tuna cactus. Like most cactus, the prickly pear didn't drill for water. It spread its shallow roots way the hell out on all sides to catch every drop soaking into usually dry soil on those rare occasions it rained. Then, being a cactus, it was able to store more water than it needed at the moment in its spongy green pads, evolved from the stems of its rose-like ancestors. Stock could feed on cactus if there was enough of it. But Caddo Flynn had allowed he'd spotted *trees,* along with green grass and even alfalfa along the bottomlands of that big box canyon or unmapped basin that the Lazy A had taken over.

Passing through, Longarm noted that the prickly pear pads had been nipped by bighorn and chawed by bugs, but there was no sign any stockmen had been blowtorching the thorns to feed stock, and by the time they'd have made her this far, those stolen mules would have been hungry as well as thirsty.

Longarm busted off some pads and commenced to peel them with his pocketknife as he led the paint on a ways, then fed and watered it at the same time with peeled cactus. The Mexicans ate the pads as well as the tunas, or fruits. Chopped up, the pads could pass for lettuce if you didn't mind the slightly soapy aftertaste. Most Mexicans swore the soap most Anglos tasted was all in their fool heads. Longarm didn't care. Not being a rabbit, he didn't much care for lettuce, neither.

Coming upon some handy rabbit bush near a jumble of boulders, Longarm tethered the paint there, murmuring, "I'd best move in the rest of the way with just this Winchester, Paint. Anyone else watching them buzzards might have noticed what a tight circle they're drawing in the sky above us now."

As he moved on, Longarm sniffed the errant dry breezes, and in spite of his three-for-a-nickel habit he was certain he smelled the shit of man as well as beast, along with some cheap pipe tobacco, sure as hell.

So Longarm slithered on his belly up a slick-rock slope to get the drop from above on whomsoever seemed to be enjoying a good shit and a foul corncob pipe just over the rise. His ploy worked like a charm. He saw at a glance he had the older rascal squatting in another clump of cactus with his pants down. Then he had to laugh like hell.

The usually more dignified livery owner from Tanktown, riding with Captain Kramer's bunch when they'd first split up, spooked like a deer, tripped over his pants and fell into the prickly pear, screaming like a drunk Comanche till he saw who was grinning down at his plight and commenced to cuss Longarm and his kin back to Mother Eve.

As Longarm rose atop the rise, he could see over the cactus, and the dismounted Captain Kramer and his bunch could make him out as well. So Kramer called out, "What's over yonder and where's the rest of your bunch, Uncle Sam?"

Longarm called back, "I've yet to cut sign and I've surely covered a heap of yonder. Alone. Sent the others back as per your orders after we'd cut the cards down to dangerous. Told 'em to wait for you all in town if they failed to meet up with you along the way. Is it safe to assume you gents cut no sign, neither?"

Kramer snorted, "Hell, no, we overtook and slew the whole bunch of disappearing stock thieves. Are you afoot or astride, Longarm?"

The younger lawman dropped back down his side of the rise, and by the time he joined the main bunch with his borrowed paint, that livery owner had his pants back up and his dignity restored, albeit he'd lost his pipe somewhere amid the tangle of squashed cactus. He intimated, as he took Longarm to one side, that he'd forgive the loss of his pipe if Longarm promised to never discuss the way he'd lost it.

Kramer led them a furlong or more through the maze of shallow dry draws, with many washing down to evolve as canyons, known or unknown, until they all enjoyed another tense moment meeting up with Sergeant Farnsworth and his few riders, coming at them out of unexplored karst terrain. So Captain Kramer decided, "Shit. This ain't getting us nowheres. Farnsworth, turn her around and lead us the hell down the way you came up."

Farnsworth was willing, and within the hour they found themselves on the bottomland trail back to Tanktown, neither worse for wear nor one hell of a lot wiser about the clifftops all around. They'd known all along what things were like up yonder. Kramer declared at least he'd made certain you needed a guide or a mighty long time up yonder before you could hope to get very far.

When Longarm pointed it out, the ranger officer agreed the mysterious stranger calling himself Clay Allison had likely been guided across a heap of limestone by a local Mex, if not an unreconstructed Indian. For the bragging stranger with the lightning draw didn't seem to want to make friends with locals of the Anglo persuasion.

They double-checked at a few spreads along the way. So it was going on *La Siesta* by the time they made it back to Tanktown and split up, with each rider free to follow his own fancy as to the next few hours of slowed down time. Texas born and bred riders were naturally likely to follow the sensible Mex habits of *La Siesta,* catching a few winks, a light snack or such slap-and-tickle as they might find themselves alone with till four or so, when things cooled down outside.

Captain Kramer never said whether he aimed to read the papers at home to his *mujer* or ravage her dog style from one room to the other. He only told Longarm he wanted to hear, later that afternoon, what his old pal Billy Vail might suggest they try next. So Longarm headed across the plaza afoot to see if Western Union had any messages saved up for him. The chili parlor next door was naturally closed for *La Siesta* and he knew better than to call on a Mex gal living alone in broad daylight. So he wouldn't have to tell Consuela about Yzabel or the fat old Widow Whitehead before he made certain he had to.

The telegraph clerk allowed he aimed to get out of the thin-walled Western Union shed and under some serious Spanish roofing till things cooled off considerable that afternoon. But he was a sport about putting Longarm's progress report on the wire while Longarm read the day letter from Denver.

Old Henry had sent it, having spent more times in their federal files. Henry seemed convinced the various rumors about Clay Allison being still at large resulted from wishful thinking and confusion about the exact time and place of his accidental death. Some folk just hated it when you told them King Arthur and Robin Hood were both dead as turds in the milk bucket. It was more fun to picture old King Arthur living in sin with his half-sister, Morgan la Fay, on the magic misty Isle of Avalon, which only meant "Apple Island" according to that one Welsh gal up Leadville way with a more practical approach to sin.

So some said Robin Hood still haunted what was left of Sherwood Forest whilst others swore Joaquin Murieta hadn't really been killed that time out California way and Dick Turpin still rode the King's Highway north of London Town because they hadn't really hung him that time. Henry's notion was that newspapermen and other taproom liars, desperate for something to pass on, kept grasping at the straws of uncertainty and decided that since Clay Allison hadn't died in *Texas* in the summer of '77 he must have died some other time, if he wasn't still alive. Nobody seemed to notice how his tedious string of gunfights ended, abrupt, early in 1877. Henry opined and Longarm found himself agreeing that had Clay Allison not died in '77, he'd have gone on to gun others since. Before his most recent outburst of mad dog gunplay, Henry meant.

Longarm resisted the temptation to wire the home office an expensive request that was likely to strike them as totally insane as well. He knew there had to be a better way. Or at least he *hoped* there had to be a better way.

Like the magic misty Isle of Avalon, the hidden fertile spread of the Lazy A could be just over the horizon if only you knew which way to look for it, and Caddo Flynn, wherever in blue blazes the fucking mutton hunter might be hunting mutton, knew which way to look for it!

Longarm was minded of those tabletop mazes college professors set to torment white rats or test their intellects. Anybody looking *down* on such a maze from above could see which way the rats should go. A rat who'd *learned the way,* like Caddo Flynn, *knew* which way to go. But a greenhorn rat, or a lawman new to the Big Bend, could run up or down one blind alley after another, missing the cheese, or the Lazy A, by yards or inches for all one could see down *in* the damned maze!

Leaving the telegraph shed, Longarm headed next for the Toro Negro to take his medicine like a man before he suffered heat stroke out in the noonday sun. Hunkered out front of the closed chili parlor was a sight so familiar along the border that Longarm barely glanced at the serape-wrapped Mexican dozing head down against the 'dobe wall with a big straw sombrero shading his face and most of his chest from the hot Texas sun. Mexicans with no place in particular to hole up for their siesta were inclined to hunker like that, albeit Longarm idly thought he'd pick a shadier spot to hunker if *he* had no place to siesta. The poor cuss was likely drunk as well as friendless in Tanktown.

Longarm had just strode on by when he spied Slim Putnam of the Tumbling Sevens riding toward him from the municipal corral. Slim had said earlier that he meant to belly up to the bar in the Last Chance. So Longarm waved a howdy at the oncoming rider, who responded with an expression of total terror and the shout of "Longarm! Behind you!"

Longarm spun like a ballerina to land out in the dusty street in a gunfighting crouch with his .44–40 in hand as the innocent-looking but oddly positioned Mex swung the double barrels of a ten-gauge up from under the folds of that doubtless stuffy wool serape. So Longarm fired first, and he was glad he had when both shotgun barrels roared at the sky above to send a whole lot of buckshot where it surely figured to do less harm than that murderous Mex had intended.

Chapter 17

Longarm strode forward through swirling snow-white black-powder smoke to see what he had wrought with three closely spaced shots. The Mex who'd been out to back-shoot him sprawled belly up with his big sugarloaf-crowned sombrero yards away along the walk and his serape now thrown up over his face to reveal the white cotton outfit Longarm had noticed by moonlight the night before. The front of the stranger's white shirt was punctuated with blossoms of blood red now. His double-barrel muzzle loader lay, still smoking, closer to his head than his big old hat. Hats flew some when a man was spine-shot. The spine-shot cuss had never gotten to the brace of Colt .45 Cavalry pistols riding his dead hips in a tooled Buscadero gun rig. By the time Longarm had decided his victim had to be that cuss who'd ridden alone by moonlight past Consuela's the night before, Slim Putnam had dismounted and others were running their way from all directions.

"I take back my warnings about quick-draw artists!" Slim exclaimed in an admiring tone, turning to another cowhand in the gathering crowd to add, "You should have seen it, Gus! That greaser had the drop on Longarm from behind and he lost just the same!"

"I seen it! I was catty-corner yonder when I heard you yell, and it was just about over by the time I figured what was going on!" the hand called Gus replied in an even more respectful tone.

Captain Kramer came down the walk in his stocking feet, albeit armed and dangerous, to take in the scene and wearily exclaim, "You surely are a boisterous youth, Deputy Long! Who might this poor unfortunate have been?"

Having reloaded and reholstered his six-gun, Longarm hunkered to flop the thick, stiff serape the other way, exposing the oddly peaceful but not too pretty face of a totally strange Mex, with features Mexicans described as "Chino," meaning nigh pure Chihuahua, a desert nation as ran to more oriental-looking bone structure than most. The Mexican phrase "¡Ay, que Chihuahua!" was not meant as a compliment. Since assimilated but not too well-educated purebloods down Chihuahua way spent more time digging ditches than teaching school, the term showed about the same respect as "Oh, you shanty mick!" or "Hey, rube!" might other places.

Slim Putnam was telling Kramer, "I seen it all! The greaser had the drop on him and Longarm cleaned his plow for him all the same!"

"I heard. I heard." Kramer sighed, adding, "Ever seen him before, Deputy Long?"

Having patted the cadaver down for I.D., Longarm rose to full height to reply, "Yep. Late last night. He rid in from the south. Not long before Andy Steiger was gunned by that other mysterious stranger. Too early to say if they were both after me in particular."

Kramer snorted, "Well, *sure* they were after you, old son! Didn't old Clay Allison tell everybody he was after you and didn't this other son of a bitch try to back-shoot you just now? What do you need, a chalked diagram on a blackboard?"

Longarm said, "I'd settle for some identities. I've yet to lay eyes on the one calling himself Clay Allison and this is the first time I ever laid eyes on *this* murdersome rascal!"

Kramer thoughtfully asked, "Didn't you just say you met up with him late last night?"

Longarm shook his head to explain, "Only saw him passing by in the moonlight, from a window as he rode up the trail from the south. Have you found out who those mules were stolen from yet?"

Kramer nodded and said, "Eight head off the Double H. Another dozen off the Bar Eleven. You say you were staring out a window in the wee small hours when this one rode in to join Clay Allison, old son?"

When Longarm didn't answer, the older lawman had the sense to let it drop for the moment, in public.

Doc Fletcher, their local postmaster, dentist and the deputy coroner, bustled through the crowd to demand, "I can see the cause of death. Who do you mean to charge with the same, Captain Kramer?"

The Texas Ranger muttered, "Hang a wreath on your nose, Doc. For your brain lies dead inside. Deputy Long, here, shot him fair and square if you know what's good for you!"

Doc Fletcher explained in a defensive tone that he had to ask before he put anything down on paper for the distant county seat and added in a more cheerful tone that since he got to bill the county, he'd just embalm the cadaver and hold it for evidence along with the others in the old smokehouse he used as his morgue. When he offered two bits a hand for help in getting the dead Mexican out of this hot sun, he had more volunteers than he really needed. He said so, protesting that it hardly took more than two strong men or boys at each end of the litter to tote your average dead Mexican.

Despite the unseemly hour, the shoot-out on the streets of Tanktown had played hob with *La Siesta* that afternoon. So, seeing they were up and dressed to go out on the street, more than one shopkeeper opened for business before two P.M. and by the time Longarm was free to go

132

on about his own business again, Tanktown was up and at 'em and to hell with August.

So when he got back to the Toro Negro the saloon downstairs was busy as a beehive, with the fat redheaded widow manning the bar and Yzabel nowhere to be seen as Longarm eased up the outside stairs to his hired room.

The match stem stuck in that bottom hinge assured him nobody had made a serious play for his sleeping form in the wee small hours, in spite of that story Clay Allison had come to town to have it out with him. It would have been easier to dismiss the brag as a big wind out of no-wheres much if an eyewitness hadn't seen the man who'd issued it beat a Texas Ranger to the draw.

Unlike that mysterious dead Mex, back by the chili parlor, there'd been nothing sneaky about the confrontation with Andy Steiger. The kid had challenged the self-styled owner of the Lazy A and been taken at his word *mano a mano* in what surely sounded like a fair fight, however unlawful it might be to shoot a Texas Ranger, fair or unfair.

Alone for the moment, out of the afternoon heat, Longarm stripped to treat himself to a whore bath and a quick shave at the corner washstand. The water provided by the big clay *olla* was almost warm after waiting for him all that time in West Texas.

Having broken out fresh socks and underwear from his saddlebags, Longarm was seated on the bed, fixing to dress, when there came a hesitant tapping on the barred oaken door.

Hoping it wasn't anybody out to kill him, not sure whether he felt up to either the big fat redhead or the little oversexed mestiza, he rose stark naked, gun in hand, to mosey on over and open wide as he threw down with his six-gun on . . . Miss Rose Bradford of the Flying B.

The willowy blonde gasped, "Good heavens!" and blushed beet red as Longarm tried in vain to cover his privates with his six-gun, a mite red-faced himself as he blurted, "Sorry, ma'am! Thought you were somebody else!"

133

Rose Bradford allowed that seemed obvious as she stood her ground in the open doorway. As Longarm had to turn his bare ass on her to grope for a towel, she calmly continued, considering, "Caddo Flynn came by our spread this morning. I thought I'd best ride in and tell you. He was . . . talking odd about having to get on up to New Mexico. I thought you'd want to know, ah, Custis."

Longarm turned around with the towel now hiding what she'd already seen if she had eyes in her pretty head, to gravely assure her, "You were right as rain, Miss Rose. For I've been up amongst his bighorn-haunted crags more than once now, and I'm in the market for a guide who knows his way across all that limestone. Didn't you tell Caddo we were anxious to question him some more about that spread in the sky he reported?"

Closing the hall door behind her, for whatever reason, the willowy blonde in beige whipcord said, "That was when he said he had to get on up to New Mexico. When I said none of you lawmen had anything against him, Caddo said he wasn't worried about you lawmen. I asked him who else he was worried about. I couldn't get much more out of him. The more I asked, the more he clammed up, until he just bolted, right in the middle of bacon with buttermilk flapjacks. One of our stable hands says Caddo was last seen headed up into the cliffs, afoot, moving as if he had a dozen devils after him."

Longarm whistled softly and decided, "Mayhaps he has, or thinks he has. By now you'll have heard about that cuss called Clay Allison and a more recent mean Mex after this child."

She nodded soberly and replied news traveled fast up and down the Tiswin Basin. He said, "Caddo Flynn might have heard he was included in the invite. I know if I had a secret spread in the sky it could vex me some to have an old ridge runner blabbermouthing about an address I hadn't offered to the post office. How long a lead might the old breed have on me, seeing somebody else has succeeded all too well in spooking him?"

Rose said, "He came by for a late breakfast. Say ten

this morning. By eleven he was long gone. I confess I took my own sweet time riding into town with the news. I'd heard you were riding with that posse and, well, my dad has been been giving us some trouble."

He said he understood and continued, "I'd never catch up with such a human mountain goat, running scared along ridges he knows better than the rest of us. It's going to take modern science to get the breed back now. If he'd headed for the New Mexico line along the ridges betwixt the Pecos and the upper Rio Grande, I could wire the BIA and have their Indian Police staked out in the Guadalupes."

He moved around the bed to pick up a shirt as he added with a wave of the same meant to be taken as a hint, "If he don't run as far north as the Mescalero Agency, we'll have to work something better out."

"Did you want to get dressed?" she asked in sudden understanding.

He allowed that had been his intention just before she'd knocked on his fool door. So she blushed some more and flustered outside to let him use both hands.

She'd no sooner done so when another familiar voice outside let fly. "Just what do you think you're doing up here at this hour, sis?"

Longarm was inspired to dress faster when he heard the younger gal reply in an easier tone, "I'm waiting out here while Deputy Long gets dressed. I'd be Rose Bradford of the Flying B and you'd be . . . ?"

The fat redhead snapped, "I know all about you and your fancy ways with men and mules, Rose Bradford. I'd be Flo Whitehead and I guess I own some property of my own! You are standing on it. Without my permit and how come you've cornered poor Custis without his clothes on?"

Rose laughed in a self-assured way and replied, "When I want a man to take off his clothes, I promise you I don't have to *trap* him! I'm here in the name of the law with information both your Deputy Long and your Texas Rangers have been after. It was Deputy Long's grand notion to take his clothes off before I got here and might *you* know anything about that, Miss Whitehead?"

The widow woman sputtered some before she demanded, "Just what are you implying about a respectable older woman, sis?"

Rose demurely replied, "You were the one who commenced this game of implications, fatso, since you choose to address me so informally!"

Then Longarm barged out the door to get betwixt them before anybody lost any hair, soothing, "Excuse me, ladies, but I got some important telegraph messages to put on the wire and are you going that way, Miss Rose?"

Rose Bradford allowed she surely was, in a tone of triumph poor old Flo just had to grin and bear unless she aimed to stake a public claim on a passing fancy too young for her by half.

She lamely tried. "I was worried about you when you never came back last night, Custis. I mean you never came back for the supper we were saving you down to the kitchen, and when we heard how Clay Allison was gunning for you, before he shot Andy Steiger instead . . ."

Longarm patted her plump arm in a way he hoped Rose might take as brotherly and said soothingly, "I was hiding out last night, ma'am. I might be hiding out later. So don't wait supper on my account. I'll grab a bite at the chili parlor whether I come back later this evening or not."

Then he nodded down at the younger gal to add, "Shall we go send them wires now, Miss Rose?"

The mistress of the Flying B took his arm with a flounce of her ash blond hair to declare nothing would please her more.

So they left the older and fatter redhead in a state of confusion at the head of the outside stairs, and when Longarm asked, Rose said the pony she'd ridden to town was over to the municipal corral.

He asked her if she minded walking to the Western Union in that case. She laughed and declared, "It's barely a skip and holler, astride or afoot. Have you been flirting with that poor fat thing back yonder, you meanie?"

Longarm asked in a desperately innocent tone what might have given her such an odd notion. She replied, "Whatever her reason, the dear old thing is *loco en la cabeza* over you! Couldn't you tell?"

Longarm snorted, "The Widow Whitehead is my landlady, for Pete's sake!" and that was the simple truth when you studied on it.

So to Longarm's considerable relief Rose Bradford switched the topic of their conversation to the telegraph wires they meant to send at the Western Union, once they got there.

Then it came to Longarm that once they got there they might well see and be seen by Consuela, from the chili parlor next door, seeing as *La Siesta* had ended early that afternoon.

Rose Bradford asked, "What's up? Why are we headed *this* way when the Western Union shed is *that* way, Custis?"

To which he could only reply, "I just thought of more important beeswax up to the ranger post, Miss Rose. I can send that wire up the line to the Indian Police at a mayhaps more convenient time."

Chapter 18

Longarm felt it safer to carry the willowy blonde up to the ranger station, where Captain Kramer apologized for having no soda pop on file as they filled him in on the odd comings and goings of Caddo Flynn.

Rose Bradford allowed she took tequila neat, without salt or lemon slice like a sissy Mex. So Captain Kramer poured three shots as Longarm marveled at how tough it could be to read a book by its cover.

At first reading, Rose Bradford seemed a perforce innocent home gal, stuck with folk as needed looking after. But the pretty little thing hadn't fainted at the sight of a grown man's dick, she'd held her own in a slanging match with an older experienced woman and damned if she didn't take her tequila clawing back at her!

As he inhaled some tequila himself, Longarm idly wondered how much adult supervision a hard-riding, hard-drinking mule breeder got from a dithering old mom and a half-cracked pop. Having grown up on a hardscrabble farm in West-By-God-Virginia himself, Longarm knew country kids got to watch critters of all shapes and sizes fornicating in all sorts of odd positions, and whilst it was doubtless true not *every* kid raised country fucked critters before they ever got around to fucking one another, country kids knew more about fucking than city kids by the time they were old enough to fuck anything. But fair was fair, and he had to allow that the notion of a curious country gal fucking a horse or even a burro seemed impractical if not impossible.

Back in West-By-God-Virginia country boys had found she-goats most willing, with bitch dogs the least. The few gals he'd ever gotten to confess such early experimentation had confided that for a country gal, critter fucking worked just the opposite, with a he-dog willing to fuck most every and anything at any time, whilst a he-goat failed to satisfy the human fancy with its skinny dick and jackrabbit on-and-off approach to the matter. So that was likely the reason she-goats seemed so pleased to service country boys whilst country gals learned dog style from the source.

Longarm warned himself not to picture willowy blondes going at it dog style whilst drinking tequila with 'em. He pretended to care more about the current market for army mules when Captain Kramer said they had a complaint about four others missing from the paddock of another spread called the Double Diamond. The missing stock not being branded, of course.

Captain Kramer poured another round as he pointed out the little lady they were drinking with that afternoon knew more about the price of army mules than he did.

Rose Bradford modestly confessed, "It's hard to say what any critter might be worth to anyone in the market for the same. The army dickers, the same as anyone else, if you follow my drift."

Longarm did. Despite the sarcastic trail song about herding Texas cattle on a ten-dollar horse and a forty-dollar saddle, things weren't that simple out this way.

Things seldom were in a rapidly changing West the newspaper men and travel book authors kept trying to simplify, sort of romantic.

It was true a mustang hunter would sell you a fresh-caught bronco, fighting like a trout at the far end of a throw rope, for ten dollars or less. But the time and trouble it took to bust a bronco, meaning wild, as in wild horse, to where it was any use at all as a saddle mount, doubled its price. If you wanted a real cow pony, trained to zigzag through brush after a cow and then skid to a solid stop and hold a good throw tight-roped to keep the cow down for you, the horse would cost you way more than its saddle. A cutting horse or a sudden quarter-miler you could win some money with was of course worth at least three figures to a sporting man with the money to indulge such tastes, and in spite of its ancestry and comical ears a young but full-grown mule was worth as much or more as a horse with the same time and trouble invested in its training.

There'd have been no sense in breeding mules if things had been at all otherwise. Breeding mules was more trouble than breeding horses. Mares didn't much cotton to mating with a jackass, and it was awkward for a runty jackass to mount a way taller mare.

Things had to be done that way, of course. It was easier for a stud horse to fuck a bitty burro, but the result you wound up with was the pathetical *hinny*—a tad bigger than a jackass but hardly worth all the trouble.

Mules and hinnies could both fuck, and some seemed to enjoy it a heap. But being they were both sterile hybrids, you had to cross the parental breeds fresh for every solitary mule you aimed for.

The mule, not the hinny, was worth the trouble and demanded way more than a scrub pony because despite its looks a mule combined the best features of the horse and burro. It was surefooted as a smaller burro whilst big as a horse and capable of packing or pulling as much or more.

After that a mule lived longer than either a horse or burro, and it seemed to stand up to hard living on piss poor fodder and way less water than any horse could get by on. So the Indian fighting army, as well as the stage lines still running and more than a few full-time cowboys, found the big old comical mule just the ticket for the rough and dry parts of the West.

Being traditional, the U.S. Cav put its troopers aboard mostly bay horses branded U.S. and used mules branded the same way to pack and haul everything from wounded men to field artillery, with most, of course, moving the tons of supplies an army in the field needs to keep it in the field.

Captain Kramer, who naturally knew all that, seemed more puzzled by the final destination of all those stolen mules than he was about any nearby hidey hole. He pointed out, "No matter where Clay Allison and his new recruits down our way have hidden that Lazy A spread he brags about, there's no money in mules or any sort of stock before you *sell* the same to somebody, see?"

Rose Bradford said, "That's easy. With Victorio off the reservation this summer and raiding back and forth all up and down the border, the U.S. Cav, the Mexican *Federales* and a whole lot of free-lance scalp hunters are in the market for mules. Aside from the usual wear and tear, it's my understanding bronco Apache *eat* mules as well!"

Longarm soberly added, "Ponies, too. The Na-déné, as they like to call themselves, hold that since we are what we eat it's better to eat noble critters. Albeit that yarn about them eating *folk* is probably a canard spread by the same Pueblos who named them Apache for us."

Captain Kramer said, "Whatever. My point is that to sell a stolen mule you have to offer it somewhere, to someone, for sale. I've sent wires in all directions, warning other lawmen to be on the prod for a tall blond cuss with a limp, offering muleflesh for sale under any old name, see?"

Longarm covered his shot glass with a hand as a signal he'd had more than enough and replied, "I doubt Clay Allison, or his haunt, will try to sell all that stolen stock, direct. Stolen goods are most often put on the market by a sneak pretending to be an honest dealer."

Rose Bradford accepted her shot, and downed it like a man, before she pointed out, "Nobody, sneaky or not, has to unload all that stolen stock in any one market. Army posts, freight outfits and stage lines in every fool direction are in the market for mules, at premium price, this summer. You can only drive a cow ten to fifteen miles a day. You can trot a mule thirty, and in less than a week you can offer a halter-trained young mule, with no brand, anywheres betwixt here and El Paso or San Antone!"

Longarm grimaced and volunteered, "You left out New Mexico and Old Mexico, *Los Federales* favoring saddle mules as well. So let's talk about *earlier* stock thieves in these parts. The Widow Whitehead tells me her man was a brand inspector drygulched by somebody running off *cows* for fun and profit?"

The willowy blonde's voice seemed a mite slurred by stronger refreshments than soda pop as she volunteered, "Poor old Danny Whitehead was *married* to a cow, and they killed Frenchy Cartier as well. Poor Frenchy wasn't married to anybody. Left his modest holdings to a kid sister called Monique. She's all right, I hear tell."

Captain Kramer, who seemed to hold his tequila better, turned to put the bottle away as he told Longarm, "That was about the end of cow stealing in this basin. They seemed to have been a Mexican gang, taking advantage of the nearest border crossing being a day's ride closer than the county seat up Alpine way. The two killings in a row inspired one hell of a manhunt." Then he said, "Sorry, Miss Rose, I meant one *heck* of a manhunt, with any strange Mex and for that matter any Anglo who couldn't account for his being in this basin in for a mighty rough time!"

Rose Bradford was staring owlishly as she recalled, "They hung an Anglo stranger with a running iron in his saddlebag from a live oak tree. I think I'm going to be sick!"

Longarm moved in to steady the willowy blonde on her feet as Captain Kramer whipped a bentwood chair from behind the desk so's the two of them could set her safely down.

Kramer smiled sheepishly up at Longarm to mutter,

"Sometimes I don't know my own strength. Tequila takes a little getting used to and she can't weigh more than a hundred pounds!"

Longarm said, "I'd vote one-twenty. She's a tad tall for a woman, and bones that show under healthy hide tend to be heavier than usual. We were talking about that earlier gang of stock thieves, Captain."

Kramer said, "Like the little lady just said, their operation was busted up, brutal, with no doubt a few innocent strangers dead and the Good Lord left to sort out the saints and sinners. When they heard how rough things had gotten out this way, Austin ordered us rangers in to tidy up and make sure nobody who hadn't stolen nothing got hung for stealing it."

He shot a wistful glance at his file drawers as he added, "I hardly need to tell another lawman how much tougher it is to deal with crooks in a constitutional manner. But I thought we had things pretty much under control until that spooky Clay Allison blew in late February or early March to cut himself into a new game entire. I was sure we'd cleaned out all them mean Mex stock thieves and things were commencing to get too good to last."

Longarm pointed out, "The total stranger claiming to be a badman out of New Mexico Territory never found, settled and improved that mystery ranch him and his *Mexican* help ride in and out from, with or without the property of less mysterious folk. So how do you like the same Mexican gang, or mayhaps its Mex or Anglo matermind, sending away for outside help when the going got rough for them a spell back?"

Rose Bradford moaned, "Oh, dear," and fell off the chair to flop on her face at their feet.

Longarm hunkered down to pick her up and spread her across the desk face down, so's she wouldn't gag on her own puke, if she had to puke, as Captain Kramer decided, "Silent partners, Anglo or Mex, could add up to an already established hidey hole off to the east. Whether the quick-draw calling hisself Clay Allison is a junior or senior partner, I can see how his mad-dog growlings and murdersome outburst could be meant to discourage others from trailing his gang too tight. What are we going to do with Miss Rose here? It don't look right to have a gal passed out across my infernal desk, and it ain't likely to do wonders for her reputation, neither. She's already living down some back-fence gossip about her and this good-looking remount officer they put up at the Flying B for a fortnight last fall."

Without moving her head as it hung face down over the edge, Rose Bradford muttered, "A lot *you* know! I never fucked that married-up soldier blue one time!"

Then she softly sobbed, "He never even tried, the confounded sissy, and those old biddy hens who say he did would lay square eggs if I ever told 'em when, where and with whom I lost my cherry! So there!"

"Mebbe if we put her back in one of the holding cells to let her sleep it off . . . ," the older lawman suggested.

Longarm said, "Her secrets would *surely* be safe back yonder, once all your help drifts in from wherever they've been enjoying *La Siesta*." He glanced at the Regulator Clock on the wall to add, "If Billy Vail was running this post, they'd have all reported in by now. What say I beg, borrow or hire a buckboard and run her on home before she can get herself in more trouble?"

Captain Kramer said he could do better than that, explaining, "I got a surrey with side curtains in the livery across the way. If we tether her pony to the surrey . . ."

Longarm cut in with, "What are we jawing about, then? Why don't we get cracking?"

So they did, getting an extra hand with the chores when Sergeant Farnsworth came in, took one look and chose not to reason why.

Hence in little more time than it would take to explain all the tedious moves, they had Rose Bradford curled up under a buffalo robe on the rear seat with the side curtains up and Longarm seated up front by himself as he drove out of town with matched bays pulling and Rose Bradford's palomino trailing.

The Flying B being north of town a piece, Longarm

got to drive silent for a spell before the gal on the backseat stuck her head out from under the shaggy lap robe to ask, "What's going on? Where am I? Where's my hat?"

Longarm calmly assured her, "Your hat's up here on the front seat with me, Miss Rose. You're in Captain Kramer's surrey. Seeing you seemed to be feeling poorly, he asked me to run you home."

She pulled the robe over her face again as she replied in a muffled tone, "Oh, I thought you were taking me some place to fuck me."

Chapter 19

Longarm lit a smoke and drove on, walking the team at say three miles an hour. When he met up with a hay wagon driving into town, likely to that livery, Longarm waved a howdy and just kept going, with the side curtains hiding any mysteriously bulging buffalo robes from the other driver.

A lone cowhand he'd never met before showed no more curiosity as they nodded neighborly in passing. He'd encountered no other traffic by the time they reached the skull-decorated gate of the Flying B. He turned to see no signs of life under that buffalo robe and just kept driving, slow, until he figured he was uncomfortably close to that Borden spread and reined in under some roadside cottonwoods to fish out and light another cheroot.

They'd been parked there a spell, with all three ponies cropping the roadside weeds and a cactus wren or mayhaps a mockingbird cussing them out from the treetops, when Rose Bradford suddenly threw the robe off, sat bolt upright and sobbed, "Oh, my God!"

Longarm quietly replied, "Howdy. We'd be a mile or so north of your main gate now, Miss Rose. Call me shy if you like, but I thought it might be best if I didn't have to explain your . . . discomfort to your hired help."

She asked in a small, scared voice, "I don't know what came over me this afternoon! Have we any other . . . explaining to do?"

Longarm said, "What came over you was hundred-proof tequila, Miss Rose. We've all made ourselves sick showing off with strong drink or our dad's cigars. You're lucky you didn't smoke one of the cigars my boss, Marshal Billy Vail, keeps on hand to trap the unwary. Are you about ready to get on home now, or would you rather just set here and listen to that tweety bird some more?"

She asked where her pony was. He told her, adding, "I follow your drift. Might save us all a heap of jawing if you chose to ride in all alone whilst I ran this rig back to Captain Kramer."

She nodded but said, "Custis, did you take advantage of my drunken stupor out here in the middle of nowhere?"

He snorted. "You don't have to be insulting, Miss Rose! I'm not one to brag, but from what I've heard from other ladies you'd likely *know* whether this child had been fooling around with your old ring dang doo!"

She laughed despite herself and asked, "Is that what you call it? I know what it's supposed to feel like down there, afterwards, and right now it feels like . . . afterwards."

He sighed and said, "Just my luck to be left out of the wet dream of a pretty lady. But you have my word I never even kissed you as we loaded you aboard back there. Could we change the subject now? Asking a man for such assurances can drift all too soon from just polite conversation to cruelty to dumb animals!"

She said, "I'm sorry, Custis. I'm not trying to tease. It's just that I can't recall whether I said some things out loud or only to myself this afternoon!"

He said, "You never said anything a gentleman of the old school might hold against you, ma'am. So just gather your wits about you and . . . Do you want to put this hat back on?"

She did, leaning forward farther than she needed to, and

147

it sure beat all how tempting tequila breath smelled when it was coming from a sort of breathless, willowy blonde.

Then she had the damned hat on, and before he could drop off to help her down, she'd sprung through the side curtains to untether her pony and mount gracefully as hell for a gal who'd just been dead to the world under a buffalo robe.

Reining in closer to where Longarm sat, Rose Bradford smiled down at him to declare, "You *are* a gentleman of the old school, Custis Long! When can a girl who owes you some explanations expect you to come a-calling?"

Longarm smiled back up to reply, "Can't say, Miss Rose. They never sent me down this way to call on any gals, and you've nothing to explain as far as I see it."

She whirled her mount around to ride off at full gallop, not looking back as she laughed or cried. It was hard to tell.

"She's been hurt. Hurt real bad," Longarm told his borrowed team as hauled their muzzles out of the roadside weeds and clucked at them to move on out. A man hardly needed a buggy whip when he clucked in a convincing manner. So it took them far less time to get on back to town.

But by then *La Siesta* was sincerely ended, leaving more than some gummy-eyed and out of joint. Dropping the captain's surrey and team at the livery, Longarm left it to the rangers to sort out who might or might not be on duty as he ambled over to the Western Union to see about those wires.

Once he had, he naturally stopped next door for coffee with chili con carne and more private words with the dusky Consuela.

He could see right off she was smoldering. He couldn't ask her why before the two others she'd been serving left. Once they had, Consueala flared. "For why you yell at those *ladrónes* from my bedroom window at such an hour, *pendejo mio*? You did not know the *bruja chingada* across the *camino* from my place is half-Spanish, half-Nahuatl and all *mouth*? Even as we speak she is shouting to the

148

four winds that I am a *puta* who sleeps with *gringos* for the *Yanqui* dollar!"

Longarm sighed and said, "I'm sorry I got you in Dutch with *La Raza, querida mia*. But you knew I was the law, and we've just agreed those riders I challenged were thieves. I had to try to stop them."

Consuela sniffed, "*No, mi friegues*. All you managed to do was for to ruin my *reputación*! Is only one way we can restore my honor among my people. You must give me *permiso* for to tell them all we have been plotting together, late at night, in *La Causa de Mejico libre*!"

Longarm wearily asked, "Have you already told the witch across the way I'm wanted in Old Mexico as *El Brazo Largo*?"

She beamed but said, "I was not sure. I thought you were. All of my people in the basin think you are. But Ricardo Chavez has been known to make things up and he is the only one who swears he is certain."

As she poured him a fresh mug of black coffee, she added, "Now that you have told me Ricardo was right, is okay I confide to only a few close friends you have been holding secret meetings in my *casa*, late at night?"

Longarm was feeling the need for black coffee after the hard day he'd just had, with hardly a wink the night before. So he thought some, to make sure he wasn't just thinking with his old organ grinder, before he decided, "Well, seeing I surely need a private place to meet with this *one* sneaky Mexican I know, I reckon you may as well swear just a very few close friends to secrecy, so they can blab it to the old witch who knows full well I've been staying at your place. But make certain you word it so's no volunteer Mex rebels are likely to barge in on us as we're holding one of those swell secret meetings!"

She glanced about, saw it was safe and leaned across the counter to kiss him, quick but French, and husked, "I can hardly wait for to meet with you in secret again, *toro mio*! You will be back here for to take me home at midnight, no?"

Longarm sighed and thought that was about the size of

it, as he wondered how he'd ever last that long without at least forty winks. As a lawman he was used to long hours on his feet *on duty.* But like actors, outlaws, railroad men and others forced to adapt to odd hours, Longarm made up for being bright-eyed when he had to be by just letting go when there was nothing better to do, and as of the moment, there was nothing he could think of doing until the Indian Police rounded up that ridge-running guide he needed. The other side had the initiative as long as it was free to sally forth at will from that secret hideout somewhere out amidst the uncharted crags of the Big Bend. Until he had a line on where the cockroaches were running when one lit the lamp, responding to challenges to a duel and chasing after night riders already halfway out of sight seemed exercises in futility.

Having sent his wires and having neither suggestions nor challenges from friend or foe to respond to, Longarm trudged back to the Toro Negro in the late afternoon light as the shadows lengthened and his eyelids kept trying to make up their minds whether that black coffee or that warm bowl of chili were having the greater effect on him.

Knowing he couldn't flop at Consuela's place before a midnight walk and at least three orgasms on her part, bless her tawny hide, Longarm decided to risk nobody coming after him earlier, with the saloon down below going full blast well into the night.

As he mosied in, he failed to see either the Widow Whitehead or pretty little Yzabel working the already fairly busy saloon. Taking advantage of the opportunity, he bellied up to the bar and ordered a tequila-laced *cerveza* off the just-as-fat but younger brown-haired barmaid on duty at the moment. He waited until she'd served him and had time to note the change he left by his beer scuttle before he remarked in a desperately casual tone that he hadn't seen either good old Flo or skinny little Yzabel that evening.

The new barmaid replied in as casual a tone, "The boss lady's in her quarters if you'd like me to fetch her. The

150

greaser quit. That's how I got this job. My name is Maggy and I'm off at midnight."

"So am I," Longarm wistfully replied, adding, "I go back on duty in a while. I'm the law. Did you say Yzabel quit, or might she have been fired?"

Maggy shrugged her plump shoulders to reply, "I wasn't there. Boss Lady says she quit. Were you fixing to arrest her for something in the name of the law? I'd heard you were in town, Deputy Long."

Longarm laughed easily and confessed all lawmen were born snoops. He didn't ask Maggy what else she might have heard about him, and inhaled enough suds to justify ordering before he excused himself to part the beaded curtain, nod to the kitchen help and mosey up the back stairs to his hired room.

The match stem he'd wedged under the bottom hinge now lay on the floor in the dim light of the long deserted corridor. A big gray cat in Longarm's guts got up to sharpen its claws and swish its bush tail as he silently drew his .44–40 with his right fist, got a good grip on the knob with his left and gave it a strong twist, with his legs gathered under him for sudden movement.

Nothing happened. The door was locked. Longarm was still training his muzzle on it when it suddenly flew open in his face.

He didn't shoot the figure standing there. He laughed like hell. For the Widow Whitehead didn't have a stitch on and Dear Jesus if old Flo wasn't *fat*!

She pouted. "You weren't so cruel on yonder bedstead with your own clothes off, you meanie! I thought we'd established that you didn't mind my, . . . weight problem."

He allowed she'd only startled him, as he moved inside to holster his gun and shut the fool door before somebody roaming the deserted second story saw them.

As she led the way to the nearby bedstead, the fat redhead confided she'd seen him coming and dashed upstairs to welcome him home at last.

As Longarm hung his gunbelt and hat on a bedpost, she added, "Where were you last night? I wait and waited,

151

hot and bothered till I just had to strum my own banjo and catch some shut-eye!"

She looked way more tempting on her back, with the folds of fat at more French postcard repose and her huge thighs spread like that to either side of her rust red welcome matt. For carrying a dead drunk willowy blonde home and setting up a later tryst with a smoldering brunette had stirred some feelings up down yonder, in spite of or mayhaps with the aid of all those hours in the saddle earlier.

So he was hard indeed by the time he'd shucked his boots and jeans to take the bawdy old saloon keeper up on her friendly welcome back, and it sure beat all how different she felt after he'd had to pull it out of Consuela before dawn like so. He was able to relish the ample charms of an experienced and willing mount fair and square, enjoying old Flo just the way she was, bless her big fat ass, until he'd come hard as hell and sincerely as a teenager in a whorehouse. After, it occured to him he could have come like so in Rose Bradford if only he hadn't been cursed with a conscience. So that sudden thought inspired a twitch Flo felt up inside of her, inspiring her to sob, "Oh, Dear Lord, you are such a darling boy and so respectful to your elders! I can't believe you want more already! For I do look in the mirror when I fix my hair and I've tried in vain to curb my appetite!"

He kissed her and began to move in her some more as he soothed her and said with a sort of guilty conscience, "I like the appetite your old ring dang doo is blessed with fine, and the way you're built reminds me of these sassy paintings by a famous Dutch dude called Rubens, I think. Whoever he was, he painted his nude ladies mighty pink and a little plump."

She offered, in that case, to get on top and offer him a view of all she had to offer, bouncing like a collection of rubber balls all wrapped up inside a naked redhead. Albeit she didn't put it just that way, and Longarm never mentioned how comical she looked up yonder. For it would have been cruel and she was being so nice to him with the way firmer flesh that mattered.

But once he'd had her that way, he faked another orgasm, dog style, to save some for later. So when the fat redhead wistfully told him she had to get back to work downstairs for a spell, Longarm sleepily asked if she'd mind waking him up around eleven.

Flo Whitehead assured him with a kiss he'd be able to sleep past midnight if they had a busy night downstairs.

Before she could make any late night plans for them, Longarm tried to sound as wistful when he told her, "I want your word you'll wake me no later than eleven. I won't be here at midnight. I got to go out again."

"In the middle of the night?" she asked, adding, naturally enough, "Where on earth could you be planning to go at midnight, Custis?"

He replied in a confidential tone, "Got to go to a secret meeting. I better not tell you more than that, lest I give away too much."

And he'd told her the simple truth, as soon as you studied on it.

Chapter 20

Nigh six hours' sleep and more black coffee had Longarm feeling as frisky as a jackrabbit, albeit, thanks to the way Flo Whitehead had chosen to wake him up, not quite as horny when he carried Consuela home from the chili parlor.

A lesser man might have had a time getting it back up on such short notice, but one of the best things about a tumbleweed job with eyes free to admire new horizons was how fresh a fresh piece of ass could look, undressing by moonlight near an open window. The way smaller but still curvacious border Mex beauty even smelled a whole lot different.

She noticed, as he rolled in bed with her, buck naked, and asked him thoughtfully when and why he'd splashed himself with lilac water.

Taking the warmer and more peppersome Consuela in his bare arms, he innocently asked, "Is that what they sold me when I asked for bay rum? I thought it smelled sort of sissy when I splashed it on after shaving this evening."

She nuzzled his bare cheek with her own to purr, "Was *muy* thoughtful of you to shave for me, *querido mio*. That big *bigote* alone feels like you are trying for to sweep my lips off when you kiss me! Have you never thought what it would feel like for to kiss a *mujer* if you were to shave all of your face?"

He answered easily, "Well, sure I have. But the reason I grew my mustache to begin with was that everybody seemed to think I was fixing to grow one a couple of hours after I'd shaved my whole face and who am I to deny you ladies a pinch of salt?"

Being Mex, she naturally knew what he was talking about, but once she'd laughed politely, she pouted. "The poet who made up those lines about kissing a man without a *bigote* being like eating boiled eggs with no salt was *en verdad* an *hombre macho* too lazy for to shave!"

Then she kissed Longarm experimentally, putting her hand to one of his cheeks to decide the contrast was as *interesante* as the way the hair around his naked *piton* felt. So he gently but firmly moved her hand down to his old organ grinder, inspiring her to purr, "Is all of this for little me?"

So he shoved it where the sun never shone, and if it took him longer than before to come in Consuela, she had no complaints. She seemed to take it as a compliment when he made her come, more than once, and just had to keep going.

But if he was low on ammunition, his head was clearer than it had been the last time they'd talked. So as he was enjoying a smoke in the moonlight, along with the moon-lit view as she took it dog style, he asked her what she'd meant about Ricardo Chavez making things up.

Arching her spine to take him deeper, Consuala replied in a conversational tone, "He means no harm. But you know how *muchachos* so young wish for to be taken as *importante*. Ricardo is always talking about buried treasures, lost mines, secret how you say hideouts and all the *peligrosos* he knows. Ricardo would have us believe he knows *El Gato,* the rebel leader, and of course he has bought drinks for *El Cabrito.* Your people know him as Billy the Kid."

Longarm thrust thoughtfully and told her, "I think *El*

Chaval would be a more literal translation. We think of him as a human kid, not a young goat."

She wriggled her hips to encourage more movement as she languidly purred, *"¿Es verdad?* We still call him *El Cabrito,* and of course our Ricardo does not really know anyone so *notorio* by any name!"

"Get back to secret hideouts." Longarm suggested, moving in her the way he sensed she wanted it as he added, "Billy the Kid ain't wanted by my home office, lucky for him. But I'm purely in the market for secret hideouts. So where do I find Ricardo Chavez when he ain't spitting and whittling over by the water tank? I ain't laid eyes on the young cuss since the first day I arrived."

Consuela thought before she decided, "I have not seen him in town for a day or more, either, now that you speak of him. He how you say bunks at the Double Stars, as a stable hand for Monique Cartier, who thinks she is so grand!"

Mere mention of another woman inspired Consuela to drop off, roll on her back and open wide in welcome. So he got rid of his smoke to take her up on such a kind offer, and a good time was had by all until he managed to come, too, before he casually asked if they might be speaking of the kid sister of that murdered brand inspector, Frenchy Cartier.

Consuela said, *"Sí,* he came down from *La Canada* and everybody liked *him.* She thinks she came down from heaven and nobody likes *her!* Ricardo says she pays well but expects everybody for to work all the time, and one can tell she has no respect for *La Raza."*

Taking a drag and blowing a thoughtful smoke ring, Longarm asked where the Cartier spread might be. He wasn't surprised when Consuela allowed it was within easy walking distance, north of town. But when he tried to picture passing it, having been up that way more than once, he had to confess he couldn't.

Consuela said, "Is on the other side of the creek, opposite the smaller *granja* of the Morenos on this side."

He frowned and said, "Do tell. How come there's no

road up the far side of the creek? I haven't seen anything off to the west but cottonwoods and cliffs on what seems a way narrower floodplain."

She shrugged her bare shoulder against him—that felt swell—and explained, "There is less room as well as no need for another *camino* west of the creek for because, as you say, is not as much bottomland on that side. So those holding land to the west of the creek hold all of it they can under grass or how you say cash crops. Is not so many and none so close together on that side of the creek for because when one holds land between running water and soaring cliffs not as far away, one must how you say extend one's claim north and south in a longer way."

Longarm caught himself about to ask a dumb question. But a fool could see that once you had a wagon trace to follow up either bank of the fairly broad but mighty shallow Tiswin, you could turn to the left and *ford* the fool creek most anywhere north or south of that quarter-acre tank dammed by Tanktown.

Taking another thoughtful drag, Longarm was fixing to ask a more intelligent question when the stillness of the moonlit night outside was broken by a loud pistol shot, as echoed from the nearby limestone cliffs, and a gruff male voice roaring out, "Hello the Lopez 'dobe! We know you're in there, Custis Long! Do you want to come out and fight like a man or do we have to smoke you out like the lone wolf you're forever pretending to be?"

Consuela rolled off the bed to fumble for her duds as a more distant female voice shrilled, "*¿Quien es? ¿Que pasa? Es muy tardes por tonterias y . . .*" before another shot and a dreadful curse in Border Mex with a thick Anglo accent silenced the nosey gossip across the way.

"This way!" Consuela whispered, half rising from the floor in a crouch with her dress back on. She added, "Hurry! Follow me over my rear windowsill and into the alameda along the creek for to hide!"

Longarm hissed back, "Stay put! That's what they *want* us to try!" as he swung his bare feet to the floor and drew his six-gun from its handy location on the bedpost. But

157

the frightened Consuela was up and running, faster, as another shot was followed by the eerie buzz of a bullet that just missed Longarm's head to thunk into the 'dobe on the far side of the bedroom. So even as he shouted out loud, "No! Don't do it!" Consuela did it.

The terrified little gal rolled over the sill to land on her bare feet and make it a quarter of the distance to the cottonwood shade of the tanglewood along the creek, when other guns on that side, a heap of guns on that side, laid her low to land face down, dead before she hit the ground.

Longarm had to figure such details out later, of course. He'd spit his revealing cheroot out at the same time he'd seen the flash of the more talkative gun east of the house. He had the cuss located in the deep shade of a roadside persimmon tree rising from the corner of the cactus hedge of the gossip across the way. The taunting gunslick would more likely be just off the older woman's property than inside her yard. But it paid to make sure. So Longarm bent to pick up his lit cheroot, took a drag out of line of the window to glow it better, then braced it on the chimney of a bedside lamp, still out of line with the window, before he called out, "Who's out there? Might you have a name of your own, boogeyman?"

When there came no answer, Longarm moved the lamp table in line with the window, and when that didn't work, he moved swiftly back to the rear window of the two-room 'dobe for a look-see across the moonlit open ground to the inky shade of the creekside alameda. When he spotted Consuela's pale form out yonder, Longarm muttered, "Aw, shit, that just wasn't fair, God!" as he held his fire and searched the deep shade for movement, cursing himself for leaving his Winchester at the Toro Negro with the rest of his shit.

He heard someone call soft and low, "Is that him? I can't make it out from here!"

A more distant voice snorted. "Asshole! Didn't you just hear him yelling out the front? You got the gal! He's alone in there now. With only one set of eyes and all four sides to cover. So what are you all waiting for? Move in on him, damn it!"

The closer voice called back, "I don't see *you* moving in on anybody. You go first if you're so brave. That ain't Little Bo Peep inside with custard pies to throw at us, you know!"

Longarm was tempted to taunt them into offering him muzzle flashes to throw down on. But he'd already made the mistake of letting them know they hadn't gotten him, and it was the simple truth there was no way in hell he'd make it if they rushed him from all sides at once.

But he knew, as they knew, he'd get anybody rushing the side he was capable of covering. So the next time that first voice called out to him with an unkind remark about his mother, Longarm didn't answer. They knew he was somewhere in the house, and he knew, now that the one with the big mouth had moved around to cover the rear, that they'd expected him to bust out from there.

So it was a Mexican standoff, even though they sounded like Anglos, and seeing he had the time as well as the probable need, Longarm moved back to the bedroom to get dressed, out of line of the bedroom window as his lit cheroot glowed temptingly.

Once fully dressed again, he braced a booted foot to either side of the doorway between poor Consuela's bedroom and the larger main room to the west, six-gun in one hand, with his double derringer off the end of his watch chain and palmed in his left fist, adding up to eight shots rapid-fire before he'd have to reload, since he'd naturally thumbed in a sixth round when he'd first laid hand on his .44-40 in the dark.

For next to walking around with all six chambers loaded and your holstered gun pointing at your own feet, there was nothing dumber than bracing for a shoot-out ahead of time with only five in the wheel.

From his central position, he had a half-ass chance of covering the approaches from east and west, but a piss poor chance of spotting a charge from either direction before the cocksuckers were right on top of him, and all bets were off if they kicked in the front door to the south at the same time.

Then, to his left, came the sound of another shot, mingled with the ringing of shattered and falling glass as the lit cheroot wound up back on the floor and somebody shouted at the top of his lungs, "He's up front, whether dead or alive!" So Longarm dashed to the back window for a blurry view of three dark figures charging out of the cottonwoods along the creek.

He fired six shots, two with the derringer, to make it sound as if he'd emptied the wheel into them. But they'd had enough, and the one Longarm had dropped wailed for them not to leave him there as they left him, with one sounding that taunting rooster laugh as they vanished back into the tanglewood's inky shade.

Longarm ran to the front window with the two rounds left, but he saw nobody trying to take advantage of his fire out the back. So he began to reload.

He just had the derringer set to go again when not far in the distance came the sounds of running men and beasts along with the rumblings of a confused crowd who would have responded to any late night emergency.

Longarm bent over to pick up the still smoldering cheroot and snuff it out before it could cause more trouble. Not knowing how much hair his unknown enemies might have on their chests, Longarm didn't go outside to meet the bunch from town until they were all around him, not sure they had the right address until a voice from out back wailed out, "Jesus H. Christ! That Mex gal from the chili parlor's out here, dead as a Confederate quarter!"

When the familiar voice of Sergeant Farnsworth called out to anybody in the house, Longarm called back to identify himself and say he was coming out.

As he joined Farnsworth another ranger and a dozen odd others out back, around the facedown body of Consuela, he had to confess he had no idea who'd just murdered the poor little thing.

He told the older lawman, "They were after me. They said so. Some voice I didn't recognize called me out by name. I knew better. But Consuela, there, being a gal, wasn't on to that old ruse, and when she busted out the back like they were expecting, they were expecting her. I had one down, over yonder, closer to the trees. I thought he was down for good. Since I see he ain't, they came back for him or he managed to get up and stagger after 'em when I ran to the front window."

Captain Farnsworth was too old a hand to ask why a man who'd just shot a man from a rear window would run to cover the front. He shifted his weight and opined, "We'd best rouse Captain Kramer and see if he wants to tag along, then. If you knocked a man down with a round of .44–40, he don't figure to get far on foot no matter where you might have hit him."

Then he asked, "What were you doing in there just now, Deputy Long?"

Longarm had been afraid he was fixing to ask that.

Chapter 21

"Secret meeting." Longarm confided, seeing that was the least he could do now for a gal who'd been worried about her rep. Aware of all the others listening and his own sworn duties to the law, he went on to explain, truthfully enough when you studied on it, "Miss Consuela allowed there were things she didn't want to talk about at her chili parlor. So I walked her home to hear her out."

Sergeant Farnsworth dispatched one of his rangers to wake Captain Kramer, and fetch Doc Fletcher whilst he was at it, before he turned back to Longarm to ask, "What kind of things?"

Longarm truthfully replied, "I was still talking to her about the geography of this basin when them night riders attacked. You ask the old woman across the road if you'd care to have her back my play. The one who seemed to be in command, he might have just been the spokesman of the one in command, called me out by name and dared me to fight in the moonlight with 'em. Miss Consuela made the mistake they'd planned on me making when they yelled in from the road with the creek side of yonder 'dobe staked out. I know for certain there were at least three of 'em. Sounded like more. Say a five-man diamond patrol."

Someone in the crowd marveled, "You're saying you and this Mex gal were set upon by a military patrol, Uncle Sam?"

Longarm said, "Not hardly. I'm saying they worked liked riders with some military training. They, or the one in command, knew what they were doing. Rough and ready owlhoot riders would have likely rid in and out shooting, with torches to throw. These bastards knew how tough it was to smoke a grown man with a gun out from under a tile roof with thick 'dobe walls around him and the light you'd shed on the subject making it advisable to stay well back, whilst, just as they did, they attracted attention in town with their gunplay."

He thought he'd drifted the topic of secret meetings safely off to one side. But Sergeant Farnsworth asked, "What was it about the lay of the land around here she wanted to tell you, Deputy Long?"

Rangers were inclined to be sharp lawmen, bless their hides.

Choosing his words with enough care to avoid dragging red herrings across the getaway trail of bastards he really wanted caught, Longarm said, "Like I said, we'd barely got here when they attacked out of the night. I can see how the poor gal could have suspected somebody she had cause to worry about might have been watching her chili parlor. I had just asked her about those other cliffs west of the creek when those night riders showed up. Can anybody here tell me what the cliff tops are like over yonder?"

A younger man dressed cow said, "I can. I been up a canyon or more after strays on that side. There ain't nigh as much of that side, for one thing. The crags roll like ocean breakers against the Mule Ear Peaks and then subside down the other way to another bottomland basin much like this here basin. No way to drive stolen stock out of *that* basin, save through an even longer north-south canyon with an army border crossing down to the far end.

163

The Mex *Federáles* have another border post directly across the ford. I doubt I'd ride that way if I was traveling incognito."

Sergeant Farnsworth said, "Lieutenant Weiner told us he was headed into the higher crags to the *east* when he vanished on us. There are way fewer canyons west of the basin because there's less higher ground to drain. But I reckon Captain Kramer will be willing to explore over yonder if you think that's the way they went just now."

Longarm truthfully confessed he had no idea which way the sons of bitches had run, afoot or on horseback for all he could swear to. The sergeant asked if he thought that could have been Clay Allison calling out to him, adding, "He bragged the other night at the Last Chance that he was out to get you."

Longarm grimaced and said, "He jumped Andy Steiger instead and that other cuss who tried to back-shoot me looked more like a Mex than the way they keep describing this Clay Allison look-alike. Since I never had a long conversation with Clay Allison before or after they buried him back in '77, I just can't say who dared me to come out and fight. I did notice he wasn't anxious to make good on his brag to come in after me, though."

Aware of the other locals listening, and knowing the local reputation the self-styled Clay Allison had been working on, he scornfully added, "I wasn't the only one who noticed. One of his own pals chided him for being so brave with another man's ass and let us not forget he ran off to leave a wounded pal behind!"

"Unless they came back for him," Farnsworth pointed out, raising his voice to declare, "I want some torchlight over amidst them creekside cottonwoods, boys. Harper, Garcia, go in the house and see if you can rustle up some rags to wrap around stove faggots, broom handles or whatever. Ought to be some cooking oil you can pour over the rags ere you light up."

Longarm said the late Consuela had owned more than one oil lamp and went in to fetch the one from her bed table as the others rummaged in less familiar surroundings. The shot that had been aimed at his lit cheroot had only shattered the lamp's chimney. The coal oil sump and the thorium-coated wick were both intact. So he cast a brighter light than anyone else as he led the way into the tanglewood with the lamp held high in his left hand and the .44-40 in his gun hand sweeping ahead of them all.

The only thing wrong with the plan was that there was nobody there. Longarm spied more than one freshly broken branch, and a ranger with a torch found where somebody had slid a boot heel down the grassy bank into the water. But that was all anyone found before they were called back to Consuela's yard, and Consuela, by the arrival of Doc Fletcher and Captain Kramer in the deputy coroner's van.

So Longarm got to tell his story over again, improved a mite since he'd had time to make Consuela sound wiser and braver without saying a thing that might help the men who'd killed her escape what everyone there agreed they had coming. By the time they had the poor little thing loaded up and on her way to the morgue the old *bruja* from across the way, along with some other neighborhood Mexicans, had joined them in the road to confirm she'd been a hardworking churchgoing credit to *La Raza* and just about their favorite neighbor of all time. The older gossip from across the way confirmed what Longarm had said about some *Anglo malo* firing on Consuela's place from a corner of her own yard and volunteered without being asked that she'd always felt as if the poor *muchacha* had almost been the daughter she'd never had.

Longarm didn't laugh. He gravely assured the older woman, who really did look like a witch up close, that Miss Consuela had always spoken of *her* with great respect. He figure it was the least Consuela would have expected him to say, albeit he suspected she was laughing like hell about now if there was anything to the promises of the sky pilots about a sweet by-and-by in the sky.

It was times like these a man hoped against hope such promises might be true and, whether they were or they weren't, he'd already promised Consuela he'd pay the pricks back for whatever they'd done to a mighty fine soul.

Captain Kramer decided there was no call to posse up in the dark. They'd just established that the jaspers had splashed down the creek, unless they'd splashed the other way. That was why outlaws trying to hide their trails splashed up or down creeks, cuss their hides.

When someone pointed out how tough it could be, night or day, to cut the sign of just a few unknown men who'd likely split up to leave the scene solo, Captain Kramer growled, "That's what I just said. Could you use a lift back to the Toro Negro in the van, Longarm?"

The younger and somewhat quicker thinking lawman said, "I could use a ride into town. But I ain't so sure I ought to go back to my hired room above the saloon. I've not the least notion what they look like, or how many of them there may be. Wouldn't be fair to the Widow Whitehead to risk her life and property. Just got one gracious hostess killed and she didn't have a dog in this fight, neither!"

Kramer glanced at the van they'd just put Consuela's corpse in, as he thoughtfully replied, "I follow your drift. Had they been worried about her telling you something, they'd have killed her earlier at the chili parlor, and you did say they challenged you from the dark by name. But it ain't but two in the morning and you got to bed down *some* damn place. Get aboard and we'll work that out on the way back to town."

They did. It was easy, once they were out of earshot of the crowd and any sneaks on the other side. Once they'd helped Doc Fletcher get poor little Consuela set to drain and embalm, Kramer led Longarm to his own 'dobe up a side street from the ranger post.

As far as they could tell, not even the deputy coroner knew where Longarm meant to spend the rest of the night, and if the murderous sons of bitches *did* guess where the man they were after could be found they were up against two experienced gunfighters and a *mujer* who was half Chiso-Apache.

The Spanish word *mujer* was simply "woman" in a bilingual dictionary. When a Mexican introduced a gal as his *mujer* he generally meant she was his wife. When an Anglo-Texican introduced the woman he was living with as his *mujer*, it was best not to pursue the matter further.

Captain Kramer called his *mujer* Juanita and she wasn't bad to look at once you got over say thirty extra pounds and smoldering sloe eyes as made a man wonder whether she was fixing to go down on him or lift his hair. She and her *hombre* had naturally been in bed when his rangers came for him. So she still wore her nightgown. Or she'd put a nightgown on for company. Her long black hair was unbound for bed to hang down far as her fat ass as she bustled at her kitchen range lest it ever be said she'd send a guest to bed hungry.

Longarm was too keyed up to fall asleep in any case, and Captain Kramer likely needed a breather before he got back in bed with such a passionate-looking *mujer*. So they got to talk in more circles as they dug into her tortillas and beans with the buttermilk she warned them to drink with the grub if they meant to sleep at all before sunup.

Captain Kramer kept asking why Clay Allison seemed to take his visit so personal and all Longarm could come up with was "Why should I be any different? He was wanted for killing a lawman the first time he was reported dead and, since he showed up down here, ain't he killed five more?"

Captain Kramer slowly tolled off the names. "Weiner, Henderson, Summerhill, Page and, right, poor young Steiger. But as far as I can tell all them killings were spur of the moment, or at least without any prior warning. So he seems to have taken a more personal interest in you."

"If that was him back at poor Consuela's place tonight," Longarm pointed out, adding, "He killed Andy Steiger after declaring his love for me and it 'pears he sent two others after me alone, whether that was him leading a bigger bunch tonight or not."

Kramer washed down a chaw of tortilla and beans with

his buttermilk and observed, "He not only loves you, he *respects* you, old son. I know *I'd* think twice about a fair fight with a man of your rep, if I was sober. So, what if he made some brags drunk and had time to consider his words before you made him eat 'em?"

He belched and added, "Works for me. Daring you to come out in the moonlight when he knew damned well you weren't that dumb adds up to a sort of four-flushing approach to a gunfight, to me."

Longarm swallowed a wad of tortilla to be polite, since he wasn't hungry and if he had been, tortillas reminded him of blotting paper more than bread. A Denver gent of the Hebrew persuasion had commented to Longarm on the way a Mex tortilla reminded him of a sort of soft and floppy Jewish matzo, only not as flavorsome. To Kramer, Longarm replied, "I'll ask him when we catch him. I'm more worried about which way they went than why he behaves so peculiar. Have you ever read up on William Teach, better known as Blackbeard the Pirate?"

The older lawman laughed incredulously and confessed, "Before my time, I fear."

Longarm said, "*Fear* was what Blackbeard was out to sell, along the Carolina coast way back before the Revolution. As a pirate for fun and profit, William Teach never *killed* all that many of his victims. They mostly gave up without a fight because of the awsome rep he'd built with his skeleton flag, ferocious threats and the firecrackers going off in his bushy black hair and beard when he came over a rail with a dozen pistols in his belt to back the cutlass in one big fist and lit bomb in the other."

"You mean the famous Blackbeard was all bluff?" asked the ranger.

Longarm shook his head and explained, "No pantywaist is about to board an armed merchant ship with a lit bomb and a beard full of lit firecrackers. When they finally cornered Blackbeard, he put up a good fight and they had a time finishing him off. He never quit fighting till they cut off his head with another cutlass. My point is that he saved himself a heap of bother by *acting* even crazier than he was."

Kramer nodded knowingly and decided, "Then it's your contention that our big blond killer raiding the basin from somewhere sneaky struts and brags like so to *avoid* gunfights?"

Longarm shrugged and pointed out, "Everyone else ran off when he shot first Henderson, then Sage and Summerhill in the same saloon. Consider how things might have gone for him if anyone else in the Last Chance had felt up to joining in."

Kramer allowed he followed Longarm's drift. Then, since his *mujer* kept shooting smoke signals at Kramer and daggers at Longarm with her big sloe eyes, Longarm allowed he was feeling tuckered and she whipped him and a candlestick into a guest room with a radiant smile and considerable speed.

The room was clean, the bed was soft, and Longarm had one hell of a time falling asleep with his mind still raging about the murder of one *mujer* and mental pictures of a mightly lively looking *mujer* under the same roof at the moment.

But sleep finally came in the wee small hours, and as ever, once he was asleep, he had a tough time waking up in spite of all the noise out in the kitchen.

He could tell something big was up, though, so he swung his feet to the floor and managed to rub some sleep out of his eyes before the door was flung open and Captain Kramer was yelling, "Get dressed and let's ride! The one you nailed never made it any farther than the Last Chance Saloon! So Liam O'Hanlon and his boys are holding the son of a bitch for us!"

Chapter 22

The sardonic Corporal Arnold was waiting for them out front with another ranger and the mounts he'd saddled for them with their own shit from the rangers' tack room. Captain Kramer's tone was also sardonic as he dryly remarked, "Glad you saw fit to grace us with you presence this morning, Jose. Where were you last night when me and the whole blamed town responded to all that gunplay?"

Arnold calmly replied, "I was off duty. This old fart I ride for works my ass off by the light of day. So I generally try to get some sleep after dark."

Kramer observed, "You sure sleep sound, Jose. Did you oversleep yesterday morn when I possed up with my *night shift* to chase after those stolen mules?"

Arnold said, "You'd all rid off by the time I got to the plaza. I reported for duty on time, dang it. Was it my fault you'd all rid out before breakfast?"

Kramer said, "It was. You weren't in your usual quarters at that boardinghouse. So where are you sleeping now, in case I need your gun hand when you're suffering the delusion that a Texas Ranger ever gets to go off duty?"

Arnold didn't answer as he mounted up. Kramer mounted his own roan, and Longarm forked himself aboard the buckskin barb they'd put his army saddle on, in time to hear Captain Kramer snap, "I just asked you a question, boy!"

Arnold sullenly replied, "I heard you. I'm trying to come up with a kindly way to say it's none of your fucking business."

Longarm smiled knowlingly when Captain Kramer nodded curtly to reply, "There ain't no kindly way to put it. But I am commencing to see the light. I won't ask if she's pretty. I don't care if she gives French lessons, but she'd better not be another man's *mujer!*"

"She ain't. I just gave her my word I was no kiss and tell. Are we all riding down to the Last Chance this morning or do you mean to beg me to fix you up with sloppy seconds?"

Captain Kramer glanced wearily at Longarm to observe, "You're right. I ought to fire him. But help's hard to find on what the state of Texas is willing to pay, so *vamanos muchachos!*"

They rode out along the trail at a trot, still shaded by the cliffs to the east, to make it on down to the Last Chance in less than half an hour. As they reined in out front, Liam O'Hanlon came out to meet them with his shotgun, saying, "Is that all the help you brought, Captain? I've one of Clay Allison's boyos in me smokehouse and it's himself we've been expecting back any minute now!"

As Kramer dismounted, he modestly remarked, "If two Texas Rangers and this federal deputy can't handle your Clay Allison, the Chiso-Apaches and the Mexican Army, I'll eat shit, O'Hanlon. How come you're holding that wounded killer in your smokehouse, for Pete's sake? That don't sound constitutional, no offense."

The owner of all he surveyed at that end of the basin calmly replied, "He ain't wounded. He'd been dead for hours when the Punchboard sisters found him in the creek by the dawn's early light. I had my help hang his soaked-

171

through remains in the smokehouse with some sides of beef and venison we're curing because it's for Chrissake August in West Texas and I've never been able to stand the smell of a gut-shot human being since I served with the Irish Brigade along the Bloody Lane at Antietam!"

Longarm smiled thinly as he dismounted, saying, "Never mind about the good old days. You say I put one in his paunch? That would account for his being able to get back up, for a spell. He'd have never made four miles after he did, of course. So he must have flopped in yonder creek and the current—"

"He was shot in the head as well." O'Hanlon cut in, motioning his kid wranglers to take care of their ponies as he indicated the way to his smokehouse.

It was around the back, closer to the cliffs than his shithouses or stables. So a long streak of smoke stain had discolored the salmon limestone all the way to the shale rimrocks above. As he trailed the burly O'Hanlon, Longarm decided, "I never put but one round in the son of a bitch. If I *had* hit him once in the *head,* he'd have never called out to his pals as they lit out."

O'Hanlon shrugged carelessly and replied, "Somebody shot him in the head. Right over the eyebrow. Blew the back of his skull away."

So Longarm felt safe in deciding, "That surely couldn't have been me last night then."

Captain Kramer suggested, "Try her this way. You dropped the poor sap like you said. Whilst you were braced for more trouble, inside Miss Consuela's place, he staggered or crawled after them. But they didn't want anybody pissing and moaning and bleeding all the way to their hideout. So they put him out of his misery down the creek a piece and, as you suggested, the current carried him on down."

"I wish he'd bobbed on down Bottleneck Canyon into the fucking Rio Grande!" Liam O'Hanlon grumbled as he threw open the door of his smokehouse, stepping out of the way of the first pungent haze of smoldering corncobs as he added, "I aint making dime one out of this deal, I hope you understand!"

As he, Longarm and Arnold gingerly entered the win-dowless, reeking nine-by-six-feet chamber, Kramer told O'Hanlon he'd write him up as a concerned citizen of Texas. O'Hanlon remained outside, and who could blame him.

The sides of beef and venison he'd mentioned hung pungent and black from overhead meat hooks, along with two hams, a rasher of bacon and a human corpse about six feet in height had his booted feet been on the dirt floor. They dangled six inches above it. The meat hook in his case was through rawhide thongs some tenderhearted soul had wrapped around his neck. It hadn't hurt him at all.

"A man who'd do that to a pal would eat shit and ped-dle his own sister's pussy!" Corporal Arnold declared, striking a match for a better look at the already somewhat sooty features of the curing meat.

Longarm replied, "You'll get no argument about that from this child. I think I may recognize this one. That bitty hole in his forehead ain't much of a disguise, and the last time I saw such a face in a photograph it went with a gun for hire under the handle of Karl Beerkeg Orbach out of Galveston."

Corporal Arnold marveled, "Another fucking Dutch-man, like that Hardpan Harry Hoffmann we tangled with just the other side of the saloon the other night! How did Texas ever wind up with so many fucking Dutchmen, anyhow?"

Captain Kramer dryly replied, "Speaking only for my own family, my daddy didn't like the way Prussia kept swallowing up all the other High Dutch–speaking states and drafting married men into their damned imperial army. I think Andy Steiger's kin came across the main ocean with that Frankonian Catholic bunch offered a land grant by the king of Spain, lest Yankee Protestants horn in where his Mex subjects had reservations about Coman-che, Kiowa-Apaches and such. I've heard tell of a hired gun called Beerkeg Orbach. Heard he had a bounty hunter's license from some fool eastern court. I wish courts back east would be less free with those hunting licenses they hand out."

Arnold asked, "Are you saying this bird was *allowed* to shoot at folk like that?"

Kramer snorted, "Of course not. You can see where such notions led to, just over his left eye. But as with the late Hardpan Harry Hoffmann, the court order allowing him to pack a gun in the pursuit of no-shows and bail jumpers made it hard if not impossible for small-town lawmen to run him in on suspicion or even disarm him if he testified he was on the trail of a want."

Arnold grinned like a mean little kid at Longarm to ask him what he was wanted for.

Longarm shrugged and replied, "I'm still working on that. Seeing as a man pretending to kill on impulse seems so concentrated on this child by name, it may be he fears I have an edge on you rangers."

Kramer snapped, "Bullshit! Clay Allison's score at present adds up to five Texas Rangers and a Tex-Mex señorita, with not one deputy U.S. marshal even scratched, so far!"

Longarm said soothingly, "Give 'em time. It ain't as if they ain't been trying. I wasn't out to speak ill of the dead, Captain. I was only pointing out how *premeditated* the attacks on me have been, next to the, no offense, sort of off-the-cuff assassinations of others."

Liam O'Hanlon called in to ask if they were ready for his own help to load the partly cured corpse on his buckboard so's he could devote all his corncob smoke to the business it was intended for.

As they stepped out into the brighter light, Kramer pointed out, "Lieutenant Weiner might have been getting warm. We only sent for you after he vanished somewhere near that secret Lazy A spread old Caddo Flynn told him about."

Arnold asked, "Wasn't Weiner a Dutch name, too?"

Kramer snapped, "I just explained all that shit, asshole,

and for the record, might you be kin to the famous Arnold they called Benedict?"

Arnold protested, "Aw, come on, there was heaps of Arnolds in old George Washington's army, and only one of 'em turned out bad."

"One was enough and the Kramers of Kassel never spawned one traitor nor a single horse thief, you asshole kid!"

Embarrassed for the both of them, Longarm asked O'Hanlon about the odd name he'd used in describing his help who'd found the body.

The owner of the Last Chance said, "The Punchboard sisters don't work for anybody but themselves. Just outside my property line, in the tanglewood along the creek."

Corporal Arnold slyly suggested, "Old Liam has tried and tried to run them trash gals off, lest customers have no place to get laid in these parts and drink somewheres else."

O'Hanlon shot him a dirty look and continued, "Whatever. What the three of 'em are up to over in their brushwood jacal is no never mind of mine, and I wouldn't fuck the youngest Punchboard sister with your dick. Or, come to study on it, eat her pussy with your big mouth!"

Longarm cut in, soothingly. "We were speaking of the discovery of the late Beerkeg Orbach's body, not his sex life. So you were saying, Liam?"

O'Hanlon moved back farther to make room for his Mexican help as he said, "I wasn't there when one or the other Punchboard sister got up to squat and drop it in the creek by the dawn's early light. First I heard of it was the oldest one ranting and raving in the dooryard about a dead man down by the canyon mouth. I sent some of my stable hands to see what she was fussing about. They hauled the soaking wet son of a bitch to my front door, and I of course had them put him in this smokehouse before I sent word into town about him."

As the hired help carried the remains outside, Longarm noticed how stiff the cadaver was. Rigor mortis started setting in three or four hours after death and lasted say twelve hours after that. So the cuss had been murdered by his own pals no more than fifteen hours earlier. But that didn't add up.

Fishing out his pocket watch, Longarm announced, "It's barely six hours since I gut-shot this bird, four miles up the creek. So say he went in the water loose-jointed around three in the morning, we are faced with *early* rigor mortis, as set in after he'd come to rest in yonder creek."

They all stared as blankly at him. It was Kramer who asked him, "Who gives a flying fuck? We know it was you as shot him the first time around two. No matter how long after that his own pals finished him off, it's obvious they did. He was floundering after 'em, hurt, and calling out to them to come back. You heard him doing so, your ownself!"

Longarm said, "I did. After I'd shown them how tough it was going to be to take me and after we all heard you and half the town headed out our way. So try to picture the scene, Captain. Try to picture three or more running like hell for wherever they'd tethered their ponies and then picture them stopping, turning around and coming back to offer aid, comfort and a shot in the head to old Beerkeg there."

Kramer stared after the stiff and straight body on the buckboard bed as he decided, "I can't. You're right. They ran like rats deserting a ship on fire or they were cool enough to come back or at least wait up for that gut-shot cuss and . . . Then what? How come none of us heard the shot if they finished him off within a mile of where you'd shot him? How come they left his body to be found if they had it at their own disposal way the hell down the creek?"

"How come indeed, and why would they have laid him out straight as a soldier blue on parade, then waited at least three hours for him to stiffen before they rolled him into the creek to float on down?"

Captain Kramer sighed and said, "They told me true when they told me you were good, Longarm. Until you drew the picture for me just now, I'd forgot, or wasn't paying attention, to the way a body stiffens in it's position of repose!" He nodded at young Arnold to add, "That's what you call the position a body settles into after it's through tumbling. Position of repose."

Corporal Arnold sniffed. "I guess I know what the position of repose is. I know how to read and I've seen some dead bodies in my day."

Longarm added, "The way I read it, somebody finished him off. Then somebody laid him out as if they meant to send for Doc Fletcher to bury their pal right. Only, once they'd taken say three or more hours to study on what they'd ever tell Doc Fletcher, they decided to just chuck him in the creek and hope for his winding up in the Gulf of Mexico by way of the Rio Grande."

Captain Kramer whistled and said, "They'd have gotten away with it had the Tiswin been at flood stage. Now all we have to figure is where old Beerkeg went in. Where are you headed, old son?"

Without looking back, Longarm replied, "To talk to them Punchboard sisters about where old Beerkeg came *out*."

Chapter 23

Captain Kramer stayed with the late Beerkeg Orbach and the way-more-talkative Liam O'Hanlon. But Corporal Arnold tagged along as Longarm strode south across the cleared approaches to the Last Chance and on into the wooded funnel leading into Bottleneck Canyon. It was wooded indeed because as usual, outlets of lakes or floodplains tended to be marshy, with high water tables all through the year.

The cottonwoods that grew most anywhere there was groundwater had alder, big leaf maple, crack willow and such horning in on them along the soggier banks of Tiswin Creek down yonder. Trailing single file along the narrow muddy footpath into the tanglewood, Corporal Arnold was softly singing, to the tune of "Lone Prairie,"

"They came by ones and they came by twos,
As far and wide they spread the news,
That she was young, and horny too,
And charged two bits, for her ring dang doo!"

So Longarm paused to turn and ask, "How well might you know them ladies in the trees ahead of us, Jose?"

The ranger scoffed. "*Ladies?* Calling the Punchboard sisters *white trash* is a compliment they don't deserve! I don't know *none* of them to *talk* to. I hear they serve greasers, and worse! They got run out of Fort Stanton for clapping up the Ninth Cav and—"

Longarm cut in, not unkindly but in dead earnest. "Since you don't know them, I'd be obliged if you'd let me canvas them alone, Jose."

The younger lawman protested, "What did I say wrong? I have only been repeating what is generally known about them Punchboard sisters."

Longarm said, "You've told me what folk say about them in these parts and I'm obliged for the insight, Jose. Now I want to talk to possibly already hostile witnesses, and with all due respect you do have a way of inspiring hostility. So I aim to move on in alone."

Arnold said, "Aw, shit, I won't say nothing to rile the raddled whores, pard."

Longarm said, "I know you won't. I wasn't *suggesting* I aim to move on in alone. I *said* I aimed to move on in alone and, like the Indian chief said, I have spoken!"

The ranger protested, "What do you expect me to do here all by my ownself, jerk off like a fool kid?"

"Whatever tickles your fancy," Longarm replied with a shrug before he suggested, "You might go on back and see if Captain Kramer has any use for you. No offense, but I don't, right now."

So each man strode his own direction, Corporal Arnold smiling mean as he sang out,

"They came by night and they came by day,
They fucked her in the barn on a bed of hay,
They gave her the clap, and the blue balls, too,
And that was the ruin of her ring dang doo!"

"Kids", muttered Longarm as he ducked under the low limb to enter deeper shade, with his derringer palmed. Canvasing for evidence with a drawn .44–40 could get things off to an awkward start. But walking cold with empty hands into the situation he suspected up ahead could take fifty years off a lawman's life.

Liam O'Hanlon had made mention of a jacal, singular, likely meaning he hadn't been over this way lately. For Longarm could make out the outlines of four such improvised shacks through the fluttering leaves ahead as he followed the well-beaten path to the Punchboard sisters' pathetic wayside diversion.

Jacal translated literally as "shack," but along the border the word most often denoted a construction combining the worst features of a log cabin with an Indian wickiup. You made one by driving saplings into the mud to enclose a modest square. Then you wove slender whips of alder, cottonwood or whatever through your upright poles to form half-ass walls offering little shelter to anything but the gaze of Peeping Toms. A more substantial roof fashioned from branches, twigs and cattail or tule reeds kept out lighter rain whilst holding in enough smoke to discourage bats if not bugs from moving in.

Considering their chosen line of work, the three sisters appeared to have built, or had built for them three little piggy shacks and a bigger shelter used for storage or to stable the mounts of customers as they enjoyed a change of mounts.

Longarm called out, "Hello the camp!" as he moved within pistol range, hoping he wasn't calling during busy business hours.

An oddly elfin dishwater-blond waif in a flour-sack shift peeked around a corner at him, saw he was alone and apparently unarmed, and grinned like hell. Not a pretty sight when a gal had a harelip.

An older, not as disfigured but not as pretty sister, with darker hair, appeared behind the first one, wearing a fancier but dirtier red kimono she hadn't bothered to fasten too securely. She was the one who trilled, "Wake up, Cup Cakes, we got a customer!"

Longarm managed a wistful expression as he strode on in, flashing his wallet and badge with his left hand and calling out, "If only I could say that was true, ma'am. But

180

I fear I'm here in the name of the law to have a word with you all about that body you found earlier this morning."

The harelipped one wailed, "I told you it would be best to shove him out in deeper water and send him on his way!"

They were joined by a stark-naked-and-proud-of-it natural brown-head with henna-rinsed hair—you could tell, when a gal stood stark in broad daylight. The almost as well-built but hard-faced older sister hissed, "Stick to cocksucking and don't spill another word, Cup Cakes! I told you both I'd do the talking and I meant what I told you, damn your loose lips!"

Then she smiled at Longarm as if he hadn't been there listening, and said, "Come on in for coffee and cake then, Handsome. For you'll find us three honest working girls without a fucking thing to hide!"

The stark naked Cup Cake started to say something but recalled her big sister's warning. Longarm laughed anyhow. It seemed obvious she'd been about to point out she wasn't hiding her fucking thing.

The older sister invited Longarm inside for refreshments or for anything else as might be his pleasure that morning.

He said, "I told you I was here on business, ma'am. I'd like you all to show me now where you found that dead man this morning."

As the three of them escorted him to the nearby banks of the creek, he got a better understanding of the way their semicircle of brush hovels nestled on a patch of cleared damp 'dobe soil surrounded on three sides by dense second growth of mostly willow, with scattered clumps of cottonwood.

He saw that despite their slovenly dress, or the lack of same, they'd recently swept the bare dirt, still damp in the shade since the rain they'd had two nights earlier, the way a house-proud homestead gal might sweep the dirt floor of her soddy. By the time they stood in the sunlight at the water's edge, he'd learned that their names, or more likely their professional handles, were Bunny, Honey and Cup Cakes. He didn't ask why they'd been given the family name of Punchboard.

Country humor could make up in pungency what it lacked in sophistication. It seemed their own notions to dub the harelip as Bunny and the well-built but spiteful older one as Honey, and Cup Cakes would have fit the henna-rinsed one had she been wearing clothes.

Honey Punchboard pointed out that where creek water was frothing betwixt two half-submerged boulders, the creek wasn't more than shin deep anywhere in sight. She said, "That's where the poor man was stuck when I came here at dawn to . . . fetch some water."

Longarm asked if they'd drug the body up on the bank and, if so, where, calmly noting, "I don't see any drag marks, heel marks, marks of any kind, Miss Honey."

She glibly replied, "I waded out just long enough to see he was dead. You don't need to be a doctor when a man's been shot in the head like so. I let him lie and fetched help from the Last Chance. You can ask them if he wasn't out there in the creek when they came down to get him. They left all sorts of drag marks, heel marks and tobacco spit by the time they were done. So we swept up after them. We like to keep things neat down here in case we have . . . guests."

Longarm nodded thoughtfully and confided, "Last time I saw the same man alive, over three miles up the creek, he was wearing a six-gun. I don't suppose you noticed one out yonder in the shallows. He wasn't wearing one in O'Hanlon's smokehouse just now."

Honey Punchboard looked away in thought and decided to say, "I didn't notice. We never went through his pockets, either, before we reported our finding him out yonder. If he went into the water with anything he hasn't got on him now, somebody else must have taken it. Can we go inside now? It's broad day here and try as I might I can't get Cup Cakes to put no clothes on."

As Longarm followed them back into the shade, Cup Cakes laughed dirty and demanded, "Why put duds on when you're only fixing to take 'em off again and it's warm inside and out?"

Longarm paid her no mind as he observed to her older sister, "I see you swept some horse apples into the creek, too. It's just as well you ladies are downstream from O'Hanlon and most everyone else in the basin. There ain't nobody settled further down in Bottleneck Canyon, right?"

Honey Punchboard stammered, "Horse apples? Who said anything about horse apples, Handsome?"

He said, "You don't have to be so formal. You can call me Deputy Long. As to horse apples, you generally wind up with some on the ground wherever you leave a horse tethered for any time. Before you dig yourself in deeper, you can tell when a horse has been tethered to cottonwood saplings because the tether rubs bark off and the horse browses all the cottonwood leaves it can get at."

She tried, "Oh, *those* horse apples? Now that you bring 'em to mind, I do recall a horny young cowboy who left his pony tethered by the brook near fodder and water so's he could take his own pleasures for some time, inside, with the three of us."

"We offer group rates," volunteered the naked Cup Cakes. Bunny just giggled. Not a pretty sight.

As they led him inside one of the jacals to sit him at a trestle table and pour him a mug of pulque, Honey Punchboard confided, "We can service any man who needs some Old Fashioned, French, Greek or Roman. Cup Cakes is our expert at Old Fashioned; Bunny there gives French lessons with her unusual lips that men ride for miles to enjoy. I'm easygoing enough to take it Greek, if that's what they want."

"Who does it *Roman*?" asked Longarm, interested despite himself.

Honey Punchboard calmly replied, "All three of us, at once, and men ride in from even farther for a taste of that."

The harelipped Bunny simpered, "I'm the one who gets to *taste* the most. Cup Cakes kisses 'em on the mouth

183

while I suck 'em off, with Honey biting on their nipples."

Cup Cakes added, "They like to feel me and Honey up as they lay back and just enjoy us Roman all over 'em."

Knowing Professor Pasteur's bugs couldn't live in alcohol, and aiming to be polite, Longarm sipped a taste of their Mex pulque, a cactus home brew that looked like watered-down okra slime but tasted like awful beer. Then he set the mug aside to tell the three of them firmly but not unkindly, "You ladies have been fibbing to me. To keep from burning all your bridges, I'd like you to listen tight and heed my words before you say one more word."

"What are you talking about?" flared Honey Punch-board, adding, "Is this the thanks we get for reporting that dead body to the law? We didn't have to report *shit,* you know! Like Bunny suggested, we could have just rolled him into deeper water and let him bob on down to the Rio Grande!"

Longarm said, "No, you couldn't. Rigor mortis had set in and the rocks half-submerged in the shallow current wouldn't carry his stiff body off as you'd planned. So you had to explain evidence you couldn't get rid of and—"

"Not true! Not true! I don't know what you're talking about! Are you some sort of do-gooder trying to run poor but honest working girls out of here? Did that Shanty Irish Liam O'Hanlon put you up to this?"

Longarm said, "I asked you to hush up and listen. So hush up and listen, Miss Honey. We both know O'Hanlon makes certain everybody who stops by his Last Chance hears how easy it is to get laid over here by the creek. But, for the record, you ladies are squatting without title on public land, not on O'Hanlon's claim. So any agent of the U.S. Government, namely me, could have you run out of here with one wire to the Bureau of Land Management. Are you with me so far?"

When she didn't answer, Longarm said, "*Bueno.* Now let's talk about the way I put things together down this way."

Taking another sip of pulque, Longarm said, "In the beginning three or four . . . customers left their ponies here in your care, where not another soul in the basin would imagine they might be. It was a long walk in riding boots, but they figured they were up against a chosen target who'd proven he was tough to sneak up on. So they snuck over three miles, shin deep in yonder creek, and used it as their escape route when things didn't go as planned closer to town."

"He knows! He knows!" whimpered the harelip. Her older sister told her to shut up and added, "He's only guessing!"

Longarm nodded gravely and said, "That's true, Miss Honey. I'm only guessing they'd have hardly told three whores, no offense, what they were really up to. I'm only guessing they'd agreed to meet back here after splitting up to get away from us. I'm only guessing Beerkeg Orbach joined them here, wounded mortal and unable to ride on with 'em. I'm only guessing they finished him off and left you ladies in a purple funk it took you hours to snap out of. Then I'm only guessing that by the time you'd decided to just help yourselves to his valuables and leave him to the creek to worry about, rigor mortis had set in and the shallow current refused to carry him away, so I guess you had to come up with another plan and I guess it just didn't work."

Honey Punchboard softly asked, "What do you guess might happen if we were to come clean, Deputy Long?"

Longarm said, "I guess I might feel I owed you something."

Chapter 24

As Longarm strode out of the trees with Beerkeg Orbach's gunbelt in his left hand, he was met by Captain Kramer, who said, "I feared you'd surrendered your fair white body to the charms of the wicked sisters. Where'd you get that Schofield?"

Longarm said, "They surrendered it to me. Let's talk about that. Know I've no authority to offer immunity from the Texas courts, but I had to tell them I'd see what I could do."

The Texas lawman said, "I know how to offer a deal for information. I figured you might. That's how come I sent Arnold on ahead with the body. Jose's a good old boy, but he did have a mouth on him to begin with and it ain't getting more discreet with experience. What did you get out of them whores?"

Longarm said, "There were five. Riding in from part unknown on Spanish saddle mules instead of ponies. I'll save descriptions for when the two of us question O'Hanlon in yonder saloon. The Punchboard sisters have been having a desperate time of it and word must have gotten around. They swear they ain't really clapped up, but whether or not they are, business has been so slow of late they've been living on beans and drinking pulque."

Kramer nodded, and as the two of them headed for the Last Chance, he observed, "Riders of the Owlhoot Trail have been known to hole up with whores when business is *booming*. Did they say how long the rascals were staying with 'em right under our noses?"

Longarm said, "From late the night before last to the wee small hours of this morning. They never served Hardpan Harry. Only those Mexicans riding with him dropped in on them the afternoon before Jose Arnold, O'Hanlon and me cleaned their plows over yonder. So the first bunch might have recommended the Punchboard sisters as a trail stop on the local Owlhoot Trail, if they were all riding for the same outfit."

Captain Kramer said, "Well, of course they had to be riding for the same outfit. That fucking Clay Allison is bossing the whole shebang if he ain't fronting for a more sneaky mastermind!"

Longarm said he was glad to see the older lawman had an open mind and added, "I agree there ought to be some common thread to all these strange riders in an otherwise remote part of nowheres, no offense. I just can't make the pieces fit into any sensible pattern, yet."

Liam O'Hanlon was waving them in from his doorway as Longarm went on, "Sticking to what's now known about last night. That last bunch left their mounts in the care of their gracious hostesses to pussyfoot on up the basin after this child. I can't say, yet, whether or not somebody else tipped them to where I was . . . interviewing Miss Consuela. They could have been watching her chili parlor, or just as likely the Western Union, from a distance. Since gunning me in town would have been more risky, they watched and waited whilst I walked the lady home. Then they waited till they figured I was . . . relaxed, and moved in for the kill."

Kramer nodded. "Killing the Mex gal and getting Beerkeg Orbach killed in the process."

Longarm said, "I never killed Orbach. I only gut-shot him. When they saw the jig was up, they scattered in the

187

dark to make it back on foot to where they'd left their mules. They waited for Orbach of course. But when he showed up too badly hurt to ride with them, the leader of the bunch, Miss Honey said he might have been a breed, shot Orbach all the way and they took his mount with them as they lit out. The confused whores layed Orbach out neater on the floor as they went through the motions with damp rags, saw they were wasting their time, and dithered until dawn about what they ought to do about him. They were afraid we'd think *they* shot him. I promised they wouldn't even be charged with withholding evidence, federal, if they'd come clean. So they confessed they'd tried to get rid of the evidence by rolling Orbach in the creek and sweeping away all the hoofprints and the mule shit. But the unbending body hung up on the rocks in the shallows, and so, before someone rode by to spot the body out in the creek within spitting distance of their camp, they decided they'd best report it, changing the details just a mite."

Captain Kramer allowed their tale was good enough for Texas, seeing they'd seen fit to tidy it up some. By then they were within earshot of O'Hanlon in the doorway. Longarm felt no call to warn a fellow lawman not to repeat their conversation to a civilian.

Liam O'Hanlon declared the bar was open for business but the drinks were on the house as he led them inside, adding, "One of my *muchachos* just told me something you might be able to use, gents. He says he might have heard a pistol shot, not too far off, around three in the morning."

The two lawmen exchanged glances. Kramer decided, "I reckon I could stagger three miles an hour, gut-shot, if I was really worried my pals might leave me behind."

Longarm silenced him with a look and asked the saloon keeper what direction that single pistol shot might have come from.

As O'Hanlon moved around to the back of the bar, he replied, "Can't say. Never heard it, my own self. I asked the kid that same question and he handed me a *¿Quien* *sabe?* He said with the way the nearby cliffs bounce loud sounds around, the shot he might have heard might have come from any direction. You want to question him?"

Captain Kramer said, "Not now. We already knew somebody shot old Beerkeg in the head betwixt two in the morning and dawn." Then he turned to Longarm to add, "What was that you said before about some descriptions, old son?"

As O'Hanlon slid his Maryland rye across the bar to him with its beer chaser, Longarm said, "You'd have said so had you known Orbach from earlier, Liam. But might you have served a hatchet-faced breed wearing blue denim much like myself, two average-faced Anglos dressed as natural looking, with the third Anglo dressed more like a Mex, in a bolero jacket and charro pants, under as Mexican a sombrero like the mysterious Mex I shot in town earlier had on?"

When O'Hanlon said, "Ain't certain. We serve heaps of riders over the course of time and I ain't always the one behind this bar."

Longarm tried, "They were riding Spanish saddle mules."

O'Hanlon brightened and said, "I'd recall saddle mules, if any had been tethered out front recent. All any of my regulars seems to talk about these days is mules. With the Apache out in force this summer and the U.S. Cav and Mex *Federales* patrolling the border like pals for a change, both armies are chewing and spitting out muleflesh as fast as it can be replaced, at a handsome price."

He poured himself a boilermaker as he added, "Since you can't sell a mule at any price, once it's been stolen, you might say mules have been a topic of interest along this bar and . . . No, I haven't seen any tied up out front of late."

Longarm asked anyone there who cared to answer about the trail down Bottleneck Canyon, explaining, "When I came up it in the mail coach a few days back, all I noticed to either side was steep canyon walls. You gents would know if I missed any side canyons, right?"

Captain Kramer flatly stated, "You didn't. The creek runs through a cleft just wide enough for white water and the narrow trail you drove in along. The canyon walls of which you speak are volcanic tufa, not Swiss Cheesey limestone. If the mule-riding sons of bitches we've been talking about lit out down Bottleneck Canyon, they had nowheres to turn off before they got to the old Spanish Camino del Rio along the Rio Grande. So why don't you and me ride back to Tanktown and wire up the border to, say, Castolon and down the border to let's say Santa Elena and just ask if anybody's seen four strangers with five saddle mules?"

"Worth a try," said Longarm, swilling some suds thoughtfully before adding, "but wouldn't you cross over into the Chihuahua Desert if you were running scared as all that?"

Kramer finished as much of his own chaser as he cared to and said, "It won't hurt to ask by wire, and I don't know about you, but I was headed back to town in any case. Are you coming with me or would you as soon ride down Bottleneck Canyon after possibles? They can't have more than a five- or six-hour lead on you, and that buckskin from our remuda can surely overtake a saddle mule with a five- or six-hour lead over rough and rocky range."

"I wish I could feel sure they'd lit out that far." Longarm sighed as he drifted for the door after the older lawman. He didn't have to explain.

Kramer nodded soberly and observed, "Clay Allison does seem to have a hard-on for you in particular, old son. What do you reckon he's so pissed about?"

Longarm thought about that as O'Hanlon's stable hands met them out front with the mounts they'd rode in on.

Once they'd forked themselves into their saddles and settled some, Longarm said, "I just can't make that piece fit. In both incarnations, quick-draw artists answering to Clay Allison have seemed way more than willing to shoot it out any time, any place, with any lawman. Before I got here, he'd shot it out face to face with three of your rangers, if not Lieutenant Weiner as well, somewhere in the

190

hills. Slim Putnam says the big blond gimp beat poor Andy Steiger face to face in as fair a fight as one can stage betwixt a young pup and a mad cur-dog. Liam O'Hanlon back yonder heard the frothing-at-the-mouth killer declare his intentions to kill me fair and square as well. Yet to date I have yet to lay eyes on the bully of this basin. Why did he issue a personal invite and then send hired guns after me? We're still working on some of the names. But the two we've names for were both professional gunfighters, as I suspect your Clay Allison by any name has to be. Does any of what I just said make a lick of sense to you, Captain?"

As they headed back to town, the sun was peeking over the rimrocks above, but the trail still ran cool in the shade of the cliffs to the east. Kramer took some time of his own to study the picture puzzle in his head before he decided, "In spite of his big mouth when he's drunk, he ain't got the balls when he's sober. At the risk of giving you a swelled head, Longarm, you've a mighty scary rep in you own right. Clay Allison's good. He knows he's good. But he's afraid you may be *gooder*. So, having made his brag and knowing others expect a man who says he aims to kill a man to *kill* him, he's sent faces you might not have recognized so easy to see if they could get the jump on you."

Longarm fumbled out a cheroot as he pointed out, "Back up and study what you just now said. I *did* recognize Hardpan Harry Hoffmann and Beerkeg Orbach on sight. They were both notorious guns for hire, and I may well have recognized others in the bunch, up closer, seeing birds of a feather ride together."

He lit his smoke and added, "None of the Mexicans I've had to shoot so far looked familiar. That hatchet-faced killer described by the Punchboard sisters as a breed could have been Mex, dressed Anglo. But, shit, we've know all along the mysterious stranger declaring himself the late Clay Allison rode into your basin with some Mexicans and . . . *What* in thunder am I *talking* about, Captain?"

Kramer said, "Beats the shit out of me. The more you talk the less sense it all makes. But where in the U.S. Constitution does it say a drunk has to make sense? We both know more than half the men hanged dropped through the trap still wondering what the fuck that had all been about! Men who think rational, by definition, don't do irrational things. Trying to fathom the motives of a lunatic can feel like chasing butterflies without a net. Blindfolded."

Longarm said, "Mean drunks acting on their own don't have to make sense. When you hire one man to gun another you have to offer him a sensible reason, Captain."

Kramer asked, "What's wrong with offering him *money*? A hired gun is a man willing to gun another man for money. He don't much care why you want the other man dead as long as you're willing to meet his price."

Longarm nodded but asked, "What would you say the current price for gunning lawmen might be, Captain? We ain't talking sheep herders or nesters underfoot here. After that, somebody with more money than brains seems to be hiring quantity as well as quality. I can't speak for the ones we haven't named yet, but Hardpan Harry and Beerkeg Orbach were in the business more for the profit than the fun, and it's way safer to gun a bail jumper for the bounty than a lawman for pure blood money. So we're talking real money for heavy labor with a gun, and leave us not forget they've been coming at this child in *bunches*!"

Kramer said, "I follow your drift. There must be more money in the stealing of mules than anyone imagined, Apache scare or no Apache scare! The son of a bitch has surely paid out a fortune in front money, and there you still are, bright eyed and bushy tailed! So by now he must be mad as hell, if not half-broke! What do you reckon he'll try next, old son?"

Longarm said, "I sure hope he doesn't come to his senses and just light out. For I've no idea what he looks like or what his real name might be, do you?"

Captain Kramer said, "Not hardly, seeing him and me

are both still alive. I'd quit whilst I was ahead and run for it, in his place. But I've always had more sense than your avearge lunatic. So he just may go on doing whatever he's been doing till we catch him doing it."

Having agreed that was about the size of it, the two lawmen rode on into town. Captain Kramer invited Longarm to dinner. He allowed he wanted to change his sweaty socks and underwear and freshen up a mite at the Toro Negro, having left his saddlebags yonder. So they parted friendly at the plaza, but when Longarm reined in out front of the Toro Negro, the Widow Whitehead was braced in her doorway, fat arms folded and scowling like she was mad as hell.

As he dismounted, she blared for all the world to hear, "How dare you darken my door again, you infernal Mexican fucker!"

To which Longarm could only reply with a sheepish smile, "Which Mexican are we talking about, Miss Flo?"

Chapter 25

Almost smiling in spite of herself, the fat redhead demanded, "How many Mexicans attended that secret meeting you told me you were headed for, you infernal miscegenist? I had your things sent over to the ranger post and I'll thank you for the key to that room upstairs, now!"

Longarm felt no call to argue. He hadn't wanted the killers after him smoking up the Toro Negro to begin with. He took out the room key, and when she refused to reach for it, he refused to be as spiteful and placed it on the flat upright post of the hitching rail before he remounted, tugged his hat brim to her and rode on. She might have called something after him. He never looked back. Nothing a man could say at such times beat leaving without a word.

When he returned the buckskin barb to the ranger post, he found his saddlebags and bedroll waiting for him in their tack room. So he lashed them to his McClellan, with his Winchester and canteens, reflecting that he was ready to go, mayhaps a tad slower, no matter which way the next red herring led him.

He might have taken Captain Kramer up on that invite to a noon dinner and mayhaps a few more winks in their guest room during the coming noon-to-four siesta. But the tack room swamper handed him a perfumed envelope he said a lady had left there for whenever Custis Long got back. That's what she'd called him, Custis Long, so he opened it up.

The vanilla-colored and jasmine-scented note inside was from Rose Bradford, out to the Flying B. Longarm knew she'd bought the perfumed, handcrafted paper off some Mex peddler. They made jasmine-scented beeswax candles and candied rose petals down Mexico way, too.

Rose had written they had something to talk about that she didn't want to put on paper, and allowed she'd recieve him any hour he might see fit to ride on out. So he borrowed a bay mare from the ranger's remuda, saddled and bridled it with his own gear and rode on out.

It was after noon when he reined into her dooryard, paying no mind to her baying yard dogs at first, but idly wondering how come Rose had not seen fit to hush 'em by the time one of her stable boys had led his borrowed mount out of sight.

At the front door, a matronly Mex maid told Longarm the old folk had been fed and put away for *La Siesta* whilst *La Patrona* saw to some mule matters out back. The *mucama* said her boss lady was expecting him and wanted him to join her out back whenever he might arrive. She whistled up a younger servant, a gal of say fourteeen, and directed her, in the version of Spanish spoken in those parts, to show their guest the way.

The *muchacha* did, and never batted an eye when they came upon a scene in the stud barn that Queen Victoria might not have found so amusing, living as she did so far removed from the grits of the late Victorian era.

Having a mind to think for himself and having grown up in the same age of steam and horsepower, Longarm understood that the late Victorians were not the two-faced hypocrites some of their own modern writers such as Oscar Wilde and Mr. George Bernard Shaw were trying to make out. They were trying to act *civilized* in spite of the natural world they were stuck with. It was all very well for dudes who dwelt where modern plumbing flowed to snicker at the way proper Victorian ladies could step over horseshit, cowshit, dogshit, pigshit, most any sort of shit in your average city street without breaking stride or appearing to notice. White-collar workers in such parts of the late Victorian world as London Town or New York City were already getting so used to riding home on commuter trains that it *surprised* them when they saw shit piles or dead cats down the road ahead. But out west of say the Hudson River, folk perforce had to just not face the facts of life going on all around them. Hence a maiden fair who preferred to have her piano legs called limbs could set a porch swing licking ice cream without seeming to notice the dogs fucking on her front lawn.

Miss Rose naturally knew that comical burro standing on a box was fucking the Tennessee Walker her stable hands were helping the burro rape. For she was supervising the operation. But she turned to Longarm as if she was looking up from knitting socks to say, "Oh, I'm so glad you got my note. I'll be with you in a moment. We're almost done here."

That was for certain, Longarm thought, trying to keep a poker face as the lathered little Spanish jackass was humping and pumping fit to bust as it hee-hawed in triumph, and judging from the way she'd commenced to move her way bigger rump, the she-horse didn't mind as much as she was letting on. He warned his own privates not to be silly as he found his curious mind wondering what it might be like to fuck a mare in heat, seeing their big old ring dang doos were so twitchy, as well as oversized for a man's organ grinder.

He knew more than one man had tried. You got twenty years and a dishonorable discharge for trying that in the U.S. Cav, whilst the British Army *hung* you. Albeit they did say Frederick the Great had decreed that any cavalryman who fucked his mount should simply be transferred to the infantry.

He tried not to wonder if the cool ash blonde, watching, as if she was window shopping, that mare taking all that jackass donging, ever wondered what it might be like to fuck anything that serious. Longarm had read an under-the-counter book called *The Golden Ass*, about an ancient Roman pimp-slave who'd trained his pet jackass to pleasure rich Roman ladies with its more than man-sized organ grinder. He wondered if Rose Bradford had ever read *The Golden Ass*, seeing she was in the business of training the critters to fuck, and if so, just how tempting she'd found the likely impractical notion.

Then he wondered if his own hard-on showed, his jeans being worn so thin down yonder, and moved off as if to light a smoke and be not all that interested in the fornication of any species.

When Rose joined him in the breezeway a few minutes later, breathing as if she'd been doing at least some of the work, her voice was calm as if she'd just put the kettle on. He hoped his was, too, as he asked what she had to declare that she couldn't put down on her perfumed paper.

She said, "Let's talk about it in the house. Is it true that big bully Clay Allison has declared a personal feud with you and sent other men right into town to stalk you?"

He allowed that seemed about the size of it as they entered by way of her kitchen door. The household help had likely retired to their own quarters for *La Siesta*, because you could have heard a pin drop in the stillness all around.

As he followed wherever she was leading, Longarm asked what the army was paying for an unbroken, unbranded mule at say Presidio or up at Fort Stanton.

She didn't sound pleased as she replied, "We can dicker up or down a mite, but they keep saying we're offering Spanish saddle mules worth no more than forty to sixty dollars. Why do you ask?"

He said, "Trying to estimate profits and loss along the Owlhoot Trail, Miss Rose. The hidden numbers mostly lie in the uncertain costs of getting livestock to market. A half-wild steer you can buy in Texas for five or ten dollars can be sold in New York City for sixty or more. But as many an optimist has learned along many a cattle trail over many a year, it can cost you modest or it can cost you too much by the time you sell your beef on the hoof at a profit."

She said, "Tell a West Texas girl something she didn't learn at her daddy's knee. We *eat* all the cows we raise along Tiswin Creek, and try to sell our far more profitable saddle or draft stock, mostly mules, as close to their home range as possible."

Longarm agreed that made perfect business sense and added, "I've been trying in vain to justify the Lazy A's margins of profit and loss. Say them twenty head they got away with the other night might have been bought by the army for say eight hundred dollars, the thieves should have quit whilst they were ahead. What are we doing in this here bedroom, Miss Rose?"

She sat on the bedstead and patted the covers beside her invitingly as she said, "We were talking about profits and loss. Don't you think eight hundred dollars is a lot of money, Custis?"

Sitting down at her side, he answered, "I'd be lucky to make that much in a year with poker winnings thrown in. That's how come others steal stock. They aim to wind up rich. Nobody with a lick of sense rides the Owlhoot Trail a mile farther than he has to. Many a present-day cattle baron got his start as a cow thief. But he knew from the start he was out to be a cattle baron, not a convicted felon. You mind the famous Uncle John Chisum of the Jinglebob, up New Mexico way?"

She wrinkled her pert nose and allowed her daddy had said bad things about the owner of the swamping Jinglebob herd.

Longarm said, "I know him. He ain't such a bad old cuss, these days. But they do say Uncle John got his start trailing Texas cows he'd never paid for up the Pecos to horn in on smaller or less ferocious stockmen. Had gun waddies such as Dick Brewer, Charlie Boudrie and the currently more famous Billy the Kid pulling his chestnuts out of the fire. But now that he's about the biggest stockman in the Pecos Valley, old Uncle John has settled back to let others call him a pillar of the community, offering proper bills of sale on all that beef he drives up the Goodnight Trail to market. Are you with me so far?"

She leaned a tad closer as she confessed she wanted to be, but had no idea what he was talking about.

He tossed his hat aside as he explained, "Men like John Chisum, who now dominates the upper Pecos Valley, or Ewen Cameron, who started the whole western cattle industry by raiding Mexican herds in the name of Texas, weren't out to be *mean*. They were out to be *rich*. They may have been mean as they *had* to be, getting started, but once they had their good starts, they tidied up their manners to enjoy the spoils of their range wars. So why ain't this cuss who calls his fool self Clay Allison following the natural progression of a serious stock thief? By now he must have thousands of dollars' worth of stolen stock hidden out in his secret canyon or already on their way to market. So why in blue blazes can't he simply lay low long enough to get rich and respectable?"

Rose said, "He's *crazy* mean, like everyone says, and it's not safe for you to board above that Toro Negro Saloon, where anybody might be planning to slip up the back stairs to slit your throat in your bed!"

He managed not to grin dirty as he confided, "I ain't boarding with the Widow Whitehead no more, Miss Rose."

She said, "I know. You'll be staying out here, with us, where they can't get at you, for as long as you're down this way."

He said, "No I ain't, Miss Rose. It ain't as if I don't appreciate such a kind offer. But two can only keep a secret if one of them is dead. So word would get around in no time that I was holed up with you out here."

She tossed her head defiantly and said, "I can deal with gossip. The good Lord knows I've had to. By now you'll have heard about me and Marv Parker, right?"

He said, "No, ma'am, and I ain't sure I want to. I've never been one for the small-town gossip as hovers around pretty ladies the natural way flies hover around other sweet things."

She said, "Marv Parker was our foreman before my daddy fired him and sent me off to a Frisco finishing school to get over him. I was awfully cross with my daddy at the time, but looking back, a thirty-year-old hand who'd deserted a wife and two kids in Tucson had no business breaking in a fifteen-year-old country girl."

Longarm cut in. "Miss Rose, I just now said I've never been one for such gossip."

She shrugged and said, "By the time I had to come home and take care of this spread and my poor old parents, I was studying art out Frisco way and running with a crowd that would have found poor child-molesting Marv a joke. So let's not worry about my reputation, and if it's your own virtue you're so worried about, that door locks on its inside and I'm as interested in keeping you alive out here as I may be in seducing you!"

She looked away and added in a small, self-mocking tone, "*Almost* as interested, anyway."

Longarm chuckled fondly and assured her, "I could top your tale of slap and tickle with older playmates way back when, and Lord knows you'd have no hard row to hoe if my *virtue* was the matter before the house, you pretty little thing. But the bunch that's after me are mad-dog vicious and coyote sneaky. So I ain't about to risk you or your elders getting caught in the crossfire, should they choose to strike again."

She said, "We heard how that poor waitress at the chili parlor was killed while you were escorting her home in the dark after midnight. But these walls were built thick with Chiso-Apache neighbors in mind, and aside from the four grown men and two tough kids I have working for me, I'm as handy with a gun as many a man, so . . ."

"So the answer is still no." He cut in, adding, "Before you blubber up and rain all over me, I like you. I like you as much as a man in my tumbleweed line of work can afford to like any gal. For I've seen how you are to your help as well as your elders, and it purely beats all how two ladies can hear the same gossip and tally it up in such different ways. The reason I ain't staying here is twofold. First off, I don't want anyone off the Flying B hurt and I don't want those mule-stealing waitress-shooting rascals to have the least notion where I might be after dark."

"You have to bed down *somewhere* after dark," she protested.

Longarm said, "There's somewheres all around in every direction when the nights are warm and dry and a man has a bedroll lashed to his saddle."

"You mean to camp out, alone, with that whole gang after you?"

He said, "Sure I do. Why should I be the only one worried after dark? Let *them* do some worrying, never sure whether I'm bedded down for the night a good many miles away or hovering just outside their hideout, fixing to bust in shooting as they lie there counting sheep and wondering how come it's so hard to fall asleep of late."

She smiled at the picture and asked, "Have you any idea where the gang's hideout might be, Custis?"

He said, "Not hardly. If I did, I'd have already busted in with the rangers right behind me. But they don't know for sure that I don't know, and why should I be the only one having a tough time falling asleep, or rising in the dead of night to pussyfoot about, should that be my fancy?"

She faked a shudder and said mockingly, "Ooh, you're so scary. I guess I see what you're talking about, but I still wish I could talk you into staying with . . . us, for just a little while."

So it seemed so natural to take her up on that kind offer that he had her in his arms before he'd studied on it. Yet just before he kissed her he felt obliged to warn, "Miss Rose, I'm down here on a field mission as might not last worth mention, and if the truth be known I've no more prospects than your average foreman, even if I was the marrying kind."

She was the one who unbalanced the both of them to fall on back across the mattress as she husked, "Oh, for Pete's sake, Custis Long, I'm not asking you to marry me. I'm only asking you to fuck me!"

Chapter 26

Judging by the position she'd suggested on her own, Rose Bradford hadn't really been feeling as detached and clinical as she let on, out back in the breeding shed. For damned if she didn't try for a tight imitation of a mare in heat, with her upper weight held stiff-armed above the matress and her bare feet planted on the braid rug and her beautiful bare back arched to thrust her beautiful bare ass up for Longarm's pleasure. He played the part of her jackass, without the need of a box to stand on whilst he held a trim hipbone in either fist, to admire the sight of his love-slicked shaft sliding in and out as she tried to dilate and clamp down in the inspiring manner of an excited she-critter.

Human anatomy dictated limitations to the fantasy, of course, and it was her idea, with his approval, to finish the old-fashioned way, belly to belly and swapping lies with their spit as they came together so hard it got scary.

She moaned, "Oh, yesss! This *is* the best way when all is said and done. Please don't take it out just yet, Custis. I'm just not ready to come back down to earth."

He kissed her throat as he rested his hips between her lean horsewoman's thighs, with his still throbbing twig up inside her toasted marshmallow, and declared he hadn't planned on riding off just yet.

Rose held him closer and crooned, "I'd forgotten how nice it could be to just *do* it, without contortions. Isn't it silly how we make up all sorts of crazy positions we're just dying to try, alone in bed with nobody to play with but ourselves? Now that I've done it, I guess mares don't have more fun than the rest of us girls, or half as much, for that matter."

He was too modest to say he hardly had to play with himself night after night. But he did ask, "You mean you've never done it . . . let's say hostile, honey?"

She laughed at the pun but said he was awful, before she confessed, "I haven't had the opportunity, since I came home from more bohemian circles to breed mules. I was . . . engaged more than once in my less innocent school days, but since returning to the basin, I've had to be more careful about my reputation as a woman of substance and a boss you don't get frisky with, if you know what I mean."

He said, "I know what you mean."

He felt no call to brag on richer gals with bigger spreads who'd been more willing to kiss a passing stranger than the local swains who came calling with flowers, books, candy and a burning ambition to better themselves.

Poor Kim Stover, up to the South Pass Range, had married more than one cruel fortune hunter since they'd first known one another, in the biblical sense. A late Victorian lady with a social position to worry about had a hard row to hoe when it came to her natural impulses. He felt sorry for old Queen Victoria herself, having to cope with all the gossip about her and the hired help since her Albert had bought the farm and left her too old to marry up with another prince and too young to just strum her own banjo, most likely.

Asking her permit, Longarm lit a cheroot for Rose and himself, promising he'd never tell a soul she smoked in private. It was odd but true that biddy hens who dipped snuff themselves would cluck like they were laying square eggs if they caught a she-male of their species partaking of tobacco in the form of *smoke*. Women weren't supposed to ride like a man, either. Albeit that notion made a mite more sense when one considered how the female crotch was formed and how young gals seemed so wild about horseback riding with their thighs wide spread. Boy kids just felt like they were getting kicked in the nuts until they learned to sit a saddle right.

As it was his turn to take a draw, with her ash-blond head resting on one bare shoulder, Rose sighed and asked, "If I can't get you to spend the night out here, darling, can I count on you to drop by as often as you can to . . . keep me informed about the progress of your mission?"

He patted her own bare shoulder to answer, "Sure. But as I hope you understand, there's just no saying how long I'll be on this odd one. For the longer I'm down here the odder it seems to be getting. But my home office only allows me a sensible amount of time in the field, win or lose, so . . ."

"You mean you don't just keep on trying until you solve all the crimes?" she asked.

He smiled wistfully and confessed, "Not hardly. I ain't supposed to tell the general public, but seeing you and me are private pals and provided you don't spread it around, most crimes are solved because there was never a mystery at all. When a lady who's had her purse snatched yells and points, the thief gets stopped half the time, and when he gets away there's most often some other kid in the crowd who knows his name and where he lives."

He put the cheroot to her lips and continued, "Murder most foul is most often committed by the most likely suspect, if not in front of witnesses. So seven out of ten killings are no mystery at all, and we usually luck out with a quarter of the cases where nobody can say right off the killer might be."

"Are you saying it's possible to get away with murder, Custis?" Rose demanded in an incredulous tone.

He nodded easily and said, "Happens all the time. Murder most foul is easier to get away with than robbing a bank, and robbing a bank is easier than stealing something easier to trace than cold cash. That's the chink in the mastermind's armor that I'm probing for down this way. Trying to get enough for conviction on that quick-draw artist drawing so quick under a doubtless assumed name could take more time than my home office may be able to afford. My boss has a back-load of crimes and misdemeanors closer to Denver, and it's an election year."

She protested, "Surely you can't mean you'd simply give up?"

To which he could only reply, "Happens all the time when they decide the game just ain't worth the candle. Governor Wallace, up New Mexico way, asked if my home office would give him a hand with that pesky Billy the Kid, seeing the new governor's had trouble with sorting the sheep from the goats around Santa Fe. But my boss told New Mexico Territory that Colorado had enough on its plate without our chasing one mean kid with a catchy nickname all over creation on a single murder warrant."

He could see she was getting upset. So he added soothingly, "I was saying it could take too long to track down a big blond gimp shooting folk under a pen name. Maddog killers with nothing else in mind tend to weed themselves out of the garden natural. The real Clay Allison fell off a wagon and busted his own neck, being such a crazy mean drunk. We can count on at least half the buscaderos simply spoiling for a fight to lose a fight before we ever have to try and convict them. But a mean drunk leading a gang of stock thieves is another kettle of fish. To begin with it's more important to stop such an operation. After that, it's tougher to sell stolen stock and just ride on than it is to gun a man pointless and scoot. So whilst the current Clay Allison stalks me, I mean to see if I can learn what he's been doing with all them *mules*."

He took the smoke back for a drag and added, "I suspect they'd as soon be able to deliver the order and net enough to make the drive worth the time and trouble, I suppose."

"How many head, where and when?" he insisted.

She said, "Custis, we're *fucking,* damn it!"

He said, "I noticed. It lasts longer when you post in the saddle and chat. After that it's really important to me, honey."

She laughed, called him a goof and crunched down with her innards as she said, "We'll be driving with other outfits down the canyon and upstream to the cavalry outpost at Castolon by way of the old Camino del Rio, come next Monday morn. With the Apache out along the border this summer, the army's not asking me to deliver at the bigger post at Presidio, so . . ."

"I want to ride along, come Monday," he cut in. "Even if I don't learn anything, riding the whole route to market from this basin, I've some notions I just might get the War Department to go along with, seeing mules meant for their Indian fighting army seem to be getting stolen right and left."

She husked, "It's a deal. You can ride with me to Castolon. You can ride with me to the moon. Just *move* that big old thing of yours and *ride* me, cowboy!"

He laughed, "Powder River and let her buck!" as he proceeded to go at it with more sincerity and vigor, until in the end it was Rose herself who murmured, "Oh, thank you, thank you, but could we stop for a while, Custis? I fear I'm just not used to this much real fucking."

He kissed her and rolled off to reach for that cheroot and relight it. A snubbed-out cheroot tasted awful for the first few drags, but at three for a nickel no man who worked for a living could be picky, and once you got it going again a smoke was still a smoke.

Blowing a thoughtful smoke ring, Longarm mused aloud, "The soldiers blue will likely think I'm crazy. But when you can't make the pieces fit after nobody else has been able to make 'em fit, it's possible you've all been picturing the *puzzle* wrong!"

Snuggled against him with her eyes shut, Rose murmured, "I know I shouldn't, but a girl has to do *something* about those feelings and it's not true it grows hairs in the palms of your hands."

He didn't answer. He kept his thoughts to himself as he smoked the whole cheroot down, and once he had, Rose Bradford was softly snoring, like a half-starved waif resting up after a thanksgiving feast.

Longarm gently eased her flat on her back atop the covers, a mighty pretty sight in the soft light from outside, and swung his bare feet to the floor to ease silently off the bed without waking her.

He gathered his duds from where they'd wound up on the rug, got dressed, strapped on his six-gun, donned his Stetson and let himself out as softly as he could manage.

He didn't encounter any of the household help as he moved back toward the kitchen. But when he got to the kitchen, Rose's mother was seated at the table, looking helpless as an old lost sheep as she bleated, "Where is everybody? I'd like some coffee, please."

Longarm moved over to the kitchen range, saying soothingly, "I'll see if I can find you some, ma'am. Ought to be a pot on the back burner and . . . here we go. Where do you all keep the cups and saucers, ma'am?"

The dotty old woman stared up owlishly to ask, "Don't you know? Do you work here, young man?"

He murmured, "Not here in the house, ma'am," as he opened a cupboard to find what he was looking for.

As he placed a cup of coffee with a sugar bowl and spoon before her—he'd found no cream, canned or fresh—Rose's mother said, "I don't remember you. When did my husband hire you, young man?"

Longarm reassured her, "He never. I'm here with the approval of Miss Rose, ma'am."

She brightened to ask, "Oh, do you know my daughter?" as Longarm dropped two spoonfuls of sugar in her cup and stirred, since she was just sitting there like a baby waiting to be fed.

He softly allowed he knew her daughter indeed and asked her permit to leave on an errand for the same.

She didn't answer. She didn't seem to be all there. Longarm ticked his hat brim to her anyway, and crawfished backward out the kitchen door. He met nobody in the barnyard. But he needed no help to find his borrowed bay in a stall, nor to bridle and resaddle her once he'd opened the tack-room door with a pocketknife blade he'd had reworked a tad by a Denver locksmith who'd said he wasn't supposed to do such work.

By the time Longarm was well on his way back to town, the cliffs to the west of the creek rose in purple shade. He hadn't thought it so late. But when he consulted his pocket watch, he saw he'd spent more time in bed with Rose, and in Rose, than he'd kept track of. So things would be shutting down by the time he made it all the way into town.

"Time surely flies when you're having fun," Longarm confided to the wide-spread ears of his mount as they passed through the tiger stripes of shade the roadside cottonwoods had painted across his path near the end of a perfect day. He knew that back in Denver his pals would just be fixing to head out across town for supper and some action, with a way duller day just ending for them.

He didn't envy the poor hard-up jaspers. For in that first flush of sanity that overcomes a man right after he's shot his own wad, Longarm could see what Lord Chesterfield had meant when he'd observed that the pleasure was fleeting, the cost could be exorbitant, the consequences could be dreadful and the position was always ridiculous.

Chapter 27

Captain Kramer had gone home for supper and fleeting pleasure when Longarm stopped by the ranger station. He rode on down to send a progress report at the Western Union, but he didn't stop by the chili parlor next door. He knew Consuela had only worked there, and as he passed by he saw they had some other gal behind the counter, but he didn't care what she looked like. He'd lost his appetite for chili con carne, at least when served across that particular counter.

He rode on down to the Last Chance, to find, as he'd expected, that the saloon was serving a fair afternoon crowd, and the free grub at the end of the bar didn't look bad. So he ordered a scuttle of needled beer, served by an Irish leprechaun he hadn't met before. When he said who he was, the leprechaun, who claimed to be a Kerry man named Kevin, said he knew who Longarm was and added that the beer was on the house and all and all.

Longarm insisted on paying, seeing he meant to dig into the free grub with a sudden appetite for pickled pigs feet and neeps that had suddenly come over him.

Neeps were a Scotch-Irish invention combining mashed potatoes and mashed turnips, which tasted better than that sounds when consumed in the company of corned beef or pickled pigs feet.

He'd barely taken the edge off the appetite his time with Rose Bradford had given him when Liam O'Hanlon returned from wherever he'd been and Kevin got back to making fairy shoes under a mushroom somewhere else. O'Hanlon agreed business had picked up since morning, thanks to the way the day had started. Longarm didn't ask, but O'Hanlon told him the nearby Punchboard sisters had just sent over for a bucket of beer and a pint of tequila. So the good times seemed to be rolling all over at the south end of the basin.

O'Hanlon added he knew all the faces in the saloon at the moment and nobody had passed by all day on a saddle mule. When he asked if Longarm had the least notion where those killers had gone after their Mex or breed leader had finished off a wounded sidekick, Longarm had to confess, "Less than I knew this morning, if we're talking about certain. We established they never rode north past the scene of that crime just south of town. I aim to ride far as Castolon with a stock drive, come Monday. I'll let you know if I spy Ali Baba's cave along the walls of Bottleneck Canyon."

"You won't," the burly saloon keeper declared, adding, "We've been talking about that. Everything and everybody goes in and out of this basin by way of Bottleneck Canyon. There ain't any caves or smaller side canyons. Are you talking about Miss Rose Bradford's consolidated drive, planned for Monday morn?"

Longarm said, "I reckon I am now. Miss Rose never mentioned mules other than her own on the way to that army outpost."

O'Hanlon said, "Safety in numbers, with Clay Allison and his stock thieves hovering Lord knows where. I have some mules of my own on the way to Castolon, come Monday morn."

He leaned over the bar to ask a cowhand within arm's length of Longarm if he'd mind fetching Slim Putnam for them.

As the willing youth turned from the bar, O'Hanlon explained, "Slim will be in charge of my modest remuda, along with the bigger shipment from the Tumbling Sevens. Not being a ranger myself, I run my own stock with the Tumbling Sevens across the basin. Slim can tell you more than I can about driving mules to market. I don't know shit about anything more complicated than the pigs and chickens out back."

Longarm didn't ask why a wayside stop like the Last Chance kept a few pigs to dispose of their garbage, with chickens to provide eggs on demand for beer or breakfast. He asked, "How come you have mules for sale if you ain't a stockman?"

The saloon keeper said, "As an investment, of course. From time to time I'm offered a cow, a pony or a mule to settle a bar tab. Other times, such as this summer with the army in the market for mules, I buy for ready cash, low, and board them over at the Tumbling Sevens until the going price is right. This summer, thanks to Victorio and the ways of green troops with army mules, the price is right indeed!"

They were joined by Slim Putnam, who asked what was up. O'Hanlon said, "Mule prices. I was telling Longarm here about the coming consolidated drive."

The tall, skinny Putnam said, "Ain't much to tell. All we got to do is code each outfit's stock with paint, seeing the army wants to do the branding, and just drive the sons of bitches from here to yonder. We're droving in strength with stock thieves red and white on the prowl. Doubt anyone will try 'cause we'll be riding with hands off the Flyin' B, Double Diamond, PDQ, Bar W and what all, with every rider out to shoot somebody."

Longarm asked who he'd see to sign on for the drive. Slim shrugged and said, "My outfit's just across the creek if you'd like to meet up with my boss, Big Roy. Come on, I ain't getting any richer in this den of iniquity!"

They went out to mount up, and as Slim promised, it was a mighty short splash across the creek and up a slight grade to where Slim kicked open the counterweighted gate and there the main house and outbuildings of the Tumbling Sevens lay, blocking the mouth of the steep-walled single entrance to the canyon complex.

The 'dobe walls and pole corrals dominated and blocked that choke point on purpose. The big tile-roofed main house stood on banked soil, with culverts running under either end of the veranda to feed the dry wash running east into Tiswin Creek in heavy weather. Someone had sure been busy with a shovel in this canyon.

When Longarm said so, Slim laughed and said, "The Lord made Mexicans to handle shovels, and Big Roy keeps a dozen or more busy all the time with drainage. Left to their druthers, these canyons would flood white water wall-to-wall ever time it rained. That's how you get these fool canyons to begin with."

The rode on in and dismounted out front. A Junoesque brunette in her late thirties or early forties came out on the veranda as if she'd been expecting visitors, to announce, "You just missed supper, Mr. Putnam, but I can tell Fong Ching to whip something up for you and . . . our guest?"

As Longarm tipped his hat brim to her, Slim said, "This would be Deputy Custis Long, Federal, here to have a look-see out back, Miss Hazel. I told him the boss would be proud to show him around."

The lady of the house said, "Big Roy's up the basin at the Cartier spread. Might not be back for a spell, unless you'd like to ride up and fetch him, Mr. Putnam."

Slim hesitated but didn't argue. He said, "I'll tell him that's what you told me to do, Miss Hazel. You want this lawman to ride with me or wait here with you?"

She trilled, "What a silly question! Would that be any way to treat a guest? You just said he wants a look around the Tumbling Sevens. By the time you can hope to be back with Big Roy, it will be too dark to see anything. So why don't you run along and leave Deputy Long to me?"

Slim shot Longarm a warning look and remounted to whirl his pony and light out for the gate as if in a hurry to get back before it . . . got too dark. A young stable hand came around the corner of the big house to take Longarm's borrowed bay in charge, as the lady of the Tumbling Sevens motioned him to follow her inside. As he followed her back through spacious 'dobe-walled but expensively furnished rooms, Hazel Wilcox said, "I dasn't ride in this gingham housedress, but we'll be more comfortable in my jaunting cart in any case. I've told my help to put a picnic basket aboard to make up for your late arrival."

He didn't think she needed to be told he'd noticed she was used to giving orders and having them carried out by her help.

She led him through a swamping kitchen, looking to neither the right nor the left, at the Chinee cook and his Mex helpers, and out to where, sure enough, another Mex servant was holding the bridle of a mule hitched to an Irish jaunting cart. The picnic basket she'd just mentioned nestled in the hollow T formed by the back of the forward-facing front seat and the back-to-back jaunting or scenery-viewing seats running lengthwise with the wagon bed betwixt the two big cartwheels. Longarm wasn't surprised when she strode straight to the driver's side. He just helped her up and walked around the Mex and mule to join her on her perch as she took hold of the ribbons and told the Mex to let go.

He didn't argue, and since Hazel Wilcox left her buggy whip in its socket, Longarm assumed the mule knew better than to argue, too. But the buxom brunette's tone was pleasant as she drove them up a wagon trace running between the canyon wall and the dry wash ditched to one side as well as deeper.

When Longarm commented on all the drainage work someone had gone to, she explained, dismissively, "Used to be part of a Spanish land grant. The grandees were a caution for keeping their Indian help busy, and it does keep our holdings dry."

He nodded but cautiously asked, "Didn't the U.S. recognize Royal Spanish grants when it took over in these parts after the Mexican War, Miss Hazel?"

She said, "Of course, and be fair, I know you've heard my husband can drive a hard bargain, but we claimed these canyons fair and square off the land office. The first Spanish settlers had been driven out by Indians, Pueblos up the Rio Grande and Chiso-Apache in these parts, long before that Mexican War or even the fight for the Alamo. When we first took over, back there, we had to just about rebuilt from 'dobe foundations up, but all that earlier earthmoving had made our little bit of Heaven a lot easier to build on."

He didn't ask if she might be part Irish. The jaunting cart had already hinted at her possible history. She was about the right age for an American-born child of Potato Famine refugees, brought up on romantic family legends of little bits of Heaven where beauties who married rich got to do most anything they cared to. Longarm was far more interested in the wider grassy glade they'd driven into, running north and south at right angles to the entrance canyon.

He said so. She reined in to wave her free hand expansively at a whole lot of scattered stock munching planted meadow grass, at least a mile in either direction, and declared, "A guest of the Hebrew persuasion remarked that our holdings are laid out in the form of something he called a *menorah*. I'm not sure what that might mean."

Longarm said, "I've seen some, Miss Hazel. A menorah is one of them Hebrew candlesticks as have seven or nine branches rising off a sort of crossbar atop the one bottom stem. I don't know why some have nine branches whilst others only have seven."

She shrugged and said, "They don't believe in Mary, the mother of God, either. But that's the way our seven somewhat higher branch canyons tumble down into what I like to call this Vale of Tralee."

Longarm asked if those seven tumbling canyons were all boxed, dead end, as Slim had said.

She said, "Of course. All the canyons west of Tiswin

Creek box the same way about the same distance west. This geologist Big Roy hired to prospect our rocky holdings says there's what he called a volcanic *duke* of harder *bastard* rock running north and south in line with the basin. He said it might have gotten there as part of the same upheavels they had around here a long time ago."

Longarm smiled and remarked, not unkindly, "I suspect volcanic *dike* and *basalt* might have been the terms he used, Miss Hazel, but I follow his drift and they'd already told me the geology was less complexicated over on this side of the basin."

She turned gracefully on the seat, obviously aware of how nicely she twisted at the waist, to reach in her picnic basket and declare, "Oh, dear, all that silly Chinee packed for us seems to be bread and wine! But it's sweet Boston brown bread and fine Spanish sherry, so we might make do."

She busted off a chunk of the dark bread, spongy and sweet enough to pass for an attempt at cake, whilst he uncorked the sherry, wondering whether he ought to. The canyon walls were getting darker and the sky above was fading from blue to lavender. There was no way to tell how close they were to sundown, surrounded as they were by looming cliffs, unless a man was rude enough to take out his watch whilst breaking bread with a lady.

But she must have been guessing at the time as she filled two folding tumblers with sherry, handed him one and without a word of warning threw back her head to sing, not badly, in a throaty way,

"The cool shades of evening, their mantle was
    spreading,
And Mary, all smiling, was listening to me.
The moon through the valley her pale rays was
    shedding,
When I won the heart of the rose of Tralee!"

A distant gruffer voice echoed along the canyon walls. "Is that you wailing like a banshee up yonder, Hazel?

What are you doing out this way at this hour, woman?"

Hazel Wilcox blanched. "Oh, my God, it's my husband! I didn't think he'd be back for hours! Let me do all the talking, Custis. He can be hard to talk to when he's in one of his silly moods."

As they perforce sat silently, listening to galloping hooves coming closer, Hazel Wilcox wearily added, "I don't know what makes Big Roy so moody at times. But that's the way my husband is."

Chapter 28

There was still enough daylight to make out details in color a furlong off. So when Big Roy Wilcox reined his cream Arab in closer, the first thing Longarm noticed about him was that he didn't sit any taller in the saddle than average. So they likely had other cause to call him Big Roy.

After that he was a still-trim middle-aged man whose mustache was bigger as well as grayer than Longarm's. Big Roy was dressed more expensive, in tailored black broadcloth as matched his ten-gallon Stetson, its tall crown creased down the front, West Texas style. His saddle gun was a Springfield .45–70 with a killing range of close to a mile. His sidearm was a French LeMat, the only revolver chambered for shotgun shells. One got the impression that should Big Roy aim to shoot anybody, he'd aim to shoot him sincere.

When he repeated his question, demanding to know what the two of them had been up to out this way, his wife calmly replied, "Nothing you couldn't have been doing with Monique Cartier, dear heart. Did the little snip offer to improve your French?"

Big Roy snapped, "She did not. Nor did she sing me

any Irish love songs. Miss Monique is shorthanded and has half a dozen mules she'd as soon sell at current remount prices. I offered to drove 'em over to Castolon with the rest of the consolidated herd and sell 'em for her as her rep."

His wife purred, "How sweet of you, dear heart. I hope she seemed grateful?"

Big Roy snorted, "I'm old enough to be her father and I'm asking the usual sales commission, you fool woman!"

Big Roy winked at Longarm to modestly explain, "Wives tend to get crazy jealous when their man still has a little spring in his stride. I've heard tell of you, Longarm. No man who gut-shoots a mule thief can be all bad, and they say you have a head on your shoulders. So I suspect we'll get along, and what can I do for you? The rangers have already surveyed all seven of our westernmost canyons for hidden exits."

Longarm replied, "Miss Hazel was just explaining about that volcanic dike all the canyons on this side of the creek box sheer against, Big Roy. I just asked your Slim Putnam to show me around over here, to see if anyone describing the layout of your big basin missed anything."

The older stockman asked, "Do you reckon they have?"

Longarm shook his head and said, "Not as far as I can tell, so far. I've been trying to form an overall big picture of the whole Big Bend in my mind, in the hopes I'd spy a piece that didn't fit natural."

Big Roy nodded and said, "I ain't certain I buy that tale of a New Mexico badman coming down this way to claim a secret Garden of Eden, way in the middle of the air. None of us pioneer stockmen laid claim to the first patch of fodder and water we came across, once the army ran the Chiso-Apache out a few short summers back. I ain't bragging I rode *every* inch of the heights all around, but I rode *some* of it and others scouted for good bottomland as well."

He waved his off hand expansively to add, "I hold three sections of damn good grass, all told, spread out in skinny canyon floors as it may seem to you. We've improved on the ditching and well drilling the old-time grandees began, and I don't mind telling you we'd have never worked that hard if we'd found that pie in the sky Caddo Flynn reported. So if it's there, it sure ain't easy to find, and how could a stranger to this part of Texas find shit?"

His wife said, "Roy! Is that any way to talk?"

Big Roy said, "I'm talking to a lawman, not a visiting spinster. Why don't you two drink your damned wine and follow me back to the house so's I can get off this infernal bronc and drink something more manly?"

As his wife reined her pony around with a wistful smile at Longarm, Big Roy fell in on Longarm's side, saying, "I've had my own hands up amid the rimrocks across the way, poking about where no rangers have been yet. They ain't found shit, and when I say shit I mean shit, gawd damn it!"

Longarm said, "There's at least one dead Texas Ranger *somewhere*. Lieutenant Weiner never came back from his proposed visit to the Lazy A, and from what I've seen of the karst geography across the basin, there ain't many patches of soil deep enough to bury a body."

Big Roy shrugged and replied, "There's many a sinkhole to drop one down, and I never said anyone's covered every square yard over yonder. It ain't that easy to ride a mile across such rocky range."

Longarm asked, "Are you saying they only explored the busted-up country on *horseback*?"

Big Roy answered, "How else would you have West Texas riders out exploring anything, on *foot*?"

Longarm muttered, "Heaven forfend," and sipped some sherry as the cart jaunted under him.

As if guessing what Longarm was thinking, Big Roy defensively added, "It's tough enough to get across that jaggedy rock pile when you *do* dismount and scamper where no hooves could go, and that scampering fool Caddo Flynn says he saw acres and acres of *mules* up yonder. How could that crazy Clay Allison drive a single solitary mule where none of my riders could get to saddled up?"

The Boston brown bread didn't set too well with sherry unless a body had a sweet tooth indeed. Longarm washed that taste out of his mouth and said he'd asked Slim to let him ride with that consolidated herd, come Monday morn.

Big Roy nodded and said, "The more the merrier, mules are harder to keep on the trail than cows, or even horses. Being they so surefooted as well as independent. But make sure you show up early. My boys will be moving 'em out at a trot down Bottleneck Canyon with a view to tiring them out and slowing them down before they reach the wider temptations of the Camino del Rio."

Longarm asked how many head they were talking about.

Big Roy said, "Six hundred and change. More than half of 'em mine. That's how come the consolidation's being formed around the core of my four hundred odd. Some of the smaller outfits up the basin have lost as much as a quarter of their saleable mules to Clay Allison's gang."

As they rode along at a walk, he added, "I'll be blessed if I can figure out what he's doing with all of 'em. There's no profit in any sort of livestock from chickens up until you sell 'em to somebody. But I've asked around, and in all due modesty, I am well known on the mule market and vice versa. But I've tried in vain to learn of any mules being sold in any unsual numbers by anyone who ain't as usual as me."

To the other side of Longarm his wife volunteered, "Didn't you say the Mexican Army was out in force along the border this summer, Roy?"

Her husband said, "I did, and had you been paying attention you'd have heard me say you can buy all the mules you want, cheaper, down Mexico way."

"Cheaper than not paying for them at all?" she demurred. Longarm had already decided she was quick-witted as well as strong-willed.

Big Roy said, "I was right, you weren't listening whilst

I was jawing with the rangers about that angle. Of *course* you can steal a perfectly good mule in Mexico. It's a national pastime. After that you have to drive it north across the Chihuahua Desert. And if you do get it past *Los Rurales,* demanding a head tax on all stock exported from stock worth more than a goat, you got to convince the U.S. Army it wants a mule marked with one of them fancy curly-girly Mexican brands!"

He told Longarm, as if a Colorado rider wasn't supposed to know, "The illiterate greasers don't brand natural with letters or numbers. They draw pictures on their stock. Makes registering brands such a bitch that the state of Texas discourages the practice."

Longarm saw they were drifting wide from the details of West Texas that mattered to him. He said, "I'll ask the killer why he steals your local mules under an assumed name when I catch him. That might be one whole lot easier if I knew where his riders were driving all those stolen mules. We know some have been loped by in the night south of Tanktown. We know none have been driven past the Last Chance. Those three . . . squatters betwixt the Last Chance and the mouth of Bottleneck Canyon told me of various riders passing through in much more modest amounts. So it sure looks like the thieves haven't run much stock down the post road to the Camino del Rio on that side of Tiswin Creek."

"Nor this side," Big Roy volunteered, adding, "I'll allow even our front gate sets back from the creek a piece on a dark night. But we ain't the only outfit on this side of the creek down to this end of the basin, and thanks to our holding the most substantial network of canyon bottom, our neighbors north and south fence all the way to the creek, which is closer on this side. That's why the post road runs up the other side."

He let that sink in and added, "If you did choose to drive stolen stock through the fenced-in meadows west of the creek you'd have to cut a heap of fences. Then you'd have to repair them after you, unless you wanted folk raising the alarm by the dawn's early light."

From his other side Hazel Wilcox told Longarm, "I was serving rack of lamb the night Captain Kramer was down here talking about that. He said he'd had his rangers search in vain for signs of cut and repaired barbwire."

Big Roy said, "The rangers agreed with me on how come nobody west of the creek has been raided yet. We're tougher to raid over this way, and after that the thieves have been loping the stolen stock along the beaten path to some secret turnoff, south of town and north of Bottleneck Canyon."

Longarm finished his sherry, folded the picnic cup and handed it to Miss Hazel with a nod of thanks before he said, "Sure looks like so. You say you have neighbors *south* of you, even closer to the funnel of Bottleneck Canyon."

His wife said, "The Spanish Hat, an illiterate dago brand proudly flaunted by stuck-up greasers who spurned my hospitality."

Big Roy chuckled and said, "Don't ever spurn old Hazel if you ain't one for lifelong feuding. When we first settled in here, we naturally sent out invites to a housewarming howdy to the neighbors north and south. The Fernandez family never even answered Hazel's invite writ on fancy stationery from El Paso. I told her it hardly mattered to white folk whether they were too ignorant to read English or stuck up as she suspected. We were only trying to act quality. It wasn't as if we *wanted* greasers calling on us."

Longarm said he'd heard mention of the Spanish Hat being down this way near the south end of the basin.

Big Roy said, "Any further south and the Spanish Hat wouldn't even be in the basin. They hold a smaller tangle of canyons than this one, draining into the same sort of funnel as the waters of Tiswin Creek run into, down the bigger Bottleneck. I've never been invited to tea next door, but it's my understanding they hold a sort of slingshot-shaped bottomland, with both branches boxing about as far west as all the other box canyons on this side of the creek."

"Have they reported the loss of any stock?" asked Longarm.

The master of the bigger Tumbling Sevens replied, simply, "I don't know. Can't tell you if they raise mules or elephants. Like Hazel says, they don't socialize with Anglo neighbors."

Hazel Wilcox sniffed. "If they did, they'd know I'm as fine a Roman Catholic as any dago don! My people bent their knees to nobody in the old country, and Roy can tell you we were married in front of the altar by a priest as fine as San Antone has to offer!"

And so it went until they made it back to the main house with the wishing star winking from a purple sky to the east.

Big Roy didn't seem to mind, but Miss Hazel seemed let down when he said Longarm couldn't stay for supper.

He made them give him his borrowed horse back and rode off into the gathering dusk. It was getting late to call on folk polite, but he was running out of time if he meant to ride with that trail drive. So he went calling on that Spanish Hat outfit next, and if they didn't like it they could lump it.

Chapter 29

Big Roy had allowed his snooty neighbors held another
canyon mouth. So that was where Longarm headed in the
gathering dusk.

He rode through more cottonwood, with some big-leaf
maple someone had left uncut because they were Druids
or didn't want to make it easy for visitors. When he busted
out the far side, he saw that another low-slung adobe complex of quarters and stables formed a defendable wall,
across a narrower gap in this case.

As he rode across their bare dooryard, a cur dog inside
the house threatened his life verbally. The pale brunette
wearing black Spanish lace over maroon gabardine threatened more seriously with the ten-gauge double-barrel Parker in her hands as she called out to him in a husky
contralto, "Go away, *gringo pendejo*. We wish for nothing
you could have for to offer. We have nothing to offer you
but both these barrels if you come one step closer!"

Longarm reined and backed his mare a step or more as
he called back to her, "I ain't about to crowd you, ma'am.
I'd be Deputy U.S. Marshal Custis Long, calling on the
Fernandez sisters if it's all right with you."

She snapped, "It's not all right with me. We know all

about those sisters across the Tiswin, and if you think we Fernandez sisters are like that, I pity you. For you are about to die!"

Longarm sighed and said he didn't want to die and so he was going back to town now, if it was all the same with her.

Then a second pale brunette popped out of the house like a cuckoo clock bird to whisper something to the one with the shotgun.

Seeing they were likely standoffish as Hazel Wilcox had warned him, Longarm reined his mount around to let them sort out whatever the hell was eating them.

But then the one with the shotgun called out, "*No, esperte, por favor.* I did not know who you were. Come back. *¡Mi casa es su casa!*"

Since it would have been neither polite not prudent to ask a lady with a ten-gauge to make up her damn mind, Longarm just rode on in to dismount and tether the bay to their hitchrail as the one with the shotgun aimed it at the veranda tiles and motioned him to follow the two of them inside.

As Longarm followed them inside, he admired the interior of their plain but well-kept *casa,* furnished in the severe style of Old Spain, with a framed coat of arms done in oils above the mantel of the cold fireplace. The one with maroon peeking from under black Spanish lace set her shotgun aside and showed him to a sofa seat, as the one with dark green under her lace tore off somewheres. By this time they'd established that the more bossy one was called Ramona Fernandez, with all those extra names, connected by *y,* the higher toned Spanish-speaking folk went in for. The other one, Carlota, was back in no time with bread, cheeses and a pitcher of sangria made with lemons, wine and cactus tuna juice.

Longarm was trying to make up his mind which was the prettiest, or the ugliest, as Ramona explained they were, alas, *solteronas,* or old maids, orphaned before their *papa* had managed to fix either up with the arranged marriages required by their fancy ways. The reason Longarm couldn't decide whether they were pretty or ugly was that they looked more *odd* than either pretty or ugly.

English-speaking folk who admired the works of the famous Spanish painter El Greco thought he painted high-toned Spanish folk with sort of greenish skin because he'd been color blind. But whilst *most* true Spaniards had natural skins of various shades, there was this one mayhaps inbred Castilian bunch that struck you as green around the edges, like a not-quite-ripe whatever, until you looked straight at 'em to decide maybe they weren't all *that* green. Longarm managed not to ask the sisters if they'd ever met that other odd bunch of Spanish gals who looked sort of like peaches, fuzz and all, with otherwise natural if not downright pretty features. Despite being smaller than Texas, Old Spain was all cut up into seperate mountain valleys, like this Big Bend country, and Professor Darwin had explained how you got sort of odd departures from the run of the mill with inbreeding off to one side of your species. He finally decided the sisters were pretty enough, and built sort of interesting if you liked women long, lean and sort of green.

The mystery of their sudden change of mood out front was solved when the greenish skinned gal in green poplin confided, "We of course know all about those agents of the evil Porfirio Díaz who are after you, *El Brazo Largo*! Is not safe for you anywhere here in this basin, now that they have found out where you are! Where did you sleep last night? We heard how they have been how you say snooping around your *posada* and how they assassinated that *mestizo* girl who tried for to hide you out. For why you stay here, knowing they know where to find you? For why you don't ride further north, where is not so easy for to murder an Anglo friend of *La Causa*?"

Longarm said, "I fear the mastermind who sent those killers after me has to be closer than Mexico City, Miss Carlota. It's true some of 'em seemed to be Mexican. But we know more than one Anglo killer in these parts rides with Mexican sidekicks, being we're so close to the border, and after that, they were killing other lawmen in these parts before I got here."

Ramona Fernandez said, "That one Mexican you shot, up in Tanktown, was a *Rurale*, or at least he used to be. Our people know more about such things than your people, *El Brazo Largo*!"

He sipped some sangria and politely replied, "*¿Quien sabe?* I take it you ladies are with *La Causa* in spite of your . . . *sangre azul* coat of arms and such?"

Ramona flared. "Is *because* we are *sangre azul* with a father who fought under Juarez that we feel nothing but contempt for the *ladrón mestizo* who made himself *El Presidente* with a gun! Are you not as *blanco* as we are and do you not fight for *La Revolución*?"

He hadn't come down their way to discuss Mexican politics. He told them he was out to find that secret spread spotted by Caddo Flynn, and Ramona sniffed and said, "*Es loco en la cabeza*. We have both been up among the rimrocks when we were small and foolish. Such wide valleys as that *Indio pendejo* reported do not occur among canyonlands like we have all around. Is nothing for you up there, and down here there are *tiros malo* who wish for to shoot you! You must let my sister and me prepare a room for you for the night."

Longarm started to say *Los Rurales* weren't after him north of the border, and then he wondered why anyone would want to say a dumb thing like that. For he did have killers after him, and this would be about the last place they'd expect him to hole up until that trail drive!

He said, "I sure could use a safe hideout, ladies. But of course you'll have to let me pay for my room and board."

They both looked like they were fixing to bust out crying, hit him with a chair, or both. So he said he hadn't meant to insult anybody and allowed he'd be proud to sponge off them, high-toned Spanish style.

On his way back to town Longarm dropped by the Twin Cs, branding with capital Cs intertwined and facing away from one another. He was hardly surprised when the pretty brunette who invited him in said she answered to Monique Cartier, the sister of that murdered Frenchy Cartier.

She sat him down by a crackling willow-root fire and her Mex maid coffeed and caked him. Monique told him some Tumbling Seven hands would be driving her few head up to that army sale because her hired hand, Ricardo Chavez, had run off to Old Mexico with his own cousin, Yzabel.

Longarm marveled, "Them two kids eloped? Well, I never. I thought she'd been fired by the Widow Whitehead for some reason."

Monique shrugged and said, "I didn't know her. My brother used to drop by the Toro Negro when he was alive. But if I had a swain to take me into town, he'd never take me to any *saloon*!"

Longarm didn't ask how such a pretty little thing had wound up with no swain to take her to town. He sensed the Fernandez sisters hadn't been getting much . . . swaining, lately. It sure beat all how riders willing to risk their health with the Punchboard sisters could leave so many lonesome singles gals just withering on the vine.

As if she'd read Longarm's mind, or reconsidered how her complaints could be taken, Monique Cartier said, "It's not that I haven't ever been *asked*. I had to slap Ricardo Chavez one evening when he commenced to talk dirty to me after we'd bred a mule. I fear that may be one of the reasons he quit on me."

Longarm pointed out, "I thought I just heard you say Ricardo ran off with his cousin, ma'am."

She said, "That was after he proposed to *me*. He said he was about to come into some money. When I told the boy not to talk silly, he got all wooden Indian, the way they do when they're really mad, and said he understood why I wouldn't marry up with a greaser. I never called Ricardo a greaser. He was the one who brought it up."

"Some young gents can talk sort of dumb when they're upset or just excited around a lady," Longarm said soothingly.

Monique sighed and said, "Don't I know it! Ricardo was just being silly. He was too young for me had he been Anglo, or even French-Canadian like my brother and me. But I do sort of fancy this Texas Ranger, if *he* didn't act like such a silly whenever he came calling on me."

Longarm casually asked, "Might this Texican swain come calling all that often, Miss Monique?"

She sighed and said, "Not as often as he used to. I think he must have changed his mind about me for some reason. Mayhaps he has a cousin *he'd* as soon run off with."

Longarm soberly suggested, "Maybe he's just giving up. You say he's another lawman, and I can tell you from experience how tracking down and beating a man with a pistol can mess up an old boy's natural charm. If you want some brotherly advice about Texas Rangers, assuming any gal with a lick of sense would *want* a Texas Ranger, you'd do best to just set the fool down and tell him how you want things to turn out. Don't expect a mere . . . Texican to make up your minds for you both."

Monique Cartier laughed, a pretty sight, and confided, "Ricardo was right about one thing. I could use a man around this house if I mean to go on working this claim. But the boy I'm talking about would probably faint if I came right out like a brazen man hunter and told him how things had to be."

Longarm asked, "How do things have to be, Miss Monique?"

She said, "A church wedding, Roman Catholic, with me in white and nobody stealing more than a kiss, with his fool tongue in his own mouth, before I have that gold band on my finger! Does that strike you as unreasonable, Custis?"

He told her, truthfully, "It's a certain way to seperate the sheep from the goats, Miss Monique. Whether a man has honorable intent or not, he's usually proud to make the acquaintance of straight-shooting women for, like sensibly courting men, they're met few and far between."

She decided, "I'll *do* it! The next time he comes by, I'll speak my mind as if I was talking to a *friend,* and if that's too rich for his blood, I'll just sell this hardscrabble spread and go somewhere, most anywhere, a girl can meet more men!"

He allowed as most anywhere might have West Texas beat and excused himself to ride on. He rode as far as the first clump of creek-side cottonwood to dismount, stick his finger down his throat and puke all that coffee and cake he'd had to force down so far.

Feeling much better, he remounted to ride on. He was nearing the low dam that gave Tanktown its name when he decided it was time to cross Tiswin Creek where it ran less deep below the dam.

As he rode up the far bank he met up with Corporal Arnold, going the other way on a blue roan with some fresh-picked cornflowers in his free hand.

Longarm had figured it was getting on toward noon. He called out, "Howdy, Jose. You'd be just the man I wanted to see. Have you time for some more fatherly advice about women?"

Arnold replied, "Not right now, no offense. Did you hear about Rose Bradford riding in at sundown all teary faced?"

"Lord, no," said Longarm. "What happened to Miss Rose?"

The ranger said, "Nothing happened to *her*. It was her folk. Her old man died sitting up as they were trying to feed him his supper. Then they no sooner laid him out on his bed and sent a hand in to fetch Doc Fletcher, when the dotty old lady took her husband's Starr .41 from a bedroom drawer and blew her own addled brains out!"

Chapter 30

It gave a man a queer turn to picture another man fixing to die any minute in another room as he was making love to the daughter of the house!

As he rode on, Longarm saw that had he stayed for supper as Rose had asked, he'd have been there when that dotty old lady he'd seved a last cup of coffee to had shot herself in front of everybody.

He told himself he wouldn't have been able to stop the old lady had he been there. He hoped that was true. He wasn't in any hurry to talk to Rose about it. But he knew he had to, sooner or later.

Crossing Tiswin Creek below the dam, Longarm reined in near the base of the open-frame water tower above a steam-powered pump house. He had passed it going and coming without thinking too much about who paid for piped water and who carried buckets to the creek the old-timey way. He didn't much care about that detail. He wanted to make certain nobody was lurking about such a handy hideout and sniper's position.

Peering through the grimy window of the pump house, Longarm could make out a ruby glow in the firebox of the steam boiler. He didn't care if they had steam pressure up or not. He was more interested in such pump house crew as they might or might not have on duty in the tricky light of the gloaming.

Using that same penknife blade, Longarm unlocked the door with his left hand to follow the muzzle of the six-gun in his right hand into the darkness. But he didn't get to use it. The place was empty and silent as a tomb, save for the soft hiss of safety-valve steam. So he backed out and locked up again.

He knew he was likely pushing it, but as long as he was there, and in no hurry to meet up with poor Rose Bradford, Longarm adjusted his gunbelt and reached up to commence climbing the ladder up one side of the water tower. Others were watching from below by the time he'd made it to the platform of the real water tank. There was no railing. But there were hand grips like you saw on the sides of box cars. So as long as he was up there and getting used to heights of late, Longarm forced himself to make a complete circuit, waving down to those below waving up in wonder at him. He wondered if he looked that purple and gold to them.

It sure beat all how a bird's-eye view altered one's mental map of even a small town. It didn't seem so, walking around a town, but most of a town was open space, with the streets wider and the yards smaller than they seemed as you were crossing them with the rooflines of the buildings looking down on you from all around.

But when Longarm gazed farther out at the cliffs all around the basin, he saw he hadn't climbed high enough to see over them. He could make out the tips of a few blood red far-distant peaks from this vantage point. That had to be Emery Peak off to the north, and if Emery Peak was higher than most anything else in these parts, a man on top of Emery Peak ought to have a bird's-eye view of everything lower.

But he wasn't going to get to the top of Emery Peak from the top of a rinky-dink water tower. So he climbed back down. It was more puckering going down such a tall ladder than up it.

At the bottom an older gent in bib overalls who said he ran the pump inside when it needed running asked Longarm if he wanted to be shown around the premises. Longarm thanked him but said he'd already seen about all he'd expected to see from on high.

They shook on that and parted friendly. Longarm next rode to the Western Union shed to find no wires waiting for him there. So he sent off a bunch, and then, having no further excuses to keep him in town, he led the somewhat jaded bay up to the ranger post on foot, and that let him kill some time, too.

But when he got to the post to swap mounts for his ride out to the Flying B, the ranger on duty at the front desk told Longarm he'd heard everybody off the Flying B was in town. He explained he'd been told they were over to Doc Fletcher's dental office cum photographic studio cum undertaking parlor. Then he asked if Longarm had any idea where Corporal Arnold might be.

Longarm said he hadn't seen Arnold around town, and that was no lie when you studied on it.

He asked if it was important. The ranger said, "More important to him than it is to me, if he means to keep his job. Captain Kramer is mad as a wet hen about the hours Arnold's been keeping, and if Arnold ain't here at this desk the next time the captain wants him, there is likely to be an opening for an all too rare promotion around here!"

Longarm asked where Captain Kramer might be at the moment.

The kid watching the store said the boss had said something about paying his respects to the Bradfords before going home for *La Siesta*. So Longarm said he'd be back later if he needed to borrow another pony, and leaving his saddle and shit in a tack room safer than anywhere else he could think of, the long-legged lawman walked slowly to do what had to be done. It sure beat all how close Doc Fletcher's layout was when you didn't really want to get there.

To ply his many trades Doc Fletcher maintained an

adobe sprawl that took up a quarter of a business block. So he didn't have to store the respectable cadavers of the Bradfords with all those dead killers they'd been accumulating, and as luck would have it, the motherly woman who met Longarm at the front door said the elderly couple were not ready to be viewed, but allowed that their daughter, Miss Rose, was with some of the help from the Flying B, inside.

So Longarm let her lead him into a dim-lit parlor as smelled of dead flowers, where he found Rose seated alone on a leather chesterfield as the mostly Mex hired help stood respectfully apart from her. Rose was dressed more for riding than a funeral. The reason seemed clear. You didn't take time to gussy up with your dad lying dead on a bed and your ma lying dead on the floor.

Doffing his dark Stetson, Longarm approached the lonesome figure at one end of the sofa. She looked up, smiled wearily and patted a space beside her shapely hips. So he sat down beside her, hat in hand, and having nothing to say that would do a damned thing for her, he said nothing.

Rose herself broke the silence, softly saying, "*Quisieramos poco intimidad, por favor*," and her help cleared out, no doubt just as glad to do so. Funeral parlors were tedious to hang out in when you *had* to.

As soon as they were alone, Rose softly said, "I'm glad you came. I don't have anybody else I could say this to, but, Custis, I am so mad I could slap Momma's face if she still had a face to slap!"

Longarm set his hat aside and took her hand, soothing. "It aint so unusual to feel mixed emotions at times like these, Miss Rose, and she must have given you an awsome jolt. But she was old and dotty, too, and might not have known what she was doing."

Rose said, "She knew what she was doing, the old bitch! She knew what she was doing the day she wired me to come home after my daddy got all banged up. It was only after I got home that she went all helpless and had to be waited on, like a child, as if my poor vegetable

235

of a father hadn't been enough for me to care for, like a fucking nursemaid!"

Longarm warned himself this was no time for levity, so he refrained from complimenting her on what a fine fucking nursemaid she'd been.

He said, "I doubt she set out to trap you deliberate, Miss Rose. She just last night proved how much she cared for your father, and it must have driven her half out of her mind to see her once strong man so helpless."

Rose snapped, "How do you think *I* felt? He was more a part of me than he was of *her*! He was my *father*! I was half *him*!"

Longarm looked away uncomfortably. He'd read how a famous doctor in Vienna Town had scandalized the shit out of everybody by intimating that the furious battles betwixt mothers and grown daughters might hark back to times when neither polygamy nor incest had been against the tribal laws and older men had been inclined to act the way older men still acted around young women prettier than their wives.

Other head doctors had assured Queen Victoria's crowd that the wars between generations were nature's way of emptying the nest for the next clutch of eggs. Those doctors held it was best for the survival of the species when kids grew old enough to care for themselves and ran away from home to go conquer Indians, eastern or western. They said human nests would turn into unhealthy ant heaps if kids didn't fuss with their elders and vice versa. They had no explanation covering those mighty close-knit clans you found in hill country on both sides of the Minni Tonka, such as the bagpipe-playing family regiments of Scotland, that James-Younger clan of Missouri or the various wandering outcast tribes called gypsies, tinkers and such. Different families likely worked things out different, in the privacy of their own homes.

But Rose Bradford didn't need her head examined by a lawman off a farm in West-By-God-Virginia. So Longarm quietly told her, "What's done is done. This too will pass and you'll go on, Miss Rose. Not having in me the power to change things back the way they were when you were little and your dad rode tall in the saddle, I can only offer to try, if you can think of anything you want me to do or say."

She looked about as if to be certain they were alone before bending closer to confide, "I wish it was all over and I was drunk as a skunk and in bed with at least three men! Does that shock you?"

He smiled thinly and said, "I know the feeling. It's come over me more than once when I've been sick as a dog or wounded serious. Our notion of the antidote to pain is pleasure, Miss Rose. The antidote to tears is laughter. That's how come so many folk laugh at funerals and gang-banging widows ain't as unusual as you might imagine. But you don't want to carry on like that in a town this size."

She said, "I'm leaving towns this size forever, now that it's possible. Hank Borden and Big Roy Wilcox have both offered to buy my Flying B. Now that it's all mine, I mean to sell out and go back out to Frisco where I belong."

Longarm cocked a brow to ask, "Who made the best offer?"

She said, "Big Roy Wilcox. I don't think our next-door neighbor will like it much, but it's his own fault for trying to take advantage of an orphan. His fool son has tried to fuck me more than once, too."

Longarm said he was glad she was so particular, or had been, up to now. He asked if she wanted him to carry her home to the Flying B after the funeral.

She shook her blond head to say, "I'm never going back there. All I'm taking back to Frisco with me is packed and waiting at the post office for the next mail coach out. I'll be staying at the Toro Negro this evening and leaving for Castolon in the morning. I have to wait there for the consolidated herd to catch up so's I can sell my few mules to the army. I already have the check for the Flying B, part and parcel. Big Roy promised the help can stay on out there. He'll be running both spreads seperate, since they're so far apart."

She caught herself and wrinkled her pert nose to add, "What am I saying? Why am I going on about the Flying B as if it meant a thing to me now? I'm leaving nothing behind out yonder but bitter memories!"

Then, though Longarm prided himself on his poker face, she squeezed his hand to say, "Not *all* my memories of the Flying B are so bad. I've a few golden childhood memories of a big strong daddy who made a swing for me out back and used to hold me on his knee and ... more recently, there was this Colorado rider who sure knew how to treat a hard-up lady."

Longarm sighed and said, "Not if you mean to spend the night at the Toro Negro, I fear. I have two good reasons for avoiding the place. Somebody stalking me with a gun knows I've stayed there in the past, and for some reason the landlady, the Widow Whitehead, told me never to darken their door again."

"Good Lord, why?" asked the blonde young enough to be the fighting daughter of fat old Flo.

Longarm shrugged and said, "I suspect she may be *loco en la cabeza*. She as much as accused me of fooling with a Mex gal working for her. Pretty enough little thing called Yzabel, I think. Last I heard of Yzabel she'd eloped with the handsome young Ricardo Chavez, but you know how older women can get."

"Good *God* I know how older women can get," said Rose with a sigh, adding in a friendlier tone, "I don't think I want to fuck you anywhere here in the basin before I've left it forever. Why don't we talk about it when you get to the army remount station at Castolon with my mules and all the others? It may take me some time to haggle a fair price, and there won't be near as many biddy hens to gossip about the way I may or may not be observing a decent period of mourning."

Longarm agreed that might be best and added he was looking forward to that trail drive. So they sealed the bargain with a kiss and a grope, with her letting him excuse himself from the funeral if he was going to help run her stock up to Castolon and meet her there, later.

It was fair dark outside now. Longarm quietly mounted up and then rode north a piece to circle the town to its east by hugging the cliffs a furlong or more east of the most far-flung shithouse, and sure enough, he spied more than one dried horse or mule apple in the dust among the roots of the high chaparral and occasional tree to be found over yonder where nobody usually rode, or drove stolen stock.

Moving back on the more beaten path along the post road, Longarm told his borrowed barb, "We're missing something, here, Blacky. There ain't no mystery as to how they run stolen stock down this side of the creek, for some distance. It's where the fuckers *turn off* with the stock that I just can't fathom."

The well-trampled dust of the well-traveled route they were following told them nothing. There was more sign of hooves and cartwheels turning off to either side than you could shake a stick at. But none of it led anywhere but to some spread the rangers had canvased over and over by the time Longarm had arrived.

Lighting a cheroot and making sure of the match stem before he got shed of it, Longarm preforce rode on, and on some more, to see if that offer from the Fernadez sisters was still good.

It was. Whether that was Carlota or Ramona Fernandez greeting him at the door with such a radiant smile and open arms was hard to tell. The two of them looked much the same, save for the colors they wore when dressed, and at the moment, the sister hauling him in out of the starlight was naked as a jaybird.

But built a whole lot better.

Chapter 31

Having nothing more sensible to say to a naked lady he'd never kissed, Longarm stammered, "I hope I haven't intruded on anybody's early bedtime, ma'am!"

Whichever pallid brunette she was demurely replied, "We feel no need for to wear clothes indoors when we do not have to, *El Brazo*—Custis."

As she shut and barred the heavy oak door, Longarm said, "Hold on. If I'm to be here any time worth mention I got to see to my pony out front, ma'am."

She shook her primly pinned-up head and replied, "Ramona will see to your *caballo*. We spun the bottle while we watched for you for to come back, and I won. I hope you do not mind, but I told Ramona she might be asked for to join us, once we how you say break some ice? With your *permiso,* of course!"

Longarm allowed he'd go along with most any notion that didn't hurt if that was what a lady wanted, as he followed her nicely put together, oddly colored rear view along the nigh dark corridor to wherever she had in mind. The bedroom was aglow with enough candles for a church.

El Greco had overdone those green flesh tones a mite,

trying for the true effect, but he hadn't overdone it much, and Carlota, as she had turned out to be, sure looked green around the gills, or in the crack of her ass and around the edges, leastways.

Longarm knew no halfways healthy human being could grow green skin. So it had to be an optical illusion, like veins filled with red blood that still looked blue under pale white skin, most of the time. He suspected there was something in the pale hide of that certain breed of Castilian Spanish that filtered in a peculiar way the light bouncing back from the innards red as any others. This biology teacher he knew in Denver, in the biblical sense as well, had explained during some pillow talk how all the feuding and fussing over racial details was based on a mighty slim deck of genetic cards. Human skin left to its druthers, with neither blood vessels to pink it nor two and only two pigments to shade it, was the color of dandruff or a head louse. It was whiter or pinker depending on how thick it lay over the blood running under it. After that each and everybody but albino folk, who only got to be pink, even if their folks were colored, grew bitty grains of carrot-colored natural pigment and a darker pigment related to the sepia ink from cuttlefish. After that, the pinkish glow from deeper and the amount of each brand of pigment added up to all the colors humans came in, from an ash blonde such as Rose Bradford to a brunette with—damn it, she did have pale green skin, and when you considered how she filled it, who gave a damn?

Carlota led him to a dimly lit bedchamber filled mostly by a big four-poster with a big top spread of Turkish toweling. He could see it was fresh, and they had towel gals in cathouses because Turkish toweling soaked up the body fluids so tidy. He didn't ask where they'd learned such cathouse notions.

They made him feel less bashful as he unbuckled his gunbelt by the bed. He'd no sooner set that aside and taken his hat off when he noticed his fly was open. Carlota had perched her bare green ass on the white toweling to

241

unbutton his fly and whip his surprised old organ grinder out before he could show it hard.

She didn't mind, it seemed, as she took it in her mouth to where her nose was inside his jeans, with her sucking it to attention.

So Longarm let her, as he undressed, or tried to. They wound up with him standing over her with his jeans around his booted ankles and his palms on her bare shoulders as he warned her to waste not and want not.

So she simply threw herself back across the toweling, and he simply mounted her with his boot tips on the rug as he strove to kick his infernal jeans off without stopping. For once a man had his old organ grinder in the tight and possibly green inside of Carlota Fernandez, he wasn't about to take it out, unsatisfied!

But she satisfied him quicker than a wink, thanks to his resisting temptations earlier and the way she could wriggle and jiggle her ring dang doo. So he left it in her, managing finally to kick out of that last denim leg as he let it soak and reached down between them to finger her clit, idly wondering if it really looked like a lima bean.

She purred, "Everything they told us about *El Brazo Largo,* I mean Custis Long, has proven to be more than true. But I do not need what you are trying for to do this soon. Would you say we had broken some ice now, Custis?"

He had to allow they surely had. So she let him sit up to haul off his boots as she yelled, "¡Ay, hermana mia! *Me maravillo que todavía estoy vivo,* and I need some *help* in here!"

That last part had been meant for Longarm so he wouldn't be shocked useless when Ramona came in, stark naked, with a tray of food and drink.

The two sisters weren't *identical* twins, he could see, as pale and sort of green as they both looked. Ramona had slimmer hips, bigger tits and a tighter ring dang doo when Longarm responded to her leaping on him that way by rolling her over to give her all her sassy sister had left him. Or did she just feel tighter because when you shoved it where it had never been before it felt so new and delicious?

Thanks to the quick one he'd just enjoyed with Carlota, Longarm was able to enjoy Ramona longer, and wilder, as Carlota cuddled close to kiss Ramona pasionately on the mouth and finger Longarm's ass as he long-donged her sister. It wasn't the first time Longarm had noticed that when gals were willing to go three in a boat they tended to act lezzy with each other. But weren't they *sisters* and . . . Where in the United States Consitution did it say spinsters dwelling in otherwise lonesome nudity couldn't experiment with lesbian notions?

As a lawman, Longarm had learned more than most late Victorians as to what might or might not go on behind locked doors and shutters. Like bestiality, consentual incest had to be a more common as well as more unreported crime than developing French postcards. For outsiders who might *talk* got to see French postcards, whilst neither family pets nor family members were likely to report such forbidden but easily obtainable pleasures as those the Fernandez sisters were indulging in at the very moment, with the one he was humping sucking her sister's tit and playing with her clit whilst Carlota, in turn, had taken her finger out of his ass to strum Ramona's clit, with his raging erection churning love foam in and about the greenish but mighty ripe forbidden fruit.

Then it was Carlota's turn to be long donged, and damned if it wasn't like starting over with somebody new as Carlota took it more down home and dirty this time, eating her sister French style as she took Longarm dog style.

So a good time was had by all, till they wound up with him on his back and pillows piled under his head, with arms outstretched and one hand pleasuring each of their groins as they knelt to either side of him to take turns sucking him off or serving him *nachos* and *cerveza*. With the sun still up outside and a whole damned night ahead of them!

Since not even green-skinned incestuous nymphoman-

243

iacs could treat a guest to such hospitality forever, the time finally came for less salty pillow conversation and reflection on what might be left to try.

With her head on his left shoulder, Ramona confided that she'd been so afraid *Los Rurales* would send someone else after him before they could shelter and protect *El Brazo Largo.*

So Longarm let them hide him out from whoever they felt like, and then it was Monday morn and time to run those mules up the Rio Grande to the army. So Longarm tethered Blacky out front of the Last Chance to spit and whittle with other early birds until the drive shaped up.

A Double Diamond rider called Luke told Longarm some jasper had been looking all over town for him the night before. Luke had never seen the cuss before and hadn't liked the look of him.

Longarm wasn't certain how he felt about the trail boss elected by the owners when he showed up full of piss and vinegar. They called him Knuckles Curtis and he rode for the Tumbling Sevens. He told Longarm he'd be riding point down Bottleneck Canyon with half a dozen others to fan out at the south exit and keep the mules from diving headfirst into the Rio Grande. Longarm figured Knuckles knew what he was doing in spite of his surly manners. So he gathered up the riders assigned to him, in a nicer way, and they were only a ways down the canyon when they heard thundering hooves and Knuckles yelling, "Move out! Move out! I got six hundred mules up my ass and you moon calfs told me you were *herdsmen,* damn your lying eyes!"

And so it went, with the mules unable to stampede any ways but down the canyon, until they were so worn down it got easier by noon to turn them at the Rio Grande and up the Camino del Rio at a steady trot.

As the drive wore on, seeing he rode close enough to talk to the now calmer Knuckles Curtis, with the twin ruts of the Camino del Rio between them so their ponies could graze roadside weeds as they held the reins, Longarm asked how anyone meant to get out *ahead* of the herd at this late date.

Knuckles explained, "It won't be that big a boo. Slim Putnam will lead the designated point riders at a lope from the tail of the column to the head, once they're *walking* up ahead where the floodplain gets wide enough to push past the lathered brutes. You'll see how we do it as we do it. This ain't the first herd I've druv to market."

Longarm said, "So I've heard. Has all this stock stealing driven the prices up this summer, what with Indian trouble and a shortage of army mules?"

Knuckles shrugged and said, "I can't say. Big Roy dickers prices with the remount officers. That Clay Allison's likely selling all the stock he's stole somewheres else."

Longarm replied, "No, he ain't. That's about the only thing I've been able to establish with the help of Western Union. The rangers tally the stolen stock at four or five hundred head, so far, with most of the spreads up Tiswin Creek suffering two or three dozen on average. Some more. Some less. The lucky ones, west of the creek, *none*. So where in thunder could that mysterious Lazy A unload four or five hundred head without any transferal of property being recorded under the stock regulation of the state of Texas?"

Knuckles said, "I can hazard two easy answers. They're selling the stolen stock to some other crooks, cheap, or they're holding them at that secret spread Caddo Flynn said he'd scouted—in either case until you lawman lose interest in all them mules."

Longarm shook his head and said, "The Texas Rangers ain't about to lose interest, now that they've lost five good men to the same gang."

Knuckles tried, "Mayhaps the gang hadn't thought ahead when they shot them rangers crowding them."

Longarm was about to observe that only Lieutenant Weiner had ridden out of the basin before he was likely drygulched, whilst poor young Andy Steiger couldn't have been getting warm enough for a sane crook to worry about. But before he could, bedraggled mules with heads down and ears back decided they'd like to go the other way and things got busy for a spell. After a mule had herded easy a spell, it changed its mind.

It seemed as many mules wanted to amble downstream as up, so it took some hat waving and hollering indeed to turn them the other way.

But as in the case of any herded critters, once they had the more adventurous mules headed the right way, the born followers tagged along after them with far less fuss and it was easy enough to keep them on the Camino del Rio, with the churning coffee brown Rio Grande to their left and to their right the same high jumbles of limestone and shale that had caused the Big Bend in the first place.

Longarm followed after Slim Putnam where the floodplain got wide enough to forge ahead of the herd. Once the lengthy, strung-out herd had human brains guiding more sensible ponies out on point, things settled down to a long weary drive on up to Castolon.

They perforce broke trail for rest and water often enough, but *just* often enough, to keep a regiment of mules in good order. So it was late in the day with the shadows lengthening and the dust they were raising starting to look pretty in the softer glow before sundown when they drove the herd into the Army Remount Service's corrals at Castolon.

The corrals around the dinky army outpost guarding a border crossing took up more space than the 'dobe military complex wrapped around a parade with a flagpole in the middle. As was ever the case, a somewhat shabbier and more widely spread shanty town inhabited by what the army called "pig farmers" or "feather merchants" fit as best it could between the corral rails, cliffs and riverbanks.

So the scene was confounding indeed as the braying mules milled and kicked up a thunderhead of sunset-gilded corral dust, while civilian as well as military rubbernecks crowded in around the few men there with any real business to dispatch. Longarm stayed in the saddle for a look-see all around as he tried to get his bearings. Across the way he spied Big Roy Wilcox jawing with a familiar figure in army blue. Longarm was glad to see his old pal Major Matt Kincaid of the U.S. Cav and meant to have a word or more with him as soon as things settled down. But at the moment he had his eye peeled for an ash blonde with a far more interesting figure than your average cavalry officer's.

So things proceeded to go to hell in a hack when a familiar feminine voice trilled, "Custis Long, you mean old thing! What are you doing here in Castolon this evening?"

Longarm turned in the saddle to regard the way shorter gal headed his way on foot in a seersucker outfit with a perky straw boater pinned aboard her more dishwater blond curls as he muttered, "Oh, Lord, why do you *do* things like this to a poor old boy who never meant you no harm?"

For the well-built blonde coming at him through the confusion was not the one who'd promised to meet him there in Castolon. She was the gal reporter they called Sparky at *The Omaha Herald* and he had to be polite to her, having screwed her silly the last time they'd met.

So how was he going to explain Rose to Sparky and, even worse, how was he supposed to explain Sparky to Rose?

Chapter 32

Longarm dismounted before anyone else could spot him from afar. He realized his tactical error when the bubbly blond Sparky stood on tiptoe to plant a far from sisterly kiss on his face. He had to kiss back with as much enthusiasm, being he was a man and she was young and pretty, too. He was hoping they could avoid mention of her ring dang doo for the moment.

When they came up for air, the newspaperwoman repeated her question as to what he might be doing down there along the border.

He said, "Working at my job, Miss Sparky. Didn't I tell you I was a deputy federal marshal? Well, I am, and I'm after outlaws down this way. So what's your excuse?"

She dimpled up at him to reply, "My own job, reporting the news for my paper, even if I have been sore-put to file any reports worth my travel allowance since the Ninth Cav decimated Victorio's band up at Rattlesnake Springs and nobody's seen him on this side of the border since. That Ninth Cav is colored, save for its officers. The Tenth and Fourth Cav, too! Do you know why we have so many darkies fighting Indians out this way, Custis?"

He nodded and replied, "Same reason we got so many

just-off-the-boat immigrant regiments out our way. The
starting pay for a buck private is an eagle a month with
a three-dollar uniform allowance. You can make a dollar
a day herding cows and up to four dollars a day down a
hardrock mine. I hear Victorio's south of the border again,
just now."

She sighed and said, "That's what I've heard, too. But
waiting for a break in the tedious saga of Mister Lo, the
poor Indian, will be easier to bear, now that you're here,
you naughty boy. Where are we going to shack up, this
time?"

Longarm laughed despite himself and said, "I just got
here. Where have you been staying, Miss Sparky?"

She confided, "You could never strum my banjo *there*!
Covering the campaign with the army, and seeing there's
no hotel in this dinky wide spot in the Camino del Rio,
I've been quarterd on the post, treated to room and board
by the colonel's lady, a dear old thing who might not
understand if I sneaked you into their guest room."

Longarm allowed that he followed her drift. He saw
she was giving such a notion serious consideration when
she added, "I don't see how I could. With all this talk of
night-raiding Apache, they have soldiers with guns standing guard all around the parade at all hours!"

He cautiously asked, "Might any other civilian ladies
be quartered on the post with you, Miss Sparky?"

She said, "No. I'm the only single girl there. But none
of the single officers have been trying too hard, if that's
what you're so worried about. The colonel's lady let it be
known on my arrival that she'd see that her husband transferred any officer who got fresh with me to a colored
regiment, the silly old spoilsport!"

Longarm tried, "Why don't I pay a prim and proper
social call on you later this evening, on the colonel's veranda, then? I'd like to jaw some more right now, but I
got some law enforcing to do and I want to compare some
notes with one of the others from the outpost where I can
call on you later. You know Matt Kincaid, of course?"

Sparky brightened to reply, "That dashing young major

down from Presidio to fetch them some mules? Of course I know him, albeit not as well as I know *you,* you rascal. Before you go punching him in the nose over me, he said he has a girlfriend in Presidio. I asked."

Longarm chuckled fondly down at her to allow as how that didn't surprise him. Then he ticked his hat brim to her and led Blacky afoot around a considerable angle to where he'd spotted Matt Kincaid looking over the newly arrived stock. Along the way he met a wrangler from the Tumbling Sevens who offered to put Blacky with the rest of their remuda in the guarded army corral.

Hence Longarm had neither a black barb nor a bubbly blonde on his hands as he mounted a bottom rail to lean over the top one, side by side with his old army buddy, saying, "Evening, Matt."

Kincaid, a tad less rustic in manner, having gone to West Point and all, but arguably Longarm's peer at gunplay and horsemanship, if nobody asked him to rope and throw, said, "Evening yourself. I thought that was you across the way, kissing that newspaper reporter."

Longarm said, "She tells me you have a gal in Presidio. So she has to be interested in you, you dashing young major. That's what she just called you, a dashing young major."

Kincaid smiled thinly to reply, "Did she now? Are you trying to fix up a pal or get rid of excess baggage?"

"You've met Miss Rose Bradford, too?" asked Longarm.

Kincaid said, "No. Is that the other one's name? She must be a looker if you'd pick her over Little Miss *Omaha Herald!*"

Longarm confided, "It ain't a matter of looks. The more serious blonde of the two has just seen trouble enough and I promised we'd meet here in Castolon to . . . comfort one another."

Matt Kincaid, a handsome man in his own right, rolled his eyes to the red sky above to protest, "Do you call this fair, Lord?"

Longarm said, "The one from Omaha really said you

were dashing, and I've never been one to hog the trough, old pard."

Kincaid said, "The *Omaha Herald* has been taken under the wing of a bird colonel's eagle-eyed wife. I already told your extra blonde a white lie to save my own soldier-blue ass! I'd like to help you out. I'd already noticed *her* ass in spite of that seersucker skirt. But it's just too big a boo for any possible pleasure to be found within a day's ride of that old eagle-eyed biddy hen!"

Longarm sighed and said, "In that case let's jaw about all those mules. Miss Sparky said you're down here from Presidio to collect some?"

The army man said, "At least enough to pack the new mountain howitzers we're expecting from Fort Bliss any day now. I pity Victorio if he and his bronco Apache ever sit still long enough for us to draw a bead on him with our heavy weapons."

Longarm opined, "He won't. Victorio is crazy mean, not stupid. No Indian with a lick of interest in his own survival aims to offer you a stationary target to aim at. That's how come you soldiers blue have been having so much luck pinning down half bare-ass Na-déné speakers mounted bareback on wirey grass-riz scrub stock they ride into the ground to eat before they steal others to ride further, whilst you boys follow them over hill and dale loaded down with for gawd's sake mountain howitzers! Don't a Springfield .45–70 still flatten anybody at any range you're ever going to spy one of Victorio's *stragglers*?"

Kincaid said, "Let's talk about that sitting down in the officer's club. Even though we've had this same dumb conversation before. All of us who've ever *fought* Mister Lo agree with you on current tactics. But political hacks with ordnance contracts to offer in exchange for campaign contributions, along with senior officers with their own fish to fry, are the ones who tell us how to chase lightly armed and laden Indians with all the expensive shit they can load us down with. Have you had supper yet? It's too

251

late to take you to our officer's mess, but I can ask them to fix you up with something at the club."

They dropped down off the rails and headed for the nearby outpost, with Kincaid leading the way. Rounding a corner of the corral, they met up with Knuckles Curtis and Slim Putnam. Longarm had to introduce them to his old army pal. But since neither asked where the two of them might be headed, Kincaid didn't have to invite either dusty rider to the officer's club. He doubtless figured Longarm would track in all the dust they'd stand for.

So they shook all around and nobody argued when Kincaid suggested he and Longarm move on, so they did, up the dirt path leading to the outpost gate say a furlong east, with the sunset at their back drawing their shadows way out ahead of them. Then, from behind them, Longarm heard Knuckles yell, "Longarm! Look out!"

So he did, whirling about as he crabbed sideways to one knee with everybody he was facing now a cutout doll of black paper, all swirling in the flames of the big fireplace in the western sky.

Then pistol shots rang out as Longarm was still clawing for his own, and one of the paper dolls seemed to char and wither to the hearth of the sunset as Longarm heard Knuckles Curtis call, "Don't point that fucking six-gun at *me*! The one you want is *down*!"

That was for damn sure, Longarm saw as he and Kincaid retraced their steps to where Knuckles, Slim and a gathering crowd stared down at a tall dark stranger staring up at the red sky with a sleepy smile and a sneaky .31-caliber Whitney pocket pistol in the dust by his gun hand.

Knuckles Curtis was reloading his more substantial Remington .45 as Slim declared to the crowd assembled, "That sneaky cocksucker at our feet was throwing down on yonder lawman, Deputy Long, when we purely caught him in the act! I never had time to *think* before this rider off the Tumbling Sevens, here to my right, drew faster than greased lightning, with results you can see for your own selves!"

Longarm nodded at Knuckles and said, "That's one I

owe you, pard!" before he hunkered by the oddly amused-looking stranger to feel his throat, nod thoughtfully and ask, "Can you hear us from down there in the well, old son?"

Without changing expression the man Knuckles had back-shot first softly murmured, *"Comé mierda, chingate y chinge tu madre, gringo."*

From which it seemed safe to assume the sleepy-eyes rascal didn't cotton much to Longarm.

Longarm asked more politely, *"¿Como te llamas y de donde eres?"*

A familiar she-male voice behind Longarm trilled, "The one on the ground just told the famous Longarm there to eat something nasty and do nasty things to himself and his momma. Longarm, as he is more often called by friend and foe, only asked him who he was and where he was from."

The dark stranger they were all staring down at had nothing further to add, ever, but as Longarm felt his throat again and muttered something really dreadful under his breath in mixed company, Matt Kincaid said, "I think I recognize him, Custis. Last time we met he was in uniform, though."

"You mean Knuckles just now shot a soldier blue?" gasped Slim as Knuckles protested, defensively, "Well, what else was I supposed to do? Let him shoot old Longarm in the back, as ugly as he might be?"

The army officer reassured him, "He wasn't in *this* man's army. If I'm right about his face alone he's a Mexican *Federale,* or he was when we met upstream in Presidio. *Los Federales* are working with us this summer, or they're supposed to be. I don't remember this one's name, if I ever caught it. But it seems to me he was in Presidio on behalf of Mexico's own remount service. As I said, we never became intimate up the river and I could be mistaken."

Longarm said, "We'd best let the provost marshal here in Castolon figure out who he was. The military police will need statements from all of us, but I doubt it'll tie us up here longer than it will take Big Roy to sell off the consolidated herd and head us all back down to the basin."

Kincaid spotted a corporal in the crowd and dispatched him to tell the officer of the day they needed an ambulance wagon and an armed detail to take charge of whoever that might be on the ground.

Longarm knew without asking the officer of the day would do just about what a field-grade officer told him to do, officer of the day being pulled most always by junior officers.

He was sure glad he had a field-grade officer on his side and hadn't been the cuss who'd actually shot a possible Mexican remount officer. For Billy Vail had sent him down this way with direct orders not to cause any more international incidents.

That was what they called it when a gringo-hating official of the Díaz dictatorship took it in his head to gun an Anglo lawman and wound up dead his own fool self— an international incident.

So he was stuck out there in the soft light of gloaming with even more who'd heard the gunfire closing in to gather round and hear the same tale that infernal Slim Putnam enjoyed telling over and over.

Longarm asked little Sparky if she wouldn't as soon interview him in depth later, on the colonel's veranda. But she said she had to get more than their mere names out of Knuckles and Slim.

So Longarm could only shift his weight back and forth like a kid who had to take a leak but didn't want to attract a stern teacher's attention, as he waited, helpless, for Rose Bradford to show up. Everybody in and about Castolon seemed to be showing up by that time, cuss that noisy Remington .45!

Chapter 33

As Longarm had hoped, the army decided that since live-stock the army was interested in seemed to be involved, the shooting had taken place in what was still for all intents and purposes a miltary reserve as far as the border crossing, and so the Castolon provost marshal's office had jurisdiction over whatever in blue blazes was going on.

The hearing in the officer's club on post was presided over by a Colonel MacArthur nobody argued with because he was the post commander.

Big Roy Wilcox invited himself to the hearing because he sold the army lots of mules and wanted to be sure his two riders got a fair break.

Miss Sparky of the *Omaha Herald* was there because she'd chosen to be there, and Longarm hadn't been the first man to notice she had a mind of her own.

With Longarm and a field-grade officer backing their stories, the panel decided without adjourning that Knuckles and Slim were telling the truth and voted whilst they were at it that until such time as someone came foreward to claim that dead Hispanic they had over to the post morgue, they'd list him as a border ruffian named John Doe and it served him right for having a fistful of dollars and pesos but no other identification on him when he chose to mess with an American lawman, bless his poor soul.

Big Roy told Knuckles, Slim and Longarm he'd engaged lodgings for the whole outfit upwind of the corrals.

Miss Sparky reminded Longarm he'd offered to walk her up Officer's Row to where she was quartered that evening.

He got to do so after Colonel MacArthur declared the hearing over and the officer's bar open. By then it was fair dark outside where the moon wasn't shedding her pale rays. So they felt safe to kiss now and again as he walked her along the ribbon of shadow on the east side of the parade, seeing she wanted him to and Longarm felt sure another swell kisser wasn't anywhere on post.

On their way to the colonel's veranda, Sparky confided she'd been set to pack it in and leave for more newsworthy parts before she spotted an old flame over by the remount corrals.

He idly asked how she'd meant to get on upstream to El Paso.

Sparky said, "Pooh, Victorio's no more likely to turn up that far west than he is down here. I've begun to doubt he'll dare to come back from Old Mexico now. They say he has a medicine man who can read and I got my own byline reporting those heavy weapons the army has been bringing out this way to shatter his nerves indeed!"

Longarm didn't want to argue guerrilla warfare tactics with a gal. He asked how she'd meant to haul out, if not by way of El Camino del Rio down by the river.

She said, "With Indian troubles shifted this far south, the army has a new mail route, up Terlingua Valley past Study Butte, then east-northeast through the Christmas Mountains and over the Santiagos through Persimmon Gap and—"

Longarm cut in. "Sounds like a fair ride."

She said, "It is. On across the Pecos, over the Staked Plains and beyond to where the army picks up its mail from the east, and I could catch a comfortable railroad ride out of San Antone, if that was where I was going, *now*!"

She hugged the arm she was holding tighter as she husked, "Where do you mean to shack up with me in Castolon, Custis?"

He said, "Ain't certain that would be the most sensible move, Miss Sparky. I doubt I'll be here long enough to risk your reputation in such close quarters. What if you were to catch that army mail ambulance as you'd planned and wait for me to join you in San Antone?"

Sparky said, "Pooh, you just told those officers back there you were no closer to catching that crazy Clay Allison now than you were when you left Denver! If you don't want to shack up here in Castolon, why not take me back to that Tiswin Basin with you? Can't you think of some place we could shack up in that Tanktown you mentioned?"

Longarm grimaced at the picture and replied, "No place where your reputation would be safe, and whether I come up with the answer or not, I can't stay in Tanktown all that long. You can't win 'em all, and as I told you before, Marshal Billy Vail is not a patient man."

He kissed her at the foot of the colonel's steps to soften her up before he insisted, "Wait for me in San Antone and I promise we'll take time out for undivided slap and tickle!"

His ploy didn't work as planned. Groping at his crotch, Sparky sobbed, "I don't want you to slap and tickle me in San Antone! Let's see if the coast is clear to the guest room!"

It wasn't. Through the lace window curtains they could see the colonel's lady waiting up by lamplight for her man to come home from the officer's club.

Sparky muttered murderously, "Oh, shit, the dragon is on watch to guard the treasures of that feather bed!"

The right handsome woman inside didn't look like a dragon to him, but Longarm recalled how Matt Kincaid had described her and concluded she was one of those nice enough looking do-gooders, like Miss Lemonade

Lucy Hayes, who refused to serve hard drink at the White House, for God's sake.

Patting Sparky's younger rump reassuringly, Longarm pointed out, "Neither army folk nor country folk are as softy-cated as folk up Omaha way, or even San Antone. When did you say the next mail ambulance to San Antone might be leaving, sweet stuff?"

She said she'd been planning on catching one come morning, just after reveille, until *he'd* shown up.

He kissed her some more, and it wasn't tough to sound passionate as he told her, "Catch that one and wait for me in San Antone. It'll take you longer to get there than it'll take me to get back to Tanktown, and I doubt I'll be there long enough to matter."

She protested, "Pooh, I'll bet you're just trying to get rid of me so you can slap and tickle some other woman again!"

He protested, "What other woman? What again? Do you see any other woman hereabouts for me to mess with again, or even the first time?"

She said, "Knowing you, I wouldn't put it past you to have some other woman lined up for tonight! Didn't you ditch me that time to make love to that French carnival gal, Lulu Blanchard?"

Longarm protested, "Is that any way to talk about a visitor to our country, Miss Sparky? All me and Miss Lulu did that time of which you bitch was to go up in her balloon, above the Omaha State Fair, for God's sake! Do you think we were playing slap and tickle in that observation balloon . . . Oh, jumping beans and Boston baked frogs! How come I never thought of that time I scouted outlaws in that French visitor's observation balloon!"

Sparky suggested, "Wasn't she a lay worth remembering?"

Longarm kissed her some more and copped a feel as well before he said, "I got to scout an army pal up before he beds down for the night, Miss Sparky. So promise me you'll wait for me in San Antone and I'll promise you I'll meet you there with bells on!"

Sensing her resolve was weakening, he insisted, "You were at that hearing in the officer's club just now. Didn't you hear me tell them I was missing some pieces of the puzzle? Didn't you follow my drift, being a reporter, when I explained how I couldn't fit the few true facts I was sure of into a sensible overall picture?"

Sparky said, "Of course I did. But how does that French hussy, Lulu Blanchard, fit into your picture puzzle? I'd heard she'd gone back to France!"

Longarm said, "Aw, Miss Lulu wasn't a hussy, exactly, once you got to know her. It's her *observation balloon,* or one as high in the sky, I have in mind right now, thanks to you."

He kissed her again and added, "Ain't got time to explain it all right now. I promise I'll explain it all you want in San Antone, if only you'll get your pretty little derrier out of my way here and let me enjoy it more thorough-some with nothing else on my mind!"

She didn't say yes, she didn't say no, when he kissed her again and left her there on the colonel's veranda, so he could leg it on back to where the colonel was still entertaining the boys with a hearty rendition of "Army Blue," off key.

It might have been just as well Matt Kincaid had consumed enough hundred proof to feel mellow when Longarm took him to one side to tell him what he wanted to try.

As it was, Matt Kincaid stared owlishly at him to demand, "Are you out of your mind or just drunk, Custis? The War Department would never go for such a crazy stunt!"

Longarm insisted, "What does your balloon corps keep balloons for if it ain't to go up in the sky to observe things?"

The regular army man said, "Professor Lowell's so-called balloon corps was disbanded before Lincoln was shot!"

Longarm demanded, "Then how come I keep seeing

259

pictures of army observation balloons in scientific journals like the *Illustrated Police Gazette?*"

Kincaid said, "Oh, the signal corps has a few experimental balloon companies. As a matter of fact the War Department sent one out west to Fort Bliss when Victorio jumped the reservation again. But as far as I know the gear was never unpacked and the enlisted personnel have been pulling regular signal corps operations."

Longarm asked, "You mean there's an army observation balloon on tap as close as El Paso? Why did they send it out to Fort Bliss and then never unpack it?"

The seasoned Indian fighter refilled his shot glass from the bottle on the officer's bar as he explained, "We were talking earlier about the idiots buying heavy ordnance to bombard Apache on the fly. Nobody out *here* asked for any damned observation balloons. They'd be useless in the field against hit-and-run night raiders. The Apache don't hold fixed positions one can map out from on high. By the time you could hope to haul a heavy gas generator and all that other shit in place to spy on distant Indians, your distant Indians would be long gone. Those signal corps boys are far more useful *signaling* with flags and heliographs across these wide open spaces, for Pete's sake!"

Longarm insisted, "I got a fixed position to scout that can't be moved an inch, Matt! I told you about that secret Lazy A spread where they say a long-dead badman is holding stolen stock. I told you how we'd tried in vain to find the blamed place, the hard way. But can't you see how easy it would be with just one observation balloon high above all that confusing jumble of busted-up and eroded rock?"

Knowing something of scouting in his own right, Matt Kincaid had to nod, even as he objected, "We're out here on a limited budget to hunt *Apache,* not long-dead badmen, Custis! How would we ever justify the expense?"

Longarm said, "Your provost marshal's office just took jurisdiction in the case of that mysterious Mex officer out to kill me before I can find out who's been stealing army mules, remember?"

Kincaid laughed and said, "That's pure sophistry and you know it! Not one single army mule has been stolen by anyone. Mules stolen before the remount service bids on them don't count!"

Longarm insisted, "They could if we could get one field-grade officer to give the right orders, and ain't you a field-grade officer, Matt?"

Kincaid laughed like a mean little kid and said, "You've got more balls than a bowling alley, and it would take at least a bird colonel to pry that balloon detail out of Fort Bliss."

Longarm glanced down the bar at the officers singing rebel marching airs with unreconstructed Texans and suggested, "Let's go ask old Mac, in that case."

Kincaid said, "I'll see if he's drunk enough. Wait here." Then he swayed some in his own right as he punched away from the bar and went to join the jollier bunch at the far end.

Longarm absently reached for the major's bottle, then reminded himself he still had to track Rose Bradford down and had likely had enough already.

A gal who'd been waiting for some all this time would have a tough time understanding a man who passed out on top of her.

Big Roy Wilcox busted free of the song fest just as Kincaid joined it, to move down the bar to Longarm—on his way out, it developed.

Big Roy said, "I've hired the top floor of the Posada de Concepcion Immaculado and the bottom floor as well. Since there ain't but one floor to the Hotel of the Immaculate Conception. Ain't that a bitch?"

Longarm laughed politely, for whatever reason, and the older man explained, "We'll be staying overnight. Mayhaps two. But I'm hoping to settle on a fair profit for all from the remount rascals tomorrow. You remember Miss Rose Bradford from that funeral back in Tanktown? She asked me to give this to you when we got here to Castolon and so, seeing we have, here it is."

As Big Roy handed him the familiar-looking expensively made envelope Longarm asked with a puzzled frown when all that had happened.

Big Roy said, "Sunday night, as me and Hazel were seeing her off from the basin. She asked if I could pay her up front for the mules she'd consigned to us as well as her Flying B. I warned her I might get a better price from the army this time than the last time, thanks to Victorio. She said I could keep any extra profit so's she'd never have to think abut mules no more. So we sent her on her way with our best wishes and a bank draft she can cash on her way through El Paso. She seemed in a hurry to get on out to the West Coast. You ready to call her a night or do you aim to cornhole one of them soldiers blue?"

Longarm said he still had business with Major Kincaid. So Big Roy asked which was the gal and which was the boy before lurching on out.

Longarm tore open the envelope to read the terse but tenderly worded message. Nothing Rose had written surprised him all that much.

Matt Kincaid rejoined him, saying, "He says it's up to the Signal Corps and my own CO in Presidio. He says he'd never advise any man to get married, go to war or go up in a balloon. What's up, Custis? You look like you're about to throw up. Had too much this evening?"

Longarm smiled crookedly and replied, "Just getting started. I forget whether it was a kindly old French philospher or a Scotchman who advised that a man who passes up a chance to pick up a penny in the dust or a piece of ass at any time and place will all too soon wish he hadn't. But damned if he wasn't right on the money!"

Chapter 34

The heaviest load they'd hauled all the way down from El Paso and up Bottleneck Canyon was the swamping Signal Corps gas generator on a Conestoga chassis pulled by six teams, empty. They'd carried barrels of scrapped nails and the demijohns of sulphuric acid in other wagons hauled by heaps of army mules. The gas generator was a lead-lined vat the size of a hotel's roof tank. Once it was set in place, for you'd never move it whilst it was hard at work, you filled it with the bent and rusty nails and poured in enough acid to cover them all as they commenced to hiss and foam before you could screw the air-tight hatch down.

Once you had, a boiler gauge told you how the pressure was building up inside. The pressure was building up as the acid reacted with the scrap iron to form hydrogen gas. You wanted it to form hydrogen gas because Professor Lowell had never found anything that had hydrogen gas beat for lifting balloons.

The Signal Corps team got the generator going before they unloaded the wicker gondola with the gas bag folded up inside it. The crowd from Tanktown got ever bigger as the troopers stretched the big black bag out on the grass to adjust its netting, securing it to lift the eight-by-eight-foot gondola squatting in the grass as if it never meant to leave. The gondola was held by its sandbags as the Signal Corps crew attached its harness to the mile of hemp cable they said they had wrapped around that spool aboard another wagon.

Seeing he had the time, as they puttered and fussed, Longarm walked up the post road to the Western Union to see if Billy Vail had ever gotten off the dime with his own damned chores whilst working a poor deputy in the field half to death.

Billy had, or more likely Henry had, being such a fuss for sending wires and waiting forever for answers. The Western Union man told Longarm he'd just taken down a day letter from Denver within the hour. He naturally knew what it said. But as he handed it across the counter, he asked, "Do you read any meat with these potatoes? I fear your home office hasn't told you all that much, or for that matter, anything as sounds like it should be your business."

Longarm read the wire before he smiled thinly and declared, "Ain't nothing as ain't my business when I'm checking out the stories I am asked to take on faith."

"You mean you just caught somebody in a lie?" asked the telegrapher.

Longarm said, "Ain't certain, yet. Forgetting to mention something to a lawman only counts as a lie if you've been hiding family secrets with criminal intent."

As he turned from the counter, he added, "What I just now learned won't matter unless and until I learn something else for certain."

He ambled back to the site of the proposed balloon launch to find that, sure enough, the big gas bag was propped up like a walrus coming ashore to fuss and fuck. By the time he joined Matt Kincaid and Second Lieutenant Morrison by the gondola, the gas bag had grunted itself up off the grass to tug experimentally on the harness attaching it to the gondola. The Signal Corps shavetail shook the rail thoughtfully and decided, "It's raring to go, soon as we get in and release the sand ballast. Permission to speak my mind, Major?"

Matt Kincaid said, "Permission denied, Lieutenant. I know how you feel. I used to be a junior officer. I know just how it feels to set things up and have a superior take over. But rank has its privileges, and had I wanted to take orders from second lieutenants, I'd have never bucked for these oak leaves."

He turned Longarm to add, "After you, little darling. Where's your Winchester, in case we see anything?"

Longarm said, "I was about to suggest we take one of your long-range .45–70 army rifles, Matt. Albeit I'll sure be surprised if we're ever attacked by eagles up yonder."

Kincaid turned to the nearest armed guard to ask, "Is that Springfield ranged maximum, trooper?"

The soldier replied, "As per orders, with Apache ghosting the horizon, Major."

Kincaid held out his hand, saying, "Give me your cartridge magazines as well. This civilian is worried about *eagles* for God's sake!"

Then they both got in. Kincaid asked how you released the ballast. The unhappy Morrison said you just yanked the slip knots holding each bag and asked how high they wanted him to pay out the line.

Kincaid glanced at Longarm, who said, "Far out as it goes until or unless I wave my hat at you. Do I wave once, it means we want to stop where we are up yonder. Do I wave like hell, it means we want to come down. Is there anything else you have to know about riding in one of these things?"

Morrison smiled dirty and said, "If the ground line breaks, pull the rip cord hanging down from the gas bag if you don't want to rise too high to breathe. We had a crew bust loose like that over at Fort Sill, and by the time they came down in Illinois, nobody could be certain whether they'd died from the thin air or the cold winds up yonder."

Longarm shot a thoughtful glance at the cliffs looming all around as he asked, "Do we spill some gas to come down sooner, how far do you reckon we'll drift across all that unmapped karst before we land?"

The Signal Corps officer shrugged and said, "Five, maybe ten miles, depending on your altitude and winds. I offered to go in your place, you know."

Longarm nodded soberly but said, "I know that. It's what I *don't* know that inspires this foolishness!"

Then he released a bunch of sandbags on his side. Matt Kincaid did the same on the other, and with an ominous shudder they began to rise slowly but surely in an asshole-puckering series of springy tugs on their ground cable.

Longarm forced himself to look down. That was the point of going up in a balloon. The folk from far and wide were already commencing to look sort of like a circle of toy soldiers staring up at them from a green rug. Longarm recognized the Punchboard sisters to the south with others from the Last Chance, along with Big Roy and Hazel Wilcox watching from that jaunting cart, with Knuckles Curtis and Slim Putnam sitting ponies to either side.

Glancing north, he saw an even bigger crowd, albeit fat Flo Whitehead's rusty hair was nowhere to be seen and he was just as glad. Some of the crowd were waving up at them. Longram was tempted to wave back, but he remembered what he'd told the Signal Corps. So he never.

Closer at hand, Matt Kincaid muttered, "Me and my big mouth! That shavetail *begged* to get in this basket with you and you heard me tell him I wanted to do this! I ought to have my fucking head examined!"

Longarm gulped and answered, "Welcome to the lunatic asylum. I knew what I was getting into and I still got in."

"You mean you've ridden in one of there things before?" marveled the army man as they rose higher than the rimrocks to either side and the dry west wind at that altitude began to lean them toward the east from the ground up, gas bag and all.

Gripping the harness ropes to either side, Longarm gasped, "I got to ride one up at the Omaha State Fair with a prettier pilot, floating free with the wind so's the gondola never *tipped* like this!"

Down below, Lietutenant Morrison could see what was happening and ordered his winch crew to pay the line out faster. It helped correct the tilt of the gondola, but scared its passengers as much or more as they suddenly soared skyward, faster, and Longarm wheezed, "Jee-zuss!"

Matt Kincaid never said that much. He'd thought charging Cheyenne contraries whilst low on ammunition was terrifying. Right now those felt like the good old days!

Then they'd risen out of the vagrant winds whipping across the rimrocks and it sure beat all how, once you got *really* high, it wasn't as scary looking down.

"Now that's really *pretty*!" Longarm said as they gazed all about across the frozen sea of limestone waves, rising higher and higher as if climbing a mast to search for pirate ships over the far, fuzzy horizon.

As Matt Kincaid pointed at features near and far, Longarm was able to name the taller peaks from the survey maps he'd been poring over of late. By the time they stopped rising to just bob at the end of their cable, he figured they were high as Emery Peak, far to the north, and a hell of a lot closer to the Rio Grande.

"So where is this secret ranch where Clay Allison has been hiding all those stolen mules?" asked Matt Kincaid, adding, "All I can see for miles and miles looks like miles and miles of busted-up limestone!"

Longarm nodded soberly and said, "That's on account of that's all there is to be seen. I had already figured as much. But I had to be certain before I accused anybody."

Longarm peered over the side at what now resembled tiny ants clustered around bread crumbs alongside a silvery tinsel string across a green desk blotter. He waved his hat back and forth as Kincaid said, "I'm missing something here. If there's no secret Lazy A, where have those thieves been hiding all those mules that were stolen down there?"

"Somewheres else, of course," said Longarm laconically, as the ground crew commenced to reel them back down faster than they'd paid out the line.

So they were nearly level with the clifftops to either side when a cotton boll of gunsmoke blossomed against the salmon sandstone to the east, to be followed by the deep-throated boom of a buffalo gun as something thunked into the gas bag above them.

"Somebody's shooting at us!" yelled Matt Kincaid as the tiny figure in a rimrock crevice on the east wall of the basin was reloading.

Longarm said, "I noticed. Hand me that Springfield, will you?"

The army man replied, "The hell you say, I've shot a possible more than once and this rifle is U.S. Army property, Custis!"

The distant sniper fired again, and the bag above them was already hissing like a steam kettle before he put another buffalo round above his first shot. So Longarm suggested, "Give him your best shot then, Soldier Blue!"

Kincaid did. The army rifle threw its slightly smaller ball as far on a flatter trajectory. Longarm said, "Nice shot, Major," as the distant sniper's own rifle boomeranged out over nothing, to spin down the face of the cliff as its owner vanished from sight in the crevice he'd been braced in.

Longarm observed, "Spine shot. They don't throw their guns away so hard when they still have any say about their spasms."

Matt Kincaid dryly remarked, "I never might have guessed. I'm as anxious to experience my first piece of ass as well. Who did I just shoot, Custis?"

Longarm said, "Too early to say for certain. But we know where you dropped him and Captain Kramer has plenty of help. So we ought to know before sundown."

"You mean you have no idea?" asked the officer.

Longarm said, "I got more *ideas* than I can shake a stick at. But I'm still working on what Billy Vail calls the process of eliminating. Have you ever noticed how you can fit the pieces as easy one way as the other until all of a sudden things snap in place and there the whole picture sets, because nothing fits any better way?"

Kincaid was still trying to make sense of Longarm's methods when they got back down to roll out of the gondola as the ground crew secured it. The gas bag kept coming down as it oozed lift out of its bullet holes. The rifle shots from on high had naturally drawn even more folk closer. Captain Kramer and Sergeant Farnsworth were coming one way. Big Roy Wilcox came frowning in from the other, along with Knuckles Curtis and Slim Putnam, both as excited as their boss.

Liam O'Hanlon joined them, along with the elfin Kevin and some of his Mexican hands, all of them looking as puzzled.

Captain Kramer called out, "Who was that swapping shots with you two from the rimrocks, for God's sake?"

Longarm said, "Ain't certain. How long do you reckon it would take you rangers to pry him out and bring him down where I can ask him?"

Kramer turned to ask Sergeant Farnsworth why he was stationary as a spot of shit on the pillow. As Farnsworth signaled other rangers and hurried off, Kramer said, "Not long. Would you like to tell us *why* he was shooting at you gents?"

Longarm saw that the Signal Corps crew were moving the deflating gas bag to lie down straight alongside the creek. He pointed with his chin and said, "He was hoping to pop us like a bubble and drop us like rocks. He didn't know how much gas he had to let out of them bitty holes in tough rubberized silk. So the *why* ain't as hard to figure as the *who*. I got me a whole bunch of pieces now commencing to fit pretty good. But they fit one way if that was Pepper MacLeod up yonder and they fit another if it turns out he was Caddo Flynn."

He took out the wire from Denver as he wearily confided, "If it turns out to be somebody else entire, I'm in real trouble. But I'm pretty certain it'll turn out to be MacLeod or Flynn. Read this and don't say nothing, Captain. I'm trusting you to see why as soon as you catch up with me a mite."

The older lawman took the wire, scanned it, whistled softly and declared, "I see what you mean. It's a surprise indeed but, like you just said, it reads more than one way!"

Matt Kincaid said, "I just got here. So what in blue blazes are we talking about? Who might Pepper MacLeod or Caddo Flynn add up to?"

"They're both old ridge runners who know their way around up yonder and I wouldn't put anything past either!" said Liam O'Hanlon.

Longarm said, "I've only met Pepper MacLeod. He might or might not have shown me the way down off his clifftops to throw me off, or out of Christian charity. I've yet to lay eyes on Caddo Flynn. He may have been murdered because he knew too much. Or mayhaps he was in on it from the first and lured Lieutenant Weiner of the rangers into a death trap with a big fat fib. There's been a heap of fibbing going on around here. Or leastways lots of folks have been hiding things they'd have no call to hide unless they were up to something and . . . Don't try it, Big Roy!"

But Big Roy Wilcox must have figured he had to try whilst the trying was good and he still had that monstersome LeMat to try with.

So things commenced to get mighty exciting in the basin for a spell.

Chapter 35

The considerable crowd assembled behaved the way crowds usually behave when hell busts out unexpected. They scattered every which way to clarify the chaos a mite for Longarm, Captain Kramer, the two army officers and those rangers and soldiers who came unstuck before it was over. For anybody who wasn't running away or on your side at such times was a target of opportunity unless he shot you first!

Big Roy Wilcox kept hauling on that massive French revolver as Longarm beat him to the draw and punched him in the nose with two hundred grains of hot lead until he back-flipped and blasted the empty sky above with buckshot.

Captain Kramer, having read the wire from Denver, slapped leather on Liam O'Hanlon to pay him back for many a dead ranger and bawled, "Aw, shit, that ain't fair!" when the burly Irishman hit the trampled grass dead as a wet dishrag beside his secret brother-in-law, Big Roy.

Neither Matt Kincaid nor Lieutenant Morrison had the least notion why they were firing on Big Roy and O'Hanlon's backup as they fired, but being trained Indian fighters they crabbed sideways betwixt shots and never missed as they just kept blazing away through the battle haze of swirling white black-powder smoke. Then the hydrogen leaking from the punctured gas bag caught fire to add to the confusion as enlisted Signal Corps and Texas Ranger guns blazed away at the wounded flopping on the grass like harpooned fur seals and Longarm shouted, "Hold your fucking fire!"

Lieutenant Morrison had little more luck shouting, "Save my balloon! If you can't save my balloon, get it the hell away from our gas generator and run the livestock into that water!"

As the firing died away and the smoke began to clear, the survivors commenced to follow orders and make more sense. Longarm saw little Kevin face down atop the bigger heap of O'Hanlon in a bloody obscene parody of that joke about the midget and the circus fat lady. One of the Mexicans from the Last Chance was sitting on the grass, hugging his waist and rocking back and forth as he chanted, *"Chinge tu madre, chinge tu madre,"* over and over in a dull, dazed way. Two others from the Last Chance lay farther out on the grass, with no further comments or signs of life to offer.

Big Roy lay spread-eagled on his back, staring up at the sky sort of cross-eyed after the center of his face had caved in that way. Knuckles Curtis lay face down on what was left of his own face, with his own gun drawn but standing like a steel-stemmed ivory flower, with its barrel driven deep in the dirt near his limp and folded-under gun hand.

Slim Putnam had propped himself up on one elbow to gaze in hurt wonder at the blood on his free hand, moaning, "Son of a bitch if I ain't been shot! This ain't right, Longarm! You had no call to gun a man who's saved your bacon from a back-shooter more than once!"

Longarm turned to Captain Kramer and said, "We might get something out of this one if Doc Fletcher can do anything for him."

The ranger replied, "He can try. But Doc Fletcher's a *dentist* and the boy may have a point. I know he rode for

Wilcox and I just saw Big Roy slap leather on you, but Slim did back your play against the men Big Roy sent to kill you."

Longarm said, "No, he didn't. He did what was only natural when he saw a man he'd been ordered to bullshit was about to be killed by a total stranger."

"Then the bunch who kept trying to kill you, and managed to kill others in the process, didn't ride for Big Roy there?" asked the older lawman in confusion.

As the army men moved to secure the burning gas bag and smoldering grass, Longarm explained, "Big Roy and his boys were almost as upset as I was by those bounty hunters on my ass. They wanted me alive, so they could bullshit me, along with you and Billy Vail, some more."

Matt Kincaid laughed incredulously, and asked, "Bounty hunters? Why in thunder would any bounty hunters be after you? You're a lawman, Longarm!"

Longarm smiled modestly and confessed, "I'm wanted down Mexico way as *El Brazo Largo*. It's an asshole Mex notion too tedious to go into in detail. Suffice to say our two-faced young Ricardo Chavez knew he could make more on my head than he'd ever make as a half-ass stable boy. He enlisted a two-faced kinswoman to make sure I was the one *Los Rurales* were after. *Los Rurales* frown on wild goose chases, and you don't want *Los Rurales* frowning on you when you have kith and kin living down Mexico way. They tend to tell Los Rurales where you are."

He spied Doc Fletcher driving out from town and waved him over as he continued, "It was easy for a two-faced señorita to make sure I was the sap they suspected. I'm a man, and she was pretty, too, and had what you call a ring dang doo. Not wanting a fuss with you rangers at a time our two countries are hunting Victorio together, Mexico sent an Anglo professional with two Mex sidekicks for openers. That plan went sour when O'Hanlon yonder spotted them fixing to ambush a man he'd been ordered to sell gold bricks to. Once Hardpan Harry Hoffmann and his boys failed, they just kept trying, with similar results you know as much as me about."

"You mean even that gang as circled in to shoot Miss Consuela from the chili parlor were only after you, not riding for Big Roy Wilcox?"

Longarm said, "That's about the size of it. Neither the Punchboard sisters nor anyone else around the Last Chance knew Beerkeg Orbach. That's why they were able to report his death to us so sincere. They were totally innocent of trying to assassinate this child. They had me sending in the very reports they wanted me sending in. Slim and O'Hanlon being so sincerely helpful had me flimflammed until I got to eliminating. I suspected at first that something bad might have happened to Ricardo and Yzabel. But once I figured they'd just lit out for Chihuahua, and wondered why, *that* piece of the puzzle was easy to fit in place, and as soon as I saw how good old boys up this way could have only been acting natural when they saved my bacon from outsiders, I had call to look tighter at all my false friends here in the basin."

Captain Kramer cocked a brow to demand, "Might your process of elimination have included the Texas Rangers, Uncle Sam?"

Longarm replied easily, "Sure did. The way it works, you start off suspecting everybody and then whittle away at motive, means and opportunity till you narrow your selection some. At the current price the army pays for mules out our way, most everybody in this basin had the *motive* to steal all those mules. Not all of 'em had the same means or opportunity."

Lieutenant Morrison came over by the listing gondola to tell him, "You and the major are surely going to have some explaining to do, and my men just pulled a pony cart off a soaking wet and screaming woman. They say she tried to drive across that creek at full gallop, to wind up upside down. I'm pretty sure she was with the one on the grass who drew on you to start the proceedings!"

Longarm said, "I know she was. Could you get Hazel Wilcox over here if she ain't sincerely dying?"

The officer turned away to do so as Longarm went on

274

explaining to Captain Kramer, "They had me flimflammed with all that bullshit about Clay Allison, even though I told you the first day I got here that Clay Allison lay dead and buried up New Mexico way."

Kramer growled, "That's the member of this gang I want! He owes us for five whole Texas Rangers, which is more than we ever lost in an average Comanche scare! I don't see any big blond bastards out yonder on the grass. Might he be the one the major shot from the balloon just now?"

Longarm said, "When they carry the body down from the rimrocks, I can assure you it'll turn out to be Caddo Flynn, even though I never saw the lying two-faced son of a bitch. I was waiting to make sure, but you saw how a guilty conscience brought matters to an earlier head."

Doc Fletcher got down from his buggy to whistle as he gazed around in wonder. Then he exclaimed, "Looks like the last act of *Hamlet* and where am I to begin?"

Longarm pointed and suggested, "See what you can do for Slim Putnam. I'm still just guessing about a lot of shit. I didn't know for certain Caddo Flynn was still alive until Big Roy played his hand to show me I was guessing right about *him*."

As the dentist-cum-deputy coroner moved away across the grass, Longarm explained, "Had there really *been* a Lazy A spread I'd have had to visit it and make certain there were no big blond bully boys with limps up yonder. Since there ain't no spread, there'd have been no call for anybody to kill Caddo Flynn to shut him up. Since it was Caddo Flynn who reported that hidden canyon full of stolen mules, Caddo had to be the barefaced liar who lured your Lieutenant Weiner into an ambush or, just as likely, murdered him for the gang as soon as they were out of the basin. Caddo just now tried to murder the major and me."

Matt Kincaid rejoined them in time to say, "I follow what you just said, Custis. I was there. But what was all this bullshit about a big bully boy with a limp?"

Longarm replied with a thin smile, "Bullshit, like you

just said. I never believed the real Clay Allsion could be up to anything down this way. But I sure wasted a lot of time and trouble trying to determine who in thunder was giving such a good imitation of Clay Allison!"

Kramer sighed. "You can say that again! Saying poor Weiner was only shot in the back by that nasty little breed Caddo Flynn, how do you account for Tim Henderson going up against *some* big blond bastard in the Last Chance, or the time they said Clay Allison or a reasonable facsimile shot it out with Quirt Page and George Summerhill, to say nothing of poor Andy Steiger, right in town!"

"Misdirection." Longarm shrugged, going on to explain, "This stage magic gal I used to . . . know told me how stage magicians make things look the way they ain't just by *telling* folk they're looking at something when they're really looking at something else."

Matt Kincaid demanded, "Are you saying five Texas Rangers were done in by *stage magic,* Custis?"

Longarm shook his head and said, "Nothin' fancy as white rabbits out of hats or quick-draw artists good enough to lick a Texas Ranger disguised with stage makeup to pass for a famous killer. Nothing more than pure bullshit. It's easy to bullshit others when they *trust* you."

Longarm pointed through the thin blue wall of smoke rising from the remains of the burnt-out balloon to add, "Yonder comes two troopers with a right mad wet hen between 'em. Let's meet her on the other side of the smoke lest she cloud up and rain harder at the sight of her menfolk."

Longarm, the ranger and the two army officers strode abreast across the trampled grass and through the stinky reek of smoldering rubber as Captain Kramer protested, "Hold on, I ain't no trusting moon calf! When you showed that photograph of the real Clay Allison, didn't some of the boys who'd witnessed the shoot-out he won against Page and Summerhill agree that was what he looked like and . . . Oh . . . my . . . Lord!"

Longarm said, "Exactly. See how clear it gets when you eliminate what you, me or a single solitary lawman ever saw with his own eyes? Liam O'Hanlon *said* a big blond cuss killed Henderson, then Page and Summerhill. None of you *rangers* saw *shit*! It's nigh certain Henderson strode into the Last Chance looking for a showdown with Clay Allison, not a point-blank execution, served with a beer across the bar!"

Kramer gasped, "Jesus H. Christ! *Now* I can see how Page and Summerhill lost that fight with Clay Allison as if I'd *been* there! They never came through the front door on the prod with their guns drawn. They got ambushed by friendly faces, just like Weiner and Henderson, earlier!"

Longarm said, "The one who murdered young Andy Steiger was most likely the man who witnessed his being beaten to the draw by Clay Allison Incorporated after *they* said, *Clay Allison* never said, he was looking to have it out with *me*!"

"But why, and where, were they really hiding all them stolen mules?" asked Captain Kramer in bewilderment.

Longarm said, "In plain sight, like that purloined letter in the story by Mr. Edgar Allen Poe. When they raided another spread as thieves in the night, they drove 'em south along the post road where they'd be toughest to trail. But they never ran 'em as far as the Last Chance or the Punchboard sisters, where some paying cusomers might not have been in on it with them. They ran 'em about as far as that narrow side canyon they wanted us to think they might have turned into. Then they turned the *other* way to drive 'em across the creek and in the front gate of the Tumbling Sevens."

"Are you saying that big Tumbling Sevens remuda Big Roy just sold to the army up Castolon way were *stolen*?" gasped the older lawman.

It was Matt Kincaid who observed, "An unbranded young mule looks like an unbranded young mule to your average remount officer, who'd have never seen a single head before he was asked to bid on them."

Captain Kramer started to object. Then he laughed sheepishly and said, "Well, shit, Big Roy kept *telling* us nobody had been stealing stock from the Tumbling Sevens. But how could we have been so . . . Never mind, I see how he slickered us, now."

The Junoesque but bedraggled Hazel Wilcox struggled with the two younger soldiers holding her as Longarm and the others joined them.

She sobbed, "What have you done to my Big Roy? What have you done to . . . the others?"

Longarm said, "Your man drew first. I asked him not to. He likely had a worried mind, Miss Hazel. Earlier this very day I confirmed by wire what I thought I ought to look into when you said you'd wed Big Roy in the biggest R.C. church in San Antone. The church register and the county license bureau confirms your story. It gives your maiden name as O'Hanlon and lists your brother Liam O'Hanlon, as a witness to your wedding before he moved here with you to be your late husband's secret partner in crime. I'm telling you how much we have on you in the hopes you might see fit to tie up some loose ends, give us some names we may have missed and so forth. Being what you are, you likely know the way state's evidence works, Miss Hazel."

She hissed at him in some unknown tongue and tried to kick him in the shins before she sort of shrank into herself with a defeated but game smile to ask, "How much time is it going to cost me if I tell you all I know?"

To which Longarm could only reply, albeit honestly, "A whole lot less than you'll get if we have to convict you on what we can prove for certain now."

To save her own desperate hide, Hazel Wilcox confirmed Longarm's suspicions, and before he died Slim Putnam backed her up on some few details. The Texas Rangers had lied when they told Slim a confession might have saved his neck, had he lived. There wasn't a thing a man who'd howdied a Texas Ranger and drawn as they were shaking hands could have said to save toad squat.

But Slim died before they could hang him, so what the hell.

From Denver, Billy Vail wired that their federal district court was just as glad to turn the jurisdiction over to Texas and the U.S. Army provost marshal, and hence, according to Billy, Longarm was to come on home fast as possible.

But travel in Texas was a sometimes thing, and it was just as easy to lose that ten-day "delay in route" he spent in San Antone. He could have likely gotten away with another weekend. But Miss Sparky had to get on back to Omaha, once he'd satisfied her curiosity about the mystery of the deadly deadman and other wonders of the Wild West she wasn't able to write about for her paper.

Explore the exciting Old West with one of the men who made it wild!

LONGARM

Explore the exciting Old West with one of the men who made it wild!

LONGARM AND THE MOUNTAIN BANDIT #267
0-515-13018-4

LONGARM AND THE LADY BANDIT #270
0-515-13057-5

LONGARM AND THE SCORPION MURDERS #271
0-515-13065-6

LONGARM AND THE GUNSHOT GANG #274
0-515-13158-X

LONGARM AND THE DENVER EXECUTIONERS #275
0-515-13184-9

LONGARM AND THE WIDOW'S SPITE #276
0-515-13171-7

*ROUND UP ALL THESE GREAT
BACKLIST TITLES!*

**AVAILABLE WHEREVER BOOKS ARE SOLD OR
TO ORDER CALL:**

1-800-788-6262

J. R. ROBERTS

THE GUNSMITH

WILDGUN

THE HARD-DRIVING WESTERN SERIES
FROM THE CREATORS OF *LONGARM*

Jack Hanson